PRAISE FOR
DAUGHTERS OF OLYMPUS

"A gripping exploration of love, loss, and the power of rage, *Daughters of Olympus* teems with the fervor of a mother, the devotion of a daughter, and the passion of lovers. Twining through these surprisingly human relationships, readers will discover a brew of gods intent on ownership and connection and, for some, growth. This story will keep you turning pages and leave you wanting more."

—Malayna Evans, author of *Neferura*

"With vibrant prose and decadent world building, *Daughters of Olympus* is a magical feast for the senses. This stirring retelling peels back the layers of myth surrounding Demeter and Persephone to touch upon their most human core. It is a stunning testament to the destructive and healing power of love to move the very earth."

—A. D. Rhine, author of *Horses of Fire*

"Hannah Lynn takes an old tale and makes it new with her brilliant retelling of Demeter and Persephone. A novel that is at once tender and rage-filled, this story delves deep into the complexities of the mother-daughter relationship in a beautifully rendered world of gods, monsters, and mortals. This is a book you'll be thinking about long after you've finished the last page! A must-read."

—Megan Barnard, author of *Jezebel*

"With her latest novel, Hannah Lynn demonstrates her deep knowledge of mythology and mastery of storytelling. Her rich, vivid details transport readers to an ancient world, one alive with danger and great magic. Although they are goddesses, both Demeter and Core/Persephone are still women, desperate to forge their own paths and make their own choices in a patriarchal world that stymies them at every turn. *Daughters of Olympus* is both a celebration of women and a testament to the importance of perspective—the untold and underappreciated stories."

—Lauren J. A. Bear, author of *Medusa's Sisters*

ALSO BY HANNAH LYNN

Grecian Women Series

Athena's Child

A Spartan's Sorrow

The Queens of Themiscyra

Standalone Feel-Good Novels

The Afterlife of Walter Augustus

Treading Water

A Novel Marriage

The Peas and Carrots Series

The Holly Berry Sweet Shop Series

The Wildflower Lock Series

The Lonely Hearts Book Club Series

DAUGHTERS of OLYMPUS

HANNAH LYNN

sourcebooks
landmark

Copyright © 2024 by Hannah Lynn
Cover and internal design © 2024 by Sourcebooks
Cover design and illustration by Holly Ovenden
Internal design by Tara Jaggers/Sourcebooks

The characters and events portrayed in this book are fictitious or are used fictitiously. Apart from well-known historical figures, any similarity to real persons, living or dead, is purely coincidental and not intended by the author.

Published by Sourcebooks Landmark, an imprint of Sourcebooks
P.O. Box 4410, Naperville, Illinois 60567–4410
(630) 961-3900
sourcebooks.com

Cataloging-in-Publication Data is on File with the Library of Congress.

Printed and bound in the United States of America.
VP 10 9 8 7 6 5 4 3 2 1

To Magdalen,
Thank you for being a true balcony friend.

PART 1

DEMETER

PROLOGUE

T HIS IS THE STORY OF A MOTHER'S LOSS AND A WOMAN SO completely torn to shreds by her family that the whole Earth would suffer because of it.

This is the story of the goddess, Demeter.

This is my story.

CHAPTER ONE

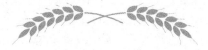

MY BROTHER, ZEUS, WAS SPARED THE FATE THAT I AND MY other siblings suffered. We were given no chance to experience the world into which we were born. No opportunity to feel the softness of our mother's lips as she kissed our cheeks or to listen to her lilting voice as she sang us to sleep. We did not spend our childhoods feeding on milk and ambrosia, or wrapped in fine threads, hair adorned with laurels as we raced beneath the great gilded arches of our royal palace.

The blazing light that should have suffused our immortal bodies was supplanted by a deep and impenetrable darkness that attended our every moment as we sweltered, limbs twisted, cramped and comfortless with barely enough room to draw breath. All because of our father, Cronus, and a future he feared above all else.

Cronus was the youngest of the seven Titans, and he was merciless and ruthless in his ambition. He thought only of power, of rising beyond the ranks of all who had gone before him. Years before my birth and armed with only a sickle, he had overthrown his own father, the King, castrating him while he slept. In that moment, he snatched the throne and had no intention of ever relinquishing it.

But a prophecy was made. One that foresaw his demise at the hands of his own child. That child would steal his throne and become the most powerful god the world had ever known. Cronus was determined that such a thing would never come to pass and hatched a wicked plan to thwart fate. Oppressive and controlling, he took his sister, Rhea, as his wife.

With her burnished flowing hair, Rhea was gentle and kind—everything that Cronus was not. She found pleasure in tranquility, contentment in serenity. She would spend her days walking, crossing fields where the wind would whip the long grasses, creating ripples like waves on a great sea. She would dangle her feet in the cool waters of the river Neda and bathe with the nymphs who dipped and dove in the soft spume that bubbled over the rocky riverbed. And she would aid nymphs and Titans alike in all times of trauma and grief, but most especially, with the birth of their children. Although by a cruel twist of fate, Rhea, the Goddess of Childbirth, endured a nightmare none could have imagined.

Whenever her belly swelled, the glow of impending motherhood shimmered on her skin. Light shone from within her, a deep luster that could have been seen by the stars above, had they cared to look down on her. She carried her children with ease, luxuriating in the time she spent with their bodies joined as one, dreaming of a future with them that would never come to pass.

For Cronus did not feel the same joy or parental instinct. He did not imagine holding his children in his arms, feeling the warmth of their skin. He did not envision a future in which we stood beside him and ruled together, one immortal and inviolable family. Instead, he felt only fear, desperation that the prophecy would soon be realized.

His savage, malevolent nature, which had seen him geld his own father, grew in malignancy, and he did not cast so much as a fleeting glance at our bodies before committing us to our fate.

Wrapped in cloth and only hours old, he took each of us from our mother, opened his throat, and swallowed us whole, condemning us to a life trapped in his belly.

All of us, that is, except Zeus.

After my sister Hestia, I was the second child consigned to Cronus's stomach, and I was not to be the last. By the time she was pregnant with Zeus, Rhea had already experienced the loss of five of her offspring to Cronus's insanity. Each time, her grief had grown, flooding every fiber of her body, seeping from her pores, dark and all-consuming, turning the joyous songs that had previously come from her lips into bleak laments.

A pain such as this is never forgotten. It simmers and grows, transforming into something much darker and stronger. With each loss, the blackness deepened. But so did Rhea's mettle. She became harder and more determined, and a fire started to burn in her that her husband did not foresee.

As Zeus grew within her, so did her resolve to rebel against my tyrant father, and she sought help from the only person she knew for certain she could trust—her mother, Gaia, Mother of the Earth. Away from the Titan King's paranoid ears, they conspired against their own blood. They plotted and planned until they knew exactly what they must do.

The night that Rhea bore Zeus, not so much as a single star twinkled above her. She had stolen away from Cronus's prying eyes to Mount Lycaeum, to a place where no creature could cast a shadow and no whisper could escape on the wind. A current of warm air blew around her, carrying the scents of sweet honeysuckle and dianthus, calming her during her labor. There, hidden from view, she crouched close to the earth and, with her mother's hand in her own, wept tears of joy, for she knew that this would be the child to fulfill the prophecy and cast her verminous husband to the depths of Tartarus where he belonged. This would be the beginning of the end for him.

When Zeus entered the world, Rhea allowed herself only a moment to breathe in the musky aroma of her newborn and feel the soft suppleness of his fingers in her own. She pressed him tightly against her skin, wishing to commit every heartbeat to memory, before placing the lightest, most gentle kiss upon the child's head. Her time with him was over, for now at least.

Wiping the tears from her eyes, she left her baby with her mother and returned to Cronus. With her head bowed in deference, she offered the King a bundle bound in swaddling clothes, in the same way that she had done five times before, so tightly wrapped that nothing inside was visible.

As with me, Hades, Poseidon, and our sisters, he ripped it from her hands and swallowed it whole, not even checking to see whether Rhea had birthed a son or a daughter, whether it was healthy and strong or sickly and weak. Never once did he suspect his wife would betray him. As Rhea wept tears of joy, knowing that her son would survive, Cronus assumed she wept from grief and believed that, once again, he had thwarted the prophecy.

While Rhea had returned to Cronus, Gaia had taken the child and fled to Lyctos in Crete, to the Aegean Hills, where she left him at the cave of Dictes, in a golden cradle hanging from the branches of a tree. In this way, if Cronus got wind of Rhea's deception and searched for the baby, he would not have found him either on the Earth or in the heavens. There, in Crete, the goat-nymph, Amaltheia, took on the role of guardian to Zeus, keeping him away from his father's vindictive eye.

As a baby, Zeus suckled milk from Amaltheia and feasted on viscous golden honey that ran in streams from beehives that dotted the land, and he became stronger with each passing day. When he was old enough, he spent his days running barefoot through the lush, rippling grass and leaping over streams. He was safe under Amaltheia's watchful eye, free to mature until he was ready to fulfill his destiny.

It was upon the hills of Crete and among the shepherds of Ida that Zeus grew into manhood, his powers more formidable than Cronus could have envisioned even in his worst nightmares. Of course, I knew nothing of him in those early days, still confined in the prison of my father's belly. But now, I can almost see him. Young Zeus, stretched out on a rock, enjoying the heat of the sun beating down on his skin, casting him in an ethereal glow while the nymphs looked in awe at a figure that no mere mortal could gaze upon and survive. I have often imagined those early years of Zeus, before he saved me.

He arrived in our father's presence as a cupbearer, only Rhea aware of his true identity. As he bowed low, Cronus could not have conceived that this man before him was, in fact, his son. In the same way, in his arrogance, he could never have dreamed that Rhea would have slipped an emetic into the honeyed drink he was being served. Cronus drank deeply from the cup, emptying every last drop. It was only a matter of moments before the effects took hold. Rhea and Zeus looked on, watching the uncontrollable spasms as the potion forced out the contents of the great Titan King's belly.

The stone came out first, rising up through his throat and nearly choking him, finally landing on the ground with a heavy thud that resonated around the hall. Then came his children.

My brothers, Poseidon then Hades, were the first gods to be

freed. Next came my sister, Hera. It was after her that I was expelled up through his gullet and onto the slippery mattress of his tongue. As his mouth opened to eject me completely, light shone in from the outside world, an intense, glaring white I had never before encountered. I squinted, trying to protect my eyes as I dropped to the ground at my mother's feet, only to be joined seconds later by my final sibling, my sister, Hestia.

The cold prickled my skin, but this was no discomfort to me. After years lost in the clammy, suffocating heat of my father's stomach, the fresh air was intoxicating. For a moment I lay there, still blinking, as I curled my fingers and toes and flexed my limbs, releasing cramps and experiencing the freedom to move that had been long denied to me.

One blink after another, my eyes adjusted to the onslaught of light. The first images came only as shadows. Black, blurred smudges that slowly formed into shapes with colors. I noted the curve of my fingers and wrists, the straight line of my forearms. Still recovering, I pushed back onto my heels, and for the first time in my life, I looked up toward the heavens. But it was not the sky that I saw.

He was younger than me but of a size and strength that I could never have dreamed of. And while my siblings and I all carried ichor in our veins, in Zeus it shone with such a vibrancy I feared I might lose my sight altogether.

While my father continued to retch, clasping his stomach in pain, my mother wept for joy at the reunion with her children.

Zeus reached out his hand to me.

"You are free from him now, Demeter," he said, the first words I had heard. "I have saved you. And I will fight beside you, always."

That was my first encounter with my glorious brother. The hero. The almighty Zeus. Oh, how naive I was.

He was right about one thing, though. For ten years, Cronus's own children waged war together against the Titan King. Battles raged and blood was spilt. But a decade is barely a breath to immortals, and the moment of our victory came swiftly. In the end, it was achieved through the alliances that Zeus formed with Cronus's enemies, with the Hecatoncheires—the Hundred-Handed Ones— and the Cyclopes that Cronus had imprisoned in Tartarus, the deepest region of the Underworld. The infernal heat of that storm-filled abyss—which is distant from the earth as the earth is from the sky—is where the vilest of creatures were imprisoned and tortured. A punishment they would have endured for all eternity had Zeus not freed them to fight beside us. And they fought with a vengeance.

Strengthened with divine food and drink, the Hecatoncheires shook the earth in their wrath. They tore apart mountains and raised the sky with winds so violent that trees were ripped up by their roots and scattered as easily as an autumn breeze flings dead leaves from branches. They caused devastation the likes of which Cronus could never have imagined. But it was the three gifts from the Cyclopes that secured our victory.

The one-eyed giants bestowed a present on each of my brothers. Hades, the eldest, received a helmet of darkness that, when placed over his head, made his image slip from sight, rendering him as invisible as a shadow on the blackest of nights. To Poseidon they gifted a trident, with which he could wield all the power of the sea, causing the water to swell and rise at his command. And finally to Zeus, my youngest brother, they gave a thunderbolt, with which he struck down our father and brought about the reign of the Olympians.

Our reign.

This was the Golden Age.

Or at least, that is what we were told.

CHAPTER TWO

T
ELL ME WHAT THAT ONE IS," I asked, pointing to a bird
resting on a branch of an oak tree.

"That," Zeus replied, "is a turtledove."

"A turtledove."

I let the name roll over my tongue as I continued to focus on its
song, which was deeper than many of the other birds' I had learned
that day. A low, resonant trill that I was certain I could listen to for
hours on end.

Zeus was already striding ahead, pointing out a more colorful
specimen.

"Come, Demeter," he called. "There are many things I wish to
show you."

After all those years confined in the rancid heat of Cronus's
belly, I continued to marvel at the wonder of the outside world and
would do so for decades after Zeus freed me. My previously suffo-
cated lungs rejoiced at the clean crispness of the breeze that wafted
below a cerulean sky, each lungful invigorating and a testimony to
my freedom.

My eyes, which had been forced to endure centuries of darkness, drank in the vivid color of sunlight reflecting off the gold-paved corridors of my palace. The marble pillars and the bronze statues dazzled with a ferocity that could have blinded a mortal but kept me captivated, as did the tinges of blue in a flickering flame, or the hundred different hues shining in every sunset. I lost days, weeks probably, awestruck by the infinite tones of blue and green in a calm sea and then the shades of gray that swirled in those same deep waters when a storm struck.

My ears, which had endured my siblings' every moan and whimper as our bodies were squeezed together, now feasted on melodies. Not just songs, but the music of the earth. The sound of water as it weaved its way down a mountainside, and the dulcet laughter of the naiads as they danced and skipped through it, were to me as any melody picked out by dexterous fingers on a lyre. I could hear a thousand notes in a flower blooming or an acorn forming, while bursts of a seedpod or the tinkle of a spray of pollen in the air offered rhythms to which my very heart would dance.

I found such joy in these gifts that I would sometimes look down from our palace on Olympus and feel a twinge of sadness at my inevitable separation from that natural world. That is not to say that I was confined. Occasionally I would leave, passing through the golden gates that marked the boundary between our home and that of the mortals, to feel again the softness of the grass beneath my feet or the coarse grain of wood bark on my palm. And though I tended to avoid mortal company, I would sometimes watch maidens picking flowers in meadows or singing as they harvested corn. And it was in those moments when I walked on the mortal lands that I found my power.

I had been raised in darkness, but now light and life surged within me. At first, my touch was required. A graze of my fingertips against a soft blade of grass would create a single flower, fully in bloom, with its petals reaching for the sun, just as I had done. In time, that same touch could transform an entire meadow into an avalanche of color. Flowers, ferns, foliage of every form would spring to life. I created life. But I did not stop there. I tended my gift. Nurtured it. And with such encouragement, my power grew so strong that I could perform such acts from the very palace of Olympus. With the whisper of a word, I could create a harvest bountiful enough for a thousand men or mold a mountainside with dense forest. I could tend to the mortals without leaving the comfort of my home. This was my calling. To bring harvests to mortals. To turn those decades of darkness into light and life, and I embraced it.

From my palace, I could see it all. I observed men and women alike as they feasted on berries, plump and lush that burst with juice upon their tongues, and pressed young olives, directing the fresh, green oil into containers, ready to use in their lamps or to season their food. I saw the pulpy meals they would feed their children and noted how similar it was to the food they gave their elderly. And, now and then, I would experience a melancholy at how detached I was from it all. But I would never leave my family. I would never leave Zeus.

Our relationships as brothers and sisters were not like those of mortals. We Olympians were gods. Immortal. Superior. Just as the Titans who had come before us, we were unique beings, incomparable to all others. It was right that we found more enjoyment in one another's company than in any others, but it would be wrong of me not to admit that, for a time, I did not merely love Zeus. I was in love with him, too.

In those early years, it was impossible to find fault in him. For those of his siblings who desired it, Zeus commanded palaces to be built, up on the great heights of Mount Olympus, beneath his own, gargantuan home. So vast was his palace that the entire earth could be viewed from his throne room. Not that mine was lacking in any way. Its bronze foundations shone like the setting sun, and vast pillars edged my cloistered courtyard, within which there was room to host as many deities as I could have ever hoped to gather.

Given that I had no intention of marrying or having children, my palace was smaller than my siblings' and those built later for my nieces and nephews, yet it was all I needed. Located on the lower south side of Mount Olympus, freshwater streams gurgled nearby as they tumbled over the rocks and down toward the earth. I could not have asked for more. Or so I thought.

Now, the foolishness of how I doted on my youngest brother sickens me to the core, but back then, I was besotted by him. I was in awe of this great god who had rescued us and created palaces for us in which we wanted for nothing. He was our savior. Our liberator. How could I not love such a being? His glory shone brighter than Helios' sun beating down upon the earth. Even when his flaws slowly became apparent, I never believed he would be anything other than kind toward me. Once again, my foolishness shows, for it had been through trickery that he had made our younger sister, Hera, his wife.

Hera had spurned Zeus's every advance. She, like myself, was intent on staying a maiden, but that was not her only reason to decline his attention. He had already taken a wife, Leto, who had yet to bear him any children. Hera was far more perceptive of Zeus's questionable behavior than I was, but like always, he managed to get his way.

He came to Hera on the hills of Crossus, disguised as a bedraggled cuckoo. With her warm heart, she took the creature in her arms and held it to her, hoping that her warmth might go some way to reviving the feeble bird. In a moment, he transformed and took her there and then, against all her protests. Shamed, Hera took Zeus as her husband.

The morning of her wedding is one I will not forget, as she wept at the future she now saw for herself, long before I recognized it. The sun shone with a brightness that only Olympians could endure, but in Hera's chamber, a dark cloud shrouded the goddess.

At her request, she had sent all her nymphs and handmaidens away, and it was I, her sister, who attended her. In my eyes, there was none as beautiful as Hera, with her tawny locks, piercing gaze, and the quiet demureness that, back then, she possessed in such abundance. Mortals and gods alike fell silent in her presence, stunned at such magnificence. Yet it was when she smiled that she was most beautiful. She could light up the whole world, more luminous than a thousand burning arrows. But on this day, darkness engulfed her.

"He still takes other women, you know."

Her eyes were fixed on the mirror in front of her as she spoke.

"I see his eyes wandering, not only to goddesses but to mortals, too."

I remained silent, braiding her hair, interlacing each gleaming twist with a pure-white lily, as I considered my answer. Now, when I think back on what I said to her, it causes me to shudder.

"You will be Queen of the Gods, Hera. Zeus will not hurt you again, nor will he betray you, when he has you as his wife."

Silence descended on us. Despite what I had said, I'd heard rumors floating around Olympus, circulating through the hallways and slipping into the ears of any who would listen. Gossip was rife, and every day a dozen new stories passed the most loquacious lips, but I knew it was one particular piece of gossip that plagued my sister.

"Leto was his wife, too," Hera said. "And I know you have heard what they are saying, that she is carrying his child, even as he makes me his wife."

Her eyes shone with tears as they fixed on mine, waiting for me to refute these words, but I could not lie to her. I had heard them myself and from sources close to Leto. Ones who had nothing to gain by spreading such falsehoods. Silence engulfed us again as I searched my mind for something to bring her at least a modicum of comfort.

"Leto was a Titan. She is not like us. Theirs was a pairing that was doomed to fail. It will not be the same for you."

"How can you be certain?"

I brushed my hand against her face, locking my gaze on hers as I spoke.

"Zeus was rash when he married Leto. He did not think through his actions. But he loved you from the first day he freed us. He chose you, Hera. He would not have been so insistent that you become his wife if he did not love you."

A half smile played on her lips, which deepened as I kissed her cheek.

"My beautiful little sister, Queen of the Gods. How happy you will be." Hiding the pain that it was she Zeus chose, and not myself, I returned to braiding her hair.

Zeus hurt and betrayed Hera more times than a mortal witnesses the sunrise and caused her to endure more torment than anyone should suffer. But this is not Hera's story. It is mine, and it would be wrong to say that Zeus hurt me.

He destroyed me.

The day that he came to me, I had been sitting on one of the rocky outcrops of Olympus, watching the life of a mortal play out beneath me. The baby was born on the island of Lesbos to a shepherd and a young woman with auburn hair. By the grace of Eileithyia, the birth had been quick, and I watched as the mother plucked the child from between her legs and held it to her breast, weeping with joy. But mortal life is so very brief to an immortal, and it felt as though I had barely sipped from my cup of ambrosia when the child was toddling between his parents and then attempting his first words. Another mouthful and he was waist height to his father and helping him guide their goats over the stony terrain. It was when that baby, now an old man with hunched shoulders, was telling his grandchild of his youth spent on the hillsides that Zeus arrived.

"You are watching the mortals again, Sister," he said.

Radiance glowed around him, and I knew from the way a smile curled on his lips that his mood was playful, and that the temper we all knew burned within him was currently held at bay. By this time, he had been married to Hera for many centuries and his indiscretions were well known, but he had achieved so much as ruler, both for the humans and for us gods, that when I looked at him, I still saw that same savior. He was the reason I was blessed with such a wonderful life. I did not know that this very day, the blinkers would fall from my eyes.

"You cannot deny you watch over them," I replied, returning my gaze to the earth to find that the old man had already passed on. His family was kneeling beside his body, weeping. The burial rites would be meticulous, with a coin placed in his mouth as payment to Charon, the ferryman, who would guide his soul across the river *Styx* and on to the Underworld, where my brother, Hades, awaited him.

"There is something so alluring about them," I said. "I find myself constantly enthralled by their ways. They live and love so fiercely, despite the fleeting nature of their lives."

"Do you not think it is because of this that they love in such a manner?" he remarked.

"Possibly, but if that were the case, what would it say about our ability to love? Cannot we feel so deeply as they do because of the gift of eternity we have been granted?"

"That is an interesting point," he agreed, and his smile broadened a little more. He paused, his gaze lingering on me, before saying, "Come, walk with me, Demeter."

He took my hand in the same way he had when he first brought light into my world.

We left through the golden gate and passed the Horae who guarded our home and privacy so fastidiously. Then, in the land of the mortals, Zeus guided me to the island of Tenos, where the crystal water shone in vibrant shades of turquoise, so clear that you could see every grain of sand on the seafloor. The scales of the fish that teemed beneath the surface sparkled as if they, too, were of an immortal nature, and the briny scent of the sea pervaded my senses.

Despite all the water surrounding Tenos, the island was, at that time, arid. The muted morning sun, which reflected on the lapping waves, found no lush pastures of flowers or wheat upon which to shine. Instead, the ground was sparsely covered in coarse brown grass that broke underfoot. Yet, as I brushed my hand across those brittle stems, they transformed. Color spread up from their roots as they thickened and lengthened, twisting into golden stalks of wheat, laden with heavy ears of corn. Wherever I touched, the barren land transformed and became fertile, and more wheat, as plentiful as any farmer could ever wish for, gleamed in the sunlight. For this is my gift. This is why mortals worship me, for I am the one who brings them their most bountiful harvests.

When the wheat had reached its full height, I pressed the palm of my hand against the tangled trunk of a withering peach tree. Leaves burst out, bright green and shining. The branches extended to form a wide canopy, which grew so heavy with the weight of amber fruit that they began to bow.

"You are magnificent," Zeus said, from behind me. "You do us Olympians proud."

Even now, I can recall the rush of deep satisfaction that surged through me at his approval, for we both knew the only Olympian he was referring to was himself and my display had been aimed to elicit such a response.

"Thank you," I said modestly, for yes, my gift is magnificent, but I have never thought highly of those who boast.

"Tell me, Sister," he continued. "Have you considered marriage yet? Do you not feel the desire to raise children, as Hera and I have done?"

It was known by this point that Hera and Leto were not the only women by whom Zeus had fathered offspring, but he was my brother and the King of the Gods, and at the time, I considered there to be worse flaws than a fondness for carnal pleasure. Now, I see that this was just one of his shortcomings, but there is not enough parchment in Olympus to record them all.

That day, I pondered his question only briefly, still thinking about that mortal I had been watching before his arrival, whose life had begun and been extinguished in such a fleeting moment. I felt a pang of sadness in my chest.

"I look on the mortals as my children," I told him, honestly. "I keep them fed and nurture them, just as a mother would. That is enough for me. I am content."

It was a truthful answer, which I believed he had hoped for, yet his face hardened.

"You do not wish to further your lineage? To strengthen our immortal family?"

I chuckled at these words.

"We already have dominion over the mortals and have defeated the Titans. What more could we possibly achieve?"

A slight wind had picked up along the shoreline, and from our place in the fields, I watched as the wave caps frothed white before rolling up onto the sand.

"They would worship your children," Zeus continued. "Give offerings and libations that would resound through the very halls of Olympus."

"I have no need for such indulgences," I said, resting my hand gently on his arm. "I am content, Brother. You do not need to worry about me. This is the life I have chosen."

I do not believe I spoke these words with any animosity, nor did I wish to cast aspersions upon Zeus's choices or invite his wrath. At first, I didn't realize that I had, for we continued to walk together through the barren fields in silent contemplation, my hands draped on the brittle stalks, creating a river of wheat in my wake. We had reached a small copse of cedar trees when, from the other side, there came the sound of laughter. Mortal laughter.

"We should not approach," I cautioned. No mortal can see us in our true state and survive; it was not a risk I would take.

"I agree," he said, but added. "Perhaps we could take another form."

I had assumed we would take a human form. This was not the only manner in which the gods roamed the earth, yet in a place where so few animals roved, it seemed the most suitable option, and it was certainly the form in which I felt most comfortable. But Zeus had other ideas. A mischievous grin crossed his face, and his eyes glinted.

"We should become serpents," he said.

"Serpents?"

"Snakes. We can move across the earth and reach their very feet and they wouldn't even know of our presence." That smile flooded through me, and in that moment, I did not view him as the great, all-powerful god, but as my baby brother, wishing to play a childish prank on the mortals. "It could be fun. Mortals are terrified of snakes. You can change into a reptile, can you not?"

Metamorphosis was not a skill I had practiced with any frequency, and before that day, I had never assumed the shape of a snake. As my immortal life would play out, it is a form I would never take again, either. But I was naive, and I wished to impress my all-powerful brother. And so, without further ado, I transformed.

The instant my scaled belly touched the ground, he lunged, pressing me into the jagged stones. I struggled against him, writhing and twisting and thrashing in my new form with all the strength that I could muster. I tried my hardest to escape him, now knowing exactly what he had planned, but he was faster as well as stronger and blocked my every turn. I was powerless against him.

My weak lungs could form no sound as he pierced my skin with his own serpent fangs, pinning me down against a rock. He held me there, my body now limp with fear and disgust until he was done. Zeus, my brother, raped me. He took me, just as he had Hera, against my will, and I knew exactly why.

CHAPTER THREE

I DID NOT RETURN TO OLYMPUS THAT DAY BUT SLITHERED AWAY and returned to my true form on the hillside, where I sat cradling my knees as I wept. At some point, Helios pulled the sun back over the horizon and plunged me into darkness while the wind rose, whipping up the grasses around me and turning the nearby sea into a wild foam. But I was barely aware of these things. I felt chilled to the bone, and a deep ache, greater even than that experienced in the belly of my father, overwhelmed me.

I could not stop myself going over and over our walk together. I had felt so at ease. Had I said something that had led to his actions? Could he have misconstrued any of my comments as an invitation? I scoured my memory yet could think of no behavior of mine that could have given him cause to use me in such a depraved manner. But of course, he had needed no reason or invitation. It was not me that Zeus had desired but my body. I was nothing more to him than a vessel that, like so many others, he had decided to fill.

The silver glimmer of the moon shone high above me when I finally found the strength to move again. Yet the moment I stood,

I felt as though I had no structure at all. As if the very fibers of my being had been shredded and then put together again but in a way that was no longer fit for purpose. I was like a cracked amphora, repaired so that no one could see the fractures, yet so weak that should it ever be filled with wine again, it would crumble.

That was how I now regarded myself—as fragile and worthless as a shattered jug—although this was nothing compared to the desperation I felt when, finally standing, I looked down. A gasp flew from my lips as I stumbled backward, hot tears lodging in my throat.

When I recall that day, I remember little of how the hillside had looked, except that there had been an abundance of yellow. Nasturtiums, perhaps, or maybe calendula. But it matters not which flowers they were. As where I stood, there was no longer any lush grass or bright blossoms. Instead, the earth had turned white and hard beneath me.

Kneeling on the spot where I had wept, I snapped the brittle, frostbitten grass between my fingers and felt the tears prick my eyes again as it crumbled to nothing. I was the Goddess of Grain. Of Agriculture. I was the one who sustained the earth's bounty, but not a single, green blade remained where I had rested my defiled body. This was when I realized my gifts had come from a place of love and gratitude. From peace and harmony. And if these emotions were overwhelmed or lost, there were consequences to pay.

How many days I remained there, I cannot say, but when I finally felt able to return to Olympus, it was early morning and Helios was once again claiming the sky. His watery rays had hidden the stars and sent out long shadows as they burned through the soft, coral clouds. Though it had taken some time, I had repaired the patch of grass that had withered at my touch and restored the blades so they once again shone in verdant green. But the image of that white earth was seared in my mind, almost as deeply as the memory of the act that Zeus had performed on me. An act I was to be reminded of the instant I arrived back at my palace.

I did not need to step inside to know that something was amiss. My home on the south face of the mountain was always filled with music and laughter. Nymphs of the forests and the mountains flocked there to sing and dance and while away the time of their near-immortal lives. Their joyous songs and innocent laughter resonated throughout the palace but most prominently in the courtyard. There, they were most carefree and contented, basking among the flora and marveling at the beauty of nature. Yet when I approached that morning, I was met with an eerie silence that made my skin prickle.

As the sun reflected off the smooth, golden floors, it seemed to have lost all its warmth, and a ripple of apprehension ran down my spine. I'd had no forewarning of what Zeus had planned for me on those meadows of Tenos, but I sensed what was to come now. I was aware of her before I saw her. After all, I had spent decades by her side.

"Hera."

Despite the abundance of seating in my courtyard, she was standing as I arrived, her eyes trained on the archway through which she knew I would enter. The cream fabric of her long robe pooled around her feet and a veil of the same, sheer cloth draped over her golden crown. But it was her face that I was drawn to. Under normal circumstances, the copper tones of Hera's irises were identical to those of her hair, brilliant and bronze. It was easy to see what had led Zeus to seek her out as his wife. But that day, her eyes were shrouded with a darkness intended solely for me.

"So, it is true," she said, as I approached. "You lay with my husband and now you carry his offspring."

As my gifts are bound with nature, so Hera's are with women, and although I had known from the moment Zeus raped me that he would have done so with motive as well as lust, Hera's words erased any trace of doubt in my mind. I was with child.

"Please, Hera," I implored, approaching her with my hands raised in innocence. "I did not lie with him. He tricked me. He took me by force."

"You wandered alone with him! You stole his attention deliberately with your trickery, with nature. You knew this would happen. You have deliberately humiliated me."

The harshness of her words stunned me. Had she forgotten how she had wept to me of her misgivings about her future husband? Had she forgotten that she was the one who foresaw the pain he would inflict upon her? And yet here she stood, with tears glazing her eyes, turning her wrath on me.

"You have always been jealous of the attention he has shown me," she continued, chest heaving. "He told me as much himself, but I did not believe him. You were my sister."

"I *am* your sister, and you are mine. Surely you know me well enough to realize that I would never cause you such grief by choice. Or myself. I did not want this, Hera. I had no desire for Zeus. I did not want him or his child."

"And yet you will raise them, nonetheless. You will nurture them upon Olympus—my home—where I will be forced to face my husband's indiscretion every waking hour. You will flaunt what you have done to me every day of our immortal lives."

There was no doubt in her voice as she spat out these words, though I myself had not had time to consider where I would raise the child, or even if I would. After all, they would shackle me to that dreadful memory that I wished so desperately to expunge from my mind. The easiest option would be to rid myself of it. Offer it to the nymphs or even to a mortal family. I would not be the first mother to do so.

Yet in that same moment, I saw clearly how wrong that would be. The child that grew in my belly had done no more wrong than a flower that grows in the cracks between the bricks of a wall. The thought of raising it so close to Zeus caused the ichor in my blood to run as cold as ice. But imagining leaving Olympus elicited almost the same response. After all, where else could I go? The world was spread out beneath me, but this was my home. The nymphs were my family. Never, since Zeus had ordered the construction of these palaces, had I ever considered that I would spend my eternity anywhere else.

Hera read my thoughts, and fury sprang in her eyes.

"So, you wish to raise them here?"

She stepped toward me, teeth bared.

"Is it not enough that I must continually suffer the presence of Artemis and Apollo? Is it not degrading enough for me that Leto's children command more affection from Zeus, have more prominence, than our own do? That he elevates the standing of his bastard child, Dionysus, to a true Olympian while our own children are not offered the same distinction? Is that not torment enough for any wife to endure? But now this, my own sister conspires against me."

Tears stung my eyes. Swallowing them back, I moved toward her.

"I have never done that, Hera. I did not ask for this. I did not seek his affection. He took me by force. I swear to you, that is the truth."

With a snarl on her lips, she stepped toward me, arms raised. The pounding of my heart felt strong enough to rattle my ribs as I believed she was about to take me by the throat, wrestle me to the ground, and deal out the same punishment as she had to some of

Zeus's other lovers. I suspect this was what she intended. She wanted to hurt me in the same way that she was hurting. She wanted the entire world to suffer.

But the instant her hands touched my skin, something happened. A warmth rose, reminding us of all the time we'd spent pressed against one another inside the belly of Cronus, and memories of how I had comforted her in his dark belly rolled between us. We were sisters.

I felt her touch change. Her hands became limp, and a choking cough spluttered from her lips. The facade dropped. It was she who fell to the ground, and the anger that she had used as an outlet for her pain ebbed away.

"I do not understand why he must humiliate me like this," she choked, and her anguish was echoed by a sudden, cold gust of wind that sent dead leaves whirling about us. "He sought me out. He forced me into this sham of a marriage. Why am I not enough for him?"

I crouched down beside her and pulled her powerful frame into my chest. She trembled against me with no more strength than a newborn.

"When will it ever stop?" she whispered. "Will I be forced to spend an eternity like this?"

I thought then of the morning of her wedding, when I told her that all would be fine, that when she was his wife, he would treat her with all the dignity and respect an immortal queen was deserving of. How I wished I could take back those words. But this day, I offered no false comfort. No assurances that soon he would grow tired of his mistresses and return to his wife a changed man. I knew that his nefariousness knew no boundaries and there was no limit to how many people he would hurt. So instead, I held her. Cradled her until she had no more tears to shed.

When I think back on that moment, how Hera clung to me in

the chill breeze of my courtyard, the aroma of acacia filling the air, I wonder if it was the last time she allowed her helplessness to show. The last time she allowed the pretense of invulnerability to drop. I wondered how many more of her husband's indiscretions it would take until she was broken beyond recovery, but I now believe that may have been the one.

When her tears came to an end, she stood and brushed down her gown. I wished I could find something to say to her. Some way to ease the pain that inflamed us both. But it was Hera who had the last word.

"You should know, you do not carry one of Zeus's children," she said. Her voice was once again filled with iciness as she offered the swiftest glance to my belly. "You carry two."

CHAPTER FOUR

I WAS WRONG TO THINK THAT I LOVED THE MORTALS THAT I SO keenly observed from above. I had affection for them. Deep affection, particularly for the young ones, of that there is no doubt. They brought me great amusement and companionship, even if they were not aware of it. But love? I did not realize what love was until I held my children against my skin and felt warmth flood from their tender flesh into my own. I did not understand the meaning of devotion until I heard those first wails echo and I knew, with all the strength that my Titan parents had bestowed on me, that I would die before I let them come to harm. I did not know that a heart could swell so greatly that it both throbbed with fear and surged with affection until I fed them from my own body. I did not know that all these things could come from being a mother.

My mother Rhea attended the birth of my twins, although I felt no need for her presence. I did not fear the pain that mortals suffer in such instances, and I knew I could not be afflicted from the sickness that often struck them after an infant's arrival. Yet she wished to attend the birth with me. Had I been filled with the same paranoid drama of my siblings, I could have seen her presence as an invasion of my privacy, or worse still, assumed she wished to act as a spy for Zeus, and garner information about my children's gifts to pass on to him, but what would be the point of such a thing? Zeus saw all. Zeus knew all. Besides, she was my mother and she loved me. So when my muscles spasmed and tensed with the ripples of impending birth, I left Olympus with Rhea and Meliae, a nymph and dear friend, at my side and traveled together to the river Pactolus, where the shallow waters washed over me, bringing the aromas of wild maple and crocus flowers from the riverbank. This was where my children were born.

When Iacchus was freed from my womb, his cries were bright and shrill, like a note from a salpinx pressed to a soldier's lips to mark an impending war. His wails stopped only when I placed him against my breast and he drank hungrily, guzzling down as much milk as his young stomach would hold. But when Core came into the world, there were no cries or tears. No angry wails of hunger at her cruel, swift removal from a place of such comfort within me. Her bright eyes were wide and open. Her fleshy limbs pinked with the heat of my body. And when her eyes met mine, it was with a look of knowledge, of deep understanding of who I was to her, and who we would always be together, and I knew my life would never be the same.

"They are gifts to the world," Meliae said as she gazed upon me with a babe cradled in the crook of each arm.

Rhea, too, looked on in awe, before meeting my eye and dipping her chin with the slightest of nods. "They are gifts indeed."

When we returned to Olympus, it quickly became apparent that my two children were as different from one another as a lion was from a butterfly. From the moment of his birth, Iacchus displayed his father's temper and restlessness. Tantrums would strike at the slightest sign of discomfort, and I found myself struggling to calm him. If I did not feed him the instant hunger struck, he would hammer his fists against me and let out high-pitched screeches that echoed throughout the halls. He was a baby who refused to sleep but grumbled and grouched every hour that he was awake from tiredness. He did not seem to want my attention yet yelled viciously if I was not in his presence. Thankfully the screaming stopped when he was old enough to walk, but the trouble did not.

As a boy he was obstinate to the core. If I asked him to remain in the vast confines of our home and play with the nymphs, he would disappear without a word and run rampant through the palaces of the other gods. He did not care whose home he trampled through and what gods might reside there, as he raced through marble corridors, running wild, knocking over vast amphorae, spilling wine, or else clanging swords and shields against the cloisters so that the noise reverberated for miles around. Of course, if I suggested he would benefit from some time outside of our home, he would lounge about for weeks on end, barely moving from the couches unless to command a nymph to bring him yet more food. And when I tried to reprimand him for his actions or insolence, he would turn his back and storm away, determined to undermine me at every turn. And I knew why: I understood from the day he was born that he knew what he was, and the pain of this knowledge had engulfed him. For though the blood of great gods flowed in his veins, Iacchus, for all his abilities, could have been a mere mortal.

My poor, poor son. How he longed to be powerful. To be immortal. To be viewed in such esteem as his half brothers, Ares and Apollo. Even many of the children that Zeus had sired with mortals possessed more divinity than my darling Iacchus, and his humanlike impotence caused him constant outrage.

No matter how much I wished otherwise, everywhere Iacchus turned, he was faced with his inferiority. It was not only his half siblings and cousins whose mere presence gloated their preeminence. Even the nymphs that resided in my courtyards could aid the growth of the flowers and fruits in my garden, displaying more divinity than him. Yet Iacchus had inherited one trait from his father: his father's wandering eyes and taste for women.

As soon he was old enough to leave Mount Olympus, I could no longer keep a rein on him. At first, he left only for short whiles, and in the company of my trusted nymphs as companions, but it did not take him long to learn to slip away from his chaperones and sneak off into taverns and bustling agoras, to places where the delicate nymphs did not dare to wander.

I must have lost fifty years of my eternal life worrying about Iacchus, scouring the view from Olympus, looking into every corner of the earth in the hopes that I would find him and be able to bring him home for good. Though at some point, I awoke to the realization that if I had ever had any control over him as his mother, it was gone.

Soon, he was absent far more than he was ever present, and he would wander from city to city, in search of unsuspecting maidens that he could charm with wit and wiles. He would beguile these innocent youths with his curling locks and talks of the marble colonnades of Olympus and tales of his great father Zeus. He would seduce them relentlessly, and once he had taken what he wanted, he left these poor innocent women without so much as a backward glance. Sometimes he didn't even bother with seduction; he merely took these women the same way his father had taken me and so many others, leaving them alone to deal with the consequences of his actions.

I was as repulsed by his behavior as any mother would be, and I tried every action I could think of to stem his ways, bribing him with gifts and promises and casting empty threats as fast as my mind could form them. But the truth was that there was nothing I could offer him. He wanted to be worshipped. He wanted sacrifices made in his name and temples raised where candles were lit in his honor and songs written about his grace and strength, but we both knew that would never be. Gradually the time between his returns to Olympus increased, and even when he did return, he would make no attempt to find me, his mother. Soon, I could barely recall when we had last spoke, and had it not been for Core, I could have gone mad with a mother's grief. But my darling Core was everything that Iacchus was not.

"You know that he will be fine, Mother," she would say as she danced to the music of birdsong in our courtyard. "I would feel if something bad had happened to him. You would too. He will return to us when he is ready."

And her words would always ease my tension, if only a little, for I knew that she spoke the truth. My beautiful, truthful, perfect Core. I do not use the word *perfect* lightly. I, who have been in the presence of all the great gods and divinities, have seen perfection in all its ruthless forms. But Core had not a hint of ruthlessness within her. Her heart was a pure as the lilies that grew in Hera's name.

"Look at the flowers, Iacchus," she would say. They were young, new to the world, and she was full of curiosity. With the touch of her fingertips, she caused a hundred daffodils buds to spring into vivid yellow blooms. She picked a handful and took them to her brother, far too naive and pure of heart to see the jealousy that was already forming a bitter seed within him.

"They are just flowers," Iacchus replied. "I don't know why you bother with them so much." His words were always biting and cold, but she would bring him the flowers all the same, before returning to the dryads with her smile, blissful and content as though her brother had thanked her for her gift, the way a generous sibling would. Core was my mirror, my daughter. She was all I could have dreamed of, and never did a cruel word leave her lips or a selfish thought enter her mind.

"Look, Mother, I have created a home for the ladybirds among the rushes," she would say, taking my hand and pulling me over to the stream so I could see the insects she had gathered there.

"Look, Mother, I have made the nymphs wreaths from the flowers you grew. Look, Mother, I have made posies for all the gods in Olympus. They will like them, will they not?"

Every innocent word she spoke brought light to the world, for despite her conception, she had not a hint of her father's darkness within her.

"The humans were created by the gods," I told her when we walked the earth together one day. A procession of nymphs trailed behind us, marveling at the trees with their gnarled and twisted roots, or the bright redness of the poppy flower as they danced at music they heard in their own heads. Often, Core would join them, her bare feet gliding over the earth as she twisted and twirled lifting her arms to the clouds above her, but just as often, she would walk beside me, her hand clasped in mine. "And as we created them, it is our duty to nourish them, to give them the grain that will sustain them."

"It is your duty and mine." She smiled at me as if she were hearing this for the first time. "And we will do this together, always."

Perhaps it is cruel of me to admit such a thing, but upon hearing words such as these, my heart would swell and even with Iacchus's absence and the trauma of how my children had come to being, I was happy. As long as I was in Core's company, I felt a sense of peace. A belief that whatever misery I had suffered beforehand was worth enduring, for it had to have brought me to this point. For a hundred years or more, I told myself that as long as I had Core beside me, then she would be all I ever needed. I had no desire to take a husband, or even a lover, to add to my company. I needed nothing other than what I had. Or at least that was what I believed, until I saw Iasion.

CHAPTER FIVE

I T WAS A WEDDING OF A MORTAL AND A GOD, AND BY ZEUS'S request, all twelve Olympians were required to attend. *Olympians.* For mortals and lesser gods, the name instilled a quaking fear. An image of greatness, impervious power infused into our immortality. But I had seen through the facade. There was no permanence in our position. No security. A child born with greater abilities than my own could usurp me in a heartbeat. Could usurp any of us. Besides, there were hundreds of nymphs and deities that considered the mountain palaces their homes. Why should only twelve of us be revered with such a title?

I will not deny that Zeus's cunning was cleverly calculated. From the moment of our release, my brother had seen what our father refused to acknowledge: that keeping his most powerful family members close and allowing them to bask in shared glory and worship brought him allies and allegiances. His own renown and stature were secured and reinforced by the renown and stature of those he kept close to him. He was made greater by our greatness. And despite this, and everything else I knew of him, I stayed close.

Hastening when I was summoned, acquiescent in his requests. Even after what he had done, I remained the doting sister.

My sycophancy made my stomach turn. The fake smiles I plastered on my face in his proximity were enough to make my teeth grind. Tension wreaked my body every second I was forced to endure his presence. I balked at the mere mention of his name and at every word that came from his lips. Yet I never let on, because even then, I knew he could do more to hurt me. For now, I had more to lose.

While Iacchus was rarely to be seen, my bond with Core had strengthened further still and the tender threads of our love were so impermeable that I could no longer imagine a life without her. Her laughter was sweeter than any nightingale songs. Her soft humming enough to draw the attention of every nymph on our side of the mountain and just the sound of her singing was enough to make my heart leap with pride.

When night fell, the pair of us would lie together on the soft grass and gaze at the stars, immune to the gentle breeze or damp as we absorbed the aroma of night jasmine that wafted thick in the air. Sometimes, the snuffling hedgehogs and ever-vocal geckos offered us their chorus. Other times, I would tell her tales from my past or sing her melodies that had drifted up from the Land of the Living.

During the day, Core wandered freely down the mountainside, plucking flowers that grew in abundance around Mount Olympus. Despite having her own chamber, her preference for sleep was always to lie with her head against my shoulder or chest. I would close my arms tightly around her, relishing the slow rhythms of her breath.

Just as I knew it would, the day arrived when Iacchus's mortal frame could no longer sustain the strength of his spirit. But my knowledge of such an occurrence did not diminish my grief. My only son was gone. Passed into the Land of the Dead, Core was all I had, and so I made the choice to no longer leave Olympus. No doubt grief played some part in my reclusiveness, for the mortal lands were full of reminders of my son, but as strange as it sounds, the more proximity I maintained to Zeus and the other gods, the more at ease I felt. That day on Earth when Zeus had taken me, he had stolen not only my body but my freedom too. He had planted within me a seed of wariness. Wariness that bloomed decade after decade.

The fear was of him but also of the Land of the Living. Merely the thought of being alone there, free to be violated and abused, caused a dark fear to rise within me. I did not tell anyone this, of course. I was a goddess. My fears were irrational. So my smiles remained fixed, and if Core ever commented that she wished to leave Olympus to walk on the fields of Lerna or Attic Colonus, I would comment on how we could see everything far more clearly from here on Olympus, or comment on how our thin air made the aromas all the sweeter and all the colors even more intense. Thankfully, my invectives worked, and Core remained upon Olympus by my side, rarely asking to wander beyond our sanctuary. That was how the centuries passed. Perhaps it was how they would have passed for all eternity, had it not been for that wedding.

I had observed mortal weddings before. I had watched the rites in a hundred towns and always fixed my attention on the women, the brides. The traditions altered slightly in every city, but some aspects were always the same. The bride would ride in a chariot to her new home, with a veil shrouding her face, and often her tears, as she sat in stoic fear or rapt elation. Meanwhile, a procession followed behind her. Full of color and music, guests laughed and danced and sang songs with such passion they roused our interest all the way to

Olympus. It was from Olympus that I hummed along to the tunes they sang, and laughed at sweet jokes the grooms told their brides, but never had I sat among mortals on such a day. Not until the day I met Iasion.

Twelve thrones were placed around the edge of the room for the Olympians. Zeus took his place in the center. I took a seat at the furthest edge. It was my desire not merely to distance myself from him but also to stay as close as I could to my daughter, although she was well beyond the age of requiring supervision.

The bride and groom sat closest to us gods, and I will confess to feeling the deepest swell of envy as I observed the pair. Radiance shone so vividly from them it was almost tangible. Their love visible to all. Dressed in the finest silk robes, Harmonia's hair was woven into loose braids adorned with pearls, while her fingers were decked with rubies and emeralds. Cadmus, for his part, barely took his eyes off his bride, his cheeks glowing with pride. Around them, music flooded the hall. Drums accompanied the intricate melodies of flutes and lyres that played at a counterpoint, while men and women twirled and laughed, pausing only to feast on the banquets, which spilled from the tables.

Core was quickly lost to the mortals, slipping between the dancers, and mesmerizing those at the tables as she spun simple garlands with her fingertips, which she draped around their necks, displaying her gifts for them all to see. Without her to watch over, I was forced to endure the company of my family.

"Look at Hephaestus. The great oaf is practically red with fury. I am amazed he is in attendance at all." A watery chill slipped down my spine as I turned to discover my brother Poseidon had slipped into place beside me. His garish trident gleamed in his hand, and a sly lopsided smirk spread wide on his face. He had picked the form the mortals revered the most—older, with a white beard that fell in waves like his hair. But there was no fatherly kindness to such a mask, and the glint in his eye confirmed that it was all for show. "What threats do you think Zeus promised his son if he were absent from today's events?"

I did not want to answer him. I did not want to be drawn into that endless web of family politics, but I knew he would not leave without a response.

"I am sure no threats were needed, it is a great honor to be here," I replied, although my eyes skimmed past Poseidon and rested on the chair at the opposite end of the hall, where Hephaestus was sitting stony faced, hands clenched on the arms of his throne. No one needed to ask why Zeus and Hera's son looked so ill at ease.

The wedding was between the mortal man, Cadmus, and Harmonia, goddess of harmony. She was the daughter of Aphrodite, Hephaestus's wife, but Harmonia was not Hephaestus's child. She was fathered by Ares, his own brother.

Sympathy surged within me as I studied the beast of a man. It was Hephaestus himself who had caught the lovers and exposed his wife's infidelity, and now was forced to watch on at this spectacle.

"I suppose it is no different from Hera," Poseidon continued to talk at me, despite my silence. "She must sit with Artemis and Apollo. It must be something you simply adapt to."

Still, I continued to ignore him, but Poseidon is nothing if not tenacious, and, as he took a cup of wine from the tray of an awaiting servant, he positioned himself a little closer to my throne. His eyes scanned me up and down, causing a shudder to run the length of my spine, though I did not show him as much.

"Why do I see so little of you, Sister? I cannot remember the last time that you and I dined alone."

"I cannot think of a time when you and I have ever dined alone," I replied truthfully.

"Then perhaps that is something I should rectify."

The temperature around me dropped, as if it were not merely the seas he controlled, but every drop of water that hovered in the air. From Cronus to Zeus, I knew that malignity ran in the blood of my brothers, and whatever plot Poseidon was hatching, I had no intention of falling prey to it that night.

"If you will excuse me," I said, rising from my seat. "I promised Core that I would find her and dance. She is fond of mortal music."

As I stepped off the dais, I did not look back to see the scowl I knew would be fixed on Poseidon's face. Instead, I felt a small sense of triumph at how my behavior was likely to annoy him. After all, he would not risk enduring Zeus's wrath in front of such a crowd, and despite his title of Olympian, Poseidon rarely stepped through the clouded gates of our mountain, preferring instead his palace of corals and gemstones that sat flush to the seafloor. He would, I assumed, be easy enough to avoid until this rebuke had been forgotten.

A rush of freedom flooded my veins at escaping his company so easily. Given that I was unsure where Core had disappeared to, my aim was simply to lose myself in the crowd until I stumbled across her or one of my nymphs, but instead, I found him. I found Iasion.

All these years have passed, yet I remember that moment so clearly. A single shaft of light cut through the courtyard, illuminating him, reflecting off his dark hair and the bangles on his arms, while everything around him was shrouded in darkness. The way he shone, it was as though he was the singular god in the room, for how could a mortal ever look so divinely perfect? His eyes glinted more shades of blue and green in the irises than one mortal should ever possess. Like the sky and seas and the fields had all combined with only their purest, most blazing tones and they were staring straight at me. My feet moved without my consent, drawn to those eyes with a power stronger than that of all the gods combined. Then in a flash, all the color was gone, and Iasion dropped into a deep low bow.

"My goddess, Demeter." Like all the mortals that attended that day, his clothing was an obvious display of his wealth, and a delicate white pattern was embroidered along the hem of his deep blue robe. The bangles around his arms, though gold, were subtle and slim, and other than a single emerald ring upon his finger, he wore no gemstones at all. "You honor us with your presence here," he said, body still bent in a bow. "I must apologize, for I am ill prepared. Had I known I would speak to you, like this, face-to-face, I would have brought an appropriate offering. Forgive me, my goddess."

"There is nothing to forgive. You are here for the celebrations, not to offer me your libations."

"Be as that as it may, had I known…had I believed you would be present…"

His words stuttered and stumbled before disappearing into the air between us, and I felt an overwhelming urge to stem his embarrassment.

"There is nothing to forgive," I repeated. "But perhaps if you feel it necessary to show your devotion, you would sit awhile and talk with me."

At first, he remained in that deep bow, his cheeks flushed with heat, those luminous eyes glinting wildly at me, possibly searching for a trap within my words.

"Of course. Of course," he said suddenly, as if deciding there was no trickery in my request, or that it was not worth the refusal even if there was. He stretched out his hand and gestured behind him, indicating a small fountain that was less crowded than where we currently stood. I, in response, smiled and stepped forward. I did not know then that I had met the only man I would ever love. And that by the end of the day, he would be lost to me forever.

CHAPTER SIX

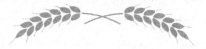

THERE WERE HUNDREDS, IF NOT THOUSANDS, IN ATTENDANCE that day, but when I walked toward that fountain, I swear Iasion was the only one I saw. Every other person, mortal or otherwise, blurred into the background. Their voices indistinct mummers, no more articulate than the gurgles of a river or rushes of the wind. Upon the realization that he was about to entertain a goddess, Iasion hurried ahead of me so he could wipe the marble slab of the fountain seat with the fabric of his robe. Even when the stone was polished to a gleam, he continued to scurry about, attempting to locate cushions for me to sit upon.

"Please, I am perfectly comfortable without cushions," I assured him, sitting down on the fountain's edge to prove my point.

His brow furrowed, unconvinced. Still, he did not refute, and took a seat a respectable distance away. Even with all the pain I associate with our moments together, it is hard not to smile at the memory of him hastily trying to wipe the dust from his robe, unable to stop his hands from trembling as the sun cast him in golden rays.

If I were forced to pinpoint exactly what drew me so intently to this beautiful young man with his dark hair and ethereal eyes, I would say it was humility. Every man in my life oozed arrogance. Immortal and mortal alike, they relied on their bravado. They would regale audiences with tales of their heroic deeds and wax lyrical about the monsters they fought and defeated to any who would listen, regardless of the truth in their tales.

At no point did Iasion try to impress me with an epic rendition of his brief life, although I will profess, I had never seen a man plump a cushion with such intensity and ferocity as Iasion did when he suddenly spotted one that was available for me.

"I do not believe you told me your name?" I said, when I took a seat for a second time, now on the cushion.

He flushed, embarrassed by such a simple question. "I am Iasion, son of Philomelas."

"You are a prince of Samothrace," I said, recognizing the name of his father. "Why did you not introduce yourself as such?" Bashfulness shone through him as he dipped his chin. While his eyes were trained down, I studied where the soft line of his jaw and the dark curls of his beard looked misplaced against the youthful glow of his skin.

"I did nothing to claim that title, my goddess. It was given to me for no honor other than my birth. But I hope to live up to the name at some point. To be a good prince to my people."

"I do not doubt that you will," I said.

On cue, a group of young children, five or six years of age, clamored toward him.

"Iasion, play with us!" one said.

"Pericles has captured a monster!"

"A monster, you say?" Iasion threw me a smile that caused my stomach to flutter in a manner I had never before experienced.

"Please, you must come see!"

It was likely that at the beginning of the wedding, these children had been immaculately dressed in fine robes and fabrics, but several hours had passed since the chariot had arrived, and by that time, in the early afternoon, many were looking as disheveled as street children. Several had abandoned their sandals, and the once pale soles of their feet were now as black as coal. Their hands were covered in earth, and the previously neat pleats of their robes crinkled and creased.

"You must tell Pericles that I am very impressed with his endeavors, but I cannot leave my company. I am sure he will catch plenty more soon." Despite Iasion's smile, the children's faces fell fractionally, but he spoke again. "Tomorrow I will catch a monster with you all. I know where the largest ones hide upon this isle."

Seemingly satisfied by this answer, the children spotted another adult whom they wished to cajole into joining them and hurriedly fled from our side.

"So you catch monsters with children, Iasion, prince of Samothrace?" I said, feeling the playful toy of a smile on my lips.

"I will be honest, Goddess. It is Pericles who catches the most, although I may have had a hand in one or two." At his words, my cheeks ached with a warmth, and a light fluttering returned to my stomach. It was a similar sensation to that I had experienced when I was first expelled from my father's stomach and the entire world was a marvel to me. When the simple sound of birdsong or rushing water had caused me to stop and marvel at the magnificence of life. That was, of course, before Zeus had claimed my body. Before he stripped my love of simple things, like the shirring rush of wind through the tree and the way light could splinter as it shone through clouds.

The dancing and singing continued around us, a constant whirring and swirling. Men and women drank and ate and reveled in the merriment of the occasion. But Iasion and I had been caught in our own current. A deep undertow that pulled me out of the room and dragged me ever closer toward him. There were no pauses in our conversations. No gaps where silence punctuated our words, or where I considered how to make my apologies and withdraw back to my family.

"Had I known the chaos the goat would cause, I would never have brought it into the palace." His eyes glaze with tears of laughter as he recounted his tale. "My mother hid me in the servants' quarters, fearing the beating my father would give me."

"Did he?" I asked fearfully. "Did he beat you?"

"No. My father puts on a good act of ruthlessness as king, but in reality he is softer than even my mother. Still, I will allow you one guess as to what meal we were served that evening?"

"Goat?"

"Yes, indeed! That very goat, to be precise."

Together we laughed so heartily I needed to wipe tears from my eyes. Never before had I experienced such frivolous joy.

A dozen times, the stories he told made me throw back my head in laughter. A stomach-strained laughter that, outside of my darling Core, no person had caused me to experience in the centuries since Zeus's assault. We must have been speaking for over an hour before the conversation took a more serious tone. The hours since our arrival had passed quickly, and most guests were so instilled with the mirth of wine, it was difficult to hear his words. I had shifted closer still toward him.

He was the child of seven, he told me, only to change his answer almost immediately after offering it.

"Six," he said instead. "Or seven."

"You do not know?" I said, assuming he had stumbled because of the normal bind of a lusty king with a string of illegitimate children.

"My brother Eubouleus was lost to us only six months past," Iasion answered. "In truth, I have been unsure how many siblings I should say I possess since then. I never wish for him to be forgotten, but nor do I wish to mislead."

"I am sorry for your loss." My heart throbbed at the pain that shone from his eyes. He did not need to speak to me to know how deeply he loved his brother and felt his absence. I had felt the loss of a loved one. It is a pain that cannot be expressed in words, even by those who have experienced it.

"What happened to him?" I said, only to realize the impertinence of my question. "You do not need to tell me. Only if you wish to."

"I do. I do," he said, almost emphatically. "I find it peaceful to do so. To keep his memory strong. But as for what happened, I can only offer speculations, for that is all any of us have."

From across the hall, laughter bellowed. Deep and raucous, it was at odds with the somber moment that shrouded us. Yet for all the solemnity of our time together, I cling to it still. And for all the shadows that crossed Iasion when he spoke of his brother, I felt only warmth at his words.

"Eubouleus was different from me, in all the best ways. He was a man who could light up a room without a word, and he could sing far more melodiously than any of our sisters. His zest for life was so infectious. I suppose that is why it is so difficult he is gone." He stopped, the smile gone, the shadows deepened. "Your brother Hades, he does not attend today? I believed all Olympians were to be present."

"Hades would not lower himself to be considered an Olympian," I replied with a smile, not sure why I felt the need to inject a hint of humor into our conversation. Iasion nodded, seemingly oblivious to my attempts to temper the moment.

"It pains me that Eubouleus did not get the burial rites he deserved. Not that I know of, at least." He still had not told me what happened, and I was tempted to prompt him on the matter, yet somehow, I knew it was the silence he needed as greatly as the words, and so I waited, aware that our bodies had shifted so close together that our knees were but a hair's width apart. "He was on a trade boat," Iasion started slowly. "My father has plenty of trusted emissaries that can trade for him and travel instead, but Eubouleus was insistent. Samothrace is only a small island, but more than once, we joked that all of Poseidon's waters were not great enough to hold Eubouleus's ego." He smiled at this, as if it were a joke he was sharing with a family member, or perhaps Eubouleus himself, and a deep warmth burgeoned within me, although it was quickly extinguished.

"None aboard the ship survived," he said. "Rumors swirled that it was Charybdis's vicious whirlpools that drafted them to their death. That they were pulled beneath the surface so quickly there was no hope of escape. I doubt we will ever know for sure, but he is gone. I feel it in my bones that he is gone."

"I am sorry," I said once again, hearing the hollowness of my words, yet Iasion lifted his eyes and smiled at me as if I had offered the most comforting words a goddess could grant.

"My mother has found it the hardest," he said, pressing his lips together as he paused. "Eubouleus was her youngest. She doted on him. She wished for more children still, but her age forbade it. He was her last baby. Now, she spends her time staring out over the sea, watching the ships as they come and go. She is empty, and I wonder if she will ever recover from this loss."

I knew that there were no words I could offer that would bring him comfort. More than anything, I wished to take his hands.

I wished to entwine my fingers with his in the hope that I could erase just a fraction of the hurt that gripped him. Yet my family was present, and even at a distance I felt the overbearing scrutiny of my brothers. And so I rose from the marble fountain and looked to Iasion.

"Would you care to take a walk with me?" I said. "I feel that some fresh air would be beneficial to us both."

CHAPTER SEVEN

THE COOL, CRISP AIR WAS A SHARP CONTRAST TO THE MUGGY heat of the hall, and it was only upon seeing the sky that I realized how much time had passed since Iasion first invited me to talk with him. Time spent on Earth moved differently than the hours whiled away on Olympus. The constraints of Helios's golden chariot slowed the pace of our existence. For that, I will be eternally grateful.

We kept a respectable distance from one another as we left the laughter and merriment of the wedding. The singers were already slurring their words, their pitch wavering from the drink, and I felt a sense of unfamiliar excitement rippling through me, growing infinitely more intense the more secluded we became. Soft pink clouds gleamed with hues of peach that shimmered as the sun sank beneath the horizon.

Step after step, the songs faded behind us, the melodies lost as they drifted away and into the breeze. As easily as the words had flowed between Iasion and me within the hall, silence swelled between as we walked together. For a moment I feared that such silence may be impenetrable, when, with the slightest hitch in his voice, Iasion spoke again.

"You have a daughter, do you not?" he said. "I believe I saw her tonight."

"I do. Core."

"Maiden," he commented, for that is indeed what her name means. Simple. Pure. Like Core herself.

For an instant, I considered remaining silent about Iacchaus. Pretending that Core, the genial goddess he had witnessed that night, was my only child. But it was Iasion's truthfulness and tenderness regarding his brother that had drawn me to him, and I was not ashamed of the path Iacchaus had taken. Only saddened that my love was not enough to keep him from it. My throat tightened before I spoke again. "I had a son, as well. Core's twin brother, Iacchaus."

Iasion's eyes widened at this news, although he did not press for any further details, as I thought he might. Had I needed any reassurance of his good nature, this was how I received it. A second or so passed, in which I let my gaze wander. Nothing but ploughed fields stretched out in front of us. Deep brown earth, rich with the scent of petrichor.

"And do you wish for more children?" Iasion said, quite suddenly.

"Excuse me?"

Immediately, his cheeks turned crimsoned. His eloquent speech transformed to a rapid stutter. "I, I apologize. That was impertinent, my goddess. Please forgive me. Forget I asked such a question." He bowed deeply, hiding his eyes and edging backward, no doubt fearing my wrath. But I did not condemn him for such words. Instead, I stretched out my hand and brushed my fingertips against his bare shoulders.

"Iasion." He lifted himself upright, and my hand fell from his shoulder, down to my side, where my fingers found his. Fingertips touching, then palms pressed together. Warm skin against warm skin. It was the first touch that we had shared. The first touch I had shared with any being in such a manner, and my body reveled in it. Sparks raced through my skin as real and hot as a thousand bolts of lightning. My lungs struggling to hold the dense air that eddied round us.

"Goddess?"

With my pulse knocking hard in my chest, we stood motionless on the soil, his own heartbeat drumming through our shared skin.

"I have never found a man I wished to have a child with," I said truthfully.

He nodded, accepting my words, but our fingers remained intertwined and neither of us moved by even a fraction.

"Iasion," my voice came out as a whisper. I feared even to blink, so terrified that so small an action could break the spell that was weaving around us both, for I knew in my heart that it was not just I who felt this deep yearning to hold him closer than I had ever held any man before. A yearning to taste the sweetness of his skin.

"Goddess…Demeter." My name, passing from his lips like a breeze, was all it took. With heat surging through me, I pressed my mouth against his and experienced the first, the only true kiss of my life, only to have him jerk away.

"You must be certain, my love," he said to me, holding me at arm's length. "I do not wish to presume. We can wait."

"I have waited longer than you could imagine for this," I said, only realizing the truth of the words as I spoke them. Now that I had Iasion beside me, I understood I had remained unmarried, not because of my virtue or morals, but because none like him had ever entered my life before. I, who had watched mortals for more hours than the beach holds grains of sand, knew there was no mistaking this emotion that flooded through me. Time did not matter. I had spoken more of my soul to this man than I had ever done before. This was love.

I knelt down on the soft brown earth, stretching out my hands and beckoning him to join me.

"You are certain?" he said again, and I locked my eyes on his.

"I am."

We made love on that ploughed earth as the sun slipped below the horizon. As stars, one by one, brightened the sky, we learned the movements of one another's bodies. I felt the smooth skin on the back of his shoulders and a scar down the ridge of his back where he had fallen in a play fight with his brothers. I tasted licorice root on his tongue and breathed in deeply the aroma of musk, so earthy it could have been created by Gaia herself. How I wish I could have tasted more of him. How I wish I could have bottled that scent and rubbed it at every place where his lips kissed me so that his sweet aroma became my own. But wishes made by gods are no more fruitful than wishes made by mortals. Now, when I catch a whiff of such a scent on a breeze, I am transported back to that field, to the pressure of Iasion's body against my own, and the swell of heat that built within me, and every moment of it is tainted with grief.

When we finally broke away from one another, our skin was slick with sweat and wheat as high as horses bulged above us from the previously barren earth.

"That was...unimaginable," he said, a boyish grin lighting his face. "To touch your body, to kiss you." He ran a stream of kisses up my arm to the most tender spot on my neck. My body grew in ways I did not know was possible. It had been reclaimed by me, for me, and now, for Iasion.

"We should return to the party," I said. "I should find Core." At my words, he moved away from me, and the light that had shone so brightly in his eyes dimmed.

"What is wrong?" I said, fearful that I had somehow tarnished our moment together.

"Nothing. Nothing is wrong. Except I do not know how I will continue to exist without you by my side. For I did not know it was possible to feel so completed by another. To love such as I love you."

Now kneeling on the dirt, I clasped my hand around the back of his neck and fixed him there so that my eyes bore down into his.

"I feel the same," I said, and kissed him again. "And we will find a way."

In my mind I envisioned the future together. A future with both my daughter and my lover and all the children we would share. I breathed in this image, basking in the unbridled joy until my heart swelled so greatly, I feared it might break free of its human garb.

When I think about that moment, the conversation that Zeus and I had held before he defiled me always arises in conjunction. Our discussion on whether our immortal lives limited our ability to love as intently as the humans. Because that was when I learned the truth. I could love as fiercely as the fires of Tartarus, and my passion could burn as brightly as the sun. Those brief hours were all it had taken for Iasion to own my heart entirely.

"Come, we should return," I said.

Upon standing, I saw the state of Iasion's body. While the ploughed earth that we had laid on was now bursting with colors and blooms and wheat twice our height, our own bodies were drenched with dirt. Smudges of soil covered his knees and back, and grains of earth were embedded into the creases of his skin.

Looking down, I saw I was in a similar state.

"Come," I said, sweeping my hands across his chest to brush away the stray dirt. "Now turn around."

We laughed like we were young children. I even had him lift his hands above his head, reminiscent of a child being scrubbed clean by a parent. And when his body was free from all except the smallest specks, he repaid the action, brushing down my body. Having his hands rub across my skin in such a manner was like bathing in a waterfall in the moonlight. It took more restraint than I knew I possessed not to encourage his groans, but I believed we had his entire life ahead of us. Longer still if I made him immortal. It would not be the first time a god's lover had been granted such a gift, although I would ensure I oversaw the transition. When Zeus granted immortality to the goddess Selene's lover, he remained in a constant sleep, and while Tithonus, the mortal lover of Eos, was granted his eternal life, he continued to age and his body grew frailer and frailer with each passing year, until he could no longer maintain a human form, and Eos turned him instead into a cicada. I would not let such trickery befall Iasion. When we were clean, we fixed our robes around us and headed back to the wedding celebrations, our hands in one another.

Having been so preoccupied, I had not considered how the party would have progressed in our absence and was surprised to find the atmosphere far more subdued. Many guests had already departed, and those who remained had fallen victim to the wine. While some of the drunks behaved raucously, others were more lethargic from their overconsumption. The children, who had been intent on catching a monster, were mostly asleep, laid out on the couches or upon their parents' laps. As I entered the hall, my aim was to find Core and to return to Olympus, with the full intention of telling her about Iasion. Not the intimate details, but that I had found a man whom I loved, a mortal who loved me with a truest heart. But before I could seek her out, I found my route blocked.

Zeus stood before me. Lightning bolt in his hand.

"You have been missing, Sister," he said.

Behind my brother, the other gods were immersed in conversation, downing one cup of wine and then another. Oblivious to us. Or at least acting in such a manner.

"Not missing, merely taking a chance to observe the island." No matter how casual I attempted to keep my tone, my voice wavered with a slight tremble. One he would have heard and reveled in. It disgusts me now, how I ever cowered to him. How I thought, even after all his deeds, that he was worthy of my respect. But back then, I was still learning my true strength. "Prince Iasion has been kind enough to show me what he knows of the island." I cast my eyes to Iasion with a slight smile, and when I turned my attention back to Zeus, the great god's chin dipped in a half nod. For the length of the longest heartbeat, I thought he was about to turn and leave me and my lover. That he would return to Hera or his children and enjoy the last dregs of festivities from the wedding. But he grabbed me by the wrist and yanked my arm upward.

"What is this?" He prodded his finger against the bony joint of my elbow. I could not see what he spoke of, but with a forceful jab, he drew his fingertip against my skin. When he withdrew it, it had darkened with a smudge of earth. I tugged my arm from his grip.

"Do not touch me," I hissed, struggling to pull my arm away.

"You are telling me not to touch you when you let vermin such as that human defile your body?"

At the insult, Iasion bowed deep to the ground. "I am a prince, mighty Zeus," he said. "I am Iasion, son of Philomelas—"

"I do not care who you are." Zeus looked only at me, as if Iasion were nothing more than a fly buzzing around him. "Why? Would you do this? Why would you befoul your body with such a man?" The hall had fallen silent. My siblings now leaned forward. Their eyes glinting eagerly at the impending foray.

"*You*, of all men, dare speak to me in such a manner?" His lips curled upward in a snarl, but I held my ground. "I love this man."

I stretched out my hand to Iasion, who rose from his bow and stood beside me. Facing the mighty Zeus, he began to speak.

"I promise you—"

I promise you. I promise. I hear those words over and over and over in my mind, for those are the last words Iasion ever spoke. Before he could utter another word, Zeus lifted his hand. The lightning bolt gleamed in vicious white. I realized too late. Too late to block the bolt of pure white light that blasted from the tip and struck my lover dead to the ground.

CHAPTER EIGHT

MY MIND COULD NOT COMPREHEND WHAT I HAD JUST seen. The white flash that engulfed the room left me momentarily blinded. The static buzzed with fierce heat, only to evaporate an instant later. My senses were temporarily numbed, but when they returned to me, the first sight I saw stole the air from my lungs.

"Iasion, no! No!"

Crumpled on the ground, his eyes were wide in confusion. No breath passed between his lips, no heartbeat, faint or otherwise, drummed beneath his ribs. His skin was as pure, as pristine as it had been only seconds ago, but there was no life left in his body. As I dropped to the ground beside him, a wail of anguish violent enough to send the birds from their roosts flew from my lungs and filled the hall. "It cannot be! It cannot be!" Never had I felt such an intense pain, so acute it afflicted my ability to even draw breath.

"Mother! Mother!" Core's voice was only peripheral to me, as if spoken through heavy fabric. Yet she dropped to the ground beside me and pulled me into her chest. "Mother, I am here. I am here. I am with you."

I am certain that more words were spoken, but I must confess, I cannot recall them. Even the embrace of my darling child failed to lessen the agony that was consuming me more and more with every passing second.

"He is gone. He is gone." I gripped my daughter with such force that it would have shattered mortal bones, though she made no attempt to loosen my grasp.

Only moments after Core arrived at my side, the nymphs flocked around us, their murmurs barely audible above my cries. It made no sense. My entire future had been ripped out from beneath me. Only a second ago he had been there, and in that brief walk to the palace, I had dreamed a new life. Now that dream had been replaced with a nightmare.

As my laments continued, I failed to hear the fresh sounds that rattled around the great hall. At the moment of Zeus's strike, the musicians had stopped playing, and children, woken by my wailing, sobbed and whimpered while their parents tried to hush them. Several of the women were weeping at the sight of the body, while more still scurried away from the hall. Yet there, motionless amid it all, stood Zeus.

"I fear the party has been brought to a close by your display," he said, raising his voice above mine. "Never mind. I was growing bored. Come, we shall return to Olympus. You can continue this scene there if you must."

His callousness alone drew me from my grief and replaced it with a new emotion. More raw and inhuman than anything I had ever known. Slipping from Core's grip, I pushed myself onto my knees and glanced upward, scouring the faces beyond Zeus. Poseidon wore only a sneer of satisfaction while Hera's eyes remained down. And so I knew what I would say. My family, my sister and those closest to me, had dismissed my lover's murder without a second's thought. Turning my attention to Core, I hoped she would read what was in my heart and understand that there was no other way.

With my shoulders pushed back, I drew on all the strength of my Titan blood and rose to my feet. Those that remained in the hall were motionless as I locked eyes on my youngest brother and took a single step toward him.

"I will not be returning to Olympus. I will go nowhere with you."

Every person in the room could have anticipated his response, and he did not disappoint. His arrogance smoldered within him, as he threw his head back and laughed. He laughed at me and my pain.

"Of course you will return to Olympus. It is your home. Come, all this fuss for one mortal man who you barely even knew. I will fetch you a hundred if that is what you want. And ones from much better stock than Philomelas, a half-wit king of a fraction of an island. Now come, my patience is wearing thin. This is not up for a debate."

He did not believe I was serious. That I might truly refuse him. After all, I had returned to Olympus after Tenos. I continued to live beside my rapist under his rule. Why would he think this should be any different? But this was different. I was different. In those few hours I had spent with Iasion, I had been transformed. Through his eyes, I had seen all the wonder and power that lived within me, and I refused to let him down again.

"I am not returning to Olympus."

Every word I spoke was punctuated with venom. No longer was Hera staring at her lap. Now her attention was on me. Hera and Hephaestus and every one of the gods and mortals alike. Every breath in the room was bated as they waited for Zeus's response. Though at first, he merely seethed. The careless laughter that had drifted so glibly from his lips had evaporated. The smile of satisfaction on his face slowly transforming into hardened stone.

"You would dishonor me. After all I have given to you?"

Oh, how he should have picked his words more carefully.

"Dishonor you? *I dishonor you?* You are the one who dishonors us all, time and time again."

His jaw snapped together. Teeth gritted as he spat. "I have given you everything."

"And what of all you have taken? Do you ever think of that? Of how much you have taken from everyone around you?"

"I am King of the Gods."

"You stole my innocence."

"I placed you upon a throne."

"And I am done with you."

The words flew into the ears of all those around me. Eyes widened. Cries were muted and in front of me, Zeus's face darkened.

"You will not survive without me," he hissed, so quiet he could have unsheathed the image of the serpent that he wore all those years ago.

"I have the whole of the earth at my fingers."

"And you will roam it alone and miserable."

"No," I shook my head. "No, I will not."

"She will never be on her own." It was Core's voice that rang out in the hall that night. Crystal clear and more tuneful than any nymph, her voice answered in rebellion to the King of the Gods. Her words rising to defy her father, where so many others had withered under his glare. My love for my daughter swelled beyond depths and heights I even knew were possible. She stood beside me and against her own father, but not only because I was her mother, but because it was the right thing to do. In the briefest second, as I watched her glow with power and beauty and saw the woman she had become, it was almost enough to forget my shattered heart.

I will not underplay the acts of my nymphs that night. With no direction from me or Core, these beautiful beings encircled us and stood beside me against the King of the Gods. Yes, they followed me, but they followed the earth just as keenly. It would have been entirely understandable for them to switch their allegiances, or to proclaim neutrality with all the gods, but they didn't. Instead, they formed a wall between my brother and me. They guarded me from his wrath in a way that my own family did not. Meliae was the first of those nymphs to turn and look the great god in his eye.

"She will not be returning to Olympus," she said.

"None of us will be returning to Olympus."

The nymphs spoke with all the conviction their delicate hearts could muster. Had I the strength, I would have applauded their defiance, but Zeus's fury remained on me. Behind him, the other Olympians awaited his response. Would he grab me by the wrists and drag me kicking and screaming through the golden gates? Or would he strike me down, murder me in plain view of mortals and gods alike? *Let him do it*, I thought. *Let him kill me.* I would rather have that than be subject to his tyranny for all eternity. But then, as he sneered down his nose at me, I saw a glimpse of something I hadn't expected. Confusion. Confusion at what would happen with me gone. Would the mortals still receive their harvests, and if they did not, would they still worship the greatest god of all? His hesitation lasted only a moment longer before he spoke.

"Do as you wish. What you do has no impact on me."

Oh, how wrong he was.

CHAPTER NINE

MY FIRST SENSE OF PURPOSE CAME ONLY TWELVE DAYS AFTER the death of Iasion. We had been in search of a place where we could settle, at least until the birth of Iasion's children, which I had known were growing in my belly from the moment we left the ploughed earth. This pregnancy was entirely different from that which I had experienced with Core and Iacchus. The humanity of my unborn infants seeped into me with a nausea I had never experienced. Waves of it swept in, leaving me unable to speak, sometimes even stand. My body was weakened by these children, not strengthened, although I reveled in it, for this weakness was the only closeness that remained between Iasion and me. Iasion was gone.

How those words echoed around my mind.

Iasion was gone.

More than once, I considered allowing my grief to overwhelm me. It would have been possible. Welcome, even, to allow the darkness to fill my lungs and draw me in as keenly as water. To let that mortal fragility within me swell until I was consumed by it entirely. I became close. Frighteningly so. I considered rejecting the immortality that had been placed upon me. I considered returning to Olympus and demanding that Zeus aim his thunderbolt at the frail remnants of my heart, the same way he had done with Iasion. But every time the shadows descended and frost formed at my fingertips, I would find Core beside me, holding my hand, abating the darkness. Holding back the shadows as if it were she, and not Helios, who had control of the golden chariot.

We traversed islands close to Crete, which we believed would offer the best sanctuary, and the archipelago offered us countless options, like the large islands of Naxos and Carpathos. There were islands inhabited with hundreds of people, where the land was cultivated and goats teetered their cloven hooves on the cliff edges, while the clanging of their bells rang out for miles around. Other islands were sparse and rocky, the ground still unploughed, little more than dry scrub and weeds scarcely scattered between stone earth. Some of these lands reminded me so greatly of Tenos, the island where Zeus had violated me, that I would lose my breath and find my knees unable to hold my weight. Core and the nymphs assumed this fragility merely another symptom of my pregnancy and hurried me to take a seat upon the same rocky earth from which I was desperate to flee. Island after island we scoured as we searched for a place to build our new home, but every time, we left almost as soon as we arrived, until my nephew found us.

The day Hephaestus came to us, we were resting on the sandy shore of Siphnos, an island that, back then, was home to less than a dozen families.

Viewed from a distance, the fine sand glittered like the purest of golds, and the deep alcoves cut into the rock faces offered shelter from any wind. Further inland, mountains rose, cutting great curves from the skyline.

As the cool lapping water shirred over my feet and disappeared back into the sea, I felt as close to peace as I could, lost in a daydream that I knew would never exist. Absentmindedly, I drew circles over my expanded belly and imagined that Iasion was with us. Like a child whose mind is full of fanciful stories, I concocted a tale in which Iasion was merely somewhere out of view. Perhaps he had taken a small boat out to catch fish for our dinner and later when he returned, I would gut them. I would scrub the hard scales with a stone before roasting the meat on hot coals like a mortal wife would do. Perhaps I imagined he was collecting kindling, or stoking a fire somewhere sheltered, to keep us warm when night fell. So many daydreams consumed my thoughts as my mind intertwined fantasy and reality with such complex intricate webs it was almost as though I had slipped past the veil of the living.

What I do remember of that day is the way the nymphs' laughter stopped. Given the dryads' affinity with the forest, it was the nereids who remained with me at the water's edge. The sea nymphs frolicked in the salty spray. Those dozen creatures, whose song was a constant, fell silent at exactly the same moment. Such an absence is enough to draw the attention of anyone, even someone as lost in a daydream as intense as my own.

"Mother." Core's voice was steady, but in the single uttering of my name, I heard her unease. Unease that ran into me like a cavalcade. Zeus. That was the immediate thought that struck me. Zeus was here. When I turned back to the shore, I saw I was mistaken, though it was an Olympian who invoked this terror.

I will make no pretense. Hephaestus's appearance is monstrous. The ugliest of all the gods, he has been constantly and cruelly ridiculed for his exterior, but his disfigurements are through no fault of his own.

Hera's son was born weak, with straggling limbs and each rib visible and protruding from his skin. More pitiful than a runt kitten, and Hera had been so disgusted by the sight of this sickly, insipid child, she had refused to accept it as her own. So rather than present Hephaestus to his father, Zeus, she tossed him from the heights of Olympus.

Through the clouds, the baby tumbled. His wails lost to the rushing wind as he plummeted down. No mortal would survive such a fall. But Hephaestus was not mortal and, as fate would see it, did not land upon hard rocks or jagged earth, but rather plunged into the sea. Protected by the soft surf, his fall slowed as he drifted downward. It was there, in the dark waters, that the gentle goddesses Thestis and Eurynome plucked him from among the corals and took him to their underwater home. There, beneath lapping water and swirling currents, they raised Hephaestus as their own. Away from the prying eye of Hera and the Olympians.

During his decades with Thestis, Hephaestus learned the skill of a smith. In the heat of his deep forge, he hammered metals and shaped fine stones. He learned practical skills, filing and lathing, shaping and melding, creating from dusk until dawn. And his creations he offered without a second's thought as gifts to Thestis and Eurynome. Gifts they accepted with pride and wore with honor, which was how Hera discovered that her son was alive.

When Hera saw what Hephaestus was capable of, she insisted he return to Olympus, where she fashioned for him a smithy with twenty working bellows. It is there that Hephaestus set about building our palaces. It is he alone who crafted the great throne room in Zeus's palace and who built the bronze pillars and detailed mosaic flooring in my own Olympian home. Oh, the creations of Hephaestus are wonders to behold. I know that over the years, the humans used to compare their own craftsman, Daedalus, to the god, but even the mortal's greatest creations do not compare to Hephaestus's work. Though even after his return to Olympus, his tale is not a happy one.

Given his role in creating the gods' homes, Hephaestus was granted Aphrodite as his wife. A wife he truly loved. Who he spoke of with nothing but genuine adoration. It is sad that such affection was not reciprocated. Still, he remained content in this new life, or so I believe. Until Zeus stole his happiness. The way he stole everything from everyone.

During their years together on Olympus, Hera and Hephaestus reconciled. I do not know the details of their reconciliation, and for mortals, I suspect it would be difficult to understand how a child could ever forgive a mother who had thrown them from the highest height. And despite our strained relationship, Hera loved her son. Though now, I wonder if she regrets that love. For it was her reconciliation with Hephaestus that lost him the use of his limbs.

Hera's affection for her own husband had been waning. Of course, given his actions, it is more surprising that any affection remained there at all, but that is irrelevant. Zeus was, as Zeus so often did, attempting to take Hera against her will. But this time, Hephaestus was there to defend his mother. The fight was short-lived, a cat toying with a mouse, and Hephaestus was thrown to the earth for a second time. Given my brother's wrath, Zeus ensured his son's landing was far less cushioned than a foam-filled sea.

The morning he walked toward me on Siphnos, feathery clouds littered the sky. His motion was stilted. An unsteady limp, aided by his leg supports, which shone like the gold of the sand.

"I apologize, Demeter," he said, bowing deeply. "I do not wish to disturb you. I have been searching for you."

"I will not return to Olympus, so your time has been wasted,

I'm afraid." I was calm yet far from amenable when I spoke, and so it surprised me when Hephaestus smiled.

"I am sorry, you misunderstand. I have come to apologize."

This I was not expecting. Gods did not apologize. I remained silent and so Hephaestus continued. "As you may be aware, I was somewhat consumed with my own ego at the wedding. Had I had an ounce of dignity, I should have stood beside you and your nymphs." Judging from the light chuckle that rose from his lips, I suspect I wore the shock of his confession quite plainly. "Our family has difficulties," he added. "I understand what is like to be favored and rejected, perhaps more than any."

"Your apology is most gracious, Hephaestus."

"The words are not my apology, Demeter." A smile now twisted on his lips. "I do not think words are a sufficient apology for what you have experienced." He bowed his head again in a show of deference before he spoke again. "It would be an honor, Goddess, to build a home for you. Wherever on Earth you so choose."

"A home?"

"Assuming you are not to return to Olympus, as you so boldly proclaimed to my father?"

His offer left me breathless. The risk he took going against Zeus in such a manner sends shivers down my spine even now. Immortal or not, I dreaded to think what great malady could befall Hephaestus if he were tossed from Olympus for a third time. Which is why I replied without hesitation.

"You risk too much, you cannot."

"Let me worry about what risks I am taking. You must only choose the place."

So on that same island, by a shallow and meandering stream, Hephaestus built a cottage. A home for Core and I and the nymphs that had bravely joined us. It had none of the lavishness of Olympus, but we needed little. Just a space to sleep, to eat and sit.

Hephaestus got to work that very same day. When he was done, I wept tears of gratitude, a fraction of faith in my immortal family had been restored.

"The children can stay here with us, even if they are mortal," Core said to me one evening as she braided my hair, weaving flowers between the strands in the same manner as I had with Hera all those centuries before. The birth was fast approaching and with each twinge, I expected their arrival. "The nymphs and I will help you raise them."

"I know you would, my darling. I know you would."

"They could fish, and swim. They would be happy here."

At that, I could not reply.

Oh, how I wished to keep Iasion's children with me. It broke my heart to know that I would have to leave them, but I would make the same choice a thousand times over. For they were only half mine. Half my lover's, and from what he had told me, they were needed elsewhere.

Their birth had been without pain, and I allowed myself one night with them on the island. One night to feed them and hold them against my skin and allow their warmth to wick into my body. One night was all I had with their father and that had to be enough. After that, we began the journey to Samothrace.

CHAPTER TEN

MORNING WAS BLEACHING THE STARS FROM THE SKY WHEN our ship rounded the island of Samothrace to make port. The babies, less than a week old, were strapped to my chest, as close together as they had been in the womb. During the journey, I had reveled in the time we had spent together: me, my sons, and Core. A small family unit, but a family nonetheless, with bonds of blood and devotion that weaved around us all.

"You do not have to do this, Mother," Core said, as she stood beside me on the bow of the boat, our destination growing before our eyes. "It is not too late to turn around."

"We have each other, Core," I replied to her. "We will always have each other." As I stood there in silence beside my child, I set myself a limit. A point from which I could not return. As the ship drew its anchor into the stony seabed, I was to be tested on it. I had fed the babies all the way to the island, but was determined that once I set foot upon the shores of Samothrace, they would no longer be mine to nurture and care for. Once I felt the soft sand of Iasion's homeland beneath my feet, I was nothing more than a nursemaid to these children. Less. A protector. An emissary. It was time I gave them to their true family.

The position of the palace upon the peak of the island offered its people a view out over the Thracian Sea, and as we departed the ship, I paused and stared in sadness at those sandy-colored bricks. The irony cut me deeply. Wherever she stood in her home, Queen Olesia—Iasion's mother—was forced to look out upon the water all day. To look out upon the sea, when it was the sea that had stolen her youngest son. Of course, it was I who had stolen another.

"You will wait here for us," I said to the captain of the boat as I took those first tentative steps onto dry land. "I will return before sunset."

He nodded to show he understood, yet remained absolutely silent in the same manner he had done the entire journey. He was a mortal who knew of his place among the gods.

From the shore, we walked onward until we reached the base of a hill. Crude steps stretched upward toward the palace. The babies had eaten hungrily in those last hours upon the boat, and I knew it would be several hours before they awoke. Still, I walked fast.

Only two others joined me on the walk toward the palace, including the dryad Meliae, who had birthed both these twins and Core and Iacchus all those years before. Meliae was closer to me than my own sisters. She had been the first to stand against Zeus, her loyalty unwavering. However, as we began the ascent to the palace, she walked behind Core and me, a bag slung over her shoulder, the contents of which I could not bring myself to consider.

When the entrance to the citadel came into view, I slowed my steps. The wind was stronger at this height. Blustering, it forced the trees to dance to and fro in the pale morning light. Light glimmered off the brass plates of the guards as they marched to meet us.

Drawing to a stop, I turned to Core and took her hands. "From here, I must go alone."

She tilted her head to the side. "There is no need for you to do this on your own, Mother. I can be with you. I want to be with you."

My darling daughter. Always thinking of me. Always thinking of others. Perhaps having her by my side would have lessened the pain I was to feel, but there are times when pain should be numbed and times when you should let it burn through you with all the fire your body can withstand. That day on Samothrace, I needed it to burn.

"It will be easier this way, for all involved." I squeezed Core's hands tightly. "You do not need to worry for me. For any of us." Since the birth of the twins, she had been the most doting sibling, cradling her younger brothers at every opportunity, often with one in each arm as she sung them to sleep. She had plucked them flowers, told them stories of Olympus and all the gods who roved there, and even divulged a tale or two of her own twin. Standing outside that citadel, I saw in her eyes how it pained her to leave them, yet such was the way of Core. Perhaps I should have thought of her a little more. I should have considered how she felt being left on the outside. But that is only one of many mistakes I have made with my daughter.

"I will wait here for you, Mother." She accepted my decision with no further objection. "If you need us, we will come."

"I know you will."

Stepping forward, I kissed her gently on the forehead, then stepped back and opened my shawl, allowing her the space to kiss each of her brothers. Her lips lingered on the soft skin of their heads, before she lowered her head further still and whispered in their ears. I did not hear what she said to them that day, but I imagine she spoke of her endless devotion to the children. No doubt she told them how she would continue to watch over them. How she would love them for the span of their mortal years and a thousand years beyond that.

With her farewell complete, Core stepped back, and wiped her cheeks with the back of her hand.

"Meliae, the bag," I said.

"You are capable of carrying it?" The dryad asked. Such a question from any other nymph would have caused a rebuke from a god. Perhaps even myself. But I knew her words came only from love for me.

"I am perfectly capable," I replied. Despite my words, my body stiffened as Meliae handed me the bag. The long strap would easily have crossed my chest, even with the two newborns tied tightly to me. But instead, I carried it at my side and kept it at a distance. The weight of the bag and its contents were light enough, yet the heaviness they placed on my heart, near unbearable.

As I separated from my small party, the guards, who had been watching our approach, left their posts to meet me. No weapons were raised, but their demeanor was far from hospitable.

"I am here to see Queen Olesia." I spoke before they question my presence.

"The queen does not take visitors." It was the shorter of the guards who spoke, spitting his words, as though I should be intimidated by such a display. I forced through my sorrow to offer a smile that even Aphrodite would have failed to find fault in.

"She will see me," I said. "Tell her the goddess Demeter requires her presence."

Had I been in a better frame of mind, I would have found humor in the moment that followed. How the facade of the powerful guard dropped entirely as the young man's eyes widened in an expression of childlike awe.

"You will need to prove such a claim." His companion moved to join us.

I had not expected the need to defend my name, and it took me a moment to consider a way out of my predicament. Or rather, it took a short while to consider a way that would not wake the babies, or fill these young guards with terror. A small sapling had forced its way between the slabs on the path to the palace. It was little more than a weed, with half a dozen willowy leaves jutting out from a spindly stalk. I did not move from where I stood. I muttered beneath my breath—purely for show, for I did not need to speak a word to actuate my powers. As I muttered, the sapling thickened around the stalk. Green tendrils twisted toward the sky, turning brown as they formed thicker and thicker branches. The two men dropped to their knees and dropped their gaze, trembling as tears filled their eyes.

"So you will take me to the queen now?"

CHAPTER ELEVEN

A VENEER OF DUST DULLED THE VIBRANT FRESCOS THAT LINED the walls of the palace, giving the impression of desertion, though I knew that not to be the case. My eyes lingered momentarily on the muted paintwork before I continued to follow the guards. Despite the cool breeze that rippled the curtains, the air felt stagnant. Unnaturally still. It was a sensation with which I was well acquainted. This palace was a home in mourning. A home from which laughter and love had been snatched far too soon.

The arrival of a god on such a meager island as Samothrace should have warranted a greeting by the king. At the very least, a fanfare by the princes. But King Philomelas was absent, hunting on the far side of the island with his sons. He would be alerted of my presence immediately, I was informed, after which it was suggested that I would perhaps prefer to wait for him than to greet the queen alone.

"I have come to see Queen Olesia," I repeated, with just enough terseness in my voice to cause the mortals to quake. "I have no need to wait for her husband."

And so five guards accompanied me. Initially, the formation consisted of two leading me through the corridors, while three followed behind: a formation undeniably similar to that in which prisoners were accompanied through the palace. As such, after hushed whispers and furtive glances, those at the front dropped back and walked parallel with me.

Other than Cadmus and Harmonia's wedding, this was the first time I had made my true self known when walking among mortals, and it came with a sense of unease. It is possible to remain ignorant of one's power when you are surrounded by beings equally powerful. Less so when you hold at your fingertips the ability to tear about a thousand lives without so much as a whisper. Not that I considered harming the mortals who resided in this palace. They were my family. Whether they knew it or not.

So far, the newborns had not uttered even a whimper as they remained strapped close to my body, obscured from view beneath my light cloak. They remained that way—hidden from sight—even when we weaved down our final corridor and reached our destination within the palace, the gynaeceum.

I had watched gynaeceums from Olympus. These rooms, which were solely for the women to congregate, were normally the heart of the house. In these places, I had listened to the bubbling laughter and raucous words of women free to speak their mind, away from the gaze of men. In this central sanctuary, they would sing and dance and weave and sew. This was where they could gossip and wax lyrical about inconsequential matters such as parties and fashion, seek confidence about lovers they had taken, or confess their fears and debate wars with as much wisdom and acumen as the men of the house. It was a place where they could come together in love and humor. Or so I had seen. But in this room, there was only grief.

A loom stood in the corner of the room, which, like the frescos, held a thick coating of dust. The fountain, while still bubbling, was green along the edges of the marble, and several of the plants had overgrown their pots, with leaves and vines stretching out and running along the ground. The place was returning to nature. Flies buzzed around the food, left untouched on platters, and a cloying, viscous odor hung in the air.

Three women were present in the room. Two sat silently on a couch near the loom, embroidering a cream fabric with blue flowers. The third sat upon her own. Her back was rigid, hands clasped on her lap as she fixed her sights out of the window to where gentle whitecaps of waves glinted in the distance.

My heart ached, not only for her loss but for mine. In my mind I could hear Iasion's voice speaking of his mother's loss, and I knew it would not be long until time had distorted his soft tone and the true timbre of my love would be lost: as ephemeral as the waves with which the queen appeared transfixed.

"Queen Olesia?" I stepped toward her as I spoke her name, although she appeared not to hear me. "Queen Olesia, I have come to speak to you." My request was met by silence, though I took her lack of protest as an invitation to move closer still. The two women who had been sewing upon my arrival were waiting with needles poised, listening in. "You may leave us," I said.

The two women exchanged a glance, deservedly perturbed by this stranger who was ordering them about in their home. Before they could protest, I spoke again.

"I suggest you speak with your guards as to why you would be foolish to deny my request." And then, purely for the pleasure, I caused the vines that had escaped their confining pots to rise further still, wrapping around one of the marble pillars. I did not need to speak again. Dropping their material and thread to the ground, they hurried out into the hallways.

With the women gone, I took a seat on a couch beside the queen, placing the bag that I carried by my feet.

"They think I am wrong." Her words were her first acknowledgment of my presence, though her gaze remained outside the room. "They think I am wrong to grieve in such a manner. I have other children. I should be a mother to them. But how can I be? I am not fit for the task. If I cannot protect them, what good am I to them? What good am I at all?"

Years later, these words would haunt me. What good at all? Had I the experience I now possess as both a mother and a goddess, I might have responded differently. But perhaps not.

"From what I hear, Eubouleus chose a life of a hero," I said. "And he received a death of one, too."

At this comment, her head snapped around to face me. She must have been little more than a child when she birthed Iasion, for even then she looked young enough to carry more children still. But her eyes held no spark of youth. They could have been as old as the Titans for the depth of grief they held.

"I do not possess my children's bones," she said coldly. "Heroes have a grave. Eubouleus or Iasion do not." She paused, only to return her attention to the water. When she spoke again, the coldness had gone, but the sorrow remained. "They say the gods took him. That Zeus himself slayed my precious son. But for what reason? For what dispute could the King of the Gods have with my Iasion? There was not a hint of malice within that boy. Perhaps that is why he was taken."

I did not wish to converse through tears, and yet the pain that throbbed behind my temples begged to be released. Drawing strength from a long and labored breath, I reached to my side and lifted the bag I had carried with me, placing it a few feet to the side, in front of the queen's feet.

"I cannot offer any comfort for the loss of Eubouleus," I told her. "But I bring this."

Wordlessly, she leaned down, loosening the strings that ran along the outside of the bag. As she pulled the fabric apart, her hands flew to her mouth.

"This is the tunic he wore the night I met him. The night he died. I have the rest too. I have what he needs for his burial."

His bones remained on the boat. If she had not accepted them—I could not fathom a reason that would occur, but I have learned not to presume with mortals—then I intended to bury them myself on Samothrace. But as she shook her head, flicking tears from the corner of her eyes, I knew I would be leaving his bones on this island.

"Thank you," she said.

This was the first time since entering the room she truly studied me. "You were with my son. You were with Iasion?" She looked again into the bag, and standing, she pulled the tunic out and stifled another sob. "Thank you. Thank you for returning him to me."

Silence in its most tense form descended upon the room and with it a static charge, so dense it felt as though I were in the presence of my brother in Olympus.

Still, no words passed between us as I pulled my cloak from around my shoulders and dropped it onto the couch, revealing the two children.

"They are Iasion's," I said, answering the question she did not have the courage or impertinence to ask. "These are your grandchildren. Your grandsons."

It was too much for her to bear. Her knees buckled. Lurching forward, I held the woman by her elbow. Yet she did not thank me; her face hardened as she edged back away from me.

"You are toying with me," she said. "I see what you are. You gods. Have you not brought me enough pain? Is it not enough that I must suffer his loss that you would torment me in such a manner?"

"There is no torment," I said, quickly reaching for the knot in the cloth that released their swaddling. Gently, I took one of my two sons, the smallest and youngest, and held him in the crook of my arms.

"Look into his eyes. Are they not the exact color of Iasion's? The way the blues and greens melt into one another." I felt a smile rising on my lips as I stared at this child, and for a split second, I feared I had made the wrong decision. For the most fleeting moment, I considered how it would not be too late. I could turn about and sail to Siphnos, to raise my children with Core and my nymphs. We would be happy. I was certain of it. But they were mortals. Their life would be so brief, it did not even compare to that of an oak tree. They needed a life with others like them. With their family. And their family needed them even more.

The queen's hand, which had trembled constantly since my arrival, was steady for the first time.

"May I?" she said and held her arms open. As I placed the child in her hold, a high-pitched mewl rose from his lungs.

"You are right. He looks so like him. The mouth too. That pursing. Iasion would do the very same at this age."

With a steadiness that came from a woman who had seven children of her own, she took a seat back on the couch, but her gaze was no longer lost and unfocused on a distant horizon. Instead, it was fixed solely on her grandson, and the sheen that glimmered in her eyes came not from pain, but from love.

"I have not named them," I said, unswaddling my second child, and placing him in the crook of her other arm. "But I believe that Iasion would have wished to call one of his sons Eubouleus."

The queen nodded, but I could tell my words were peripheral to her now. Everything was peripheral to her. Her world was once more filled. For several minutes, I stood there and watched on as a heart that had been emptied and shattered re-formed crookedly, piece by piece. It was only when I shifted slightly, ready to retreat, that she once more noticed my presence.

"I am sorry, forgive me. We must sort you a room. I will call the king now. We will have a celebration. Shall we place the children in your chamber? I can call for wet nurses if you prefer. I am certain there will be some in the village."

Her words spilled from her at such a rate it was as if she had only just remembered how to speak and was fearful that at any second she may once again lose the ability.

"The king...their uncles... We will raise a feast to you, my goddess, that would rival Olympus itself. And you will be here. You will be with us." If her hands had been free, I have no doubt that she would have grasped mine and pulled me into her chest, but her hold on the twins remained unflinching. "There are not words for what you have brought this family. What you have brought back to me."

Never, in all the offers I have received, have I experienced gratitude akin to that which I felt that day. Which was why I kept my words brief.

"You are kind, Queen Olesia, but I cannot stay. I must return to my ship. Please instruct one of your men to come fetch Iasion's body."

The confusion that had plagued her when she spoke about her sons returned, and with it, fear. Her skin paled as the blood drained from her cheek.

"But...but his children. They are... They are—"

"They are yours now," I said. "They will stay here, to be raised by you. If that is acceptable to you?"

At this, the queen dropped back onto the couch and made no attempt to stifle the tears that rolled from her in great gulps.

"My goddess. I cannot... I cannot... They are mine?"

I looked at my sons, both at peace in their grandmother's arms.

"They are yours."

I think about that day often. How happiness can be so deeply intertwined with grief, so it would not be possible for the joy to exist had the pain not been present beforehand.

By the time I left, the queen was fully attended to by servants and maids who hurried about at her will. Her voice barking orders as though she had never once been silent.

And as I walked the path down the sloping hill and back to the ship, the thinnest sliver of frost glinted in my wake.

CHAPTER TWELVE

L ITTLE WAS SPOKEN ON THE JOURNEY BACK. I STOOD ON THE
stern of the ship and watched the resting place of Iasion's
body grow smaller on the horizon. Waves broke against the
hull while gulls circled the ship, squalling with excitement in their
misplaced belief that we were a fishing vessel that would soon provide
them with their supper. The crew felt keenly the absence of the twins
and barely dared look at me, for fear of how a grieving god might
react. But there was one person upon that ship, beyond my daughter,
who viewed me with no fear at all. Only compassion and concern.

We had left the harbor, and the sails were taut with a strong wind
when Meliae came and stood beside me. I did not wish for company,
but to be alone in my solitude. Her presence alone was enough to bring
a tingle of cold to my fingertips. Her words pushed me further still.

"You have given this family a gift that has rewritten their future.
I believe your lover would be proud of you." She meant to offer
comfort, but those words shot through me like a blade between my
ribs. I snapped my head around to face her. That icy tingle was now
a frost that bled onto the wooden planks beneath my feet.

"Do not speak to me of Iasion. You did not know him." The bitterness in my voice would have sent the other nymphs scurrying from my sight. But Meliae was not like the other nymphs. She was as close to a true friend as I ever had, and she turned her face out to the sea before she spoke again.

"You are right, Goddess. I did not have that honor, but I consider myself fortunate to know you. And for you to offer this mortal your heart, I already know that his love for family ran almost as deep as your own." I stayed silent, desperately clinging to that bitterness that had filled me only moments before. I did not want to thaw. I wanted to find strength in that cold. Yet Meliae continued. "I know that for you to have given up your own flesh and blood, for the goodness of his kin, he must have shown a pureness of heart that even we nymphs rarely possess. And I know that to stand up to your brother, where even gods cower, he must have loved you with all the strength of an Olympian. So I will stay firm with my choice of words. He would be proud of you."

My throat tightened as the heat of tears pricked behind my eyes, and as I stood there, with no more words to speak, Meliae's hand slipped into mine, and there we stayed until Samothrace could be seen no more.

The absence of Iasion's body on the boat was almost as keen to me as the absence of my sons. An absence that became worse still when we arrived in Siphnos.

The grief that I had put on hold for my sons alone struck me like a fresh tidal wave. Every waking minute I was in agony, each breath tearing apart the threads of my heart. I regretted my decision to return Iasion to his family and wished instead that I buried him in Siphnos. I chose the exact place I would have buried his body: at the top of the hill, where the sun hit the earth at such an angle it glimmered like molten metal. There, a singular cedar tree of peridot green stood. This place, I decided, and that tree were sacred to Iasion. A place where I could forever recall the love we had shared.

Every day, I would walk to the cedar and talk to Iasion as though he was still there. I would tell him about the nymphs and Core and how she pestered me to leave the island. I would talk about all the festivals I wished we could attend together or describe his mother's joy at the union with her grandchildren. Some days, I would arrive before sunbreak and would not leave until the moon shone silver above me. Sometimes, I would not leave even then. Hours, days, weeks. I lost track of it all. For what did they matter without Iasion?

Core and the nymphs thought my behavior irrational. I was not immune to their whispers and glances. But what right did they have to comment? They had never loved. Nor endured the agony that comes with a love that is lost before its time. Besides, it was more than that. They were naive of the world in a way that I was not. We were safe on Siphnos. Together and safe. And what else mattered but that?

"Perhaps we could visit Delphi." Core asked me, on more occasions than I cared to count. "The mortals there revere you so greatly, and I am certain Apollo would be gracious of your presence."

"Perhaps, but not yet," I responded with variations of the same words, over and over again. "It is not safe for us to travel too far. Zeus will be looking for me."

"Then perhaps just to a nearby island."

"We are safe here. We have everything we need." Each time the conversation swayed in such a manner, I placed my hands on her cheeks and locked my eyes on to hers. "Believe me, my love, when you have seen as much as I have, you all realize what a blessing we have here." Sometimes she would sit with me a little longer, staring at the branches of the tree, offering sweet condolences about a man she knew nothing about. But mostly she would leave me be, and I was grateful for that. In my heart the cedar tree was a place for Iasion and me alone, and even Core's presence there felt unnecessary; she had an entire island to roam. Now, I realize how foolish I was.

"It does not do any of us good to stay in isolation on this island." This was another line that she proffered time and time again. "If I was to go alone, you know I would never leave you, like Iacchus. I would leave for a few hours at most." Yes, Core tried every approach that she could, but only one of the four children I birthed remained by my side, and it was not a risk I was willing to take.

"My answer is no," I would say with just enough firmness that she would cease her pestering for a short while.

In the hours spent away from my shrine to Iasion, the home Hephaestus built for us was a sanctuary. It may not have had the opulence of Olympus, but it had beauty in abundance. We felt no need to prune back vines as they twisted around the pillars of the courtyards, nor to confine them to the trellises and pots. Fruit grew so heavily that branches bowed, while flowers and buds teemed with life—butterflies, dragonflies, hummingbirds—you could find them all, flitting between the flora that grew denser and more vibrant with every passing year. For Core and the nymphs, it was indeed a paradise, which was why I disregarded her requests to leave. She was too young. She simply did not understand how fortunate she was.

Year after year, Core and the nymphs bathed in the streams, basked in the endless sunshine, and absorbed the scents of cowslips and apple blossoms that grew day after day without fail. Some days, dolphins would come so close to the shore that the nereids would swim out to meet them. From my place upon the hillside, I would observe from a distance as Core splashed into the shallows of the sea, watching the nymphs dip and dive beneath the blue water, their laughter as nourishing for the soul as any food could be for the body. The nymphs, loyal to me and my child, were in as great a bliss as possible. The lapping waves were a home for the nereids, as the fresh water running through mountain groves was for the naiads, and the forest for the dryads. We were a family.

As the decades passed, I worried less about my brother. I did not doubt that Zeus had long learned of our location. After all, it would have taken little effort on his part to gaze down from the heights of his palace to see the nymphs and Core singing amid the corn. Yet he made no attempt to contact me. Not to apologize and reconcile our tattered relationship, nor to demand my return to Olympus. But perhaps it is unsurprising, considering how greatly he benefited from our absence.

My presence on Earth had caused the mortals' harvests to flourish like never before. Wheat grew taller than a grown man, thick with seeds and more than they could harvest each year. The animals were so well fed that the offerings and sacrifices were the most excessive experienced outside of war. Libations were constant, not only for myself but for all the gods, including Zeus. And any acts that increased his reverence, he was unlikely to disrupt. And so we remained at peace. But that does not mean our lives were not tainted by sadness.

It was nearing a century since Iasion's death, yet I felt the pain each day as if it was fresh, and had been spending great hours beneath his tree, reminiscing about the brief moments we had together, dreaming of how I would have spent any more if we had been so fortunate.

The landscape of the island changed greatly in the century since our arrival. Partially, that was due to the passing of time, partially gifts bestowed by Core and me, but mostly it was the nymphs who brought about this transformation. Dryads formed connections with trees: birch, beeches, olives, or great pines. Each had their own to which they were linked. Their presence caused the trees to thrive on every corner of Siphnos. Nymphs are phenomenal. But they are not immortal.

I had been sitting underneath Iasion's tree, basking in the shade created by the canopy, when Core called my name and raced up the hillside toward me.

"Mother!" Her voice bounced off the hillside. "Mother!" I will confess the sight of her irritated me. Oh, how callous a mother that makes me sound. There had been a time when I found joy in every breath she took, but now I feared she would begin her pestering. That she would list the places, far less verdant than Siphnos, that she wished to visit, not understanding the extent of the luxury that she had been granted. Every time I was forced to reject her wishes, it gnawed away at me, so much so that occasionally I retreated to Iasion's tree not to converse with my lost love but so I did not have to repeat my rulings to Core.

But as she came closer, I saw that the smile that normally glimmered in her eyes was replaced by a deep darkness. Her brow wrinkled in anguish.

"Mother, you must come. It is Meliae. I believe she is dying."

CHAPTER THIRTEEN

I T WAS THE ONLY TREE IN THE COPSE—ON THE ENTIRE ISLAND—
that was not alight with green. Bare branches, dry and brittle,
stretched up to the sky, while patches of bark peeled off in great
chunks. And there, sat at the base of the trunk, was Meliae, as youthful in appearance as the first day I saw her.

The sight rendered me paralyzed. How could I have missed this?
A tree that barren must have been shedding its leaves for months, if
not years, and yet I had been oblivious to it. So absorbed in my grief
that I had not noticed death was to strike yet again.

While I watched on, dumbfounded, Core stepped forward and
knelt beside the dying nymph, cupping Meliae's hands. I do not
know what words were exchanged by the pair. All I know is that
when they broke apart, Meliae's gaze was fixed on me, and I had no
choice but to go to her.

"Darling Meliae," I dropped to the ground beside the nymph,
suppressing the iciness that was clawing at my fingers. "Why did you
not tell me? Why did you not let me know this was happening?"

She smiled so softly, and her eyes stared so deeply into mine it forced me to wonder when I had last allowed someone to look at me in such a manner. I knew, of course, the last time that had been, and it caused that frost to once again tingle at my fingertips, though through love for my nymph I drew it back inward.

"What good would it have done?" she said, quietly. "It was inevitable. And I am at peace with it, as you should be."

My gaze shifted upward as I forced back tears that wished to tumble free.

"Tell me," I said. "What can I do? Is there anything I can do for you, or is it already too late?"

I do not know what request I expected of her. Her parting was imminent. Yet as she opened her mouth to speak, she shifted herself so that she was speaking into my ear.

"Give her freedom," she said. For a moment I did not know of whom she spoke, but as Core's soft sobs reached my ears, I understood. And the thought alone was enough to clamp a vise around my chest.

"She is all I have. I cannot lose her," I began, but Meliae would not hear it.

"There are worse ways to lose someone than by giving them their freedom," she answered me. "She is a goddess of a world you have kept hidden from her."

"For her own safety," I said, but Meliae smiled as she saw though my poorly veiled lie.

"She is a grown goddess of the earth, Demeter, yet think of all she has not seen."

As much as I wished otherwise, it required little on my part to consider the things I had kept hidden from her. She had not seen the slopes of the Pindus mountains turn violet with crocus blooms or held the velvet petals of a cerulean anemone between her fingers. She had not brushed her palm across a sea of ripening corn while absorbing the pungent, bitter aroma released from the vivid pink flowers of the oleander trees or walked on the carpets of blossom that covered the stone steps of the temple floor in Delphi.

"If you do not do this, if you do not allow her to leave this island, she will leave of her own accord, and it will be far more difficult to convince her to return," she continued. "You, of all people, should know that."

Nymphs are not regarded for their wisdom. They are known for their frivolity, their love of life, yet I knew every word Meliae had spoken was the truth.

Choking back the tears that filled my throat, I nodded so slightly I do not know if she even saw. I hope she did. I hope she knew that her words struck me in my heart, for before I could speak again, Meliae was gone, and in her place a thousand fluttering leaves.

CHAPTER FOURTEEN

I SUSPECT MELIAE HAD SPOKEN HOPING I WOULD ACT UPON HER words with some impetus. That perhaps that same day, or at least the same year, I would grant Core that freedom she had begged me for. But no matter how much I wished to, each time I believed I was strong enough to let Core go, the thought of losing her caused the words to stick in my throat, and I would hurry back to Iasion's tree, and weep to him of my weakness.

One evening, when the sky had turned a deep shade of scarlet, she came to me. Rather than speaking, she took a seat on the grass and crossed her legs. Brushing her hand against the blades, a stream of purple flowers rose in the wake.

"They are beautiful," I said truthfully.

"Thank you. Meliae told me once of a peony that grows on Mount Parnassus which has petals as deep purple as the richest wine. I believe I have captured the color, but the scent… I did not think to ask her of the scent."

She let her words drift into the air. The silence bursting with all that was unsaid, as silence so often does. Normally it would be

Core who broke the mood. Who would think of something genial to say, before excusing herself and returning down the hill. That time, however, it was I who spoke.

"You should go. See it. Smell it for yourself."

Her head snapped around to face me.

"It grows upon Mount Parnassus," she repeated, assuming I misheard her.

"I know. You should go there, capture the scent. Meliae would have wanted such a thing."

I expected my comment to elicit a response, but Core's mouth closed, and her eyes remained unblinking, as if any movement would cause my words to evaporate. And so it was I who spoke again.

"I believe the flower she described only blooms for a short while. Perhaps you should go tomorrow. But you should take some of the nymphs with you. Please. I am certain they would like to see them with you."

Before I could finish, Core had leaped from the ground and wrapped her arms around me in a tight embrace. So often had my daughter held me to her, but never like this. Never with such pure unbridled joy. I knew there would be no going back on my word.

The following day, I stood with her on the shore, three of the youngest nymphs at her side. Aglaope, Peisinoe, and Thelxiepia. Unlike Meliae, they had been near newborn when they left Olympus, following their sister nymphs as much as myself. As such, it was little surprise those were the ones who chose to go.

"Remember to keep your true self hidden." I clutched her to my chest, desperate to recant what I had said and forbid her to leave, but I bit down on my tongue and recalled the way Meliae's leaves had skittered across the fields to become lost on the horizon. "And keep your eyes and ears open for other gods."

Breaking away from my grasp, Core held me at arm's length and planted a kiss upon my cheek.

"I will be fine, Mother. And I will be back before you even have a chance to miss me."

"I will miss you the instant you leave."

She turned to go but I reached out and gripped her wrist.

"Remember, do not show your gift. Even if no one is in sight, the gods may be watching. You must hold it within you."

"I know, Mother."

With that, she kissed me again, and turned to face the sea.

She was gone for mere hours, returning just after midday, yet during that time my anguish grew so acute that an entire crop shriveled on the nearby island of Seriphos. Those poor farmers. I can only imagine their faces as their healthy plants withered and blackened into nothing but mulch before their eyes. (You can be assured that I repaid their adversity with harvests more bountiful than they could have dreamed for decades that followed.) For their part, the remaining nymphs entertained me the best they could, singing songs and persuading me to dapple my feet in the water with them. But my gaze remained fixed on the horizon, and it was only when I saw Core's silhouette appeared upon it that a true breath of air filled my lungs.

"Mother!" Core ran to me upon her return. "It was beautiful. Everything Meliae told me and more."

"Is that so?" Pain and joy flooded the very marrow of my bones.

"Exactly as she said, the color of wine. Here, see for yourself. I have brought you a posy."

She stretched out her hands, and offered me a small bunch of flowers, so deep in color they absorbed all the light that shone upon them.

"Mother, you must come with me next time. There are such wonders beyond this island, you will not regret it. I promise."

"Soon," I said, taking her by the arm and turning her toward the house so that she might not see how desperately I was stifling my tears.

"Thelxiepia told me of another place near Sparta where the wild thyme grows so densely that you can smell it in the air all the way from the shores. We are to go tomorrow."

"Tomorrow?" Anguish and pain hitched my voice so fiercely that Core stopped midstep.

"You do not mind, do you?"

How I wish I'd had the strength to respond with the answer that burned in my heart. Perhaps if I had at least limited the freedom I gave her, then I would not be burdened with my current existence, but as any parent knows, to snatch happiness from their child is to break their own heart, and so, with my throat burning with tears, I forced myself to smile.

"Of course you must go," I responded. "I look forward to hearing all about it."

CHAPTER FIFTEEN

S HE WOULD LEAVE AS DAWN BROKE, ACCOMPANIED BY ANY number of nymphs, and return before sunset. Always I watched for her silhouette moving back toward me from the sea. Always she held in her hand a posy of flowers she had plucked for me. Colors so exquisite, they mimicked every shade of a sunset and the ombre tones of the deepening sea.

Then each evening, with the blooms set in a vase of fresh water and a simple meal placed before us, she would delight in telling all the sights she had seen that day.

"There is honey on Andros that is unlike anything you will have tasted before. It is not like our honey here. Not that ours is not delicious, but this tastes of thyme, for all the bees there feed upon it. I will bring a clay pot with me tomorrow so you can taste it too. Unless you wish to come with me? There is a temple there that they have built in your name. You could visit it while we are there."

"Soon," I said, offering her a broad smile, attempting to sound convincing. "I will come with you soon. Though I do not think tomorrow would be best for me."

In our hearts, we knew that the chance of me leaving Siphnos grew less and less likely with each passing year. I had become a recluse. I had always been one to shy away from crowds. To prefer the company of myself and a select few trusted companions, even before Core was born. And afterward, when I left Olympus to go in search of Iacchus, it was a task I dreaded, not only because my son was pulling away from me but because of the places I was forced to look for him. Dense taverns and bustling agoras, filled with jostling bodies, shrieks of laughter, and wails of pain. The fetid scents and clamoring sounds so overpowering that I would need to hold a cloth to my mouth and even then, my eyes would prick with tears. Now, merely the thought of ploughed earth roused images of Iasion falling dead to the ground. My lungs would seize and constrict as I reimagined the moment over and over again. Suffocating in the memory. A glimpse of a boat in the distance stirred memories of my sons, all lost to me. My heart throbbed with such intensity that I would double over and clutch my knees. And still, after all the centuries that had passed, I saw my brother in every shadow, leering at me, ready to pounce. Ready to pin me to the rocky earth for all eternity. Roaming the earth had brought me rape and the murder of my loved one, and every landscape I looked upon reminded me of it. But in Siphnos, I had no bad memories. Siphnos was my sanctuary.

As the years passed, Core was gone as many days as she was present, although not all of them were filled with sweet honey and fragrant bouquets. There was one incident, I recall quite clearly, after which I had thought—or rather hoped—she may never leave the island again.

The incident occurred after the festival of Thesmophoria, the three days in the year where all the women in Hellas worshipped Core and me. These were the days where offerings—sacrifices and libations—were raised to our name. When the mortal women would pray to us to bless their crops and their fertility, and we would respond with all the gifts we could bestow upon them. No matter how often Core left Siphnos, which had become nearly daily by this point, always we spent those three days together. That festival we had laughed as I had not laughed in years. Together we drank uncut wine and sang and danced. Only three nymphs remained, for the rest had succumbed to the inevitability of time, but that did not temper our joy. On the fourth day, after the festival had ended, Core skipped back to continue traversing the world beyond Siphnos, but the goddess who returned was not the one who left.

I knew something was wrong the moment her silhouette appeared on the horizon. Normally she walked in front of the nymphs, her hands swinging the flowers she had plucked during her travels. But there were no flowers in her hand, although that was the least of my concerns.

"Core!"

Her body was slumped forward, her feet dragging as Thelxiepia took her weight. Fear surged through me. Was she wounded? She looked wounded, but by what? Not a mortal. A god, perhaps. Had her father found us? Had he threatened her, or worse still, assaulted her like he had done with me? The nymphs would have had no power to fight him off had he set his mind to it. All these thoughts rushed through my head as I splashed through the water. Pulling her out of Thelxiepia's grips, I ran my hands over her face and body in search of signs of trauma. Though I quickly found no physical marks, her tears continued to stream.

"What happened? What happened to her? Are you hurt? Core, my child, are you hurt?"

Her eyes were red, gleaming bloodshot, though her skin was as pale as a wraith. My vision muzzled and blurred as the worst images flurried through my mind.

"There was a child," Thelxiepia's said, stepping forward, drawing my attention away from my daughter. "There was a child in one of the meadows. He had been abandoned by his mother. Left to the wild. It was…upsetting, for us all."

"A child?"

"Yes," she said. The other nymphs nodded quickly in agreement, though Core herself could make no noises other than sobs.

The image of what Core must have seen rippled through me. Mortal death is something I know about from my darling Iasion, but to bear witness to a baby in such a state, their innocence taken before they were old enough to form their first true laugh, was enough to cause my own heart to break. Still, I was relieved.

"She is not harmed."

"She is not harmed," Thelxiepia assured me. "But she was the one who found the child. The body…" The sentence did not need to be finished.

I wrapped my arms around my child and offered her the only comfort I could offer.

"My darling. I'm so sorry. I'm so sorry you've had to see such a sight."

"I should have saved her. I should have done something to save her," Core stuttered, the image of the baby etched so fiercely in her mind she could speak of nothing else.

"They are mortals, my darling. It is the hand they have been dealt. Give it time, you will forget it."

I brushed her hair with my hand, wishing I could draw away the grief with my touch, yet at the same time, I felt a sense of vindication. My poor Core's sensitivity ran so deep that even the death of an unknown babe wounded her. She could not have survived a life like other gods, weaving paths between the mortal world and our own, constantly exposed to death and anguish. She was safe with me. That is what mattered the most.

"Come, we should take her to her bed," Thelxiepia said, stepping forward, taking control of the situation. "She needs time alone. Time to grieve what she has seen."

As Thelxiepia had said, time proved a healer for Core, though not a swift one. What my child had seen that day caused her grief so great that for nearly a century she remained on Siphnos, never venturing even to near islands.

"Perhaps a short stroll to Seriphos," I suggested, crouching beside her bed, for she did not have the strength to even sit upright. The words I spoke were so at odds with everything I had said before they felt like needles in my heart, but they were all I could think of to try to coax her from this state. "I am certain Aglaope would accompany you? All three nymphs. Perhaps I could even come."

Had any words warranted a reply, I was certain it would have been those. She remained silent.

Never had I felt so at a loss as a mother. Never had I felt more desperate to help her, and yet no words reached her. More than once I wondered if perhaps she had known the child's mother, or she had been exposed to more of her death than she and the nymphs had revealed to me, but I did not press, for I knew in her own time, she would return to me, and return she did.

"Mother, I wish to leave the island today. I assume that will be agreeable?"

She had come to me so early that I was still asleep. My face crumpled on the soft cushion of the couch where I rested my head. I blinked, confused by the sight before me, before I hurried to my feet.

"Core, my darling. You are up. Let me fetch something for you to eat. Or drink. You must be hungry. Tell me, what can I fetch you?"

"I am fine, Mother. I will have something on my return. The nymphs are ready. They are waiting for me now. We are leaving immediately."

"Oh…" I had no more words to say, so stunned was I by this sudden transformation. She smiled, tight and forced, yet a smile nonetheless, before kissing my cheek and heading to the shore.

After that day, the grief receded, almost as though it had been stripped entirely from her being. I thought of asking her how she had managed to push it aside, for I still thought of Iasion daily. But the opportunity never arose. Then, a little over a century after she regained herself, she was taken from me, and this time it was more than grief that had stolen my daughter, and time alone would not bring her back. No, that was up to me.

CHAPTER SIXTEEN

THAT DAY STARTED LIKE ALL THE OTHERS. WHILE CORE AND THE nymphs disappeared for their day of basking on newer grasses and unfamiliar waters, I spent the day as I so often did, listening dreamily to the praises of the mortals, thanking me for the endless crops I provided for them. Ensuring that the mortals were well fed and their crops sufficient was not a job I took lightly. I had the power to ensure their lives were filled with health and sustenance. I could ensure their futures were rich and blessed. I was not like my brother Poseidon, who transformed the seas from gentle billows to crashing thunderous waves at the slight indignation or a misconstrued insult. I had no great desire to cause suffering and torment purely for entertainment.

I suspect my mortal lover and sons had played a part in the constant compassion I felt for the rest of their kind, but in my chosen exile, I had become even more generous and fruitful with my gifts. Those late years upon Siphnos were the most bountiful that humans ever experienced. In return, they offered me the first corn of their harvest and sacrificed their most prized swine in my name. If only it could have lasted.

When the sun dipped toward the horizon, I ceased my listening and breathed in that warm evening air. The open roof of the courtyard allowed the muted afternoon light to cast long shadows along the marbled floors. Readying myself for the others' return, I filled five cups with wine, taking a long sip from mine, before refilling it and leaving the house to head outside.

This time of day, where I waited for Core's return, was a moment of indulgence. Sometimes I remained in the courtyard, but normally I would stroll up the hill and sit in the shade of Iasion's tree. My visits there were not so frequent as they had once been, but even so, each day, I would visit for a short while at least, to reminisce about that single evening we had spent together. I would bring to the front of my mind the sparkling gleam in his eyes, and the shy smile that twisted at the corner of his mouth, and I would imagine he and our sons now together in the Underworld. That, for its part, offered me a little comfort.

Slowly the sun sank lower and lower, until it clipped the horizon, and a deep sweep of magenta arced across the sky. It was peculiar for Core to be this late to return, but not unheard of. As such, I strained to hear beyond the island, searching for the laughter and singing of the nymphs to indicate their impending return. Upon hearing nothing but the shirring of wind through the grasses, I stood and walked toward the shore, my eyes locked on the sea. Any second, I expected to see her silhouette gliding toward me, yet even as I reached the sandy cove where I had waited for her in those early days, the view remained empty of her form.

With long, deep breaths, I tried to steady the nerves that had frequently overwhelmed my body in those early days of her excursions. Core was trustworthy. And what's more, she had company. Only Thelxiepia, Aglaope, and Peisinoe remained, but those were the nymphs to whom Core was closest. They would risk their lives rather than let anything happen to her.

When the circle of the sun bisected the horizon into a perfect arch, the first sparks of true worry lit within me.

She always returned before nightfall. No matter how far she traveled, no matter what meadow or orchard she gathered flowers in, she was always under my roof by the time Selene's moon appeared in the sky. Yet a pale crescent was already present, making her claim for the sky as Helios drew his chariot downward.

No longer content to sit and wait, I turned back and headed toward the home Hephaestus had built us.

She must be on the island already, I tried to convince myself. She must have slipped past me when I was not looking. A game perhaps. A cruel game that she and the nymphs had decided to play upon me. With my heart hammering, I quickened my step, calling her name as I rushed up the stone pathway.

In minutes, my calls had turned to screams as I shouted her name from the pit of my guts. The palace was empty. The view in every direction, clear. The sun was setting, but Core was not on Siphnos.

My legs now burned as once again I ran to the water's edge, but this time I did not stop until the water reached my knees. The frothing white foam splashed up with an icy spray that soaked my face and hair.

"Core! Core!"

I screamed until my voice was hoarse, and then screamed louder still, turning one way and the next, praying to deities older and fiercer than me that this churning, curdling dread filling my gut was unfounded. I prayed that the fear clawing at the very cells of my existence was nothing more than a mother's baseless anxiety. Yet I knew in my heart of hearts that it was not the case. Returning to the hillside, I continued my search in all directions.

The last rays of sun were glancing off the earth, scattering weak watery light in thin rays, when several silhouettes finally came into view on the far side of the island.

Never before had I run like I ran then. I ran as mortals run, with my muscles straining to keep each stride longer and faster. I ran so my feet barely grazed the earth. I did not stop, even when I reached the group gathered on the shore.

A group of three. Three nymphs.

Fear pierced my very bones as I forced myself to speak.

"Thelxiepia? Aglaope? Peisinoe? Where is Core? Why is she not with you? Where is she?" I scanned the three of them before settling my gaze on Thelxiepia. "Where is she? Where is my daughter?"

Even before the nymph opened her mouth to speak, I knew what she would say. I knew that my heart was to be broken again, yet I could not have predicted all the ways my life would be forced apart because of the words she spoke.

"I am sorry, my goddess. I am sorry, I do not know. We do not know where she has gone."

CHAPTER SEVENTEEN

THE TEMPERATURE PLUMMETED AS A SEA OF ENDLESS SHADOWS shrouded my view. This was not a coolness that had come from the mere departure of the sun. This was a chill that sank into my bones and pierced through my fingertips. One that caused my breath to fog in the air and the nymphs to recoil in fear.

"Where is she? Where is Core?" I repeated.

I looked between them all, like she could have been standing behind one of them, hiding, as a small child would when playing a game. "Where is my daughter?"

The three nymphs stood with heads bowed, eyes trained to the ground, and a sound, more guttural than Cerberus himself could produce, rose from my throat. I had trusted them with the most precious thing in the world to me, and now I was ready to snap their necks, if that was what it took to get an answer from them. I believe they sensed as much. For Thelxiepia stepped toward me, her hands raised like I was a wild animal intent on attack.

"We were hoping she had returned here to you, my goddess," she said.

"You were *hoping*?" My voice cracked with a high, angry pitch that sounded more like my sister Hera than myself. "Why is she not with you? Where is she?"

Since that day when the nymphs had formed a barrier between myself and Zeus, I had never doubted their loyalty to me. They had protected me from my brother, and in return, I had kept them as equals in my home. Viewed them as friends, not followers. Yet as we stood there in the water, with the waves turning icy around us, I saw that it was all a lie. They had never viewed me as an equal, or a friend. Just a god that they followed dutifully, perhaps the lesser of the many evils that held a throne upon the summit of Olympus.

"Where is my daughter?" My voice bellowed and every green leaf on the island shriveled. This was not a small patch of ice, like that which had formed on the island of Tenos. Not a single hint of color remained. A gust of wind blew in, scattering the white, frozen leaves around us in a whirlwind.

Aglaope and Peisinoe stepped backward, but Thelxiepia held her place, although the tremble to her hand did not escape my notice.

"She did not return to meet us, Goddess. We searched for her. We searched, but she was not there."

Her words were pounding behind my eyes, spoken in riddles, designed to confuse me.

"Return? You were with her, were you not? You were with her?"

The guilt that flashed in her eyes caused a wave of nausea to strike so fiercely it was a miracle I remained standing.

"Why were you not with her?" I spat.

Thelxiepia looked at her sisters, willing them to come to her aid. In the end, it was Peisinoe who took the burden upon herself.

"It has been that way for many years, my goddess. Centuries.

She prefers the solitude of traveling alone. It has been the goddess's request."

"The goddess's request?"

I gawped at the words tripping from my lips. Core made no requests of the nymphs. Not that I had ever seen upon this island. She spoke to them as sisters. Friends. Equals. Besides that, she knew my stipulations when it came to her leaving the islands. It had never even needed to be discussed. The nymphs went with her. Always.

"She prefers to be alone," Thelxiepia repeated her sister's words.

Silence swilled around us, broken only by the crash of the waves behind us.

"Go on," I said, my words more forceful than any wave Poseidon could conjure.

Thelxiepia clenched her hands in front of her. Around us, the last leaves fluttered to the ground. A confetti of the dying. Centuries of life upon Siphnos and, in one instant, it had been transformed. It was a carcass of an island, derelict and devoid of life. My heart should have broken at the destruction I brought to my home, but there was far, far more destruction to come.

"It has been that way for decades, my goddess," Thelxiepia continued. "We leave together and sometimes we will walk together, too, for a while at least. But then she will leave us and we wait. We wait and once she joins us, we return here together."

The words were so utterly bemusing, she could have been speaking to me in a different tongue.

"Well, where does she go?" I asked, thinking of Iacchus and his revelries, while also recalling the blooms that she greeted me with when she returned from her travels. Blooms from the entirety of Hellas. Were these just a ploy to distract me? Random flowers she had snatched hurriedly so that I did not become wise to her lies and deceit?

"She would tell us where she had visited upon her return. Sometimes she would stay close by, perhaps traveling to the next island. Other times she had been further afar. Anatolia. Macedonia."

The confession felt so absurd, I could barely believe it was true. What on earth could Core hope to find in such solitude? Siphnos was not a large island, but certainly large enough that she could find a quiet corner to remain undisturbed, if that was what she desperately sought.

"And none of you thought to follow her? To stay close by in case she had needed your help?"

I stood, rendered mute, struggling to comprehend the enormity of what they were telling me. Core, my darling daughter, who I trusted explicitly, had lied to me for centuries. Not only that, but they had left her alone, where she could be exposed to the worst of humanity. Day after day, year after year, they had risked her innocence.

Without warning, Peisinoe dropped to her knees. "What do we do, Goddess? Tell me what we should do."

Any compassion I had felt for these creatures abandoned me. I did not see them as I had once done. Sisters, daughters, my kin. Instead, I saw them for what they were. Beasts who had taken my trust and betrayed me. Creatures as vile as Zeus himself, who took advantage of the life I had offered them for their own gain. Monsters.

"You have done enough," I said.

In my past, I had learned how fear can weaken. I had seen the effect upon myself; how dread and anguish had caused me to shrivel, cower, and recoil into a shell of my own creation. But I learned that day I could find strength in those same moments. That fear, when mixed with anger, could transform into something more formidable than I could have ever dreamed. The nymphs' betrayal brought about my darkest, most vengeful attributes, which I cast upon them all so that they would never be the same again.

CHAPTER EIGHTEEN

I HAD NEVER USED MY POWER FOR ANYTHING OTHER THAN GOOD. From the moment Zeus had freed me from Cronus to walk on the earth, and I saw the pitiful and weak state of mortals, I vowed that I would protect them. I pledged my existence to nourish them. Even when my brother wronged me, I took that hate and turned it inward, transforming it instead to love for my daughter. But there was no way to transform the betrayal of my nymphs. No way to see the good in the light of their actions.

I did not know what the outcome of my words would be as I muttered beneath my breath. The hard hiss of my tongue smacking my teeth reverberated around my skull as spittle flew from my lips.

"My goddess," Thelxiepia lifted her hand, fear fast in her eyes as she pleaded. But I did not hear her words. I heard nothing but the vengeance I was conjuring.

"Please, my goddess." They exchanged fearful glances as they stepped backward. But I did not let them go. I inched closer, and while their hands were raised in deference and defense, mine were poised toward the earth, calling forth the power I possessed.

There was no bolt of lightning here. No massive waves, a hundred times the size of a man crashing like thunder to the sea. No, for me the power came from the very earth, which trembled beneath our feet. This was not the icy chill that had coursed through my veins before, this was red-hot rage that radiated from my very core. And I fed on it. Breathed in that fury and let it erupt.

"Please!" I heard their cries again, but either I did not care or I was too far gone to stop myself. You must decide which you view as the truth, if there even is one, for I myself do not know.

As the power surged within me, the nymphs dropped to the ground, crying as their hands clawed at the earth. Only they did not stay as hands. Talons stretched out where their fingers had once held fast. Their cries rattled on the mountains behind us, stirring up a breeze strong enough to rip the fabric of their robes, but I was not done yet. No. While they were bent over, unable to move, I transformed their bodies. Giant wings erupted from their backs. Not lightly feathered wings, like those on the giant horse Pegasus or the sandals of the messenger, Hermes. These wings were black and scaly, slick with a dark sheen, like oil pooled deep beneath the earth's surface. Their beautiful faces could have been a mirage, for how in contrast to their monstrous bodies they were. Though their eyes had changed. Gone were those bright colors of light and joy. Only blackness remained.

"Goddess!" Aglaope croaked, black tears pooling where her claws dug into the earth. My nymphs. Those who I had considered my companions, my friends even, were no more. The Sirens were born.

The Sirens—the beautiful monstrous creatures that lure sailors to steer their ships onto the jagged rocks of the western sea with their enchanting songs so that they can feast upon their bodies—are of my creation.

There have been times when I considered whether I was wrong to react in anger. Without my rash response, those sailors would never have succumbed to the alluring tunes and their untimely death. Hundreds of wives and children would still have their husbands and fathers. But I do not dwell on such things often. Those nymphs wronged me. They wronged me and put my daughter at risk. They deserved to be punished.

As the Sirens tested their wings and took to the sky, I fell to my knees, taking gulping breaths of the bitter air. Loneliness swept in like a cloud. A mist so dense that no light could penetrate it. Core was more than my daughter, more than my heart. She was every part of me. I could not live without her, and certainly not without knowing what had happened to her. But to find her, I would need to leave Siphnos.

It was a battle of fears, but a brief one. When I weighed the options—leaving the safety of my island or risking an eternity without my daughter—I knew what I would do. And I did not wish to wait until morning.

Not once during those first days of my search did my lungs rest. My throat may have bled, and my tongue grown weak, but nothing could keep me from calling out my daughter's name. I did not care who heard. I did not care if every god was looking down on me from Olympus laughing. I needed to be reunited with my daughter. So I screamed her name with as much force as my Titan blood could muster.

Knowing Core's love of meadows, I started my search in the lushest lands of Hellas. On the peninsular of Hermione, I shouted across the waves, where my calls were met by only the crash of water on rocks. I did not waste time meandering between the lines of trees. Core may have disobeyed me in heading out without the nymphs, but I knew she would never be so emboldened as to ignore my calling directly.

Tear-filled, but still hopeful, I headed to the verdant hills of Pheneus, where my voice echoed off the mountains. Beneath my feet the grass froze and died, but I did not bother to turn it back to its former, verdant state. Instead, I kept moving, regardless of the cold chaos that I left in my wake.

I did not cease my walking, all my wails, nor did I eat or drink. Had it not been for the alternation of Helios and Selene, I would not have even registered the passing of time. For what did time matter to me? An hour when Core was missing felt to me like a century.

I reached the land of Mysia long after nightfall, when milky clouds masked the sky. No stars or moon shone above me. Darkness was all that was to be found. I had traversed through night and day without stopping, using Selene's light and the glimmer of the stars to guide me. No matter how muted the beams she provided, I continued on. Yet that night darkness descended on me in its truest point, and I could go no further.

"Core! Core!"

I searched blindly, hoping that my voice alone would be enough to guide her to me through the black. Hoping that perhaps she was hidden in the endless shadows that surrounded me. My feet tripped over tangled roots, my hair caught on low-hanging branches, yet I stumbled forward, when two pinpricks of light in the distance caught my attention.

I stopped and watched as the two pinpricks grew brighter and larger. Whoever or whatever it was, it was encroaching on me. Then, without sound or warning, those two lights became four, then six. It was then I knew exactly who was watching me.

CHAPTER NINETEEN

I HAVE MENTIONED BEFORE THAT ONE OF MY BROTHER ZEUS'S greatest skills was keeping those with power close to him. Any immortal who he believed could at some point be of benefit, he kept within his inner circle, or at least in a peripheral circle in which they still felt the strength of an allegiance. While he imprisoned or killed most of the Titan gods during the war with our ancestors, there were those for which Zeus made an exception. Naturally, he saved our mother Rhea from the fiery depths of Tartarus, as he did the Titan Epimetheus and his brother Prometheus, who allied with Zeus, buying them their freedom—for a while at least. Metis, who, for a short while, Zeus claimed as his wife, was also spared the fate of the Underworld. But there was one Titan whose wrath he did not dare risk. One goddess whose powers were linked to magic so strong that he adorned her with gifts, giving to her a share of the land and the sea and the heaven. She who gives, and she who takes. Hecate.

The goddess approached me, torches in both her hands, which flickered with every step, illuminating her face and the faces of the two dogs that walked on either side of her. Though we had never met, I did not need an introduction, nor did she offer one.

"Goddess," she said. "You have been calling into the night."

She had already heard my words and did not appear angered by my presence, so I did not feel the need to lie to her.

"My daughter, Core. Have you seen her? She is missing. She left our home in Siphnos and has not returned. It has been days now. It has been days." It is not in my habit to disclose the location of my home. Indeed, I had never done so before, but my mind was addled from exhaustion and grief. All of which Hecate saw as she hooked one torch in the crook of a branch and stepped toward me, offering out a flask.

"When did you last rest?" she said. I shook my head, declining her offer of the flask, but she persisted. "Sit, please, sit."

"I cannot. I cannot. I must find her."

"And I will help if I can, but you must rest, if only for a minute. You will be of no use to anyone in this state."

Only when I noticed the tremble of my hand did I realize she spoke the truth. My head pounded with such ferocity; it was a miracle I could hear anything other than the drumming within my skull. And so, without further objection, I took the flask.

Even with the light provided by Hecate's torches, the land was mostly shadows, and I could see no place where I could easily sit. So I dropped to the ground like a pebble falling to the bottom of a lake and found myself resting on soft, cold earth as I lifted the flask to my lips.

Never had water tasted so sweet, yet it stung the tender flesh of my throat, which was raw and hoarse from days and nights of shouting. Still, I drank through the smarting, gulping back the unending supply that this flask appeared to contain. Only when I could take no more did I push myself back onto my feet and hand the flask to Hecate.

"Thank you," I said, with a small nod of gratitude. "Your kindness is appreciated, but I must continue my search. Core could be anywhere by now."

I did not feel the need to say more. I had no relationship with the goddess and expected nothing from her. Given how freely she had offered me her flask, I assumed that she wished for nothing in return, yet as I turned to leave, she grabbed me around the wrist.

"Wait," she said.

Though her face was that of a young woman, with lushest black hair and fresh dewy skin, her hand told another story. Liver-spotted and sinewy, the wrinkled fingers gripped me, not tight enough to cause alarm, but firm enough to stop me from moving away immediately.

"When was this? When did your daughter disappear?"

Though her question was a simple one, I struggled to offer her an answer.

"I, I am not sure." I had traveled from shore to mountains, but how long had that taken me? Several days for certain. As I stood there before the goddess, I forced myself to recount in my head each time I had seen the sun set and compare that to all the times I had watched Selene's moon rise.

"Nine days ago." I said with certainty with my calculation. "For nine days and nine nights, she has been gone." Beside Hecate, one of her dogs raised her head and looked at the witch. In turn, she looked at the creature by her side, as if the pair were exchanging words.

"Nine days ago, you are certain?"

I was. It may have taken me a moment to gather myself, but I was correct about this.

"Yes, I am. What do you know? Tell me. Do you know something?" Had I displayed such desperation in front of any other gods, I dread to think what reaction they would have had. Certainly, compassion would not be their choice of response. Probably ridicule, if not outright disgust. But Hecate nodded and spoke slowly, as if she were uttering words to a child. A child she did not wish to disappoint.

"I know nothing for certain," she said. "But there was a cry. I heard a cry of rape from the fields of Eleusis. Or at least I believed I had. When I reached the sight, there was no maiden to be found."

My heart clenched. Was this news of Core, or just an old witch toying with me? Had I heard this news earlier, then perhaps I would have been more inclined to believe her, but I had yelled Core's name countless times in the land the witch spoke of. She was not there.

"I have already traveled through the fields of Eleusis. I found nothing." My tone was bitter.

"Perhaps if we go together, we may see something we missed when alone."

My fingernails dug into my palms as I bit down on my tongue. It would do me no good to make an enemy of Hecate, particularly given her offer of aid. But no matter how brief this conversation was, every minute not searching for Core was a minute wasted. And for that she invoked my wrath. "If you have nothing else, I need to find my child," I responded. Her hand was no longer on mine, and so I turned and she did not attempt to stop me, although she spoke again.

"I can help," she called as I walked away from her. "You should not go on alone."

"Alone is all I have until I find my daughter," I called back, without so much as turning my head.

Regret stems from this conversation with Hecate. Perhaps if I had accepted her help, then things would have ended differently. Perhaps I could have saved my daughter. But I was too blinded by my grief to see that. Grief and stupidity, for the days that followed were a nightmare Morpheus himself would have struggled to create.

CHAPTER TWENTY

A s I WANDERED FROM THE WITCH, MY MIND TRIPPED AND stuttered, swaying between anger and confusion at the encounter. Why would Hecate think that a single voice calling for aid would be my daughter? She had no further evidence. A single voice calling rape could have come from a hundred maidens across Hellas. It could have come from myself at one point. My only explanation was that she meant to send me on a fool's errand. That she somehow sought to gain something from my distraction. After all, I visited Eleusis and found nothing, despite my thorough search. To go back would prove a waste of time. I needed to keep moving. Which is why I headed to Onceium.

The small village near Thelpusa was by Oncus, a son of Apollo, and though I knew little to nothing of my nephew's child, I knew this land had one feature unique to all the places I had traveled: the horses that roamed upon it.

Great herds roved across the fields and into the forests. Bays and piebalds, duns and palominos. Every color of creature could be found wandering across the groves and between the trees, or else standing knee deep in the rivers.

I was mesmerized by the ease with which these creatures moved. Transfixed by the way they combined such grandeur and regality with such agile and free spirits.

One particular dapple-gray mare looked as though she had been painted with clouds, created by Eos herself. With my gaze lost on the animal, I forgot the urgency with which I had been desperately searching for Core and trod quietly up to the herd and placed my hand against the flanks of the mare. Her nostrils flared and I feared that perhaps she might bolt, but her ears tipped forward and her eyes surveyed me, her great round pupils a gateway to her soul. Who knows how long I could have stayed there, staring into the heart of another. Too long, most probably, but I was not given the chance, for a voice stopped me cold in my tracks.

"Now I know you have not been hiding here all along, Sister."

Centuries had passed since I had heard his icy timbre, yet I knew his voice. It sent the water in the air into crystals around me as ice formed beneath my skin. Trying to disguise the mixture of revulsion and fear that mingled within me, I fixed a genial smile, lowered my hand from the mare, and turned to face him.

"Poseidon." His eyes were as gray as a storm-filled ocean and carried within them the same sense of unpredictability. I edged away, hoping to find security with the mare, but instead she reared, observing my brother with all the caution he deserved. A second later, she fled into the forest behind us.

"I am surprised to find you so far away from Siphnos, Sister," he said, a knowing tone in his voice. "That is where you have been living these last centuries, is it not?"

He was toying with me, waiting for my reaction, yet I had long assumed the other gods knew of my home. I could only conclude that respect had allowed me to maintain my solitude without being disturbed. It was I who broke the terms of that agreement when I started wandering the earth.

"If it is conversation you are after, I am afraid you have caught me at an inconvenient time, Brother. I am afraid I cannot stay. But perhaps I will see you upon Olympus soon."

"Olympus? You must hope to rid yourself of me if you are suggesting you will return to our brother's kingdom to see me. I heard you were still mourning that mortal he disposed of all those centuries ago. But perhaps as you are here, gallivanting through the countryside, that is no longer the case. And what of your daughter who normally clings to your side? I assume she is here, somewhere, is she not?"

Though my heart raced and hands shook, when my voice left my mouth, it was low and smooth and without a quiver.

"Core is back on Siphnos, with my nymphs. It's why I must return. I do not wish for her to be on her own for too long."

"But she is not on her own. You said that yourself. She is with the nymphs. It is you who are on your own, Sister."

I remained rigid. Fixed to the spot. The sun rolled down toward the peaks of the mountains, while a herd of horses strolled lazily toward the river. In a movement as fluid as the water he thrived within, Poseidon slinked toward me.

"You know, there were rumors in my palace that you birthed children from that mortal. And that you returned them to their mortal family." He took another step closer. Every cell within me was desperate to retreat, to flee as fast as I could, and yet if I knew anything of my brothers, it was that the chase would only excite them more. "I understand that. Imagine, if you had shackled yourself in such a manner to a mortal, as to have birthed more of his offspring. A body such as yours, Demeter, it's not meant to birth frail mortal children. We are the children of Titans. We are meant to birth gods. That was why Zeus gave you such a gift, allowing you to continue our line with him."

His words repulsed me so deeply that my throat stung with the acrid taste of bile. But I forced against it. Forced against my repulsion and the desperate urge to flee. It would not help to run, I told myself, again and again. Fleeing would only make matters worse. But what other options did I have?

"I still recall those days, don't you?" he said, relaxing the space between us slightly as he took a nonchalant step away.

"Which days?" I asked. If I could keep on talking, then perhaps my mind may figure out a way to escape this situation.

"The days within our father's belly, of course. We were all so close together. So very, very close, back then. I think it is a shame such a distance has grown between us. Do you not think so?"

"I think distance is inevitable after such a time." I spoke mildly, without animosity.

"I disagree. I think the distance makes us weak. Distance is the start of decay. It allows others to sneak in between us and cast shadows on our greatness. It is when we are together, as close as we can be, that we are our strongest. That is one thing our great brother and I agree upon."

He took another step forward, a single step, and he was so close to me that I could smell the briny tang of his breath, and see the salty spray that had settled on his skin.

"Our children will be magnificent, Demeter."

The instant he made his intentions clear, I could hold back no longer. I would not let it happen to me again. I would not let another of my brothers violate me. I knew that he expected me to put up a fight. Perhaps he had Zeus had laughed together over cups of ambrosia as they recounted all the women they had raped. But I had no intention of fighting. No, instead, I ran.

CHAPTER TWENTY-ONE

I DID NOT WAIT TO SEE THE LOOK OF SURPRISE AS I SPUN ON MY heel and darted away into the thicket of the forest, following the same path the mare had taken only minutes before.

My feet slammed against the stones as I dipped and ducked beneath the branches, trampling over leaves and twigs as I twisted and turned, my mind racked with indecision. Did I stay on the main path, the easiest route to run, or veer off it, into the undergrowth where my path would be more difficult, but so would Poseidon's pursuit?

In the end I let my feet make the choices; I ran until my legs burned, and further still, refusing to slow my pace, believing that if I could make it to the far side of the forest where caves were carved into the mountainside by locals, I would be safe. There, I could hide in the shadows and bide my time until Poseidon grew bored with looking.

I was deep in the forest, hearing the crunch of the branches behind me, when a thought struck. I wished to move quickly, so why was I maintaining this human form? Why was I running in this cumbersome, two-legged frame with thin skin that bled at the first sign of a thorn or prickle? Surely there was a better way to retreat.

In all my years in Siphnos, I had been so opposed to transforming that I forbade the action to Core and all my nymphs, despite the powers they had been blessed with. After all, my overwhelming experience of transformation happened that day on Tenos. But this was not the same. This time, I chose my form.

The instant my hooves hit the ground, a rush of air flooded through my lungs. The gallop came as easily as breathing. My mane whipped in the wind behind me. I could run like this for all eternity, I believed. I could run like this and even Hermes, with his winged sandals, could not have caught me.

As I approached the edge of the forest and saw the herd of horses knee deep in the foaming water of the river, I found myself questioning my initial plan. The caves were predictable. To shelter in shadows, hidden away, was what Poseidon would expect of me. If I were to outwit him, I would need to think beyond my limited naivety, and where would be more hidden than in plain sight? While mammals scurried in the undergrowth and birds flitted in the trees, no footsteps reached my ear. No warning of Poseidon encroaching upon me, readying to attack. Slowing to a gentle trot, I left the safety of the trees, and headed toward the stream and the other horses.

Only one stallion paid me any attention as I approached, yet for all the tense distrust he eyed me with, he made no movement as I dipped one hoof and then another into the stream. My new thickened hair and skin protected me against the chill as I moved deeper and deeper. Though even as I sidled right up next to the rest of the herd, I did not allow myself to breathe a sigh of relief. Poseidon would not give up his hunt that easily. I knew that. I would have to wait.

I cannot say how long I stayed there, nestled between the bodies of foals and mares, their warm breath against my flanks a contrast to the water that broke on my legs, their soft nuzzling, a counterpoint to stony pebbles beneath my hooves. But I can tell you that as hours passed, my fear began to fade. Poseidon would have found pleasure in terrorizing me. Joy in watching me race away from him. Perhaps that would have been enough. Perhaps he had already returned to Olympus so that he could drink with our brother and laugh about how I had been so pathetic and fearful that I bolted into the undergrowth like a startled rabbit. The more I repeated these thoughts in my mind, the more certain I became that they were the truth and the more confident I became that I would be able to continue my search for Core.

Eventually, the sun sank to a deep orange orb, cut by the jagged landscape of the horizon. As the water cooled, the horses grew restless and began climbing the riverbank into the long grasses. I, too, was about to follow when I saw him, standing there on the steppes silhouetted by the fading light.

There is no point asking me how I knew that the stallion standing on the hillside was my brother, but I assure you there was not a shadow of doubt within me. With the sun directly behind him, a black image was all I could see, his mane billowing as his tail flicked in the air. Yet I knew it was Poseidon, and even though his eyes were lost to me in the shadow of the evening sun, I knew he was staring at me. He had not given up the fight at all. He had merely been waiting.

Nausea churned within me with increasing acridity. The stallion of the herd had noticed him, too, and, instinctually, knew he was a threat. As Poseidon galloped toward the water, the stallion, rather than stepping forward in protection of the herd, drew backward with a whinny as he bucked high into the air. The rest of the herd quickly followed, racing out of the water and retreating to safety. Finally, I was the only one who remained.

"A horse," Poseidon spoke as he reached the riverbank. "You would mock me by taking one of my own forms?"

I wished I had bolted. Followed the rest of the herd. But that would not have stopped my brother. He would have slaughtered every one of them to get to me.

"Please, Brother, Core is missing. I am out here searching for her. I only wish to find my daughter."

"Is that so? Then perhaps you should keep your family onside. We could be of help to you, you know. If you would only be more obliging."

My mind raced. Perhaps it was a fight he wanted. Perhaps he found his pleasure in the struggle. Perhaps if I did not create the drama he so craved, then he would lose interest and leave me. I could but hope.

"You have not seen me in centuries, Brother. Perhaps I am not the innocent goddess you still believe me to be."

"Is that so?" He drew so close to me I could feel the flick of his tail against my skin. His nostrils flared as he pulled in a long breath, so deep it was as though he was pulling my scent in from the air. I fought the urge to kick out, or snap, or bite. He would grow tired of the tease, I told myself, repeating the words over and over in my mind. He will get bored. He will leave me. If I just stay quiet. If I do not put up a fight.

"You ran away from me," he said, rubbing his head against my neck. "Why would you do that? Are you afraid of me, Sister?"

"I told you, I only wish to find my daughter. You understand, I need to find her."

"I understand," he replied, taking a step backward.

"You do?" Disbelief rattled in my voice.

"Of course. Which is why I will make this swift."

CHAPTER TWENTY-TWO

NIGHT WAS UPON US WHEN POSEIDON FINALLY RELEASED me and wordlessly retreated into his true form. For a short while, he watched over me. My scratched and bruised body crumpled on the damp earth.

"We should not leave it so long next time, Sister," he said. A second later, he was gone.

The moment he left, a wail shot from my lungs so thunderous the earth shook.

"No! No, no, no!" I cried, glancing down at my already-swelling belly.

Once again, I was with child.

It is common knowledge that the births of gods vary greatly. My first pregnancy had been swift, though slow enough that I had time to notice my belly swelling day by day. Far quicker than mortal gestation, but I was still proffered the time to ready myself for their arrival. Time to prepare for what was to come. But with this pregnancy, I was afforded no such luxury.

The instant I heaved myself to my feet, I felt the enormity of the growth within me. My mare's body, previously taut and muscular, now sagged in the stomach, and each step caused a violent burning to spread outward from my belly. The birth would be soon.

It was not only the speed of my impending labor that shook me but also the fact I was alone. During Core and Iacchus's birth, my mother had been present, while my daughter and the nymphs were there to aid me in the arrival of my second twins. But there was no one with me that night. I was truly alone.

My legs barely felt attached to my body as I dragged myself back into the stream. Already my stomach was squeezing. Contracting in ripples that set my head spinning. The water. I remember thinking so vividly that if I could only reach the water, then it would cool this burning heat that was coursing through me. I would reach the water and an answer would come.

I pushed myself down the bank, slipping in the mud and tumbling downward so that I entered the water not upon my hooves, as I had hoped, but with my front legs sliding flat against the earth. Pain ripped a scream from my lungs. Louder than the screams of Tartarus. So loud that it did not go unnoticed.

They came with thundering hooves. A drumming that caused the earth to tremble beneath me as they churned up the earth. A hundred horses galloped from the hills toward me, a mare in distress.

To this day, I do not know if the stallion that led that herd was the same who had stood for all those hours with me in the water. I believe it may have been so, but my mind was clouded and Onceium was rife with horses. Either way, it was a dark bay mare with amber eyes who first broke away from the group and watched over me.

Horses prefer to birth in privacy. They shy away from watchful eyes and bring their foals to life in secrecy, which has led me to believe that they knew—the same way they had known that Poseidon was not as he appeared to them—that I was different. They understood what I needed.

Two mares took a place close to my side as the surges cut through me, one after another, until they were too close to be distinguishable. It was then that my fourth child was born. Yet he was unlike any of the children I had birthed before. So much so that I could not stem the gasp that flew from my lips.

His coat was as black as a starless sky as he slipped from my body. His form entirely that of a horse. Fear gripped me as, for an instant, his body slid into the water, but he was steady on his feet. Not a foal, but a stallion. His wet mane shimmered with water as though it had been dipped in the light of the stars. His pale eyes gleaming.

Silently, we observed one another. A heartbeat of recognition for what I was to him, and for what I could never be. With only the slightest of wobbles, he shifted toward the herd. The mares dropped from my side, and I saw it was not me they had come to aid, but my child. And so, with barely a glance over his shoulder, Arion, my child, thundered away into the night. But I was not done. Another child remained within me still.

Oh, how in those moments I prayed that child would be a horse. How I wished as the wind shirred through the grasses that I would be graced with another horse from my womb. Or a serpent. A monster even. All I knew was that I could not birth a child that would require my love or companionship, because I could offer it neither. I could offer it nothing.

As the horses' footsteps faded away from me, my strength faded further and I returned to human form. The water, that had been so cooling to me before, was now icy, turning my skin into a mass of goose bumps. As I dragged myself up the bank, the surges started again, yet no horses came to my aid. I had no nymphs to hold my hand, no mother by my side. And so, truly alone, I birthed my second child by Poseidon. Not a horse, but a baby. A daughter.

Despoina.

CHAPTER TWENTY-THREE

To talk of Despoina is to force me to delve into the darkest recesses of my mind. The mere mention of her name sets my skin into prickles and calls forth an icy regret that clings like talons to my very insides.

For many years, I did not say her name out loud, or even in my head. Even now, it does not flow as easily from my tongue as it should. It is not that I am ashamed of her. Please, never believe that. She is my daughter. I do not hold her conception and her father against her any more than I ever did Core or Iacchus. I do not consider her lesser in any way. No, I do not speak her name because of my own shame. That is the reason my lungs chill at the thought of that child. The reason that frost forms at my fingertips. I was too blindsided to be the mother she deserved. To be a mother at all. And the truth is that if I were faced with the same decision again, I would make it a thousand times over. All eternity has done nothing to change my mind about that. No, I did the right thing. Abandoning her was the right thing to do.

Oh, you may judge. I am sure many of you will. I birthed this child, grew her in my womb. She was my responsibility. But this was not like when I had my other children. I was not greeted by a flood of love. With Despoina's birth, I felt only numbness and overwhelm. The inexplicable burden of a task I was not able to fulfill. Had that child stayed with me, she would have endured a life of suffering. My misery and guilt would have bled into her little by little until she believed it was her own. Or worse still, she would believe she was deserving of it. Deserving of the blackness her mother displayed in her presence. Perhaps she would even believe that she was the cause of this numbness that consumed me. No, no child deserved that. Even with my mind as muzzled as it was, I knew that was the truth. She was better without me. Still, I did not abandon her then in the cold waters of Onceium where her brother roamed the hillside as a horse. I found her a home.

Fatigue drowned me. I cannot say what thoughts were running through my head. Or if any thoughts were there at all. Exhaustion had dulled every action. It had slowed my steps and turned me deaf to the sounds of her cries. Yet I knew I had to find her a place. A family. Someone to feed her. For I had no intention of feeding the child myself. No, this child would know nothing of the woman who abandoned her. Not even a mouthful of my milk.

With my daughter swaddled close to my body, I stumbled on as the morning light bleached the stars from the sky. I have endured so many endless nights in my immortal life. So many long, long nights where it has felt like the sun will never rise. I have wept a torrent of tears in the infinite moments that span between dusk and dawn, and more still while the moon faded from my sight. But that night, with Core still lost to me, Poseidon's teeth marks still raw upon my skin and Despoina in my arms, was the longest of them all.

I am ashamed to say that I do not know the name of the village where I left my daughter. It was not in Onceium, I know that. Perhaps it was closer to Ellis or Messenia, but I cannot say for certain, and it does not matter that the specificities are lost to me.

I found a house with lamplight flickering in the window. There was nothing special about this house. It was of moderate size, with a fountain gurgling out the front and chickens stirring in their roosts. I recall thinking to myself that if the family could afford oil for their lamps all through the night and even when the sun was breaking on the horizon, they were worthier of the title of parent than I was.

My footsteps trod the cold crisp ground beneath my feet as I approached the doorway as quietly as I could, attempting to hush my child. Yet in those last moments, there was no quieting Despoina. It was as if she knew what I was about to do. Her wailing rose in a crescendo as I placed her on the doorstop and backed away from her.

I did not even kiss my child goodbye. I did not wish her the best for her future, or promise, once I had found her sister, that I would use a fraction of my infinite life to come and find her. I offered her nothing, and I did not look back.

CHAPTER TWENTY-FOUR

I WALKED AWAY FROM THE WAILS, ONLY HALF HEARING THEM. AS IF I was wrapped in a gauze that somehow separated me and the true meaning of those cries. On and on, I moved one foot in front of the other until the wild laments faded beneath the whirring of the wind. I walked until I could no longer hear them. Not upon the air, nor in my heart. No, my heart was too broken to feel. Numbness gripped my very soul, for after all I had suffered, my darling Core was still lost to me.

Onward I walked, with no direction. The memories of my brother's actions and the pain I endured eddied in currents around my stomach. Yet these pains were secondary to the one that continued to grow in my chest. And this pain was entirely physical.

I had, to a lesser or greater extent, breastfed all my children. Of course, the duration had been brief given how quickly Core and Iacchus grew, and how fleeting Iasion's twins had remained with me. But I had never relied on a wet nurse, finding joy in the togetherness. As such, I had never experienced the pain of milk swelling within me as it did that night with no child there to relieve the agony. Pain that only increased as I forced myself to keep moving. For a full day, I walked, dragging my body on. Grief and exhaustion caused me to stumble and trip, but it was the burning in my chest that truly weakened me. With every breath, the throbbing grew and spread until finally, I could walk no further.

I did not see where I was when I dropped to the ground. I did not care. I had lost my beloved daughter and given away another. I was empty.

Sometimes I consider what would have happened if she had not approached me that day. If I had been left cradling my knees in agony for all eternity. Perhaps, like a victim of a gorgon, I would have turned to stone. Perhaps I would have stayed so still that moss would have grown over my body while the wind and water slowly weathered me away. I did not care. I cared of nothing, including the woman's voice that spoke beside me.

"Oh gods. What have we here? A woman such as yourself should not be out like this. Come, come." I did not register how she aimed the words at me until she hooked around my waist and pulled me off the ground. "You can't stay here. Come, come with me."

"My child, my child," I repeated, failing to express myself any further, unaware even of which child I referred to. "She is gone. My child is gone."

"Hush, shush. I know. I know, but I have you now. You are in safe hands now. Don't you worry."

So many parts of that night are hazy or else blocked from my memory in their entirety. But the face of that woman who guided me upward on a rocky pathway that led to a citadel will be forever etched in my memory. I recall how her body stayed close to mine, protectively so, as she weaved us a path between the stalls and helped me one by one up the steps to the palace. Still, I can see the creases swept around her eyes, and the vertical lines that spread out from around her weathered lips.

Baubo was the woman who found me that night. A woman whose opinion of me is deservedly sour, but whom I can think of with only compassion and regret.

As the walls of the palace appeared around us, Baubo's arms remained gently looped around mine, her hunched body low to the ground as she pulled me forward.

"My child," I said again, failing to convey any more.

"You are not alone, my poor thing. Come, come with me, child. I have you now. I have you now." Whether it was judgment, lack thereof, or simply the reality that I was truly alone, I made no protests as she guided me through the palace. The morning light poured in through the large archways in wide sheaths, while delicately woven tapestries hung on the walls, interposed between the painted frescos. Not that I noticed then.

She led me to a room where, in one corner, a fire was lit with orange flames while in the other was a long couch, which Baubo lowered me onto.

"You are safe here. I will fetch you a drink. You will be safe here, child."

For an instant, I considered punishing her for addressing me in such a manner. If any being, mortal or otherwise, had spoken to any of my siblings in such a way, they would not have lived to repeat the word. But that night I was helpless.

I did not notice that she left me, only that she returned with a cup of warm goat's milk in her hand.

"Drink this," she said. "Come, drink up, and we will find you something warm to wear."

"My child."

"I know. But here is a good place. Come, drink."

Shadows lingered in the doorway, yet none approached, and Baubo did not leave my side again while I drank. When my cup was finished, she waved her hand and one of the shadows stepped into the light. In their hands, they held a bundle of clothes.

"You are nearly dry," she said, taking the cup from my hand and helping me to her feet. "You will feel better soon."

While I stood with my bare feet on the cold tiles, the old woman began to undress me. The depths of humiliation should have seen me rush from that chamber, or at least push her hands away from me, but I did not have the strength for such action. Even as the old woman's eyes were drawn down to the engorged mounds of my breasts, I remained stoic and unflinching.

"She was still a baby. A newborn?" she questioned. When I didn't reply, she cupped my chin in her hands.

"I have been where you are. More than once. I know better than many that the pain is great, but you were lucky I found you. We will ease this for you. We can ease your pain." Then she tilted my forehead, and placed a kiss there as if I were a child and, when she had wrapped the robe loosely around me, she turned away.

"I will return shortly. Just sit and rest. I shall not be long."

As Baubo retreated, I did as she said and took a seat, though not, as I suspect she intended, on the couch, but on the stone floors near the fire. The yellow tongues flickered onto my skin, but I did not feel the skin singe the way a mortal would have. Instead, I raised my hand, thinking that if I plunged it deep enough within the flames, it might distract from the agony that writhed within, but no sooner had I flexed my fingertips, a voice spoke behind me and I snatched my hand back to my side.

"Child, I have someone who wishes to speak to you." Baubo was standing straighter than when she left me, a slightly deeper spring to her step. "This is her. This is the one I found," she said to the woman at her side.

You do not need to have spent decades watching mortals from a palace upon Olympus to know when you are standing before royalty. Her finery shimmered as she stood with perfect posture. I, in turn, was a crumpled mess. All my powers and immortality meant nothing when they had failed to keep my darling Core safe.

"Baubo tells me that you have lost your child," the queen said, crouching down beside me only to shift a fraction away from the heat. "I understand the agony we mothers go through. I myself am suffering, though not of the same measure. Not yet, at least." She paused, possibly expecting me to respond, yet she had not offered me a question.

Silence stretched between us before the queen continued. "My fifth child is not yet two months old, but my body has refused to produce the milk he needs to sustain him. We have tried him with milks from goats and sheep, but they cause him great sickness, and while we have another wet nurse, my son's hunger is too great to be abated by one woman alone." Another pause perforated her speech. I knew then why I had been brought there. And it was laughable. Still, I kept my tongue in my mouth and waited for her to continue. "I see that the great goddess Rhea favored you greatly. If you would use this favor to aid us, I would compensate you well. You would live within the palace. Never need to pay for food or drink. Speak to Baubo. She will tell you that we are good people. My husband the king and I." At this point she paused and turned her attention to the elderly nursemaid, who nodded hurriedly.

"They are the best of people. Most generous. I have been in service to them since their first child was born. Over twenty years.

And there are no kinder folk. My milk has long dried up, but still they found a place for me in their home. They would do the same for you, I do not doubt it. If you are obliging."

The queen nodded, visibly satisfied by Baubo's response. Her focus was once more on me, awaiting an answer. An answer I could not form. As silence swelled in the room, she repeated her request, albeit more succinctly than before.

"Would you stay here and be a wet nurse to my son, Demophoön?" the queen asked, before adding. "It is a great honor to nurse the son of such a revered house."

As great an honor as raising the daughter of two gods? I wanted to ask. Did Despoina's new family have any idea what honor had been bestowed on them? If they did not know now, they would learn soon enough.

"Why not stay here until your strength returns?" Baubo said, sensing my hesitance. I suspect she had promised the queen a solution to her current predicament and now feared I may disappoint her. "You do not need to agree to stay here permanently," she continued. "Just until you have a little more strength. Is that not right, my queen?" The old lady held the gaze of her superior in a manner I have rarely seen. Their eyes locking, a hundred thoughts passing between the pair in that single moment. A single moment after which the queen turned back to me and smiled.

"No, of course not. Just until your strength has returned."

This was not altruism; I could see that. Still, I dipped my chin in a manner that they read as agreement. Before another word was spoken, Baubo's hooked arm was once again lifting me up to my feet.

"Come. Come, we will take you to the prince now. You will love him. He is the dearest thing. Just you wait and see."

CHAPTER TWENTY-FIVE

ANY PERSON WHO HAS RAISED A CHILD WILL TELL YOU THAT from the instant they are your responsibility, in whatever capacity, you are forever changed. You no longer hear wailings sounds as earsplitting annoyances but as anguish and torment, which you alone must heal. And in a ball of tender, wrinkled flesh, you see all those things that flesh may grow into. All the incredible wonders that they may achieve. The hardships they will overcome.

No sooner had I dipped my chin than I was swept up and ushered to a nearby chamber further into the palace. Once again, a fire flickered in a hearth, though the flames were starting to dim, while the couch was covered with cushions and blankets. But the couch was not the only piece of furniture in the space; a wicker crib sat a safe distance from the fire. And in that crib, a baby, several months older than the one I had left only hours before, yet tiny and helpless nonetheless.

"I will leave you to get acquainted," the queen said, stepping back out of the room almost as soon as she arrived. "You will come and fetch me if I am needed?"

"I will," Baubo replied.

I had always thought my maternal instinct was bound by the blood I shared with my children. I thought the bonds that entwined us had grown in my belly with them and that the fierce love I felt was seeded from the fact they were mine and mine alone. A mother's love. Not once did I consider the ability to feel such deep affection for one that was not my blood. But the instant I saw Demophoön, that belief was gone.

Baubo was true in her word: he was the most beautiful of children. His thick crop of black curls, far darker and denser than any of my children had been born with. His rounded lips, plump and pink, his skin as smooth as porcelain.

"We have been feeding him goat's milk the best we can," Baubo told me. "But as the queen said, it makes him sick."

I will recall that moment for all eternity, just as I recall the first time I laid eyes on Core and Iacchus. I do not doubt my recent losses played some part in the immediate affection I felt for Demophoön, but the instant I saw that child, a warmth I had not felt since Core had left returned to me.

His legs were clusters of squishy rings, pale and dimpled fat that invoked an overwhelming desire to squeeze them. Having picked up the child, and holding him in the crook of one of her arms, Baubo had unclasped my robe, exposing my left breast, the skin of which was now so tight with milk that the veins, filled with ichor, glowed beneath the surface. I do not believe the old nursemaid could have noticed such a thing, for surely she would have spoken, but instead she merely handed me the child.

The instant his warm lips latched on to me, the bond was complete. His scent pervaded the air, sweet and earthy, like the root of a licorice plant. He drank greedily, barely pausing for breath.

It was like the world condensed around us, until we two were all that remained, and as my eyes closed, I found myself drawn back to those days upon Olympus with Core and Iacchus. I recalled the warmth of their small bodies pressed against mine and the sweet music of my daughter's gurgles, which filled the air. Baubo spoke again.

"I will fix you a bed in this place," she said. "No doubt you will wish to sleep when you have fed him. And I will get someone to fix this fire. We do not wish for the room to grow cold."

I glanced at the glowing embers in the fireplace, though I did not notice the lack of heat. My warmth came from inside. From the earth and this child.

"I can fix the fire," I said, not bothering to lift my gaze from the child as I spoke. "I am well versed in such things." It was hardly a chore. On Siphnos, we did not have slaves or servants to do our bidding, and we had never felt the need. Yet Baubo shook her head forcefully, causing the loose skin of her jowls to flap as though they were made of leather hides that had been hung up in a strong wind to dry.

"Don't be silly, you are a guest here, for now. You will take the hospitality that is offered to you."

There was an edge to the words *for now*. As if it were not the gods who might see my fortune change, but her king and queen, and perhaps even herself. Of course, I said nothing. As Demophoön guzzled away, Baubo continued to linger over me, until a little while later when she spoke again.

"He has taken enough for now. Come, we should move him to his crib. No doubt he will sleep for hours. And you should do the same."

The child's eyes were now fully closed, and his mouth had

dropped away from my nipple, although his lips continued to twitch; even in his dreams, milk occupied his mind.

Without waiting for me to rise, or speak, Baubo plucked the child from my arms and laid him down in his crib, kissing him as she did so. It was not only me who had fallen in love with him.

"I will come back when you are both rested," she said, nodding to the couch behind her. "Sleep well. He will need food again soon."

With that, she left me alone.

I lowered my body onto the couch, desperate to fight against the weariness that was gripping my muscles and mind. *What was I doing here?* I asked myself again and again. I should have been looking for Core. I should have been searching every corner of the earth to find her. But where else was there to look? And how would I be of use to her when I barely had the strength to keep my eyes open?

My mouth stretched into a yawn as I willed myself to stand back up, yet my legs refused to comply. I could not move anymore. With one final glance at Demophoön, I succumbed and allowed my eyes to close.

"Forgive me, Core," I said before I fell into the deepest slumber.

CHAPTER TWENTY-SIX

I DREAMED OF MY BROTHERS AND MY DAUGHTERS. OF MONSTERS that came from the land and sky and sea. I cannot be sure what those monsters were, but when I woke, the sheets were soaked in sweat, my heart drumming as though it wished to flee from my chest.

Panic filled me as I opened my eyes, only for it to subside at the sight of Demophoön now awake in his crib.

From all I had seen of mortal children, it was a surprise that the child had not woken me with his cries, until I understood that the accolades Baubo had placed upon this child were not simply idles of a doting elderly nurse, but the truth. I stretched out my legs, rolling my neck from side to side as I moved across to him. His sapphire eyes stared up at me, and upon seeing that he now had my attention, he moved his lips in a familiar sucking motion.

"You recognize me already, do you?" I said, unable to hide the sense of joy I felt. "I know what you want. Come here." This time he fed for even longer, only occasionally stopping his suckling to take a breath or swallow the mouthful that he had taken far too greedily.

"No wonder you have such delicious legs." As I squeezed his pink flesh, a smile flashed upon my cheeks. It was fleeting and shallow, but immediately I wiped it from my face. I had nothing to smile for. This child had nothing to smile for. His life would be so brief, so fleeting.

It was a few moments later that the tapestry on the doorway was pulled aside and Baubo stepped inside the room. In her hands, she carried a plate of fresh fruit. Plums, damsons, figs, and apricots. Even from the edge of the room, their sweetness swilled in the air.

"You two have slept late." The folds in her skin deepened as she gazed at Demophoön. "But it is a good thing you are awake now. You will need to have a proper scrub before the feast tonight."

"Tonight?" Guilt ripped at my insides. I could not stay. I had to keep searching for Core. And yet, Demophoön needed me. And I, in some part, needed him too.

"You are to dine with the king and queen tonight," Baubo continued, oblivious to my distress. "They wish to thank you. They are holding a feast."

"A feast?"

She took the child from me and busied herself with the swaddling.

"Thanks to the goddesses, Hera and Eileithyia. It is unlikely you will have attended a feast like they hold here. The king has ordered a dozen swine killed." From the pit of my stomach came a gnawing growl. When had I last eaten? Not since Core had vanished. I am ashamed to say that my mouth watered at the thought of a decent meal. A decent meal and a bath.

While the fruits Baubo had brought went some way to satiate my hunger, it was not until midday when I received a chance to bathe.

Groaning, I dropped into the water. The heat sinking into my muscles as I closed my eyes and absorbed the scents of lavender and thyme. I scrubbed my body clean, picking out dirt from beneath my nails, and watching the water turn gray with the black grime from the soles of my feet.

"There is a robe for you in the nursery," a maid said as she wrapped the towel around me.

"Thank you," I responded, pulling the towel tighter. My body had already healed from the physical wounds Poseidon had inflicted, yet I kept myself covered nonetheless.

Back in the nursery, Demophoön was waiting for another feed.

"Look at how he smiles to see you," Baubo said as she handed me the child. The words were not false flattery. There he was, looking up at me with a sense of knowing. Of love.

"I shall leave you both, just for a short while," Baubo said, retreating from the room. "I must find someone to fix your hair."

With Demophoön and I alone, I once again fed the child.

"You are blessed," I told him, stroking my hand over the downy softness of his skull. "Don't tell them, but you have been fed by a goddess. That is a luxury indeed. You will grow strong and fearless. A hero, I suspect."

At this comment, the baby waved his arms and legs with elation. His reaction implied so keenly that he understood what I had told him that a laugh broke free from my lungs. A laugh that I immediately quashed. I did not deserve joy. Not while Core was still lost to me.

Minutes afterward, when tears had once again replaced the happiness, Baubo returned with a maid to fix my hair.

"Are you not attending the feast?" I asked, as the final braids were placed in my hair. Baubo was kneeling on the ground, stoking the fire. However close her relationship was to the king and queen, I found it difficult to believe they would allow her to attend a feast in such grubby attire.

"Not tonight," she said. "I will stay with the child. Perhaps you can bring me a plate when you are done. Duck or goose if there's some to spare. Fatty bits too. Don't let the men get all the fatty bits."

I nodded, only half-listening as I observed my reflection. Little more than a slip of eyes remained visible as I pulled the veil across the rest of my face. It would have been so easy to slip into this role that had been pressed upon me, that of mortal wet nurse. I could stay there until Demophoön was grown, I thought. Longer still. Perhaps find other queens who required my services. It would surely be no worse than the life of loneliness I was burdened with now.

"Come," Baubo said, standing up and wiping the soot from her hands on to the seat of her robe. "You should not keep them waiting. Eat, be merry. We shall both be here when you return."

CHAPTER TWENTY-SEVEN

I HAD ONLY ATTENDED ONE MORTAL FEAST BEFORE, WHEN I WAS placed on a throne and all in attendance knew who I was. This was a very different affair. Had my true identity been known, I should have taken a seat higher than that of the king and queen, and yet I realized only as I stepped inside the room that I did not know where my current place should be among the tables and long benches. Although that was only one of my concerns.

The cacophony of the crowds hammered against my ears. The percussive clattering of the plates. The raucous laughter and high-pitched squeals of children. My muscles clenched beneath my robes as I fought back the urge to race in the other direction. How was it possible, I wondered, for me to hear the libations of ten thousand women, singing my name and praise around the world, and yet being seated in a hall with a fraction of that number was enough to set my head swirling with dizziness.

Men leered and shouted, and each second searching for a seat caused the tension to rise within me. The air grew hotter and hotter with every breath. So thin that I thought I was sure to pass out, when a finger jabbed at my side.

"You sit there." The finger pointed to a table on the other side of the hall where a cluster of women with veils over their faces were gathered and talking. Without so much as a glance at the owner of the finger, I hurried across to the table.

It is not fair to say the other ladies were unwelcoming. One passed me a plate, and another filled my glass promptly with wine. But they did not invite me into the conversation. I was not told names, or where people had come from, or how long they had been in this house. I was not even asked what my name was or where I had come from.

As the wine began to take hold, the men wandered away from their seats, jostling me from the left and the right as they tried to push in and take a seat by these women. Had I had any of the forthrightness of Hera or Athena, these men would likely have regretted their presence at our table greatly, but I did not wish to draw attention to myself. And so when my plate was clean, I stood up from the table and picked my way out of the hall and back to the nursery.

"You were faster than I expected," Baubo said upon my return, before her eyes moved down to my empty hands. "You did not bring me anything to eat?"

"There is plenty of food left," I told her, praying she would not ask me to return to the crowds of people. "I thought that perhaps you might like to join the others, rather than remained trapped in here."

I made the comment purely for my own benefit, rather than Baubo's, for I wished to be alone.

"I told the queen I would watch the child," she said, although her tone implied she was less than enamored by this instruction.

"But I am here now. You have already seen what a bond he and I have." I watched the contemplation shadow her face and attempted to reassure her further. "You could always bring your plate back, if you prefer? That way, you do not need to leave him for too long. Or you could take a bath," I added, indicating the soot that still covered her hands. Finally I piqued her interest.

"I will be swift," she said brusquely, once again wiping her hands on her robe. "Perhaps I'll fetch myself a glass of wine if they haven't brought out the cheap stuff already."

Her footsteps retreated, the tension flooding from my shoulders. I dropped my hands into my chest and breathed my first full breath since entering the dining hall.

For several minutes, the sound of my breath filling my lungs was all I focused on. When I looked up again, my eyes fell on Demophoön.

"You sleep well, don't you, little one?" I said, stopping forward to stroke his soft downy hair. His cheeks had pinked from the warmth of his sleep as his chest rose and fell softly. Watching that child brought me peace. Seeing him calmed the agitation that writhed within me. Yet as I stared at him dreaming, a sense of unfairness built within me.

His life would be so brief. It was likely the status of prince would shelter him from the worst aspects of humanity, but still, he would be gone from this world far too soon.

Then a single ember flickered from the fireplace and caused an idea to alight in my mind.

It was a thought I had never considered with my Iacchus, for his grievances came not from his lack of immortality but from his lack of powers, which was something I could not change. Nor had I considered it with my twin boys, for their place was with their family. Iasion's family. But this young child, who was untainted by mortals and gods, had allowed me to feel again. This child had brought warmth to my heart when I had believed it turned to stone. I had lost so many of my children. All my children, and while he may not have been my blood, I was determined not to lose Demophoön like I had lost the others.

Hastily, I moved across to the fire. The flames were contained, trapped between the crisscross of wood and kindling, but as I lifted my hands, they rose into great pillars.

"This will not hurt you, my child," I whispered as I lifted Demophoön into my hands. "This will mean we can be together forever."

He was hungry, and wished to feed, but I kept him a distance away from my chest as I muttered the words of the spell. The fireplace flickered, as if an open breeze had fanned the flames, which turned only the very tips from a glowing red to a vivid blue.

It was not a spell I had done before, but the words were fresh on my tongue and rolled forward unceasing. They were part of me.

I tilted him further still until he was within the fire. Fire that, together with my incantation, would burn away his mortality. As I held him in the heat, I felt it. Felt his frailness seeping away from his frame, and strength, strength beyond any mortal filling him. A few moments were all I needed. A few moments and he would forever be safe. But they were moments I did not get.

CHAPTER TWENTY-EIGHT

A SHOVE FROM MY SIDE HALTED THE INCANTATION AND THE split-second break was all it took.

The aroma hit instantly. That bitter unmistakable charring of flesh followed immediately by the screaming wails of the child. His agony was louder than a siren as it shot up in the air. His skin blackened, but his eyes remained wide and wild. There was still time, I told myself. There was still a chance I could save him. I concentrated on the flames, willing them to grow. Willing the magic that flowed through me to seep into the fire and the child. And for the briefest instant, it was there. It was back. The purple sparks. The glittering green. But no sooner had I placed the child back within the magic than he was snatched from my hands.

"What have you done? What have you done?" Baubo screamed as she poured an amphora of water over Demophoön's blistering skin.

"You fool! Let me take him. Let me do this."

"You are a madwoman. You are a murderer! Guards! Guards!" She shrilled at the top of her voice. "Murder! Guards!"

I moved to wrap my hands around her mouth and silence her as my siblings would have done. But that was when the quietness struck me. Demophoön was silent.

I stumbled back, my body shaking with anger and disbelief.

"You silly old woman. You *fool*. You have no idea what you have done. I was saving him. I was giving him a life. An eternal life."

She did not hear the words I said. I suspect she could not hear anything other than her own choking sobs.

"We invited you into our home. You monster. You beast. You murderer. You will pay for this. You will pay with your life as he paid for my foolishness."

"You are not listening—"

It was true, for her eyes were solely on the baby.

"There is no punishment you do not deserve. I will see to it myself. You will burn in Tartarus."

The thundering feet of the guards racing along the corridor joined her bellows. Thundering like those horses who had raced to me in the river. Thundering like the flapping of wings as my nymphs, forever changed, took to the sky. The noises compounded within me, all of them hammering around my skull. It was too much. Too much for me to bear. I clutched my hands around my head, rocking back and forth as I tried to see myself upon my island. I tried to envision myself in my home, with my daughter and nymphs. I needed my daughter and my nymphs. Yet there were gone. They were gone, and I was here alone.

"Seize her!"

The clattering of shields and spears crescendoed as armed guards surged into the nursery. If they came for me, I would hurt them. I could feel it. I could feel the power running through my fingers. That same burning heat that had struck on Siphnos when I learned of the nymph's betrayal flooded me. I would do whatever needed to be done.

"Stay back," I yelled, yet they didn't even blink at my words. Not one of them even slowed. "Stop!" A barrier of thistles sprouted from the tiles, cracking the earth beneath their feet. The guards in front tumbled back, their eyes widened in terror.

"What is it?"

"A witch? We have a witch?"

Confusion caused them to shout over one another, as they desperately sought an answer for what they were seeing. Some stood transfixed, but others backed away. *Good*, I thought. *Go now, before I hurt any more of you.* But they had not backed away from fear. They had moved to make room for the queen.

Fear and confusion flashed across her face at the barricade of thorns, but neither lasted long. For as her gaze moved across the room, it landed upon the bundle in Baubo's arms.

Her mouth fell open in a gasp. Her body lurched forward as she scrambled over the thorns to reach him.

"Demophoön. Demophoön, my son. My love." Her body trembled as she spoke his name over and over again. If only words had been enough for him to open his eyes and respond. I should not be ashamed to tell you that this moment broke me. Shattered my heart beyond all form. More so even than when I had left Despoina only hours before. After all, that was my choice. This mother had lost her child through no choice of her own. I know how that feels better than any other.

"I don't understand, what happened to him?" She continued as tears poured down her cheeks. "How did this happen?"

Fearful of what she had seen me do, Baubo offered me only the swiftest of glances before she bowed low.

"My queen. Queen Metaneira, the nurse we brought into the home. She has...she is..."

Her words fumbled as she pointed at the purple thorns, hoping they would offer an answer she could not find. As she had hoped, the queen followed her line of sight.

The blood drained from Queen Metaneira's lips as she turned to face me.

"Whatever you are, you will answer to the gods for what you have done here. To harm a child, to break Xenia, this is unforgivable."

I did not drop to my knees, as mortals would have done in such a situation. Nor did I rise above her and demand her undying respect, as I know some other gods would have done. Instead, I lowered my head slightly.

"Queen Metaneira, I would never hurt a child or a host. I assure you, my intentions were pure. I wished to honor you. To give your child the greatest gift. To offer him immortality."

She frowned, and stared at the dead bundle in Baubo's arms, as if he might break out of his burned shell, awake and living. I only wished that was possible.

"If that is the truth, then why is he...gone..."

So much pain shone through her at that word. *Gone.* I had spoken the exact same word to myself time and time again. Why were they gone? Why was Iasion gone? Why was Core gone? Though I had no answer for myself, I could at least give the queen one.

"The spell was nearly complete. A minute longer was all it would take, but Baubo did not know what I was doing. She assumed I was trying to hurt the child."

"Is that true?" The queen stiffened as she offered the question to her nurse. "Is it true what she says?"

"He was in the flames, my queen. She was holding him in the fire. I thought… I thought—"

The queen raised her hand to strike the old woman. After all, slaves had been beaten to death for far, far less, and I readied myself to step forward and intervene. After all, it was not Baubo's entire wrongdoing. But the queen placed her hand on the nursemaid's shoulder and offered a single nod, the sign of her entire forgiveness. And when it passed, the queen turned back to face me.

"Who are you, to come into my house and declare the strength to grant immortality? What is it you want in this place? What do you want from my family?"

"I want nothing from you, Queen Metaneira." For the first time since entering the palace, I stood up tall and allowed the smallest flicker of my strength to shine outward. "My name is Demeter. I am the goddess to which you offer for the first crops of the season. The reason your harvest grows high and bountiful, and you have food to feed your children and more still to sell and barter. I am the sister of Zeus, daughter of the great Titan King Cronus. And by my words, I meant no harm in this house."

"Demeter?" The queen repeated, stepping backward.

I nodded. "That is the truth."

The guards did not wait for an order before dropping their weapons and falling to the ground on their knees. A second later, the queen followed.

CHAPTER TWENTY-NINE

SILENCE DESCENDED. SILENCE I WISHED I COULD BREAK WITH some words of comfort. But there is no comfort to one who has lost a child. No cure for the despair that will haunt that parent every remaining hour of their existence. Slowly, the queen rose to her feet.

"You will return to the hall, and dine with us," she said. The words cracked in her throat. "Arrangements will need to be made. Demophoön was only a baby, but he was a prince, and he deserves the most gracious of burials. I will need to make arrangements and I would like for you to be there. You were his nurse, if only for a short while. As your host, that is my request."

It was a request I knew I could not refuse.

Though I had despised the noise of the dining hall, it was nothing compared to the silence of it. As I walked back into the hall, not a piece of bread was broken, nor a single piece of cutlery cluttered. All eyes were upon me. Judging me. In my fingers, I felt the sharp prick of ice. Folding my arms, I tucked my hands under my robe. You may ask why I did not leave. Why I did not say to them that this situation was unworthy of my presence or why I did not bring down my power upon them. But Xenia is a bond that requires all guests and hosts to be protected within a house. And whether deliberately or not, I had broken that bond. The suffering I had inflicted on my host had deepened my own grief, yet I knew my pain at the loss of Demophoön was only a sliver of what the queen, his mother, felt in that moment. And so if she required me to share a meal with her to help repair that bond that I had severed, then the least I could do was oblige.

There was no searching for a seat this time. No scouring between the heads for a gap on a bench where I could slide in surreptitiously. The chairs at the top table had been shifted, a new empty place set centrally. An empty seat awaiting me.

There is nothing to be afraid of, I told myself over and over. *I will be gone from here, and there is nothing to be afraid of.* It is bizarre to think of a great goddess fearful amid a gathering of mortals who could do her no harm. But mortals are afraid of all manner of beings that can do them no harm, snakes, spiders, rats. Irrational thought is not reserved solely for humankind.

I held my breath steady as I took my seat. Immediately, a platter containing a pig's head was placed in front of me. Fruit was stuffed in the animal's open mouth, its once bright eyes now muted and dull.

I had no desire to eat such a thing, and yet I pulled a chunk of pink flesh from its cheeks. Only when I forced several mouthfuls into my stomach did the queen speak again.

"Would you grant us the gift of explaining how you came to be in our halls?" she asked. "We have not hosted a goddess before, and would certainly have shown you a greater level of respect had we known whose presence we were in."

"I could not ask for more respect," I replied swiftly. "To entrust me with your child is the greatest level of respect one could show." I did not mean my words callously, nor did I consider how they could be interpreted in the light of Demophoön's death.

Somehow, Queen Metaneira forced herself to smile. Perhaps it was a strength she had gained from years living in a house full of men, or perhaps it was delusion caused by the loss of her child that made her feel that she could speak to me with such confidence and absolution. But I could not help but wonder if there was a little Amazon in her blood.

"What is the reason for your visit?" the queen asked again.

Different thoughts cross my mind as to how I should reply. It was known that gods took human forms and traveled the Earth frequently. I could pretend that I was behaving in the manner as my siblings so often did, simply scouting through villages and towns, testing men and women alike for their loyalties to the deities. I could have said I was there to test them, and that their graciousness would ensure I blessed them from this point on. But this was a mother who had just lost a child at my hand, and if anyone could have comprehended my actions, I believed it was her.

"My daughter Core has gone missing," I spoke quietly, but the hall was cavernous and that even at the back of the room, wives and husbands strained their ears, waiting with bated breath. "She has been missing for ten days now, and I can find no trace of where she has gone. I have scoured from Encheleans to Carpathos and every scrap of land between."

"What was she doing? Where was she when she disappeared?"

"I only wish I knew," I said truthfully. "She had taken to wandering in the meadows of the mortal lands at her leisure. Islands, mountains, anywhere flowers grow. I cannot say where it was she was last and therefore I do not know where to continue my search."

The queen's eyes locked on mine, and as she gazed at me, I felt a bond grow within the pain. But it was not she who spoke next, but the king. As was often the case, King Celeus was several years older than his wife, though his jaw was still square and his head still dark with curls. When he stood up, he balanced his weight on the table and tilted his head to the side.

"Triptolemus," he said, calling down to the end of his table. "Come. Come here."

At his command, a young man rose from his seat. His skin was deeply tanned and unspotted in the manner of one who spent his life outside. His chin was square and his hair tightly coiled close to his head, and there was no doubt of his parentage. He was a prince. A brother of Demophoön. "Triptolemus, you heard what the goddess just said about her daughter?"

"I did, Father."

"Do you think it is possible?" There was an urgency in the king's voice that I did not understand, yet it was clear Triptolemus did.

"I do. I do, Father." I did not appear to be the only one confused by this conversation of riddles. For the queen looked between her husband and son, bemused, before Triptolemus turned his attention to me.

"Goddess, I believe I may have seen something of significance. Ten days before this, I had been out in the fields with my brothers. The land in Eleusis is rich with grasses and meadows. And the swine and cattle that we farm here are some of the plumpest and most juicy that you will find in all of Hellas." I could not believe that the boy would think it an opportune moment to sell his cattle, so I remained silent and let him speak. "We were sitting beneath the trees, the cattle and swine, content in the grasses, I will admit, I was near to dozing off, when a great rumbling awoke me. And there, not too far from where I had been lying, the earth opened up."

He paused, and such I felt it necessary to repeat what he had told me.

"The earth opened up?"

He nodded his head. An entire herd of swine and cattle went down this chasm. Now I was certain he was telling me out of a desire for money. Perhaps he thought the loss of his brother could be negotiated to counter the loss of the beasts.

"I am sorry for your loss. I am sure that must have affected you greatly. If you are wishing to be recompensed in some way—"

"Oh, my goddess, no, that is not what I'm saying." His cheeks colored with embarrassment. "As the swine disappeared before our very eyes, a chariot drawn by black horses appeared in the sky. The chariot driver's face was invisible to me, and he quickly disappeared back down into the chasm, but his right arm was tightly around a young girl. A beautiful maiden."

Numbness swept through me, for I could not believe what I was hearing.

"A chariot drawn by black horses, dove beneath the earth?" I repeated slowly for fear of what the words meant.

Triptolemus nodded. "I believe my brother sketched a drawing of it, if you wish to see, my goddess, for we were so taken aback by the sight."

I shook my head. There was no need for me to see any drawings these princes may have done. For now I knew who had my daughter.

CHAPTER THIRTY

WITHOUT WAITING FOR ANY FURTHER WORDS, I TURNED and walked from the hall, though when I reached the corridor, I faced the issue of where I could retreat to. I would certainly not return to the nursery with scents of charred flesh still lingering in the air, yet solitude was what I required. So, with no real purpose, I weaved a path through the palace until I found myself on an open balcony. The narrow space was decorated with an ornate mosaic flooring and tightly packed with plants. The vines in the pots grew high up, though the leaves were yellow and insipid as though they had received far too much water on the roots. I placed my fingers on the stem of one of the plants and felt the life returning to it. If only it had been that simple with the child, I considered. One by one, I worked my way through each of the pots and had less than half a dozen remaining, when a voice spoke out to me.

"I am sorry, I have interrupted you. You have found the place that I come to seek solitude. No doubt for the same reason."

I turned to the voice, finding myself face-to-face with the queen.

In the pale light of the courtyard, her tears shone so brightly her entire being could have been made of water.

"This is your home. You do not need to be excused."

She nodded, her lips tightly pressed together.

"You will excuse my impertinence, Goddess, but do you not have people that will help you? Other gods that you could seek aid from to help bring her back to you? Your sisters, perhaps?"

Her words were said with such earnest innocence, I knew in my whole heart that what Baubo had said about this king and queen was true. They were good people. Good rulers. And yet her comment aroused in me a laugh. Genuine, yet bitter. Painful in the truth it exposed. To think other gods would help me was comical. Who would I go to? To my sister, who disowned me the instant her husband laid his hands on me? To my mother, who I had not heard from in centuries, even with the death of my beloved? Even Hephaestus, who had been so gracious to me in private, could not risk his parents' wrath by aiding me openly in public. No, there was no one I could go to. There was no one who would offer to help a goddess who had spited their company in favor of nymphs and her daughter. Nymphs whose lives she had destroyed and a daughter whose life she had failed to keep safe. No, there was no one I could call upon to come to my aid, I wanted to say to her. I was on my own. I had always been on my own.

I was about to say so much when a flickering light out on the horizon caught my attention. I cannot say what that slight twinkle was. A fire, lit to cook food outside, perhaps. Or a single torch, carried through the night. It did not matter. It was one single light, but I imagined how easily that single light could split and become two pinpricks, or perhaps even four. And in that instant, a fire was lit within me and I turned back to the queen.

"Yes, yes, there is someone I can contact. Someone I can ask for help. And if I have your blessing, my queen, I would like to invite them into your home."

CHAPTER THIRTY-ONE

ASKING FOR HELP IS NOT A GIFT OF MINE. THERE ARE MEN and women, gods and mortals, who do not think twice about seeking aid at the slightest hint of discomfort. But discomfort is the world that I was born into. It is a place of familiarity. Comfort, almost. But I needed help. I needed a being on my side whose word even Zeus would not refute. I needed Hecate.

I cast the spell, summoning the witch in the same fire where Demophoön had met his death. I thought it only polite to the queen that I did not tarnish her palace with my presence in other rooms. It also offered me the opportunity to rid the room of the thorns I had cast earlier.

Queen Metaneira and Baubo remained, hovering over my shoulder as my face remained hidden from them in the shadows of the flames. The crackles and hiss of wood grew deeper as I chanted, whispers like melodies drifting through trees. Sparks whistled as they darted up into the air. White, gold, violet, and green and then, no sooner than they had started, did they stop, and the fire dropped to nothing but smoke, leaving a cold chill in the air.

As the silence lingered, I turned to the women waiting behind me. "She has heard my summoning. And now all I can do is wait."

I will never forget the graciousness of Queen Metaneira and King Celeus for the part they played in hosting me. Of course, their actions may have been from fear of retribution, but I do not believe that is so. Queen Metaneira displayed a compassion I have rarely found in mortals or immortals, and her calming presence silent beside me was one I will forever be grateful for. A calmness that remained even when I brought a witch into her home.

As I have learned is the way with Hecate, I saw her lights long before I was blessed with her presence. Pinpricks that shone in the distance. There were one or two false alarms. A shepherd's fire, lit on a mountainside, caused my heart to leap, as did a distant merchant's lamp. Now I look at these moments with mild amusement, but back then, the truth struck me with a deep disappointment.

She came in the darkest hour of the night. Clouds shrouded the moon and stars, a dense blanket that offered not even a smudge of light to help us see. The queen had requested two seats on the balcony, which offered the largest views over their lands. While I remained standing, resting on the cold stone pillars and craning my neck, she fell into a deep sleep, no doubt fueled by the tears of her lost child. It was only when I saw a single light in the distance, moving closer and closer to us, that I roused her.

"She is here. She is here," I said, sounding more like an impatient child than a goddess. "The witch Hecate has heard me. She is coming now."

At this the queen stretched out slightly, with a grace that would offer Aphrodite jealousy, as she rose to her feet.

"Then we should go to meet her."

I myself had been unsure how I was to approach Hecate,

considering how curtly I had responded to our previous meeting. Given Zeus's deference to the witch, I could hardly laud my right as Olympian above her. Making demands would likely go poorly. And so as she approached in her flowing cloak, steady and stately, despite the whipping winds that tossed around the branches and leaves, I felt I had no option but to be truthful.

"Please forgive me for our previous meeting," I said, when she approached the steps to the palace. An apology from the gods is rare, and even more so when it is the first thing from their lips. "I was not in my right mind. The grief of losing my daughter caused me to forget myself."

"You called me. You summoned me and I have come," Hecate said, before shifting her gaze to the side of me to our host. "This is your home?"

"It is, and you are most welcome here." Queen Metaneira said, her courage and strength just as forthright as it had been addressing me. "Shall we head inside, to the gynaeceum? We will not be disturbed."

It was a peculiar mix of women. A queen, a goddess, and the witch. I considered asking the queen for privacy, but quickly dismissed the thought. Without her, I would not have even considered seeking Hecate's aid. She deserved her place by our side.

We walked in silence. There was something peculiar about the way Hecate's posture changed so fluidly, moving in one moment as though she were hunched, bones curved and as crooked as an old crone, and then in the single breath standing tall with the posture of a dancer. Her face, similarly, moved with the air, appearing momentarily as though it was formed from pure silk, only to turn gray and coarse with a shift of angles. An aroma of the earth emanated from her presence. Damp leaves, and rich soils. Aromas that reminded me in some part of Iasion.

When we reached the gynaeceum, I felt the need to offer my apologies again.

"I am sorry for any discourteousness I may have shown you," I repeated as I offered Hecate a seat.

"You do not need to explain yourself. You have called me, and I have come. There is no animosity between us. I assume you have news of your daughter, and that is why you require my presence?"

I was grateful for her abruptness and that she required no more groveling on my part. With an equal desire for haste, I began.

"There is a prince here. A prince who believes he saw my daughter with Hades. He believes he saw my brother snatching Core and taking her away to the Underworld."

"Which would explain why I could see no trace of them when I searched for the source of the cries," Hecate answered promptly. "So, how can I be of service to you?"

Mortals view us gods as bold and brash, but for me, even asking something of someone who had offered their help caused a tightening within me. Never before had I asked anyone for help. But I could not do this alone.

"I need to know if it is true. If Hades truly snatched and stole my daughter. I cannot accuse Zeus of being complicit in such a crime until I know for sure."

Hecate clasped her hands, which were clawed with protruding nails, but in a blink, there was nothing there but smooth palms and gentle curved fingertips. She did not ponder the question long before she offered her suggestion.

"We shall go to Helios. He who sees all."

Helios, God of the Sun, was another of the Titans that Zeus allowed to continue his role after Cronus's demise. It is unsurprising, because without Helios to ride his golden chariot across the sky from east to west each morning, the mortals would have been plunged into eternal darkness. But he was not a god with whom I had socialized. Even on Olympus.

"He is of my lineage," Hecate said, sensing my reservations. "He will listen to me. If we leave now, we can meet him at the eastern point of the sky. We can be ready for when he brings his chariot."

CHAPTER THIRTY-TWO

Having departed Eleusis, Hecate and I traveled to the island of Rhodes. Green blades of grass were damp with dew. The fading heat of the earth ready for the rising sun. Had I come to this place in search of Core already? It was difficult to tell. I believed I had traveled the whole of the Earth, but places transform. Shadows lengthen, shores retreat. Landscapes shift even to us.

We waited in a darkened field, where the silhouettes of trees were barely visible against the blackness of the night. I was impatient. Never had I so greatly wished for dawn to come, nor had I been so fearful of the news it would bring me. Above us, the stars dissolved, the faintest fading first, until only the boldest constellations remained. And then, when all had gone, the thinnest sliver of bright light appeared on that imperceptible line of the horizon, where the sky meets the Earth.

"It is Eos. She is painting the Dawn," Hecate said.

And what a painting she made for us that morning. The deep, impenetrable blackness faded into a burning crimson. Brushstrokes of clouds, luminescent with the light of Helios, glowed as if they had formed upon Olympus. Had my life allowed it, I would have watched every second of that masterpiece. I would have committed to memory the way the colors blended so seamlessly, and the chorus of the first birds taking flight. It is no wonder people worship us. Not when you see what we are capable of. And then from that strip of light came the first simple splinter. A lone ray, breaking into the world.

"We must go now. We must meet Helios."

Hecate's pace was faster than I expected, her long strides racing across the fields to reach that point on the horizon. Together, we were standing upon a mountain, when out from the curtain of dawn came the golden chariot.

I have seen the artwork that mortals have created depicting the Titan Helios, but no paint could ever do justice to the fiery golden chariot that rose above us. The old god showed not a hint of his age. His muscles rippled as he held the reins of his four horses and his eyes glowed. Horses that found their path blocked by the hands of an ageless witch.

"Hecate, what is the meaning of this?" Helios yelled from his chariot. "I must ride. Eos has already painted the dawn."

"I understand, Brother, but please, we wish to ask you something. The quicker you answer us, the quicker we will be on our way."

His eyes burned with frustration as they skipped beyond us to the western sky, which remained shrouded in a blanket of darkness.

"Be brief."

With the swiftest of glances in my direction, Hecate nodded, and I scuttled forward, like a child.

"My daughter is gone," I told him. "Core, daughter of Zeus and Demeter, is missing. A farmer of Eleusis says he saw the earth splitting open and a chariot of black horses rise from its chasm. He says he saw her taken beneath the earth with a cloaked figure. I need to know if this is true. I need to know if my brother Hades has taken my child."

"Your daughter. She is the one who wanders the earth, tending to the flowers in the meadows?"

"She is," I said with a sharp pang in my chest. If Helios knew of Core, then he had likely seen me, refusing to leave my little island. Terrified of what I might find beyond my sanctuary.

His eyes locked on me, his irises the same white blue as the manes of his horses.

"It is true," he said. "The earth did open, and it was Hades's chariot who raced forward into the sky, and snatched your child. Now that I have told you, I can wait no longer. I cannot be of more aid to you. I am sorry."

My knees buckled beneath me, though Hecate was there to catch me before I tumbled. With my breath staggering, I straightened myself back to standing, only to find my voice catching on a lump in my throat. A lump that caused tears to flow freely down my cheeks. Tears of hope.

"Thank you. Thank you."

Helios locked his eyes on mine as his horses pulled against their rein and tugged upon their bits. Considering the urgency with which he had wished to take to the sky, I was confused by his hesitation to leave.

"I have seen you with your daughter," he said eventually. "I have seen the bond you two share. For someone to separate the pair of you…" He shook his head as if the thoughts were too painful to voice. "I only pray I never have to endure what you are experiencing. To lose one's child is an agony I cannot imagine."

Sometimes I think back on his final words to me and wonder

if one of the other gods had heard his utterings and sought to bring about his pain. For Helios did lose a son, Phaethon. A mortal child, Phaethon, like so many children, pestered his father for gifts inappropriate for his age and skill. And like so many doting fathers, Helios had relented. Giving in to his son's pleas, he allowed him to take the reins of his golden chariot. But Phaethon did not have the strength to command it, and certainly not the immortal horses that pulled it. Any fool, immortal or otherwise, knew how that day would end. As the horses galloped across the sky, they bucked and bolted and changed their course. The child's strength was not enough to hold the steeds as they plunged toward the Earth. The flaming chariot drew so close to the Land of the Living that the tops of the trees caught alight and Phaethon fell to the ground and was lost to his father.

But this is not Helios's story. This is mine. Now I knew where my daughter was, and I wanted her back.

PART TWO
CORE

CHAPTER THIRTY-THREE

Y OU WASTE YOUR POWERS," IACCHUS SAID TO ME ONE DAY AS
we were sitting in the courtyard, sunlight streaming through
the open roof. In the center of my hand, I held a cluster of
perfectly dark miniature pearls, poppy seeds. As I cast them outward,
they landed in an arc upon the ground and sprouted deep red flowers
that bloomed in front of us, a waterfall of the deepest crimson.

"If I had power like yours, I would not waste it on flowers." The
scowl on his face deepened. He was plumper than I was. Round-
faced and chubby-limbed, yet his cheeks always sank inward as if he
were sucking upon a sour lemon, and his lips turned downward like
they had never learned to smile. "I would raze the Earth, like Father.
I would send thunderbolts shooting down into towns, or create
storms so big the greatest ships were smashed into a million pieces.
The mortals would know of my true power."

"Brother, I do not believe the mortals would worship you for
smashing their ships." I replied. I did not mean to hurt him with
my words. I was merely confused. Besides, the mortals would never
worship Iacchus, for he had no power. And this was the root of his

unhappiness. This was the constant churning, stomach-curdling injustice that ran through his every thought. I could see that.

During those first decades upon Olympus, we were inseparable. We would laugh together and sing together and bathe in the cold fresh streams that meandered down the mountainside. Gradually, though, that laughter faded.

For even with the whispers that rattled between the bronze pillars of our home—whispers that taught me the truth about how Iacchus and I had been conceived—Olympus was still paradise to me. The glorious sunshine. The myriad of flowers. The songs of the nymphs. To me, there were so many sources of love and joy. To Iacchus, it was a reminder of all that he was not.

He aged so quickly, and not with grace. When his bones broke, they took months to re-form. His speed was slow and clumsy, and he failed to impress with strength or wit, and he soon saw this. He was mortal, and not even a spectacular one. For all his bloodline, Iacchus was mundane.

Before I had even contemplated a role beyond the palace walls, he was wandering down to the mortal lands, determined to lose himself in drink and women the way so many mortals did. How I fretted for him during those years. I worried that one of these women might conceal a knife within their robe, sharp enough to slit his throat, or that he might start a brawl that he could not finish. But I could not ask him to stay with me.

"Perhaps I can come with you?" I suggested once. He had been away from Olympus for several years and returned an older man. A cough had settled in his lungs. Hacking and phlegm-filled, it affected him both day and night. I had made my suggestion, believing that my presence with him, in the Land of the Living, might deter him from visiting the seediest of establishments and allow me to create some final happy memories together, but my mother shook her head, barely allowing me to finish.

"There is nothing good to be found from roaming the earth as he does," she said. "You will remain here. It is safer here."

I understood her worry. Iacchus's days with us were fading fast, but I knew no matter how much I begged him, he would not remain upon Olympus in his final years. And so I tried to appease her.

"I am not like him, Mother. I am a god. I have powers."

At this, she grabbed my wrists and squeezed so tightly her nails dug into my skin.

"Those are the words of the foolish," she snapped. "There is always someone who is more powerful. Who will use trickery and cunning and manners you could not even think of to get their way with you."

We both knew who she meant, and so I did not ask again. I did not question my mother.

At some point in their lives, most daughters believe their mother is the most beautiful creature to have roamed the earth, but during those early years on Olympus, Demeter truly was. And though that beauty was visible to all who laid eyes on her, to me, her real beauty was in her love alone. Love for the mortals she doted over, providing them rich harvests year upon year. Love for the nymphs she held in her company and for the flora that grew in her wake. And love from me and my brother. So much love.

No ease comes with talking of Iacchus, which is why I supposed my mother stopped when he left for the Land of the Dead. She refused to even mention those fleeting early years when we were together. But I think of my brother. Perhaps not as often as a sister should, but I think of him still.

With Iacchus's death, my mother's watch over me became more

and more oppressive. I feel guilty choosing such a word, when her only desire was to keep me safe. And my only desire was for her to be happy.

In the hours I carved out for myself, I would look down from the palace of Olympus. From such a view, I saw lavender buzzing with bees and longed to brush my hand over those buds and send their scents spiraling into the air. I wished to take the hard spines of rosemary and crush the herb between my fingers to let their aromas flourish around me. I wished to feel cold waves lapping over my toes and feel the chill of fresh spring water running down my throat, but I never pressed her to leave. I had an eternity. I had every year I could wish for to visit these places. Besides, I was not without company. Nonetheless, the rush of excitement that flooded me when Mother arrived back in our palace that morning after a summoning from Zeus was irrefutable.

"Mother?" I said, taking her hand and noting the chill that rose from it. "What has happened? What is wrong?" Of course, I assumed the worst, for her skin was pale, her eyes glazed as if seeing only inward. "What do you need of me?"

I ushered the nymphs away, giving her the privacy I assumed she required. Slowly, the light returned to her eyes, and she lifted her head to face me.

"Zeus has made a request of me. Of us. All of us."

Fear surged within me as I considered all the atrocities he could have demanded from his kind, which I why I faltered when my mother continued. "We must attend a wedding down in the land of living."

"A wedding?"

"A wedding of a god and a mortal."

CHAPTER THIRTY-FOUR

Zeus has declared the Olympians be seated on the dais," my mother said as we entered the palace. She was dressed in the finest garb I had ever seen her wear, with gold jewelry dripping down her arms in wide bangles, hammered into the shape of ears of corn, while more gold threads were woven into her braids. Never had I seen my mother so ostentatiously dressed, and I wondered if this was, once again, a request of Zeus.

"Where am I to be seated?" I said, my nervous excitement growing infinitely at the realization of just how much freedom I was to be granted that night. For while I was a god, and one who resided upon Olympus, I was not an Olympian and there would be far fewer eyes on me. I would be able to dance with the mortals, to perhaps even display the small limits of my power, for it paled in significance against my mother's.

"Do not worry, you will not be far from me," Demeter responded, misreading my question. I was not worried. I was ecstatic. I was going to dance. I was going to feel the warmth of a mortal's hand in mine. I was to taste their food, drink their wine. I was, for the first time since I had been born, to experience something new. And I was ready for it.

I sat at a table with three mortal queens. Frail and stunning, they looked at me as if I were the greatest being they had ever seen. They hung up on my words. Fetched their servants to fill my wine. They laughed at my jokes, regardless of how feeble they were. And to me these women were mesmerizing, their transient life as compelling to me as my immortal one was to them.

"Core, your name means *maiden*, does it not?"

"It does."

"Goddess Core, do you dance?"

Oh, how I danced. One song followed and then another, and with each the rhythm seeped deeper and deeper into me. With the queens' hands in mine, we span and swiveled, turning and turning so that our skirts fanned out into plates around us. After every song came the desire for another. My senses reveled in it all, even as the air grew muggy with sweat and the queens began to tire, I did not stop. Truthfully, I believe I could have danced for all eternity.

I was busy spinning, lost in the music, when a voice bellowed out from the front of the hall.

"You let vermin defile your body."

The room snapped into silence. Every dancer had stopped, every musician poised, and every pair of eyes turned to the source of the shouting. All the warmth evaporated from my body.

You cannot underestimate my shock at seeing my mother standing in the center of the room. Demeter did not stand centrally. She would grow corn higher than pillars, if she believed it would mask her presence. And yet there she was. But my eyes were tuned to the man beside her, and my fear was replaced by a deep-rooted hope.

Like most people who knew her well, I had assumed Demeter

would never find happiness with a man or a woman. While she had not defined herself as chaste, like Athena, or Artemis, there were unspoken words upon Olympus that she would never take a lover. Yet there she was, radiating energy.

Zeus was on his feet, his white robe grubby, smudged with food dropped from his hand. Far from the immaculate being the mortals envisioned him as.

The man by my mother's side bowed deep to the ground. A warm glow colored his skin, and a gentle light shone in his eyes, though beyond those features, he was entirely ordinary. Plain, in fact. As he lifted his foot from the ground and slowly stepped forward, I wondered how he would dance. A strange thought perhaps, but that is the one that ran through my mind. He spoke slowly, his words clipped with an accent that I suspect came from one of the islands, but I was not knowledgeable enough to know which.

"I am a prince, mighty Zeus," he said, addressing Zeus from his lowered posture. "I am Iasion, son of Philomelas—"

"I do not care who you are." The tension rose. Men and women exchanged hurried glances, or took shuffling steps backward. But I remained unconcerned. My mother was in love. That was all that mattered to me. I did not care about Zeus's tantrum. Zeus always had tantrums. Still, when his eyes narrowed on my mother, as if he was squinting in a bright sun, I inched further toward him.

"Why? Would you do this?" Spittle flew from his lips as he spoke. "Why would you befoul your body with such a man?"

"Befoul myself?"

I awaited the inevitable. During all our centuries on Olympus, Demeter had bowed to every one of Zeus's commands. She had attended every feast he asked her to, taking a seat wherever he commanded. She had taken every insult he threw, every word of humiliation, and so when her back straightened and her eyes gleamed with a fire I had never seen in her, I did not feel fearful. I felt proud. This was the mother that I needed. The mother who could see her strength and mine. The mother that would allow me to run about the Earth. I cannot say how much she grew in that moment, but I could not look away, her power glimmering like an aura of white frost.

"You dare speak to me in such a manner?" Her words punctured the air. "You speak of verminous men when you are the most abhorrent of them all." A collective gasp shot through the air. Zeus *was* verminous; it was likely every man and woman in that hall knew as much. But Demeter had said it to his face. Only then did a slight flicker of fear alight within me, though it was dim compared to the admiration I felt. Demeter was the daughter of the Titans, and she was claiming her true throne.

"I love this man," she said. "I love him." I am sure that there are some who ridiculed her feelings, but human lives are fleeting, so it is no wonder that their passion ignites so quickly. Without another word to Zeus, she stretched out her hand to the man beside her.

Strengthened by the goddess at his side, this mortal man tried once again to speak to Zeus. He edged forward and opened his mouth, though I did not hear what final words passed his lips before the bolt of lightning lit up the hall and he dropped to the floor, like a pebble from the edge of a cliff.

"Mother!" I pushed my way through the guests and ran across the floor. Demeter had crumpled the moment her lover did. Her howls were instant. A cry of a shattered soul that resonated through the very foundations of the hall and struck me straight in the heart. I dropped to the ground next to her side, attempting to make sense of her unintelligible whimpering.

"Mother, I am here. I am here."

At times I resented the childlike perception she held of me, but in that moment, that is how I felt. Like a child, unable to help the most important person in my world. I was still struggling to find my own composure when Zeus spoke again.

"Come, we shall return to Olympus."

How I prayed. I prayed in the pits of my hearts to deities beyond my knowledge that she find the strength to fight him. That she would not cave and cower at his words. How I begged of her, through my thoughts alone, that she would not retreat to her subservient state. Then, engulfed in the pits of despair, my mother rose to her feet.

"I will not return to Olympus."

Pride and fear overcame me. Where would we go? How would we manage? I thought only of we, for I could not imagine a world where we would ever be parted. And yet, while my uncertainty grew, her resolve remained.

"I have the whole of the earth at my fingers," she said, a chill crystallizing in the air.

"And you will roam it alone and miserable," Zeus replied.

"No." She shook her head. "No, I will not."

I knew then that my time had come. I stepped forward, my gaze fixed on this monster who had given me life.

"She will never be on her own," I said. In that moment, I felt a power I had not experienced before. A sensation of the future that was to come. Hope. My mother had found a strength she did not know was possible. The world, as she said, was at our fingers. Little was I to know I would trade one golden prison for another.

CHAPTER THIRTY-FIVE

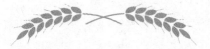

THOSE FIRST FEW DAYS AWAY FROM OLYMPUS FLEW BY IN A frenzy. A blur of emotion, both for me and my mother. We were not alone in our absconding of Olympus, as several nymphs also stood beside her, but it was I alone who bore the weight of my mother's grief. Raw and unfettered, it was unlike anything either of us had experienced, even with the loss of Iacchus. Still, I did my duty the best I could, but it is hard to be lost in the sorrow of another when your heart is bursting with happiness.

In those first days upon the Land of the Living, I experienced what I had dreamed of for centuries: I was walking on the earth. I felt sand slip between my toes, watched dolphins dancing in the water. I sailed on a ship and heard the songs of fishermen catch on a far breeze and sweep across an open sea. I smelled salt air and caught the scent of winds rich in the humus of the earth. Even as I kissed my infant brothers goodbye to leave them with their grandparents, I could not help but think of the future that awaited me. A future of excitement and adventure. But how wrong I was.

Siphnos. Now the island's name is enough to cause a shudder to run through me. An invisible vise to clamp tight around my ribs. It was not like that at first, of course, and even now, I cannot objectively deny the beauty of those shallow beaches where the light would catch the waves and transform the iridescent fish beneath the surface into a rainbow of color. I, too, see the appeal in the gentle slopes of the rolling hills that would turn into a waterfall of color with flowers at the touch of my hand. But even paradise can become a prison.

The day we returned from Samothrace, my mother did not head straight to the home that Hephaestus had built for us, as we all expected her to, but walked up to the highest point of the island, where a lone cedar tree broke the skyline. There, beside the tree, she dropped to her knees and spoke to the branches as though they could understand her every word. The sun fell, and still she did not leave her vigil.

"Should we go to her?" asked Thelxiepia. She was one of the youngest nymphs to shun Olympus in solidarity with my mother. Back then, I knew little of her. That changed over the years, of course.

"She has gone there to be on her own," Meliae replied, with her opinion carrying far more weight than the younger nymphs.

"That does not mean it is wise of her. Surely company helps in such a situation."

Of course, it fell to me to approach her.

The sun had already sunk beneath the horizon and the once blue sea was cast in gray, with thin slithers of silver rippling in the distance. A swath of clouds moved silently above, and the chorus howl of a wolf pack masked the sound of my footsteps as I climbed the hillside toward my kneeling mother, still unsure of what I should say.

"This is where I would have buried him," she said, her eyes remaining fixed on the ground before her. I had made no attempt to make her aware of my presence, yet she could sense me there. "I should have buried him here, on this island. That way, at least part of us could have been together for always."

"It is a beautiful place," I said, still uncertain how to comfort her best. "Perhaps tomorrow, in daylight, we can come back here together so I can see the place more clearly." A moment passed, the growing volume of the wolves emphasizing the silence between us. I opened my mouth, ready to beckon her down the hillside, when she spoke again.

"I should have stayed for his burial. I should have ensured it was completed correctly. Queen Olesia will be too concerned with the twins. She will be distracted."

Under my mother's instructions, I did not get to see the queen, and yet I doubted these words were true. I may not have had children of my own, but I had watched enough of the mortals to know that the birth of one child did not erase the loss of another.

"She will ensure her child receives the proper rites. He will have passed through to the Underworld."

"He will walk in the Elysian Fields. He was loved by an Olympian. He will reach the Elysian Fields and he will roam there with the heroes. He was a hero. He died as a hero for my love."

"He did, and I am certain he will have his place among them." I placed my hand on her shoulder, although my touch did not offer the comfort I had hoped. She jerked upward, spinning around, and for an instant, when her eyes met mine, all I saw was the torment whirring behind her pupils. So much confusion. So much pain. I did not see my mother, the maternal, doting Demeter, but the daughter of a Titan. I saw my father and the terror that he was capable of inducing, and knew that should she ever be pushed to such a point, my mother could tear the world apart with all the fury of Zeus and Poseidon combined. I lifted my foot from the ground, ready to retreat, when in a single blink all that anger was gone and burgeoning tears gleamed in her eyes, before she hurriedly wiped them away.

Swallowing back the fear that had grasped me, I slid my hands down into hers and squeezed them tightly, forcing a smile to my lips.

"After we have visited this place tomorrow, I thought you and I could take a stroll. Visit Mount Athos, perhaps? The helichrysum will be in bloom, and you know how I have always longed to see them."

The small daisy-like flowers had never grown in Olympus, and it seemed as viable a reason as any for me to suggest to my mother that we leave Siphnos. As a distraction, at least. Wordlessly, she raised a hand and placed it against my cheek, the slightest of smiles only accentuating the bleakness of her gaze.

"You are so fortunate, my darling daughter." She shook her head, her fingers pressing into my skin as her smile widened. "You are so blessed, for no harm will come to you here. Not while I am by your side. I promise you that."

Had I realized how those words would forge my future, I would have pushed back harder. I would have told her how she was fortunate too. I would have told her that she was blessed for the love, however brief, that she had found with Iasion. That she was blessed for this home we had been given so generously by Hephaestus and for all the children that she birthed, regardless of their mortality. She was blessed for the nymphs who faced the wrath of the most feared god to stand by her side. But I did not say that. Instead, I took her hand and lifted her up to her feet.

"Come, you should sleep now. You can return to here tomorrow, if that is what you wish. Mount Athos can wait."

And oh, how long it waited.

CHAPTER THIRTY-SIX

URING THE FIRST FEW DECADES, I WAS PATIENT WITH HER behavior. Perhaps indulgently so, for never did I once suggest Demeter stop her grieving and address the needs of the mortals who worshipped her. Logically, I considered how long she had grieved deeply for Iacchus. Was it a decade or two? Maybe it was closer to a century, but however long, I had assumed this would be similar. It was foolish, I know, to put a finite estimate on how long grief would keep its hold, but I was naive to love. Besides, it was not as though I had time to languish in my mother's apathy.

With Demeter present only in body, it fell upon me to fulfill her duty to the mortals. I continued to bless the Land of the Living the way she would have done. Ensure they had the towering wheat they required to thrive. I enriched the earth and blessed their harvests while she spent decades staring at the same tree, which became more and more windbeaten and slanted with every passing year. Part of me suspects it only remained standing because of her powers. She would have conversations with an apparition of her mind, knowing full well he was gone. While ignoring the daughter who stood only feet from her and neglecting the friends who had given so much to stay by her side. Friends who remained steadfast in their loyalty to her, but also, their love for me.

"It has been years, Meliae. How long will it go on?" We were sitting together on the fountain Hephaestus had built for us outside our home, our eyes trained up toward my mother. The nymph did not ask me to clarify what I was referring to, for it was a conversation we had shared several times.

"I cannot answer that, Goddess. Some hearts never heal. Or so I have heard."

So I have heard. Those words rattled around my skull, like a clanging anvil, invoking an anger that I could no longer keep buried. Not in front of the nymph who, in many ways, now knew me better than my own mother.

"Do you never wish to learn about such love for yourself?" I asked. "Surely you must wish for more than a life trapped on this island."

She placed her hand on my shoulder. "How could I be trapped on a place I chose to come to? A place my feet could carry me away from, if I had such a desire?" She removed her hand, only to wince.

"Meliae?" I said, as she inhaled sharply. "What is it? Is something wrong?" Fear grasped at me, yet she simply smiled.

"All is right, Core, my darling," she said, shrugging away my concern. "And to finish my answer to your question, I do not feel trapped here, my goddess, but if you do, it is your mind that has made your cage."

I searched her face for any trace of that fleeting pain, but it was gone. She was Meliae, as smooth-skinned and bright-eyed as always. All that remained was the weight of her comment in my mind.

Despite what Meliae had said, I knew the cage was not of my

creation. It was of my mother's. But just like Meliae, I had followed her there on my own two feet. So why couldn't I leave? I did not ponder the question for long. I knew the answer. Demeter had already lost so much. Besides, I was immortal. What was a few more years spent comforting my grieving mother?

I am not asking for your pity. Nor do I view my mother as a selfish, irresponsible parent. I am immortal, not a child, and by this point, I was centuries old. Lesser gods, younger and with far less power than I, were out making grand statements. Demanding shrines and offerings and even, in some cases, a seat in Olympus. I do not begrudge them that, as I did not begrudge my mother. But I longed for her, as I longed to see the world.

"You are all I have. You are all I have," she would say each time I raised the subject of leaving Siphnos. "You are the only one who will never leave me, as they have left me. We will be safe here, together forever, you and I." She would grasp my hands, the desperation in her tone echoed in the tightness with which she gripped me. As she spoke, my heart would ache for both her and myself.

"You shall never have to endure what I have endured." That was another of her favorite phrases that she would utter on the rare occasions that she would braid my hair. "You will never experience any of it. I will make sure."

Yes, they were her words of protection—her assurance that I would never have to go through the horror my father afflicted upon her—but as Helios's chariot rose and fell, and she continued to utter the same words, they took on a new meaning. And certainly not the one she had imagined. I would never experience anything of life. I would never know love so passionate I would abandon everything I had ever known. I would never feel a kiss on my lips or experience the heartbreak of losing a lover. I would never truly feel. I felt that lack like a constant itch beneath the surface of my skin. An incessant gnawing that knew no relief.

With all this said, the same thing that caused me to lose my mother and my freedom also brought it back. Grief.

It is easy to ignore the passage of time if leaves never fall, and hair never grows white. Years slide through one seamless sunrise into another. Tides rise and fall as the breaths of the ocean. Time for my mother and me was insignificant. But nymphs are not immortal, and Meliae was the first to show us that.

All forms of nymphs followed us to the island, bringing with them trees and flowers and life that my limited knowledge of the world could not have anticipated. The color of the gentle mountains and vibrant meadows was dictated more by them than by either me or my mother. As such, had I been observant, I should have seen it coming. I should have noticed how the ash tree that grew near one of the coves had started to change. The leaves were sparser. There was a bow to the trunk, which was now gnarled and knotted. I would have thought more deeply when those sparse green leaves turn brown and began to fall to the ground and how one day, finally, there were no leaves at all.

"Mother!" I raced up the hill to find her gazing at the knots in the bark of Iasion's cedar tree. "Come. Come quickly. It is Meliae."

"Meliae?" The name was spoken as a question mark.

"Please, she has asked for you."

With a nod of her head, my mother rose to her feet and followed me down the slope to where Meliae lay, propped up against the trunk of her ash tree. A wistful smile rose on her lips as she saw my mother.

"My dearest friend," she said quietly. At the sight of her companion, my mother's step faltered. Her skin turned ashen.

"No, it cannot be. Not so soon. Not so soon," she repeated, unable to move.

Even in her final hours, Meliae had not aged. Her skin was as fresh as the day she had first entered the world. Her eyes glimmered as she forced her smile a little wider and stretched out her hand to me.

"Core, my dearest goddess. You have brought me more years of joy than I could have dreamt."

The lump that formed in my throat was so large that when I finally swallowed it down, the effect was immediate. Tears tumbled down my cheeks.

From the ground, Meliae raised a hand, which she rested against my cheek. "Come now, there is no need for tears. Go, pick some flowers to lie here beneath this tree for me, for I wish to speak with your mother."

My eyes moved between Meliae and my mother. Fear was etched in Demeter's expression, and I knew she did not wish for me to leave her, but for once it was not her wishes that mattered. And so I rose, kissed Meliae lightly on the forehead, and turned my back on her.

I waited until I reached the edge of the cove and then I turned back and looked at the two figures. My mother knelt, her head buried in Meliae's robe, a frost spreading out on the ground around them as the last of the leaves fluttered up in the air. She was gone.

CHAPTER THIRTY-SEVEN

I DID NOT FIND OUT WHAT MELIAE SAID TO MY MOTHER THAT DAY, but I have my suspicions. For when Demeter left the blackened and brittle tree, she did not return up the hillside, but joined the rest of the nymphs and me in the house to drink wine and share stories of Meliae. While the nymphs spoke of adventures they had had upon our island, swimming with dolphins, bathing in the moonlight, my mother spoke only of their time on Olympus, and I watched as the realization sank beneath her skin; she had missed so much. I saw the change in her that night, as visible as the constellations that swept across the sky above us, yet I did not dare hope to believe what it would mean, not until that day she came to me.

Meliae's death was still fresh on her mind, though I suspect a year or so had passed. My mother was returning to us. No longer did she ignore the mortals and leave their harvests solely to me. No longer did she spend every hour from dusk to dawn wearing the earth thin beneath the cedar tree. She laughed with the nymphs, listening to their songs and watching them dance the way she had been on Olympus. She braided my hair, not because I required it, but because she once again longed for the closeness between us. Meliae's death was still raw, and I had not broached the subject of leaving the island again. Naturally, it had continued to linger in the back of my mind, but I was patient, for I, too, was grieving the loss of a friend.

The evening she came to me, the sky had turned a deep shade of scarlet, and rather than speaking, she took a seat on the grass and crossed her legs. I was creating flowers, brushing my hands against the long blades and pulling forth purple blooms from beneath the earth. It was not a skill I had perfected. Since my birth, the nymphs had watched with pride and glee as I practiced my gifts, while Demeter's response differed greatly and her reactions had worsened since our arrival on Siphnos. Now, she would watch on, narrow-eyed and nervous, as if my making a single bud burst into bloom would be enough for the gods to come crashing down to earth to drag us back to Olympus. If I had had my way, I would have changed the color of the island every day to reflect the colors of my mood, or the tones that danced in the sea and sky, but back then, my talent was not sufficient for such an act. I could create a harvest for every village from Gallia to Sarmatae, but my talent with blooms was no more advanced than it had been all those years ago on Olympus.

When I noticed her presence, I hastily stood upright, my heart drumming as I awaited a reprimand. Wordlessly, she reached down and plucked one of the flowers.

"They are beautiful," she said.

I waited. Expecting more. Expecting a rebuke. When it did not come, I spoke again.

"Thank you. Meliae told me once of a peony that grows on Mount Parnassus which has petals as deep purple as the richest wine. I believe I have captured the color, but the scent... I did not think to ask her of the scent."

My words drifted, and tension began to weave a web between us as I considered what I should say. It was my habit to offer some benign comment about the nymphs or the weather to ease the tension between us. But before I could offer either, Demeter spoke.

"You should go. See it. Smell it for yourself," she said.

I smiled softly, assuming she had misheard me.

"It grows upon Mount Parnassus," I repeated, keeping my tone as even as I could, but when I lifted my eyes, I knew that she had heard exactly what I had said.

"I have heard it is beautiful there. Though, if you would do me one small kindness and take the nymphs with you."

"To Mount Parnassus?" My face must have been a picture, for she smiled at me then like she had all those years ago when I was young.

"If Mount Parnassus is where you choose to go. Take the nymphs and stay together. And you must be back by sunset."

My voice caught in my throat, fearful that a single word from my lips could break the spell that had somehow enchanted her and cause her to change her mind. Yet a minute ticked by and Demeter's hand was in mine. My heart leaped from my chest as though it had wings. I jumped to my feet.

"I should tell the nymphs," I said. "We will leave first thing in the morning. If that is all right with you?" I added hurriedly. Demeter's smile tightened.

"I had assumed you would wish to."

I ran down the hill toward the house, my feet thundering against the grass, my hair spraying out behind me.

This is the start, I wanted to scream loud enough for Olympus to hear. This is when I would finally start to live. And what a life was waiting for me.

CHAPTER THIRTY-EIGHT

Intense anxiety took hold that first time I left Siphnos, and I was grateful for my mother's insistence that the nymphs stay with me. Had it not been for my sense of pride—after all, I had spoken so much of this moment—then I may have turned back before we arrived on the neighboring island. But the instant my feet touched that ground, the fear disappeared.

"How can it be the water is so much bluer here than on Siphnos?" I said, as we stood upon the peak of Seriphos, staring out toward our homeland. I had stood on the mountains of our island countless times, but never had I seen the waters glimmer the way they did that day. The rugged coastlines cut deep coves into the dense ocher landscape while the gentle sloping sea was darkened only by the sinking shadows of the morning sun. I could have spent a decade watching those colors shift from turquoise to indigo and back again. "It is bluer, is it not? And the color of the leaves, it has a much darker tint, do you not think?" Some of the older nymphs mocked me a little, but I did not take it to heart. Nor did I have time to brood over their words. "Come, we should head to Mount Parnassus directly."

That day, I picked those deep purple peonies and held them to my nose and breathed in the scent, committing it forever to my memories. But those flowers were just the start.

For centuries after that day, I would continue to take trips in such a manner, and for the first time, I felt *freedom*. Yes, I was still bound to my mother, and to the hours by which I would have to return to Siphnos, but there is so much that one can see between dusk and dawn, particularly if you are a god. I watched murmurations of starlings form images of gods and beasts upon the sky and saw newborn lambs stagger to their feet and take their first mouthful of milk. I saw waterfalls cascade down rock faces and turn barren lands into an oasis. And of course, I saw meadows.

There are so many wonders to behold, yet to me there is little as beautiful as a perfectly formed flower, and wherever I went I would ensure that I plucked a handful of the blooms to take home to my mother, taking each one carefully from the stem so as not to disturb the petals.

"Perhaps you would like to join me when I next visit," I would say without fault as I handed her each bouquet.

"Soon," she would always reply.

"Perhaps I could go on my own then, instead?" I tried, hoping to inch a sliver more independence from my mother's grasp. "I do not wish to drag the nymphs to places they do not wish to go." While I did not doubt the nymphs' loyalty to me, I knew their love for my mother ran equally as deep and I had strong suspicions that she sent them with me not only as guides and companions but to keep me in rein and ensure I did not test my powers or expose myself to the mortals and gods alike. It was sometimes hard not to resent their presence.

"The nymphs are blessed to be in your company, Daughter."

Demeter would reply. "They would never feel anything but joy to travel with you."

And so I would bite my tongue and ignore that itch that was once again budding beneath my skin.

I had been leaving Siphnos for nearly two centuries when I started separating from the nymphs and traveling on my own. It was not a conscious decision to disrespect my mother's wishes. Instead, I hoped only to ease the strain on my friends. Only three nymphs remained. Three nymphs who found as much pleasure lying in a poppy field as they did running through it and dancing. While they never complained about their duties or how time had afflicted them, they had grown slower in recent decades, less eager to spend the days traipsing up and down mountainsides.

The first day I left them we had reached Kynthos, a small island still a fair distance from the mainland. My intention was to visit the waterfall of Polylimnio, a place of verdant green. A bright gorge filled with the most turquoise of water was hidden from view. The rushes that grew in such a climate were fascinating to me, and the way the trees clung to the cracks in the rocks, standing firm despite their vertical platform, could captivate me for hours.

"Why do you not stay here and rest?" I said, when the nymphs finally joined me on the island. "You do not need to come with me. I am only going to Polylimnio. We have been there a hundred times, at least."

My eyes went to each of them individually, and they looked to one another before Peisinoe elected herself the speaker.

"She will not have it. Your mother will not have you traveling alone. And you need not worry, there is plenty of life in us yet."

She smiled broadly, though I noticed the tightening in her lips.

"I will go alone," I said again, lifting myself up and making my posture as grand as it could be. "The village is quiet, and we rarely see more than a handful of mortals. Wait here for me and I will return before Helios reaches the peak of that mountain." I pointed to the west, where a mountain protruded into the sky. At such a height, the sun would most certainly clip it long before it sunk below the horizon. "I promise I will return before you barely even miss me. My mother will never need to know."

My heart hammered as I said those words, half-convinced that the nymphs would rally against me and drive me back to Siphnos to tell my mother of my betrayal. But instead, Thelxiepia stepped forward and bowed to me. A sign of deference she rarely showed.

"You should return here before Helios reaches that peak, Goddess." Her voice was commanding. "If you do not, then we will return alone."

I nodded frantically, terrified that she would change her mind. "I will be back. I will be back." Leaning forward, I kissed each of them on their cheek before I turned toward the sea and ran.

I did not get as far as Polylimnio. I cannot even tell you how far inland I went. All I can say is that never had sights been more beautiful than those I saw that day. The cornflower-blue sky shone above a hundred blossoms, the scents of which swirled around me with dizzying intensity. I plucked every stem I could, pulling some with such force I ripped their roots from the ground. Such was my desperation to capture the memories forever. Sap coated my hands, thorns pricked my palms, and I relished every moment of it. I felt as elated as my very first visit to the Land of the Living. I wanted to breathe it all in. I wanted to dance and scream. I felt so alive.

I will confess that I was so overcome with my newfound freedom that I was a moment later than expected reconvening with the nymphs.

"I am here, I am here," I gasped, racing toward them. All three were on their feet, scanning the horizon in different directions.

"Helios has dipped below the top of the mountain," Thelxiepia said, with a flicker of fear in her reproach.

"He was at the peak of the mountain when I set foot on this isle. I assure you I was here. I was here."

Thelxiepia observed me, as unblinking as one of Medusa's creations. Yet when the stone broke, it was not to be smashed into rubble, but into a small smile.

"I take it you enjoyed yourself?"

"In ways I would not have dreamed possible."

After that it was a habit we fell into. Each morning, we left Siphnos and traveled together for a short while, often until midday, and when the nymphs' singing would wane, we would stop in the shade of a grove and forage for food. Then, once we had eaten, the nymphs would lie down in the grasses to rest and I would go wherever the day took me. Each place I visited, I would stop to pick fruit or flowers. Enough to give to the nymphs and Demeter so my mother did not grow suspicious. It was manipulative. I see that now, but back then I did not think of anything other than how I could ensure that I did not lose my freedom.

Sometimes I would head to mainland Hellas, other times I would travel further south, or catch a tantalizing scent on the wind that beckoned me east. I traveled wherever my desire took me, and in all those lands, my presence aroused no suspicion. On the occasion that I found myself in a misguided location—such as a busy agora full of bartering men—I could slip into the shadows and be forgotten from sight within an instant. Such are the luxuries of godliness. Sometimes I would stay there, listening to the discussions of the mortals, reveling in the complexities of such a life so unlike any I could ever imagine. And when I tired of their ramblings, I would walk on, only resting when I came to a meadow or copse where I could pick fresh flowers for Demeter. I was happy. Truly. And I could have stayed that way for as long as the nymphs remained, if I had not met her.

CHAPTER THIRTY-NINE

THE HEAT WAS STIFLING THE MORNING I MET HER. THE SUN'S arc so close to the earth that the plants cowered. Even my mother was lethargic in the heat. The beauty of Hephaestus's design allowed air to whip through our home in great billows straight from the sea, cooling the seats upon which we laid, but that was not enough to abate the constant insufferable stuffiness.

It had been the same way for several days, and I had stayed on Siphnos, bathing in streams there, even heading to the sea and allowing the waves to rise up and over my thighs. But in all my travels, the island had grown small, and confinement made my temper grow shorter. The world called me.

"I think I shall head to the river in Tegea. The water there is always cool," I said to my mother. The dawn chorus was yet to begin in full, with only a lone bird waiting for another to complete its duet, but I was already tired of the tedium I knew would await me, and ready to leave. The nymphs, too, hurried to their feet.

"Are you sure you do not wish to join us?" I said to my mother, in the same farcical manner I always asked her. And just as always, she pressed her lips together as if she was considering the idea. This was the game we played, pretending she might one day actually join me.

"There is a village holding a feast for me today," she said, casually offering one of the generic excuses she frequently supplied us with. "I must listen in, offer them my gratitude. But let me know what the waterfalls are like. Perhaps if it is as cool as you say, I will join you tomorrow."

We all knew that she would not.

I kissed her swiftly, then turned to the nymphs and left.

Our first destination was always Aegina. This island close to the mainland was rich in flora and fauna, and as such caught the attention of both Athena and Apollo in the later years. But back then, it was known only to us, and the nymphs would pass the hours in the streams or the forest, awaiting my return. Now that so many years had passed, they rarely asked whether I wished for company, although occasionally they joined me. That day, however, they made their intentions perfectly clear, and we had barely placed a foot on the island when they dropped in the shallow water of a drying stream. For a moment, I considered joining them. The river was shallow. It would have been the perfect depth to lie down flat with its gurgling brook, but I wished for people. Not to talk to, but to listen to. Watching families playing in the water was something that brought me great joy to observe. The frivolous laughter. The shrieks loud enough to shake leaves. There was always joy to be found by a river on a hot day, and that was what I went in search of.

As I reached the land of Tegea, I was dressed simply, as a young woman in her twenties. It was my standard fare. I wore a white veil that floated down over my face, embroidered with deep green flowers and ears of corn. My feet were bare, though I wore simple bands around my wrist.

Just as I had expected, several families had gathered by the river, attempting to evade the heat. I cannot say how many people were present, but certainly more than I had ever encountered there before. The women huddled in groups, fanning themselves while young children clung to their breasts. Men threw one another from their shoulders into the water, while children clambered over their parents, splashing and shrieking.

I adore the sonority of a family playing in the river, but that day the noise was close to a cacophony. The water was crowded, and I could see no way for me to slip in with ease among the women. I had not yet been brave enough to strike up a conversation beyond a simple greeting. If I were to sit with the ladies, gathered as they were in such a manner, they would likely ask me questions: where I had come from, where my family was. All questions I couldn't, or rather wouldn't, answer. And so I turned my back on the large gathering and headed downstream, where the water weaved between rocks and well-rooted trees. I would find a quiet place to bathe and cool off before I returned to the nymphs, I decided. Enjoy the pleasure of my own company. However, when I reached the coil of the river where I had planned on bathing, I discovered I was not as alone as I had expected.

I had seen the naked form of a woman before. We would all take such forms to bathe on Siphnos, and there were several on Olympus who shunned clothes in favor of letting their skin be free to the elements. But never had I seen a body like this.

She was half-submerged in the water, with only her head and back visible to me, yet as I inched toward her, she stood, oblivious to my presence. Water weaved in rivulets down the curves in her spine. Her skin was deep as the wood from a cherry tree, the curls in her hair fighting the weight of the water that pulled it down. I could only see the back of her, and yet I was mesmerized. I stood watching, silent, aware of the pounding in my chest. I should speak, I told myself multiple times. Alert her to my presence. But then she might disappear. She might disappear and be lost to me forever.

Then, without warning, she plummeted and disappeared beneath the water.

I gasped, the rush of air from my lungs pinning me to the spot. Had something sucked her beneath the waves? Were there river monsters in this area of Hellas? Certainly none my mother had ever told me off. Then what? A strong current? An invisible undertow that had dragged her under? Time expanded as I stared at the water, which showed no signs of struggle beneath the surface. *How long had she been gone?* I asked myself. Too long. That was all I knew.

I cannot say why I ran. Why I bolted toward the stream, but before I had scrambled through the rushes, she rose from the water, her eyes staring directly at me. And once again, I froze.

"Are you going to stand there and watch?" The glint in her eyes was as bright as the water that ran down her neck. "Join me. It is perfect. Assuming you can swim?"

Yes, I could swim. But I had difficulty saying so.

"If you walk down the river a little way, there is a low bank," she continued, despite my silence. "It is far easier to get into the water there."

She spoke as though we had exchanged words, as if I had accepted her invitation to join her in the water. And in my heart, I had.

Moving back out of the rushes, I followed the river further downstream. There, by the gentle slip of the bank, I saw her pile of clothes, folded and placed in the shade of the willow tree. It was some walk from the tree to the water. A walk she would have made naked. A walk that I would have to make naked if I were to join her. Nervousness fitted through me, though I tried to push it back as quickly as possible. What was there to be embarrassed about? I was a goddess. Besides, we were just two young women seeking respite from the heat. That was what I told myself as I dropped my robe.

CHAPTER FORTY

THE WATER MIGHT HAVE BEEN BRACINGLY COLD. IT MIGHT have been as frigid as that what had melted from a glacier that very morning. Then again, it might have possessed a heat from the depths of the earth. I am afraid I cannot tell you because at that moment, all my senses were too preoccupied to consider my own body. For my eyes were locked on hers.

"You need to come a little deeper in," she said. "The water moves fastest at the edge. You are likely to get pulled downstream." She spoke with such confidence, as if we were already friends. As if we had spent our entire lives growing together to reach this point. But then she tilted her head to the side, and my skin tingled under her gaze.

"I have not seen you here before," she said. "You are not from the village, are you?"

"No." In later years, she would laugh at this. Laugh at how muted I became. So terrified, all I could manage was a single syllable, and even that left my tongue in a mumble. Yet this did not deter her. Unfussed by the brevity of my answer, she stretched out her arms and turned a great circle in the water before she spoke again.

"Where are you from? I assume you have relatives in the village?"

The questions encircled me in confusion. Where was I from? My mind whirred as I tried to record the name of another village in the region, I could not even recall if we were north or south. "I am from the east," I said slowly.

"There are many places east of here. Where exactly?" Her eyes bore into me with such intensity that I could barely look away, except to note the small smile that twisted at the corners of her lips.

More than anything, I wanted to offer her an answer that she would have approved of, but my mind refused to cooperate.

"I should go," I said instead.

I stumbled backward, scraping my heels on the sharp stones of the riverbed before scrambling upward on the bank, where I picked up my clothes and held them to my body. All the while, my eyes never left hers. Yet she did not say another word. With my skin still dripping, I placed my robe over my body and ran all the way back to Aegina and the nymphs, where I arrived flushed with a heat that had nothing to do with Helios.

All that night I tossed and turned, unable to shift her image from my mind; the way her hair flowed was like molten metal down her spine. The way her skin caught the light, turning it as iridescent as a gemstone. How I longed to run my finger across that smooth line of her collarbone, to feel the softness of her touch. Whatever it took, wherever I had to go, I would see her again, I promised myself.

Unlike so many of my kin, patience had always been considered a gift of mine. But it is easy to be patient when you have nothing to wait for. It is easy to be patient when each day is the same as the last and the future stretches out indefinitely. So if I had ever possessed the virtue of patience, as so many thought I did, that night it abandoned me. I longed for the painted sky and the birds' duets and all the signs that would let me know I could leave. I willed the stars from the sky, and when I looked upon the moon, I did not see its beauty, but viewed it with restless irritation. Unable to even close my eyes, I tossed and turned, angered by the blackness of night that taunted me beyond the window. As such, by the time dawn broke, I was waiting by the water, drumming my fingers impatiently on my side.

"You are eager to leave this morning," my mother said as I hurried the nymphs, trying and failing to coerce them from their states of lethargy.

"There is a harvest in Boeotia," I said, the lie tripping easily off my tongue. "The peaches there are supposed to be the best in all of Hellas. They offered us libations for a great bounty. I thought it would be prudent of me to taste the fruits myself."

"You are a great maiden for your people," Demeter replied, and I kissed her cheek only briefly, afraid my deceit might cling to my skin as a wretched, putrid aroma.

In the same manner as the day before, I left the nymphs in Aegina and headed straight to Tegea. No longer drawn to the raucous laughter and singing coming from the families gathered by the river for breakfast, I did not stop to watch the children playing and laughing and throwing handfuls of water over one another. Instead, I walked, almost ran, toward the weeping willow.

I knew she would be there. It was though she altered the air in a way that only I could see, perfuming it with her song and skin.

Once again, my voice stuck in my throat, as I reached the place beneath the tree where I could see her. Unlike the day before, she had pinned her hair to her head in a pile of swirling braids, although several soft tendrils had escaped and had fallen free over her bare shoulders.

As she turned to me, her smile broke, gleaming in her eyes.

"I was hoping I might see you again."

CHAPTER FORTY-ONE

S HE MADE NO ATTEMPT TO TURN HER HEAD OR OFFER ME
privacy as I dropped my robe, although it felt as if I were
peeling off so much more than clothes. Her eyes never faltered
as I stepped into the water, holding my breath and steeling myself
against the cold I knew would shock my body. Whether it was a test
I cannot say, but she did not move toward me. Instead, she remained
on her side of the river. I was the one who was forced to move to her.
And I did. My body sent out ripples on the surface of the water as I
pushed myself through it.

"I was saddened you had to leave so quickly yesterday," she said
when I reached her. "I did not even have a chance to ask you your
name."

"My name?"

"You do have one, do you not?"

What a question to be posed.

"I am Core."

"Core?" Her eyes narrowed in confusion. "All maidens are Core.
Do you not have a name of your own?"

It was a similar comment to that made at the wedding of Cadmus and Harmonia, and back then I believed my name had suited me: the eternal maiden. That was who I was destined to be, yet here I was ashamed by such a title. As she spoke it, it indicated an absence. A lack of any more substance than that of a young girl. And I was not young. Far from it. Just innocent and naive. And never had I felt more so than in that moment.

"My name is Core," I repeated, humiliation washing through me.

"Well, Core, I am Ione."

Ione. Violet. A flower, small and unsuspecting, yet it can blanket entire meadows. Its honeyed aroma was enticing. Its flavor sweet with a strength that could linger on the tongue.

"Ione," I said again.

"Have you eaten?" she asked, stretching her arms and pushing off the bottom of the riverbed. "Come, I have brought plenty." A thin stream of ripples spread out in front of her, which she followed to the riverbank. The current was gentle, barely enough to cause me to sway, and without waiting for another word, I followed her.

Together, we climbed out of the water and lay down beneath the shade of the willow tree.

"I was surprised to see you yesterday. Even more so today. It is unusual to see someone I do not know here." She retrieved an embroidered bag from the grass and pulled out a handful of apricots, which she placed on the grass between us. "Please, help yourself."

My heart was a flutter of nerves. Something about her presence drew me into her, and I reached across to take an apricot for myself not because I desired the fruit but because it was she who offered it.

"It is not so long a stroll from here to my home," I told her, though I instantly regretted the decision.

"So you live close enough to walk and to the east. Is that correct?"

I bit down on my lip, fighting the torrent of lies that were ready to spill from my tongue; my elderly father was a trader, and we had recently moved here? My husband was from these parts, and he had wished to return home after our nuptials? All were viable reasons for my presence, yet all sounded trite and contrived. Besides, I did not wish to lie to her. If anything, I wished to tell her the truth, but instead I did as I had seen mortals do for all eternity. I averted the question.

"Does your husband not mind you being on your own like this?" I said instead, taking a leap of faith. Without doubt she was old enough to be married, old enough to have birthed several children, and I did not doubt that someone of her beauty would have had a hundred suitors lined up before she had even reached a suitable age.

"My husband is grateful that I am out of the house, and not causing him torment," she said with a smile.

"You do not see eye to eye?"

"We do. But our marriage is one of convenience, as I'm sure you understand."

From the way her eyes glinted, she assumed I understood her meaning, but I knew too little of the world to understand. My throat was drying, but I needed to learn more about this woman.

"You have a husband, so you have responsibilities? Children?" I asked next.

"I have never felt a great longing for children of my own," she replied, with a swift sideways smile.

To me, this added only more confusion. Yes, there were goddesses who had taken vows of chastity. Who did not wish to share their body or bed with a man, but I do not believe I had heard a woman so openly voice her lack of desire for children before. Particularly not with one who had already spoken of her marriage.

"Your husband, surely he must want children?" I asked someone imprudently.

"I mentioned it was a marriage of convenience, did I not?"

Sensing my confusion, she sat up on her elbows.

"At fourteen years, I was married to a man three times my age," she began. Considering the relationships of my kin, such a thing should not have surprised me. And yet it did. The thought of perfect Ione, my Ione, as I had already come to think of her, so young and thrust into the arms of some wrinkled old crone sickened me to my stomach. Clearly, I displayed such emotion on my face as she threw back her head and laughed.

"It was not as terrible as you are imagining," she replied when the laughter died away. "Many women are not blessed with husbands with such a temperament as mine. Nor ones who have so little desire for my type of body." I did not understand what she was imply-ing, but I sat straighter, desperate to hear more. "He was a good man. Flawed, as we all are, but a good man. Even when others in his circumstances would not be so...understanding...even when the sickness came." A lump formed at the base of my throat as I waited for her to continue. "When he knew that he would not recover, he made it his dying wish that his brother would marry me."

"You were passed from one man to another?" I said, the sicken-ing in my stomach surging.

"I have been blessed with the safety of one good home and then another," she countered. "My first husband's brother was twelve years his senior and lost his own wife in childbirth. But prior to this, she had borne him three sons and two daughters, and he had no desire for any more. He did, however, desire my first husband's fortune, which was offered to him when he married me. Believe me, the situation has proved most favorable to both of us. Being married stops the constant wagging of tongues, and theater of looks in our direction, but leaves us both free to follow our own indiscretions."

"Indiscretions?"

Ione smiled, her lips pursing before she spoke.

"You really are quite remarkable, Core." She shifted again, exposing a length of skin inward of her knee. My eyes followed that line upward. Ashamedly, I suspect I could have stared at that bare patch of skin for an entire lifetime, had her voice not snapped me back into reality.

"I have spoken too much. Now I would like to know something about you. After all, I have plied you with stories of my life, and yet you remain a near mystery to me," she said. "Perhaps you could tell me the name of the village to the east where you have walked from."

A pause formed in the air, and for a second I feared it would close around us, cornering me into a web of lies for which I was ill trained, but before I could fumble some weak words, she was laughing. "Forgive my impertinence. According to both of my husbands, my lack of boundaries is one of my failings. You deserve your secrets. We all do. Now let us eat more. I am famished."

I had slipped from my life into a dream. One where scents eddied around with dizzying intoxication. The distant cries and shrieks of children and men were as mellifluous as music. Though Ione spoke directly to me, I often found her words drifting out of focus as my attention fixed on the way her lips moved as she spoke, or how she carelessly brushed her hair behind her ears. Little by little, the sun crept in its downward curve until she sat upright and brushed the grass from my knees.

"I must return home. My husband is hosting guests. But will I see you again? Tomorrow? This is the place I always come to if the sun is shining."

I nodded, swallowing down my heart, which had pushed itself uncomfortably high.

"I will see you again," I replied. Knowing in my heart that nothing in the world could stop me.

CHAPTER FORTY-TWO

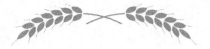

OVER THE NEXT MOON, A ROUTINE BEFELL US. OR AT LEAST it did for me. I would bid my mother farewell, kissing her lightly on the cheek, while offering vague insinuations as to where I might go. Then, once we reached Aegina, I would leave the nymphs, again kissing them before racing to Tegea and the part of the river where the willow tree draped its leaves in the fast-running water.

Each day, Ione was ready and waiting, regardless of how early I arrived. More than once, I considered what would happen if I escaped Siphnos before dawn. Would she still be there, submerged and waiting? What hour would I need to arrive to watch her drop her robe and descend into the water? Or to watch her silhouette growing closer and closer as she came from the village?

I longed to surprise her by arriving early, greeting her in the same manner that she met me, but I knew to leave at such a time would arouse my mother's suspicion, and so I held on to the hours we had been given, using them to absorb every morsel of Ione's life that she offered me.

"This has become my most favorite part of the day," she said, once, as she greeted me with a smile so bright I felt as though I was Icarus, dangerously closer to the sun, where the light was simply too mesmerizing to ignore. "Seeing the happiness on your face when you greet me."

Always I joined her in the water. That initial blast of cold offered me an excuse to gasp the way I wished to at the sight of her. Once in the water, we talked a while before we retreated to the shade of the shore, where she would share with me whatever food she had brought. While the wind shirred through the trees, she would talk of trivial topics: *the next festival of Hera. The offerings her husband had prepared for Poseidon.* Sometimes she would delve deeper into her own life, telling me of her stepchildren, several of whom were older than she was, and married with their own children already. I listened intently, absorbing every word she said, fearful of when the questions would turn and she would ask me about my family, or future, and I would be forced to lie. Thankfully, though, she seemed happy enough to talk and let me listen.

"You have been singing all evening," my mother remarked when I returned to Siphnos one evening. "I do not believe I have ever heard you sing so beautifully. You will attract the other gods' attention if you continue in such a manner." She laughed as she spoke, yet I could hear the concern in her voice. The edge of fear that scraped in her throat. I did not think of other gods or their attraction to me. How was that possible, when my head was entirely filled with Ione? Still, I quieted my singing for my mother, keeping the melodies tucked inside.

I recall the first time our hands slipped together. Our fingers had intertwined as we lay on the grasses. It was such a simple action, yet for me, it was the greatest intimacy I had experienced. The pressure of Ione's palm resting on mine remained so strong her touch could have made a permanent indentation. Her words blurred before they reached my ears for the dizziness she caused me. The next morning, as I bade Demeter farewell and began my journey back to Tegea, all I could think about was how I could engineer another opportunity to touch her. To brush against her skin. That was all I let myself hope for. Yet that day, it all changed.

When I left the nymphs on Aegina, I did not head straight for Tegea but instead went to Scheria. The orchards there were renowned for their pomegranates, and given how gracious Ione had been, sharing her food with me day after day, it seemed only right that I should repay that generosity. Through the thick skin of the fruit, I could taste the sweetness of the seeds, and a light lifted in me as I imagined the pleasure that Ione would get from my gift. But that light which had filled me faded the instant I arrived at our river.

A blanket of cloud shrouded the sky, so dense and black, barely a sliver of sun escaped. Rain drizzled down, filling the air with a chill so cold that even I, with my immortal ways, shuddered. No laughter floated up from the river. No great splashes of water as the children leaped from the riverbed and into the stream. The only sound was the constant patter of rain, which grew harder and harder as I stood there. A weight sank deep within me. Ione would not come to the river in weather such as this. In the mere minutes that I waited, a strong wind bolstered down the mountainside and battered the trees. Gazing at my hand, I attempted to feel the presence of Ione's fingertips, pressed up against my palm as it had been the day before, but it was as if the rain had washed the memory away.

"Core!"

Her voice was half drowned out by the rain and wind, but a whisper was all it would have taken to hear her. There, between the river and the village, she stood drenched to the bone, water streaming down her face and hair. Without hesitation, I ran toward her. The rain had soaked through my robe, causing the fabric to cling to my skin, and my feet splashed in mud-filled puddles, yet the chill that only moments ago gripped me had gone.

When I reached Ione, she did not speak, but she took my hand and pulled me with her as she ran. The laughter that broke free from my lungs then soared like Pegasus; if anything were to attract the attention of the gods, it would have been that. Not my singing, or my beauty, but that unadulterated freedom. I had lived for so long, but only now was I starting to understand what it was like to be alive.

I followed her, half-dragged, half-skipping as she led me across the meadows. The drenched grass reached my knees as my free hand skimmed the tips of the flowers, releasing their aromas. *Was this what it was like to be a child?* I wondered. To be free of inhibitions or fear? Or is this how the other gods truly felt? Those who were not held captive by the love of their mother. We headed away from the river and the village, and I thought at first that her entire aim was simply to run with me in the rain, when a small shepherd's hut came into view.

"We can shelter in here," Ione said, dropping my hand to open the door and beckoning me inside. And naturally I followed.

CHAPTER FORTY-THREE

T HE AROMA OF STRAW AND ANIMAL FEED CLOYED IN THE HOT
and muggy air of the shed, yet I barely registered them as we
stepped inside and pushed the door closed behind us. With
only thin slits of light seeping through the wooden slats of the wall,
the darkness was unexpected, and it took time for my eyes to adjust
to the lack of light. When they had, I looked up and Ione's gaze was
fixed on me.

"I am afraid it isn't the standard of shelter you are used to, Core,
daughter of Demeter."

I froze, hoping that perhaps I had misheard her. Or that the
comment had been said in jest. But only a fool jokes when it comes
to the gods. "Daughter of Demeter? Child of Zeus," she said, shifting
closer to me. "I am right, am I not?"

I was penned in. Not by the door, which I could have easily
pushed open, but by her words that anchored me to the ground.
Outside, rain pelted down, the wind now howling as it cut a draft
through the wooden planks.

"I assumed you would deny it," she continued, as I remained

unable to form words. Had I thought more quickly, then yes, denying was what I should have done, but my mind was awash with terror.

"How long? How long have you known?" I asked, my voice barely audible above the drumming rain. She turned and brushed her hand against the walls of the hut.

"Do you know that the flowers grow where you lie? They grow on earth that has been barren for years. Leaves glimmer. Wheat and grass have grown higher before my very eyes when I am in your presence. The earth is music around you. How could I not know?" She stepped forward and placed a hand against my cheek. "How could anything as perfect as you possibly be mortal?" she whispered.

I closed my eyes, letting the weight of my hands fall to my side as I savored her fingertips against my skin. This was a touch I had not let myself dream of. One that had lurked in the back of my mind, for to release it would open the floodgates to something that could never be locked away again.

"What are you doing here with me, Goddess? Why do you seek my company?"

My lips and mouth fumbled to find words.

"Do you wish me to stop seeing you?" My voice was a sad, scared whimper. "If you wish that, I will not come again."

She was barely a hair's breadth from me now. Each breath of mine shared with her own.

"I wish I could keep you here forever," she said instead.

All I could feel was longing. Longing like I never knew was possible. Desire burned through the very depths of me. Desire to hold her and kiss her, to make her fully mine. But fear came with such desire. Should she reject me, then what? I would return to Siphnos empty. Hollowed out. And so I stood fast, not daring to breathe.

"There is nowhere for us to go, in such weather," Ione whispered. "We must stay."

"That is what I want. I want to stay. I want to stay with you always," I whispered. And then I could speak no more, for my lips were upon hers. Or perhaps it was she that placed her lips upon mine. I cannot say, and it did not matter. For from the instant they touched, all my fears flooded away from me, leaving my desire to rage. I was a virgin goddess. As pure as Artemis and Athena. Never had I so much as kissed a man or a woman before, yet I did not fear inadequacy, for it was with instinct that my hands reached up to the clasp on her sodden robe and let the fabric drop to the floor. I stared, transfixed, at the body in front of me. In all her bare beauty, she may well have worn the girdle of Aphrodite, for how else was it possible to become so intoxicated?

She did not reciprocate the action of undressing, but watched as I dropped my own robe.

Only when I stood exposed to her in the nakedness of my human form did she take my hand.

"Come," she said, pulling me on to the mattress of the hay.

It was as though my fingers had been made to touch her skin, to seek out every inch of her like no other had before. I watched her body tremble and quiver. Her pupils expand with pleasure as her head tipped backward, each moan from her lips more intense than the one before. And she, in turn, transformed my body in ways I did not even know were possible.

At every point, I believed I could feel no more, but she was there to bring me to a higher level of ecstasy. Her fingers, her lips, her tongue, all there to serve me again and again. So absorbed was I in her body that I did not notice that the rain had stopped. Or that the clouds had drifted away, and the sun had started its downward arc with diminish ferocity. I noticed only her.

"Is this love?" I asked. We lay upon the straw, Ione's head against my chest, rising and falling with my breath. *Poets should write songs about the hours that had passed*, I thought. We should be written on parchment and sung in taverns and last for all eternity.

"If this is not love, then I fear I will never know what is," Ione laughed sadly, but when she caught my eye, her glimmer faded by just a fraction. "If you intend on destroying me, Goddess, I would rather know now."

Destroy her? The thought that I, or anyone, would ever cause her pain was enough to seize my heart with terror. Freeing myself from her grip, I propped myself up onto my knees.

"Come with me. Come to Siphnos. I can make you immortal. We can be together forever."

She did not speak at first, but a small smile twitched on her lips as she leaned forward and planted another kiss on my lips. Entirely unexpectedly, flowers erupted in the hay around us. Ione stilted a laugh at the sight.

"You are magnificent," she said.

"So you will do it. You will let me make you immortal?"

"Let us talk about this another time," she said, kissing me again. "We do not need to rush this."

By the time I left and met the nymphs, they were pacing the ground of Aegina.

"Where have you been?" Aglaope said. "It is nearly sunset. Your mother will never let you out of her sight again if we do not return immediately."

Perhaps before, I would have felt some remorse, but her words washed over me. I was in love.

CHAPTER FORTY-FOUR

SOME DAYS WE WOULD MEET AT THE RIVER, BUT NO LONGER DID we keep a safe distance. Now our hands met beneath the surface of the water, and our legs wrapped around each other's hips as our bodies balanced upon one another in the soft current of the river. I lost count of the number of times we made love beneath that willow tree or in that same shed. Each time, my tongue would seek a new tender spot of flesh to excite. Or I would spot a new mark on her skin, a new slight scar or wrinkle I had not noticed before.

"I assume you do not wish us to come with you?" Aglaope said one day as we reached Aegina. For a moment, I could have sworn a twinkle glimmered in her eye, but before I could respond, it was gone. Never once did they ask where I went or question why my robes would be dirtied, or on one occasion, torn, when I returned. They were content with the freedoms they gained beyond Siphnos, as was I.

"These are stunning," Ione said one morning, as I handed her a small posy of flowers that I had plucked on my travels to her. For Ione I traveled further than before, desperate to bring all the wondrous beauties of the earth to her, for she refused to leave no matter how often I asked her.

"I will take you there if you wish. The meadows in which they grow are remarkable. The scent, divine."

She smiled, the fine lines around her eyes now deeper than they had been in those early days.

"I have a family here, Core. I cannot simply leave."

"It does not have to be for long."

"You and I have very different ideas of time, remember?" She cupped my face in her hands, the manner she always did when she wanted me to pay attention to her. "And we are happy like this, are we not?"

"I am happier than I could have dreamt," I replied honestly.

"Then let it stay this way."

We did not spend every day together, as much as I wished that could be so. There were days when Ione's husband and children required her to be present, to host guests or hold feasts for the gods. There were weeks when she was traveling to meet family. And those single mortal days—days that upon Olympus had felt like a mere blink of an eye—were now agonizingly slow. But the bliss of reunion was inconceivable. Every day with Ione felt like starting life over again, and even after a decade together, I felt like I had barely scratched the surface of our relationship.

"Have you considered my proposal?" I asked her, though the question became less and less frequent as the years passed. "Us, together for all eternity. How could anything be more perfect?"

"Eternity is a long time, Core. Besides, how would you explain my sudden presence to your mother?"

Guilt tumbled like waves inside me. So many times I had opened my mouth to tell Demeter of Ione. So many times I wished my mother could meet the woman I loved. Laugh with her, sing with her. For if she knew her as I did, then how could she not love her as I loved her? But this was my mother. As scared of her shadow as she was strangers. She would see a plot in Ione. Find a reason to fear this perfect mortal, to tarnish our relationship through her own fear.

"Let us pretend we only have this moment," Ione would say, whenever she saw the melancholy of my mother seep into me. "Let us pretend that we are both mortal, and this is the only life we get to spend together."

Oh, I was wise to her tricks. I knew the exact response these words intended to elicit, but I would fall prey to them without fail.

It was not only Ione who had other obligations. There were days where my thinly veiled excuses of plucking flowers in meadows were not a sufficient reason for me to leave Siphnos. Festivals for which my mother expected me to be present. For her part, Demeter would push her grief and anxiety aside during these days so that it was almost as if Iasion had never existed. It was I who grieved instead in those early years.

I tried to convince my mother that perhaps we should attend some of these festivals in person. That we should greet and thank those mortals who gave gifts to her so generously. Perhaps, I suggested, making our presence known to them would ensure the offerings grew each year. I should have known that such incentives would mean nothing to her.

"We do not give out of greed," she replied. Her tone was that of an adult chastising a young child, rather than addressing me as a millennia-old goddess in my own right. "We alone offer a gift to strengthen the mortals, more powerful than the other gods. Do not let vanity get in the way of that."

I closed my mouth and stared out at the sea, willing the hours to pass. I should confess that during those first years, I would always listen for Ione's prayers. I would strain to hear beneath all the thousands of voices, that singular, mellifluous voice that spoke only to me. I would imagine her smile as she spoke, relishing the knowledge of exactly who was receiving her words. For an immortal, those days without her felt like decades. Each second would drag, like a pebble tossed by a soft wave on the shore, destined to turn and twist with the illusion of freedom, only to be trapped by the same water that moved it.

As the years passed, I did not need such confirmation of Ione's devotion. I would relax, and like my mother, bask in all the offerings we received. My deep love for Ione gave me a deeper understanding of my mother. My patience with her grew. I would listen to her repeat those same tales of Iasion over and over again. And smile, knowing that she believed their brief time together was real love.

Two decades after that first meeting in the river, Ione met me by the willow tree, but there was no smile gracing her lips. No twinkle in her eye. For a second, I feared the worst. That I had been wrong to trust her affections for me was as strong as mine were for her, but as she fell upon me and wept, I knew that was not the case.

"My husband is sick," she said. "It is the same sickness that affected his brother, my first husband. An illness of the heart. He will not last to see another festival of Thargelia." My relief was short lived, for Ione's distress quickly became my own.

"What does that mean? What will become of you? I can stop it. Do you wish me to save him for you?"

She took my hands and pressed them against her lips. "This is life, darling Core," she laughed sadly. "I will be fine. I am an old maid now. Twice married with no children of my own. No man has an interest in me. But his children are good. They will see that I am adequately looked after."

"Adequately? What does that mean?"

"It means we do not need to spend the time we have together worrying. Now come, I have brought some pomegranates with me."

That incident, though it pained me, I remained silent. There were times, however, when I did not hold my tongue so successfully.

"When I am gone, do you think you will love again?" I recall her asking some years after her second husband had passed into the Land of the Dead. We had walked through the village together to reach a waterfall a short distance away. These moments in public I always viewed with mixed emotion. For as much as I reveled in being seen by her side, it was not enough to hold her hand in friendship. To appear as two aging women, content with each other's company. Her laughter lines had been swept there by hours spent giggling together, as if we were both still young girls. The graying plait that now weaved down her back was twisted by my own hand. But I saw the other changes too. Those hidden beneath the fabric of her robes and saved only for my eyes. We were more than mere friends, and I wanted everyone to know it. But that was not safe for her, and her safety was what mattered the most.

When we reached the waterfall, I caused the grasses to grow so high around the edge of the water, they created our own barrier from the world. Inside this space, the clear spring fell like a constant torrent of rain. A shower of pure delight, which we had stood beneath and laughed.

"Why do you talk about such a thing?" I responded to her. "You know I never loved before. I cannot love without you."

"Perhaps now that I have taught you to love, you will find others for whom you can feel the same."

She ambled from the waterfall to the bank as though her statement had been nothing more than a passing comment. Her step was unsteady as she entered the water. Frail even, though I paid it little mind, for anger flowed like acid in my veins.

"Why do you say such a thing? This does not need to end. *We* do not need to end. I can make you immortal. I can make your youth return."

"Is that what you wish for?" She turned to face me. "For my youth to return? I always believed it was not my youthful skin that made you love me, Core. Perhaps I was wrong."

I bit down on my tongue hard enough to draw the tang of blood. Furious that she could say such a thing.

"I love you now a thousand times more than I did the first day I saw you," I said, "and I will love you a thousand times more each lifetime we spend together. Every hair on your head could be white, or fallen, and I would love you. You know that."

"I do. I am sorry, my love." As she lowered herself to the ground, she patted the earth beside her gently, hoping I would join her, but I remained in the water, fixed with my scorn.

"Perhaps it is you who does not love me. For it is you who refuses to consider an eternal life together."

Contemplation shrouded her expression. She pressed her lips tightly together, allowing the sounds of the waterfall to fill the silence before she spoke again.

"You live in paradise with your mother. Is that not correct?"

"You know it is." I had told her all of Siphnos and the nymphs that lived there with us within the first year of our union and had spoken about it freely since. There was not a moment of my existence I had not told her about.

"You have everything that you need, yet you still needed a new escape. A place to be free. Me. But what if you were to tire of me, the way your father has done with all the mortal women he has taken?"

"I am not Zeus." My fury grew further as I stormed from the water to her side. "He and I are nothing alike."

"I am not saying that you are, my love. Believe me. But that does not mean you will not tire of me."

"I would never. I could never."

"How many of your gods have shown monogamy to their spouses? Mortal or otherwise? How many claim love unending and stay true to that claim?"

It was true that monogamy was not a skill possessed by my kin, and that, based on the evidence, her fear was well placed. But though my anger diminished, I refused to relinquish my point.

"Will you not even consider my offer?" I said.

She smiled at this comment and took my hands. Though I wished to resist, I allowed my fingers to unclench and slip between hers. I had taken an aged form like Ione. My knuckles were lost in folds of frail skin, and bold blue veins ran like tributaries beneath them. But appearance was where the similarities ended. For when my hands held hers, it was still with the grasp of a goddess, and not of an old woman. The same could not be said for Ione, yet in the blindness of love, I barely saw it.

"I have. I have, my love," she whispered, her lips brushing my ear as she spoke. "From that first day and every day since. But one life is significant enough for me. But just because I will cross the river to the Land of the Dead, you will not be lost to me, I swear. Please, my darling, let us not talk of such things. There are much more pleasurable ways we can spend our time." She brought my hand to her lips and began to trace a line down my arm with kisses.

Of course, I had not been so easily distracted as to forget our conversation but remained certain that with time I would persuade her. Alas, time was something we did not have.

CHAPTER FORTY-FIVE

MOTHER HAD INSISTED WE GATHER ON THE HIGHEST peak, ready to watch the dawn together. It was our way for the festivals, though none of those were as important to my mother as Thesmophoria. The festival of Demeter. Each year it grew and grew, though I was equally to credit for such proliferation. Unbeknownst to my mother, I had been using my travels to provide the lands with the most abundant harvests I could. Each region I visited, I cast my blessings over. Each field of corn I walked through flourished. The love I felt for Ione transposed into love for all the mortals.

With Ione at my side, I had learned so much more about the mortals we kept fed. I had met her step-grandchildren, and her nephews, who occasionally came down to the river to bathe with us. She had taken me into her home, where I had met her friends and maids, introduced to them as *an old friend*. On the rare occasions that Ione had been unable to meet me, she would often send one of her young relatives to pass on her messages and I would talk to them. Learn of their likes and dislikes. Speak to them as a friend. I was bonded to mortals in a manner that my mother could never dream of. That is why our blessings grew.

The day before, Ione and I had made love in that shepherd's hut again, for the first time in nearly a decade. She had taken me there, quite unexpectedly, and though the wooden walls were now rotten and poorly patched, I built us a wall of wheat. Afterward, we had lain in a blissful silence, watching as swallows dipped and dove above us. We did not need words. Did not need promises of a love eternal. We already had that. We were utterly content in one another's company. Yet during that festival of Thesmophoria, as I took my mother's hand on the top of the mountainside, I offered Ione only a passing thought. After all, we had years left to enjoy our love.

Oh, how callous and ridiculous that sounds now. And how I wish that was not the case. How I wished I had listened in on all her words, like in those early years. But there was no longer the need. She was, in all but name, my wife, and I looked forward to regaling to her the events of the days when I saw her again. ·

And what a festival it was. Aglaope played the lyre as Thelxiepia sang. My mother and I, too, shared tunes as we danced barefoot on the grass, with corn rising up around us. And the wine. The first day of the festival, we were moderate in our consumption. Sipping away as we listened to adulations rolling in off the hills from the far corners of the world. But as the worship continued, our moderation slipped away. Amphora after amphora was emptied into our cups. Oh, the amount of wine we had drunk over those three days would have put the followers of Dionysus himself to shame. Sweet wine, not cut with salt water the way the mortals would drink it, but fruity and rich. For the first time since arriving in Siphnos, my mother and I giggled and laughed like young nymphs. I cannot say where the frivolous nature came from.

"I wish for every day to be like this," Thelxiepia said as she finished a song and collapsed onto the grass.

"Every festival," Peisinoe corrected. "My body will need at least the year to recover."

By the end of the three days, we had placed blessings on all of Hellas, and I was dizzy from the euphoria of the worship. Euphoria I wished to share with Ione.

I had intended on traveling before heading to Tegea, to fetch Ione a gift of fruit or flowers, but my yearning to see her was too strong, and when I reached Aegina, I continued straight onward.

"I will be back before sunset," I called to the nymphs as I went.

The sky was feathered with white clouds, which did little to diminish the sun's fury as I skipped barefooted through the long grasses, brushing my hands against the seed heads. It was disappointing, but not unsurprising, to find that I reached the river before Ione. As the years passed, her need for sleep had grown longer. The death of her second husband resulted in her presence being required more at home, and it would often not be until midmorning when she strode down to meet me. But I was not concerned. When the midday sun shone directly above, however, a knot of concern tightened within me. Had she been required to spend another day with her family? It was not beyond the realm of possibility, but had such an event occurred, where was the young nephew given a coin in exchange for running to the river to tell me? The longer I waited, the tighter the knots twisted. Something was missing from the air. No, not from the air. From the world. To others, it would be so small as to be imperceptible, but to me, the planet had shifted off its axis and the movement forced an emptiness in its place. Even before I picked up my feet and ran toward the village, I knew what I was to find.

CHAPTER FORTY-SIX

MY FEET SLAMMED AGAINST THE ROCKY EARTH AS I RACED toward the village, shouting her name. From behind me came a gust of wind. Blackened crops followed in my wake. Birds circled overhead. Clouds with gray underbellies swollen with water shrouded the sky. I was wrong; I told myself again and I again. I had to be wrong. She was barely fifty. We had spent less than thirty years together. It could not be. As I approached the village, my pace slowed and my eyes scanned the whitewashed walls of the buildings.

Ione had taken me to her home on many occasions after her husband's death, though always under the guise of an old friend. Positioned on the far edge of the village, two olive trees whose trunks had entwined marked the southern corner of their land and offered a view from her veranda that spanned out over the mountains. I had stood on that veranda with her. I had looked out at that view, as she stood behind me and planted the gentlest of kisses upon my neck. I had imagined what it would be like to spend the night there, to wake up next to her each morning and watch the sun rise, with our fingers interlocked and the scents of each other's bodies still clinging to our skin.

But there were people on the veranda that morning. Too many people.

Whether I wished to or not, I kept walking. My feet dragged on the earth, sharp stones stabbing my soles as I made my way up to the steps to join the prosthesis for my love.

I had observed endless mortal burials and knew well of the three stages that occurred before a soul was laid to rest. First came the laying out of the body so that mourners could come and pay their respects; the prosthesis—the procession of the body—came three days after death; and then the burial, where the body was placed with Charon's payment to cross the river Styx. I had seen countless of them before from Olympus. But never like this. Never as one of the mourners. And I mourned.

Mortals are born crying. For a short while, it is the only form of communication they have, before the slight flickers of a smile and urging laughs begin. But I am not mortal, and the only true anguish I had ever felt was my mother's. I had lost my brothers, of course, but that had been expected. A pang of sadness had reverberated through me when we left the twins, knowing I would not see their first steps, or what kind of men they grew into, but sadness is not heartbreak. Disappointment is not desolation. And that day I was desolate.

The sound of tears choking in my lungs was so alien to me that as I ascended the steps to Ione's home, I was forced to stop and search for this source. When I realized that it, like the wheezing of air as it struggled down my throat, came from within me, the tears flowed faster still.

Ione's body was cleaned and dressed, laid out with the feet pointing toward the exit of the house. My heart was shredded: desiccated and destroyed. No part of me spared. I stepped forward and placed my hand against her cheek, gasping at the cool dampness of her skin.

"Ione," I whispered. She was gone. My hand hovered, suspended by invisible threads, before I dropped to my knees, not even aware of Ione's family and friends also present.

I regret this. I regret my selfishness and how I did not even consider the grief of others. But grief, I had learned from my mother, makes you selfish. My mother left Olympus and never returned after the loss of a man she spent one mortal day with. How could that compare with my loss? I didn't believe it did.

"You knew my aunt well?" I turned to see a woman standing over me, a veil was over her head, but her eyes were in view.

"Your aunt?" I scrambled to my feet, so that I could search within this woman's eyes, desperate to see a hint of those deep irises that I had gazed into for hours upon end. But there was nothing. No similarity between the pair at all.

"I loved her," I gasped. "I did not know how to love until her." I did not consider how my response may be received, but if this woman did not know her aunt truly in life, then why should she not learn who she was in death? With a worried look, she dipped her chin, leaving us once again alone.

As time passed, footsteps padded quietly around me. Whispers floated between doorways. Yet no person approached me again. I sank back to the ground, my grip still firm on Ione's dead hand as the cold stone stung my knees and the shadows grew long. The light that shone through the open window grew muted and watery. Yet I did not move. I think perhaps I would have stayed there, my body stuck to the ground for all eternity, had it not been for the hand that rested upon my shoulder.

"It is time you left, my child. It does you no good to stay."

My head turned, not to see who the speaker was, for I knew the voice with absolute certainty, but out of shock that they should be here with me.

"Thelxiepia?" The nymph's dark skin glimmered even in the lack of light.

"I'm here."

"She is gone, Thelxiepia. She is gone."

"I know, my love. I know. But you should come with me now. We cannot stay in this place. We need to let the mortals grieve."

"I cannot. I cannot leave her."

"They will see to the burial rites, child. We need to leave her now. This is not our place to be."

No nymph's strength is comparable to mine, and yet Thelxiepia lifted me from that ground, as if I were as feeble as a newborn. With one hand still in mine, she wrapped her arm round my waist and brought me to my feet. My eyes, however, remained fixed on Ione for as long as they could, for I knew that this would be the last time I ever saw her.

As we made our way to Tegea, the grief came in surges, sometimes so overwhelming that it would steal the breath from my lungs and weaken my knees and cause me to drop down. But Thelxiepia caught me each time and held me steady until I could carry on again.

"We are nearly there. We are nearly at home," she told me time and time again. "We will be there before the sun sets. It is not far now."

At Tegea, the other nymphs did not speak, but helped their sister, guiding me home to Siphnos.

I do not know how we made it back to the island, but we did.

"Core..." My mother was waiting on the shore for me. "Core, my child. What is it? What has happened?"

I could not speak. Tears lodged in my throat, rendering me mute. The pain they caused burned down to my chest. How could I tell her? How could I tell her that the woman I loved was gone when she did not even know that such a woman existed? How could I say that the grief she felt for Iasion I now understood and felt a thousand times over, for that is how many more days we had together? How could I say that? I could not.

"Are you hurt? Are you hurt, my child?"

Her hands ran up and down me, twisting my body as she searched for some sign of injury, but a broken heart cannot be seen. Even by those that love you the most deeply. Still, I did not resist her.

"There was a child," Thelxiepia's spoke beside me, my mind not yet registering the meaning. "There was a child in one of the meadows. He had been abandoned by his mother. Left to the wild. It was…upsetting, for us all." She turned her head quickly behind her to where Peisinoe and Aglaope were standing.

"It was distressing," Peisinoe said with unwavering certainty. "For all of us. But Core, she is the one who found the child. Is that not so?"

All three nymphs' eyes bore into me. They had embroiled me in a lie, a lie to save me from my mother's wrath and anger. They had risked the wrath of an Olympian, for me. When I am alone, I think of those three fearless creatures. How they were willing to risk so much for me. But I cannot think of it for too long. For I know. I know what happened.

"I should have saved her. I should've done something to save her." I said, finally finding words to speak.

My mother's arms enveloped me. The warmth of a hug. A shoulder to cry upon.

"They are mortals, my darling. It is the hand they have been dealt. Give it time, you will forget it."

I did not offer another word but waited until her arms dropped, then walked silently past her and into the house. I would not forget. I would never forget. At least, not on my own.

CHAPTER FORTY-SEVEN

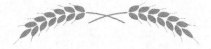

I DO NOT KNOW WHAT WEB OF LIES THE NYMPHS WEAVED FOR ME during the days that followed, what reasons they gave for my inability to speak through the tears.

Anger surged within me. Anger at Ione. I do not believe it was the gods' will that she left me that day. It was her will. Her will to leave me at the one time she knew I would not be able to put up a fight. The one time I would not know. I was angry at myself for not making her immortal, angry at her for the betrayal of not choosing eternity with me. Never in all my days had emotion swelled and surged within me in such relentless torrents.

My mother was more attentive to me in those days than at any other point during our time at Siphnos. Her vigils at Iasion's tree were cut short, as she alone cared for the needs of the mortals. And though she tried to speak to me, and offer comfort, I could not respond, for fear of what words would tumble from my lips.

No particular incident invoked my decision to finally leave my chamber, though I chose an hour close to sunset, when I knew my mother would be by her tree. Galvanized with a sense of purpose,

I marched to the water, where the nymphs were lying in the grass, their eyes in the distance.

"How did you know where to find me?" I offered no formality or greetings. Nor, to my shame, any thanks for the aid they had offered me. "How did you know where I was?"

The three women exchanged a glance, full of tightened lips and unspoken words. In the end, it was Thelxiepia who spoke.

"You are not the only one who has wandered to new places. Who enjoys privacy and solitude. We have all spent time wandering these lands at some point or another."

"On your own?" The surprise hitched in my voice. It is ridiculous to have assumed I was the only one who sought freedom from the binds that my mother placed upon us. Still, Thelxiepia's answer had offered me no clarity as to how she knew of Ione until the realization sank through my skin, chilling the blood in my veins as it went.

"You saw us?" I said, my breath gasping. "Ione and I? How many times? Did you follow me?"

"I did not." Thelxiepia said. "I promised you your freedom, and I meant that. I was walking, that was all. And you spoke so fondly of the river in Tegea, and I thought to see it for myself. I stumbled upon the pair of you. You were laughing. Holding one another's hands." She opened her mouth as if there were more to say, and I imagine there was. Kisses, if nothing else. A flush of embarrassment rolled through me, yet I quashed it as quickly as I could. What was there to feel embarrassment for? I loved a woman. I was not the first, and I knew I would not be the last. "When I realized your relationship with the mortal, I left quickly, knowing you had not seen me and not wishing to disturb your privacy. I knew that if you had wanted to tell her of us, then you would have done. She was your secret. I wished her to remain so until you felt comfortable sharing her."

My relationship. My secret. She was my world. She was not some fling, the way Thelxiepia made it sound. Ione was not some brief dalliance that was to be forgotten. Some one-night salience. She was the one who made me see light in the world. And now that light had gone.

"It might help to talk of her," Thelxiepia said. "The way your mother speaks of Iasion."

At this I snorted. "What they had did not compare to us."

Thelxiepia nodded slowly, her movements cautious, as if I were an animal she feared provoking.

"You have loved, Core," she said quietly. "You have experienced a devotion that so many, mortals or otherwise, only dream about. You can find strength in that. You can find joy in the memories you have."

"Strength?" I was aghast that she would suggest such a thing, yet the nymphs stepped forward and took my hands.

"Goddess. I will tell you now, this pain you are feeling is a gift. This pain shows your fortune. Why do you think the nymphs and I stood with your mother that day of the wedding? Why do you think we follow her so loyally? It is not solely because of her powers. I can assure you of that." I paused my sniveling, merely to catch a breath, though Thelxiepia took it as a sign to continue. "Your mother felt true love. True love that ascended status and birthright. True love that would give a scrawny mortal prince the courage to stand up to Zeus himself. That love is a wondrous thing, a powerful thing. And you, too, have experienced it."

Had I? I wondered. Would Ione have stood up against Zeus himself? Yes, I laughed in my mind as I considered it. Of course she would have.

"Draw strength from the pain that you feel," Thelxiepia continued. "Know that it comes from a place of power. You will be better
for this loss."

Perhaps if she had not said that final sentence, I would have
considered the truth in her words. But I had seen what grief did.
How had my mother been better for her loss? How could I possibly
be better for mine?

"You do not know of what you speak," I said, turning on my heel
and retreating to my chamber.

For days on end, I remained there as bound to my chamber as
Danae was her tower. I did not rise with the birdsong, did not wish
to see light sparkle on the smooth sea. I did not want to hear the
prayers and adulations given in my name. I did not eat, or drink,
but merely existed, as much a shade as Ione herself. As those who
have lost will know, grief has the ability to twist time. To make every
second feel as though it is an eternity, and for those with an eternity
to spare, the magnitude of this cannot be understated.

My mother did not know the truth. She had marked me as a
sensitive soul from those first days on Olympus and bought fully
the story of the abandoned child. So much so, that often as she sat
by my bedside, she would talk to me about my brothers and other
mortal children and how it does not help us to grow so attached to
ones whose lives are so fleeting. Perhaps I had once been the soft soul
she saw me as. The delicate bud, that, when pressured, was forever
so deformed that the petals would never open. But those years were
behind me.

Some days I would venture out of my room, to stand on the
veranda, and gaze outward at a world that no longer contained Ione.
I would close my eyes and pretend the whispers of the wind carried
her voice from the Underworld to me.

"What am I to do?" I asked Peisinoe one day. I had ventured as far as the courtyard, although that was enough to stir a thousand memories. The way vines twisted on trellises reminded me of the way Ione would braid her hair so that it crossed over the crown of her head, and the clusters of oleanders brought me back to a day when I had picked so many, and my arms were so full that I dropped a trail all the way to Tegea. "What am I supposed to do without her?" I repeated to the nymph, feeling the tears burning behind my eyes.

"That is up to you. If you need all of eternity to grieve, then you take it. Look at your mother."

She had meant the words as comfort. To support me in my heartache, but my response was the opposite. They twisted like a knife in my side. Is that what I were to become? My mother? In that moment, it was as if a great cloud passed from my eyes and illuminated a bright burning light.

"I wish to go to Tegea. I must go. I must go now."

Light-headedness engulfed, like a sudden rush of blood had flooded my head, yet I maintained my balance.

"Perhaps we should spend the day here, outside first." Thelxiepia suggested, having joined us. "We can take you to the waters. You can bathe in the river. Or the sea, if you prefer?"

I shook my head.

"Tegea. I need to go now. I cannot... I cannot."

My throat refused to release the words, but they did not need to be spoken for the nymphs to know what my heart felt. I would not allow myself to become like my mother. Locked away. The reclusive god, with little more presence in the world than Hades. I remember genuinely having that thought. The comparison between myself and the God of the Underworld. I have wondered if my father was watching down on me, smiling as it raced through my mind. It is not without possibility.

"We should tell your mother where you are going. Or at least that you are leaving," Peisinoe said, sensing my galvanization. Once again, I shook my head.

"We will be back by sunset. I need to go. To see the place again."

Tension rippled in the air, wrapping itself like a breeze around us. As we stood there, Thelxiepia spoke again.

"You can go, but we will come with you. We will not let you go there on your own."

"We will go as we always go," I said, hastening to the coast, but Thelxiepia's hand fixed around my wrist.

"No, we come with you. All the way. You will not do this on your own."

I wished to object and fight her, but I did not have the mental strength.

"We leave immediately," I said instead.

CHAPTER FORTY-EIGHT

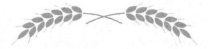

THE TRAIN OF NYMPHS THAT FOLLOWED ME ALL THE WAY TO Tegea did little to comfort me. For centuries I had traveled everywhere on my own. I did not require an escort. Despite my mother's constant concern, my presence aroused no suspicion. On the rare occasion that I found myself in a misguided location— such as a busy agora full of bartering, angry men—I could slip into the shadows and be forgotten from sight within an instant. Such are the luxuries of godliness. Not that I ever needed to hide in Tegea. No, here I wished to be seen. For reasons I cannot say, I fixed my eyes forward, the nymphs' footsteps behind me the only sign of their presence in this place I had tried so hard to keep private.

I walked straight toward the riverbank, the same way I always went, yet there was something unfamiliar about the landscape. The grass was longer than it had been, skimming my knees, and full of the buzz of crickets, while the scent of lemon balm and marjoram muzzied the air. My eyes found the path I frequently took carved out between the grasses, yet as my feet followed it, something felt different. The ground was harder than I expected. Or perhaps it was the aroma that was unfamiliar. Perhaps it was the presence of the nymphs that made the place feel so peculiar. I could not tell, but when we reached the river, that confusion deepened.

I scanned my gaze up and down. Willows continued to line the banks, and one particular specimen caught my eye; its branches flourished upward before cascading down into the water. It was similar in size to the willow that Ione and I would meet beneath, but the leaves were yellow, rather than green, and the bark of its trunk peeled and cracked in a way that ours did not; it barely had any life remaining.

I turned in a circle, trying to gain my bearings. So much was familiar, and yet it was distorted. As if I were not in Tegea, but a place drawn from a description of it. The village remained in the correct location, but it was larger than it had been. The meadows that we had danced in were now ploughed and planted with grapevines; straight lines interspersed with wheat to make the most of the land. I moved further down the river to where a small bridge stood. One I had not seen before. It was not a modern addition; the wooden planks no longer lay flush to one another, and rain, wind, and the river itself had worn down the wood so that it warped and tilted to the side, while moisture allowed a dark green moss to grow on the underside. It must have been there decades, but how could that be? How could a place I knew so well have changed in so many ways? I had been here at the river less than a moon ago. Had I not? A tremble afflicted my lungs, which caused me to breathe in wheezing gasps of air.

"Thelxiepia, where are we? Where *are* we?" My voice quivered, the strength in my legs draining into the earth beneath me.

"We are in Tegea, Core."

"That cannot be. It is not right. It is not right."

"Time has passed, Goddess. Time has passed."

"I don't understand. I don't *understand*."

My words were not the truth. I knew exactly what she was saying, but I refused to accept it. To admit it to myself.

"I am so sorry, goddess." To see a nymph cry is to see the most beautiful creature in existence shattering open before you, and yet tears glazed her eyes. Tears not for herself, but for me. "It has been many years, my child. For the mortals, it has been many years."

"No. No, it can't be." My throat closed tight. The heat of the morning now suffocating. Stifling me as I tried to draw a breath.

"It is what you needed. You needed to grieve, that is all." Aglaope tried to take my hands as she spoke, but I pulled away from her.

"How long? How long has it been?" I stood, but I knew the answer would be enough to floor me, yet I needed to know. When they did not speak, my voice rose. "How long has it been?" My voice raged in the air. Birds flew from their roosts as the branches of their trees turned black beneath me. The nymphs exchanged a look. One of the deepest, heart-wrenching sympathy and guilt.

"A century, or thereabouts."

My knees buckled beneath me with such a speed that they could not catch me. I plummeted downward, no breath in my lungs as my hands struck the cold stones of the earth.

A hundred years. The time spun around in my mind as I thought of my last conversations with her. How she had made me promise to never stop picking flowers, to never stop singing and dancing. How I had promised I would continue to live even when she was gone. But I had agreed because I had barely even contemplated that a world without her would be possible. We were supposed to have had decades left together. Decades in which I watched as the frailness of age wore away at her bones and her stubbornness and she succumbed to my wish to make her immortal. But that had not happened. Instead, all I had done was break my promises to her.

It was then I realized the truth. I had become Demeter. I saw my entire eternal future stretched out in front of me. Perhaps I would place a shrine on the island, for Ione, like my mother had. Perhaps I would pretend to find joy in life, listening to the mortals' adulations at the festivals and feasts, but in truth, my heart would break a thousand times over, as among those voices, I searched only for one. One I knew I would never hear again. I would be imprisoned on Siphnos once more, and I would not fight it. Why would I, where there would be nothing to leave my prison for? Then and there, I made a promise to myself that I would not become my mother. I would not spend my life lost in grief, yet I could not erase Ione from my mind. I could not, but there were those who could.

CHAPTER FORTY-NINE

I DID NOT WAIT TO PUT THE WHEELS OF MY PLAN INTO MOTION. Fear drove me forward. Fear of what I would become, but also fear that if I did not act swiftly, I might lose the courage to act at all.

On the journey back to Siphnos, I took Thelxiepia's hand and slowed our steps so that a distance stretched between us and her sisters. I am certain I could have involved all the nymphs; none of them would refuse me. They kept secrets from my mother all those centuries when we had gone our separate ways. They had kept hidden from her the love I had for Ione. But this was about more than merely omitting details to Demeter, and I did not wish to endanger any more of them than necessary.

Besides, it was Thelxiepia who had found me at the prosthesis. She was the one who had witnessed my heart break. Who saw the rawest, freshest wounds as they seared through my skin. It was she who I could feel staring at me with worry etched in lines on her perfect skin. Who always paused before speaking to me, with more that she wanted to say, though she remained fearful of crossing a boundary. But the boundaries had all been crossed that day she found me broken, and so she was the one I chose.

"I need to ask something of you," I said, slowing my pace even further to extend the gap between us and the other nymphs. "There is somewhere I must go. Somewhere we must go. And something I must ask of you before we go there."

"Of course." Her voice was more tentative than her words. "Can you tell me where we are headed?"

"Certainly." I glanced forward. We were close to Siphnos now, and though I knew we would not be overheard, I lowered my voice. "I will need you to leave your sisters, though. It has to be you alone. I am to travel to Mount Helicon. You will go to Olympus."

For a moment, Thelxiepia remained silent. Her lips pressed tightly, and I watched as the threads of my words weaved together to form an image in her mind.

"You wish me to send a muse to meet with you? You wish me to go to Olympus to seek them out for you?" The muses. Goddess of Dance and Music. But so much more. They alone remembered everything. Every act that had come to pass was etched in their memory. There was a reason my father kept them in his favor, and it was not for their lyrics and melodies. Power came with recalling the past. Yet for me, power would come from forgetting it.

"It is too great a risk for me to go myself," I said, confirming Thelxiepia's thought. "Should my father or another god recognize me, I cannot predict how they will behave. But you are insignificant to them. They will think nothing of another nymph." I had not meant my words to sound cruel; they were simply the truth. "You are the one I trust to do this. Thelxiepia. I know how much I ask of you. How much we have asked of you, staying on Siphnos all these years, but I cannot go another century with this pain. I cannot go another day. Please."

Silently, Thelxiepia nodded.

"And which muse it is that I must summon to Mount Helicon?" she asked, though I suspect she already knew the answer.

"Mnemosyne. The Mother of the Muses."

"And the Goddess of Memory."

Without the need for words, I nodded. "I need this. I need to forget her."

Like all the gods, Mnemosyne was my kin. Her parents were my grandparents, and her power so great that, like all those Titans whose gifts could be of benefit to him, Zeus allowed her to reside on Mount Olympus. But she and the other muses had two homes. Free to come and go as they wished, they would split their time between the bronze and gilded palaces of Olympus and the fertile lands of Mount Helicon. There she and the other eight muses were free to pursue their arts and passions, surrounded by their sacred springs.

"I wish to go as soon as the sun rises tomorrow," I told her. "If Mnemosyne is not present in Olympus, then come straight to Mount Helicon and join me there. I will need you with me either way."

I prepared myself to move. Ready to quicken my pace and join the nymphs so that we could return to Siphnos together, but Thelxiepia caught my hand.

"Goddess, I will do this for you. Of course I will. But have you thought what will happen if Mnemosyne refuses your request? She is not known to remove memories from gods."

I nodded, lowering my head to the ground. Beside my feet, a small patch of daisies was blooming. Their perfect bright centers gleaming like tiny golden suns. As I stared at them, I recalled the crown I had made for Ione one morning when the grass was filled with these little white flowers. I had made her a hundred crowns over the years. Crowns filled with all the blooms that I had gathered on my travels. But as I placed that single loop on her head, she clutched her hands to it as if it were made of gold.

"This. This is my favorite," she said, her eyes alight and glowing.

"You say that with every gift I give you," I snorted.

"Yes, but this time I mean it."

I shook my head, with my laughter only ceasing as she planted a kiss on my lips.

I blinked, and the daisies on the ground beneath my feet were wilting and brown. It was a short while more before Thelxiepia's question came back to me and I lifted my head and met her eyes firmly.

"She will say yes," I replied. "She has to."

CHAPTER FIFTY

WHEN WE LEFT TOGETHER THAT MORNING, I EMBRACED my mother tightly, wondering if I would ever see her again with the same eyes. I learned of love through Ione. I understood grief through Demeter. Because of that, I did not know how greatly my relationship with her would change when my memories of my lover left me.

"I love you, Mother," I told her, then turned my back and walked toward the sea without waiting for a reply.

When we reached Tegea, I turned to the nymphs. "Thelxiepia is to join me today," I told them. "We will meet you here as usual, before sunset,"

Peisinoe looked at her sister before speaking to me. "We are all here to aid you, Goddess. Whatever it is you need, we can help."

"Thank you, I know. But you have already helped me so much."

Sensing that there was nothing they could say to dissuade me, they dropped back, allowing Thelxiepia and I the privacy we required.

"Thank you. Thank you for this."

"If your mother finds out, I cannot lie to her."

"She will not. She will not think to ask. But find Mnemosyne quickly. Tell her how we are bound by sunset to return to Siphnos."

"I will tell her."

"And you will join us there afterward."

"As you wish, Goddess."

With that, we parted ways.

It was easy to see why the muses chose Mount Helicon as their home. The lush lands were richly fertile with a view that spanned out over the archipelago below. Dense and verdant trees offered them all the shade and privacy they could require, while the two springs, in which they bathed and drank from, ran with water so clear that every single pebble on the riverbed was visible from above the surface. The air was filled with birdsongs in much the same way as upon Siphnos, but there was a coolness to it here. A breeze that ensured the heat did not become stifling. Had it been any other time, I would have plucked flower after flower and weaved the stems into a crown, or else tied them into a posy. But that morning, my hands could not remain still enough to do such a task, and I found myself constantly shifting my position and gaze, though the tension remained however I stood or sat.

I was sitting upon a broken tree trunk that lay flat on the ground, gazing out at the clouds that drifted over the hilltops, when a voice spoke behind me.

"Goddess, she is here."

There stood Thelxiepia, the nymph I had seen day after day for centuries, and beside her stood Mnemosyne.

I had seen the muse before during those years upon Olympus, but only ever at a distance. Understandably, my mother did not integrate us at the gatherings Zeus held, and Mnemosyne, like other muses, had always been swamped with admirers. Never had her attention been solely on me, and now that it was, it felt as though the entire heat of the sun blazed down upon me. She wore a green robe, brighter and more luscious than the hills upon which we stood, and her loosely waved red hair flowed past her shoulders and down to her waist. And though she stood no taller than me in stature, I felt dwarfed by her presence.

"Daughter of Demeter." Her voice was as soft as a breeze. "You have requested my company, and it is an honor to respond." I doubted her words were true, but the flattery helped ease the tension that had held me relentlessly. "Your mother, is she well? It has been some time since I saw her on Olympus."

"I am certain you are aware of the reasons behind my mother's departure," I said, my voice gentle. Nonconfrontational. After all, there was no confrontation to be had here.

Mnemosyne nodded solemnly. "It was many centuries ago," she said. "Is she still afflicted by grief?"

"Grief does not know limits on time."

I had not meant to sound curt or discourteous, yet I heard the sharpness on my tongue. Thelxiepia stiffened beside me, although Mnemosyne showed no indication of indignation at my reaction. Rather, she softened.

"So that is why you are here? You too have fallen in love and wish to forget the grief that you must endure. I assume the one you loved was a mortal too, like your mother. You poor child."

Throughout my entire existence, I had abhorred how my mother treated me as a child. I had despised the way that, despite all my powers and strength, she viewed me as less capable than her. She saw me as frail and childlike, despite being a goddess centuries old. Yet standing before Mnemosyne, my tongue twisted and my heart raced and I felt that same sense of inadequacy and inexperience I had felt the first time I saw Ione. Mnemosyne's age and wisdom shone through from the depths of her gaze.

"I cannot take the grief alone," Mnemosyne said, placing her hand on my arm. "You must lose the love that came with it. Every second which passed between you and this mortal will be gone forever. Is that truly what you want?"

All of Ione, gone. It would be as though she had not existed. Could I do that? Could I return to a world where she did not even exist? My heart throbbed, my lips sealed tight, as if to utter the words would be a betrayal of all we had. But Ione had betrayed me too. She had betrayed me when she slipped away from the Land of the Living without even offering me the opportunity to say goodbye. And so I dipped my chin into a nod.

"Will it hurt?" I said, my words sounding more like a mortal child than a goddess, but Mnemosyne only smiled.

"No, it will not hurt, but there are some things I wish you to know first." I nodded. I do not know when it happened, but Thelxiepia had slipped her hand into mine and now squeezed tightly. "Once these memories have been taken from you, only the gift of a muse will return them."

I nodded again, swallowing as I found my voice.

"Then please, tell your daughters not to approach me. It is not what I wish for. I wish for them to be gone."

"I will do so."

"And what of a sacrifice?" I asked, straightening my posture. "A payment for your time and gift?"

To my surprise, Mnemosyne shook her head. "We are placed upon this earth to share our gifts, my daughter. Especially with those who need them as deeply as you do. I will take no sacrifice, but I will tell you this: nothing will erase this love from your mind a second time. Not a blessing from me, not the water of the river Lethe. If these memories are returned to you, they will be fixed for all of eternity, you understand?"

Again, I nodded my response. "I understand."

"In that case, my child, drink."

CHAPTER FIFTY-ONE

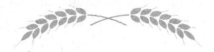

The cup Mnemosyne offered me was made of dented brass. The long stem worn so thin in the center it was a wonder it did not snap between my fingers. Filled to just below the brim, the liquid inside was as transparent as air.

"Water?" I questioned.

"Spring water from our stream, blessed by me, child. This will do as you have requested, though once you start to drink, be sure that you finish it all. Otherwise, memories might remain."

At this, I turned to Thelxiepia, daring to hope for some hint of approval on her face.

"This is what you wish for," she said. When her words finished, her eyes remained on me and I saw behind them all she wished to say. She had told me before how I was lucky to have loved so deeply and so fiercely. How love such as ours was a blessing and that I should draw strength from my grief. But I could not do that. Whatever strength Thelxiepia saw in me, I did not see in myself. Which was why I drank.

The water was as pure as I had ever tasted. The subtleties of hillsides steeped within the flavor. Tangs of mint and lemon balm tingled softly on my tongue, more delicate and appetizing than any wine I had tasted. As delicious as the ambrosia upon Olympus. Still, I did not revel in the taste, but drank down one mouthful and then another. Large gulps, which emptied the cup. As the drink grew scarce, I tilted the stem higher and higher, tipping my neck back to drain it fully, and even then, when I was certain that every last drop had fallen into my mouth, I ran my finger around the inside, ensuring that none remained. Only when I was certain the cup was empty did I hand it back to Mnemosyne.

"How long will it take to work?" I said. I could still see Ione as clearly as a morning crocus in my mind. I could still hear her laughter and feel the soft pressure of her lips against my neck. And I wanted to hold on to it. I wanted to cling to those feelings. Fear of what I had done flooded me, and I grappled to recall those early meetings in the river. Or was it a lake? I was not certain. As I stood there, images began to fade. As I begged to keep Ione within me, I struggled to remember why the name Ione was important, and my hand went up to my neck, as if there was a shadow there. A faint presence of something that had once touched me deeply, but made no mark at all. And her face? Whose face had it been I was thinking of? For a moment, I attempted to comprehend why I had come to this place and what I had been thinking of, but before I could voice my confusion, other questions rose in my mind, for I did not even recognize where I stood.

As my eyes scanned the scene, I struggled to make sense.

"Daughter of Demeter. This is a lovely surprise. Your companion tells me you have come to pick the flowers from the steeps of our Mount Helicon."

Wide-eyed, I stared at the figure in front of me. She stood in mortal form, as did I, but the glow of light beneath her skin that emanated out into the world told me she was no mortal. This was a god. Her red hair tumbled down past her shoulders, reflecting the midmorning light as vividly as a sunset. And I had memories of this goddess. Not firm ones. We had not spoken before, I did not think, but I had seen her. On Olympus.

"Mount Helicon," I said, her words finally taking root. "You are a muse?"

"I am Mnemosyne," she responded, and she reached out her hand, waiting to accept something from me. That is when I noticed the brass cup in my hand. Dented and worn thin, it could have been as old as the gods themselves.

"My daughters are constantly leaving their belongings lying about in the meadows," Mnemosyne said, taking the cup from my hand. "I thank you for retrieving it. Now, come, let me show you the stream. I believe you will be enamored with the rushes that grow there. They are quite unlike anything you will have encountered elsewhere on your travels."

She looped her arm into mine, and with Thelxiepia trailing behind, we walked through her meadows.

"Of course, I wished to come to the mountains of Helicon," I said to myself.

When I returned to Siphnos that evening, my mother was seated beneath Iasion's tree. As I glanced up at the mountainside and saw her there talking to a figment of her imagination, a stab of anger struck me. After all, it was ridiculous how greatly she grieved this mortal, at the expense of the life before her. I knew I would not fall folly to such a thing.

CHAPTER FIFTY-TWO

L IFE CONTINUED FOR ME, A DAY-AFTER-DAY EXISTENCE OF festivals and flowers. For decades, I continued on, my only concern for the nymphs, who I knew were growing older around me. Of course, my concern was as much for myself as it was for them, for I knew not how I would continue my lifestyle of traipsing between meadows without their illusion of a chaperone. Still, this was but a distant concern. They had been near newborn when they came to Siphnos with us. They had plenty of life remaining. And so I had assumed my future was set, for the foreseeable at least. How wrong I was.

It would be remiss to say I had not thought of Hades before that day. Of course I had. I had thought of all my family. With each scream of a new mother, my mind would dart to Eileithyia, my half sister and the Goddess of Childbirth, and I would hope she was there, watching over the woman, granting her a swift and gentle birth. Aphrodite would be at the forefront of my mind every time I saw a couple in the grasps of love, casting each other sly glances, or surreptitiously brushing one another's hands under the oblivious eyes of their friends or family. When I passed the seas and watched a great swell of waves toss fishing boats, I would think of Poseidon, I would think of the nymphs, I would think of all my siblings and half siblings and cousins from a hundred mortals, many of which I would not know had they approached me and kissed me on either cheek. I saw my family and the gods in everything around me, and that included Hades.

Hades came to my mind with every glimpse of a funeral rite, or gravestone, be it newly erected or condemned to the long grasses, submerged in undergrowth, sinking beneath the Land of the Living. These sights triggered images of his dominion, God of the Underworld, master of the dead, although I had no image of him in my mind. As ruler of the dead, his requirement in the Underworld proceeded any desire Zeus had to call him to council on Olympus, and so we had never met.

I thought of him greatly after Iacchus, hoping that my brother's continued existence in the Land of the Dead would offer some comfort to my mother. Of course, had I retained my memories of Ione, I suspect I would have thought of him far more often. Possibly I would have been jealous of his proximity to her, or that I spent a few mere decades with her, while he had been granted an eternity. I'm certain that was how I would have perceived matters, only I did not think of Ione. She did not enter my dreams. Not her face. Not her voice. Occasionally, when I would hear the name mentioned in a busy agora, a sharp pain would flicker in the pits of my mind, but the moment would be gone even quicker than it formed. And that is how it would have stayed had he not come for me.

The day the earth opened, I was in Eleusis.

There was a light breeze that day. One that ruffled the leaves from the trees and carried on it a scent of thyme and chervil. Bitter herbs that held a hint of uncertainty, like a storm brewing out of view, behind the peak of a mountain, or beyond the horizon. The birds' chorus echoed the irresolution in the air as they altered their melodies and soloists, diminuendoing and crescendoing even before a discernible tune could be grasped.

The flowers of Eleusis have always been a sight to behold, with their explosions of color. I believe that there is not a single shade you could not find in that meadow, had you the tenacity to look long enough. The bright and pale pinks of the mondara complemented and clashed with the vibrant oranges of the crocosmia and the red of the hibiscus. Blues from the deepest azure to the palest violets flooded the area. Chloris had worked her magic in those fields, so much so I wondered if perhaps the Goddess of Flora was present, casting her magic over the place as I watched on. Though if that were true, she did not make herself known. In the distance, two shepherds were at work. Or rather, talked to one another while their herds ambled, but that was the way of life.

I was debating how long I could stretch my time out simply strolling, when the rumble began beneath my feet. I had heard many an earthquake in my years. A sharp strike of Poseidon's trident against the seafloor could cause the earth to tremble and quake, and with those first judders, I assumed that someone had, once again, invoked my uncle's wrath. Yet the rumbling did not pass. Instead, it grew faster and harder, and when I fell to my knees, I realized that this trembling of the earth was something altogether different.

With an almighty crack, the ground ripped in two, as though it was nothing more than a veil of silk, torn by a seamstress. The petrichor of that clear day was replaced by a heady swirl of musk that came deep from the earth. But the tearing of the land did not stop there.

Gasping with panic, I tried to flee, but every step I took away from the chasm was curtailed by another slide of the earth. When I opened my mouth to scream, dirt and dust filled my lungs, choking me. I was on my hands and knees, grappling at the stems of flowers, but they held no more purchase than I, and so I held in my hand little more than roots and petals, and all the while, the world was caving inward.

I was going to fall. I was going to fall into the abyss and be trapped beneath the earth and lost forever. I was to be the goddess buried beneath the meadows and not even the flowers I had plucked would mark my grave, for they, too, would be lost with me. As I struggled against the sliding earth, I thought of my mother. Of the pain that losing me would cause her. I thought about how she was right to fear the world beyond our island. How she would wait, for all eternity, on the island for me to return, too fearful ever to go in search of me. *I'm sorry*, I wanted to cry to her. Forgive me. Those were the words that formed on my lips, ready to spill out, but then, in an instant, it all stopped.

The silence was absolute. The earth had stopped shifting. My ragged breath pounded against my ears as my heart knocked against my chest. Grunting and wheezing, I dragged myself forward before I found within me the strength to stand and lift my feet, ready to run. That was when he came in his chariot. The black horses galloping forward. His single arm wrapped around my waist as he heaved me up from the earth, and into his chariot.

"Rape! *Rape*." I cried with all the strength my lungs could muster. "Rape," I cried again, praying that Helios himself would look down on me and rescue me with his golden chariot. Or perhaps the shepherds would arrive and possess a power strong enough to save me. And my wish was granted, partly. The young men heard my screams. Their head snapped toward me. The one closest dropped the bleating kid he was holding and raced toward me. My eyes locked on him. The fear lodged in my throat, still screaming that word over and over. "Rape. Rape!"

He had seen me. He was coming. He was coming. That was what I believed, but before he could reach me, the chariot I was in dove deep beneath the ground, and with a rumble loud enough to reach the depths of Tartarus, the earth closed behind me. I was gone. I had been taken to the Land of the Dead.

CHAPTER FIFTY-THREE

F EAR. IT HAS GRIPPED US ALL, MORTALS AND GODS ALIKE. ZEUS
himself is not immune, for why else would he have thrown all the
most powerful Titans into Tartarus? He feared that they would
one day overthrow him, the way he had overthrown Cronus. Hera,
his doting, faithful wife, constantly feared that she would be replaced,
which of course she was, frequently. My mother, as you well know, was
afraid of many things, but above all, losing another loved one. And I
was fearful that my life would remain stagnant for all eternity. But what
I would have given for stagnation then. What I would have given to be
trapped on Siphnos, in the safety of my overbearing mother. What I
would have done to have returned to a life of monotony.

The arm around my waist remained fixed, though even if it had
lessened its grip, it would have made no difference, for there was no
way for me to escape. To leap from the chariot would be to plunge
an unimaginable depth into…into…what? Down and downward we
went, beyond the depth of the longest tree roots and further still.
Even if the earth had not been sealed shut above me, I doubt I could
have glimpsed the sun, for how far down we traveled.

For a short while, I continued my screams, the singular words of *help* and *rape*, over and over. I writhed and twisted, beating my fists on my captor's arms, though he did not so much as flinch. Any sounds I made were swallowed by the rock that surrounded us, and my captor seemed as impervious to my shouting as he was to the constant slamming of my knuckles against his side. And so, when my throat was raw and fists throbbed, I focused solely on the hooded figure and lowered my voice.

"You will pay for this," I hissed. "I am the daughter of Zeus, and you will pay. I will make sure of it." Never before had I referred to myself in such a manner. Always I had chosen to be the daughter of Demeter, never of Zeus, but I needed the strength that came with my father's name. He was the god whose wrath and fury knew no bounds, as opposed to the goddess who feared even a crowd of mortals. Yanking my arm from my captor's grip, I snatched at the creature's hood, determined to expose him fully, though before I could pull on the fabric, his arm flung outward and knocked me down into the seat of the chariot. His head snapped back to face me, to study me through the shadows of his cloak, and for the briefest second, I believed he was to apologize for his action.

"Stay where you are," he said instead.

Those were the first words he spoke to me. His voice, low and gravelly, rumbled in my ears. In my heart, I knew. A chariot with four black steeds could mean only one god, yet I could fathom no reason he would have taken me.

We must have been traveling for hours, when the first glints of light glimmered. Ephemeral and so infrequent, I initially doubted what I was seeing. My eyes had struggled to adjust to the lack of light, but the deeper we went, the brighter the lights became, sustaining for longer and longer until slowly but surely, images formed in the distance. First came the two moats beneath me. The outer ring was only fractionally wider than the streams that ran down the mountains in Siphnos, but the inner moat, smaller in circumference, was at least twenty times as wide. My eyes were fixed on the sight, the way the lights shimmered on the water appearing as though it had been whipped into a foam by a stormy wind. And there in the center, a sight that caused the air to freeze within my lungs.

I had heard rumors of my uncle's domain. Of his palace built from obsidian, carved into pillars and arches more gargantuan than even Olympus. And why not? After all, Zeus may have been considered the king of gods and men, but mortals spent only a finite time on earth before they are claimed by Hades for all eternity. Yes, with a kingdom of numbers like that, Hades deserved a palace that marked his dominion.

The sight of the palace erased my last traces of doubt. It was Hades who stood beside me in his chariot, commanding his steeds. Hades, who had taken me, snatched me from the earth. And as his horses' hooves came to a clattering halt on those gleaming black stones outside the palace, I began to understand the extended terror of this knowledge. No person, living or dead, could find this palace without Hades's say-so. And no person could leave it. I drew my eyes from one side to another.

To the left of the palace, great white cypress trees cast their shade over a dark, glimmering lake. It was the same effect that I had seen from above, where a frothing foam transformed the air above the water to mist. As I leaned outward, wondering what phenomena could cause such an effect, realization struck with a crippling fear. It was not the pool that was glimmering at all but rather those who crowded around it. Souls. Translucent souls. Wraiths.

When his horses were stationary, Hades slipped out of the chariot and took two paces toward the palace gates before he stopped and turned to me. Though his face remained covered, in his hand he held a gold scepter: the tool that had allowed him to open the earth and split the land between the living and create a pathway to the dead. For a moment, I stared at that object, unable to grasp how one single instrument could harness so much power.

"It is this way," he said, then continued onward. I still find it amusing how he assumed I would simply follow him. How he thought his words would be enough to make me walk through those colossal gates. Instead, I dug my heels into the wooden floor of the chariot and refused to budge.

"Why have you brought me here?" My voice echoed around the space, releasing a reply of a thousand moans. A chill spread down my spine, yet I did not show this with so much as a shiver or a blink of my eye. I remained upright, my gaze fixed on the god in front of me. "What do you want from me?"

His face was still hidden by the hood, and shadows of his beard were the only facial feature I could discern. Still, he stopped, and I heard the way he sucked in a lungful of air and ground his teeth, before he spoke.

"You will come inside. I have prepared a chamber for you there."

The way he spoke reminded me of my mother. He assumed I would follow his orders without question. But he was not my mother. I did not owe him life or protection. I owed him nothing.

"You will return me to the Land of the Living," I said, my voice conveying far more confidence than I felt. "And while we journey back, offer me the courtesy of telling me why you have brought me here."

Silence followed my comment. Silence that I wish had never

ended for the reply he offered sent a bone-deep chill shuddering through me.

"You are here because you are mine." His words struck me square in the chest. So simple. So coolly said, yet they released in my heart a heat as strong as if he had struck me with his palm. Fear transformed into fury.

"I am nobody's," I spat at him, with the same ferocity and fire that I spoke back to Zeus all those years ago at Harmonia's wedding. "I am certainly not yours."

I braced myself for his wrath. Expecting him to explode with the same anger my father would display when confronted in such a manner, but instead, he pulled back his hood and frowned. His face was a canvas of shadows. Large, dark eyes stared back at me from the palest of faces, while his sharp angular cheekbones cut down to a tightly clenched jaw. His brows, the same black shade as his beard, knitted together as confusion marred his face.

"Tell me," I said, speaking before the bravery could flicker out. "Tell me why I am here. Tell me now."

CHAPTER FIFTY-FOUR

S WEAT CLUNG TO MY BODY. A STIFLING HEAT, AS INTENSE AS A midday sun, caused beads of perspiration to bud on my skin and run in rivulets down the curves of my face and body, yet I did not move even to wipe my eyes. I remained fixed, unmoving, waiting for my abductor's response.

Hades himself showed no indication of feeling the heat, with the hood of his cloak now resting on his shoulders, his face exposed to me. Had he stood straight, his height and stature could have rivaled Zeus. Yet the King of the Dead was far from the imposing figure of his brother. The way his shoulders curved felt learned, a concerted effort to minimize his presence.

"Explain yourself," I said again, a fraction more quietly. His own reluctance stealing my fervor. Yet no matter how faintly I spoke, I was determined, and when I folded my hands across my chest, I saw the resignation cross his face.

Hades's words came out as stutters and broken sentences, constantly dipping in volume, every now and then becoming entirely inaudible as if they were obscured by a great distance or a raging wind. But there was no great distance between us, and even with the light winds, I could hear the clattering of metal and occasional shouts inside the palace. I dared not dwell on them.

"Zeus." That was the first word he said intelligibly. Although it was still so quiet, I repeated it to him.

"Zeus?" I pressed the great god's name in the hope it might spur more words from the God of the Underworld, but his eyes were still trained on his feet. "Zeus allowed you to take me?" I pushed again, hoping that such direct questions may garner a response faster. Though Hades did not speak, his head jerked down in a nod. Fear surged in me. Fear, which I fixed in the clench of my jaw before I spoke again.

"For what purpose? For what purpose did Zeus allow you to take me?"

The frown line deepened between Hades's eyebrows. A deep crevice that reminded me of the gaping mouth I had fallen into. He cocked his head to the side.

"As my wife," he said.

As his wife.

Why laughter was my response, I do not know. I certainly did not choose it to make light of my situation. Nor to mock Hades. But once that first titter had escaped on my breath, air rolled from me faster and faster until I could not stop. Great bellyaching laughter rocked from my lungs, echoing in the great cavern around me until it was not only my voice I heard, but a chorus of my own echoes. Tears accompanied my laughter, and I think even now that it may have been a moment of insanity. Perhaps I was due one after all I had been through. Gradually, though, when my laughter diminished to a throaty chortle, Hades spoke again.

"I... I... I thought he would tell you." So many pauses

punctuated between his words, and my laughter filled them all. "He is your father. I believed he had told you."

"My father? He is the man who raped my mother. The only fatherly action he has done for me is leaving my mother to raise me. I am no daughter of his."

Hades's jaw wobbled wordlessly, bobbing up and down in search of words as he wrung his large hands out in front of him. "Demeter, then. He would have told Demeter? He must have told her of our impending marriage?"

At this, my laughter rose. I did not mean to sound so cruel, but the naivety with which he spoke, it reminded me...it reminded me of myself. Of how ignorant I was in my knowledge of the earth. I stemmed my laughter and drew in a lungful of the tar-rich scalding air, restraining my bitterness the best I could.

"My mother has not spoken to Zeus since the day he killed her lover. Centuries ago. Millennia, even. She does not leave her island. And he does not deign to visit."

At these words, Hades's confusion was replaced by something deeper than concern. Fear of my mother, perhaps? Of some form of retribution, at least. Whatever it was, I saw weakness and pounced.

"You must take me back now," I said. "I am not yours. I am not free to be given. I am not some mortal whose life can be bartered for cows and coins. You need to return me. Now."

For an instant, I watched him consider what I had said, and the smallest glimmer of hope flickered within me.

For the first time since he had taken me, his back straightened, and his gaze locked on mine. His eyes were deep, the same color of obsidian from which his palace was made.

He shook his head, frown lines once again formed on his pinched brow. It was not a simple shake, but a rapid motion, as if he was trying to dislodge an uncomfortable thought from his mind.

"No. I cannot. You must stay, that way you will see."

"See what?"

"The reason for this marriage. My love for you."

Perhaps that would have been the time for laughter. It was the most humorous thing I had ever had the misfortune of hearing, and certainly as ridiculous a joke as even the nymphs could tell. But there was no joy. No laughter to be found.

"Love me? You do not know me. I have never even spoken to you."

"That is not true." He took a step toward me, animated. "On... on Olympus. When you lived upon Olympus. I visited. I visited to speak to Zeus. I saw you; I saw you and your mother. You were singing." I waited. Tension pricking my skin as I anticipated the great revelation. The recount of some deep and meaningful conversation that had somehow been stripped from my mind. But what he said was, "You smiled at me."

"I smiled?" I whispered.

"And then you bid me a good day."

I pressed my hand against my head, certain I would feel the type of fever that sends humans into a delirium, for what could this be, if not an insanity of the mind?

"I have not lived upon Olympus for millennia," I said, exasperated. "I cannot have spoken more than three words to you." A polite greeting. That was all I imagined it could be, for I could not even remember that moment, yet I saw in his eyes the earnestness with which he spoke, and I softened only slightly. "What you think you feel for me is not love. Do you understand that? You do not love me."

I watched his lips part and waited for those jagged dislocated words to stutter toward me in an apology. An admission of regret and anguish that would see him return me instantly to the meadow from which I was taken, for already I believed I had a gauge of this god. Not of his strength, but of his weaknesses and of the insecurities that plagued him. But rather than an apology, he grabbed at his hair and paced back and forth, muttering to himself. "This is not how it was supposed to be. This is not how it was supposed to be." The words rattled around him, softly, like the pattering of his feet. As he pounded the earth, I studied my surroundings, hoping, naively, that a chance to escape might make itself apparent, but such a thing did not occur.

When Hades finally stopped his pacing, he turned to face me. He was nodding slowly, forcefully.

"Do you know of my sister Hera?" he said.

"Hera?" The question seemed so absurd, I could not discern where he hoped to go with this, yet he took my response as confirmation to continue.

"Hera had no love for Zeus before they were married. She was against the union, but now it is she who fights most fiercely for it. It is she who is most devoted to her husband."

My confusion only deepened at his response. Hera? The epitome of the jealous wife. To say she had given me a wide berth when I lived upon Olympus would be to grossly underestimate her response to my presence, for she avoided even being in the same room as me. Any relationship she and my mother had shared dissolved the moment of my conception. Could this abduction somehow be revenge on her part? It would not be the first time she had punished one of her husband's offspring for his misgivings.

"Hera, is she the one who told you to do this?" I questioned, trying to understand why Hades would feel the need to speak of her. Yet again, he was shaking his head, clutching at his scalp.

"No, no. That is not what I mean. That is not…" He stopped again, only inches away from me. "I mean, their love grew. Her love for him grew. Love can grow. She wanted nothing of him, and now she weeps every time he isn't faithful to her." Had I had known how he would act next, I would have moved quickly, but his actions were as unexpected as the apparent marriage that I had found myself in. He dropped to his knees and grabbed my hands. I tugged, trying to pull myself out of his grip, but it only fastened. "That could be us. Only I would not be unfaithful. Never. I would never disrespect you the way Zeus has with Hera. Let me show you. Let me prove my love. And in time, you, too, will love me."

The enfeeblement from the God of the Underworld emboldened me. With a sharp tug, I pulled my hands from his grip and pushed my shoulders back.

"If you truly love me, as you say, then you will return me now."

Yes, my tone was harsh, yet his actions thus far had led me to believe he would be far more biddable than rumors I had heard of him. Immediately, he stood, his eyes flashing with a fury I recognized from my father. His face sharpened, his chin jutting forward, and with a flick of his hand, he snatched his hood back over his head.

"You are my queen. Your stay here is not negotiable." And with those words, he turned on his heel and marched into the palace.

CHAPTER FIFTY-FIVE

I WOULD LOVE TO WRITE THAT AS HADES MARCHED INTO HIS palace, I snatched the reins of the black steeds, clambered upon that golden chariot, and drove those horses all the way up to the Land of the Living myself. Perhaps you are thinking that my strength, as a daughter of Zeus and Demeter, would cast itself forward in some magnificent manner that allowed the roots of the trees to burst downward, smashing into the Underworld before coiling around me and pulling me up to safety, knocking aside my captor and all those who aided him in the same long sweep.

It would have offered a romantic end to the tale, to see Hades's palace fading into the distance behind me, that day just a juncture of my eternity. But I knew my predicament could not be solved by rash actions. I did not possess such a power nor even the strength or skill to contemplate managing his immortal horses. I did not hold Hades's scepter and would not be able to open the Earth and return to the Land of the Living. Even I, who had spent so long isolated from other gods, knew that there was only one way for me to leave the Underworld: with Hades's blessing. And so, with a final glance upward, to where the sky should have been, I followed him into his palace.

Hundreds of pairs of eyes watched me as I walked toward the palace gates. I could not tell who they belonged to. Servants, attendants, aids to the dead? Wraiths? Warriors? I did not know, but I made sure that I did not lower my head as I walked. No, I let their eyes fix on me. I allowed their stares to strengthen my resolve. *Look,* I wished to spit at them. *Look for as long as you wish, for you will not see me again.*

And yet, with all those words of courage, there was a truth I could not ignore. A notion so chilling it beat down every hopeful thought I had. *Zeus had granted me to Hades. Zeus had given me as a wife. Why?*

At the palace gates, Hades retrieved a ring of tarnished brass keys from his cloak. The selection jangled in his hand, some as thin as a wire, whereas others were as thick as a man's bone.

"You will not wander outside the palace alone. For now at least," he said, turning a key in the lock. The gate ground open, the creaking groan of the metal sending a shudder deep into my core.

The palace opened into a portico, where light from oil lamps battled the darkness of the obsidian. My eyes were well adjusted to the dark, and I saw clearly what awaited me. Knowing there was no choice, I followed Hades inside.

My sense of smell was attacked within the first footsteps. The odor, which I had expected to be fetid and overwhelming, was certainly pungent, though not in the manner I had anticipated. Aromas of rot and decay were entirely absent, with much sweeter scents in their place. Burnt-orange flames released a bitter yet not unpleasant fragrance of citrus fruits—clementines, grapefruits. Aromas that I would have never suspected in such a place. Mint, in all its forms, thickened the air. The aromatic coolness of the herb almost overpowering, yet it was subdued by the dense pollens that eddied in the motes. For only a fraction later than the aromas hit, I laid my eyes on the scenes that stretched out into the palace. Barely a fraction of the obsidian was visible beneath the blanket of flowers that smothered the walls. More flowers than in the meadows of Eleusis.

It was not natural, the way that flowers grew in our home in Siphnos or on any of the lands I had visited. There was nothing organic or haphazardly wonderful. No, it was unearthly. Too pristine. Too ordered. But that is not to say that it was not beautiful. Manicured, yes, but beautiful. The pillars of the portico had been wrapped around from floor to ceiling. Green vines spiraled upward, the large leaves covered with blooms. Transfixed, I studied the purple flowers, the petals of which turned outward to reveal a deep golden stamen. While I did not have my mother's knowledge of flowers, I did not believe these to be native to any island in Hellas. The vines and blooms together continued their path upward until they reached the ceiling, where they created a canopy above us.

"Does it meet your approval?" Hades said. I had not realized I had stepped away from him. My hand, which was currently reaching out toward one of the flowers, snapped back to my side.

"Meet with my approval? This is prison. You have taken me to a prison."

He stuttered, shaking his head as if he could beat my words away "The f-flowers. You love flowers. There are more. Here, here, this is for you too." He took me by the wrist and pulled me deeper into the palace. Never had I faced such an action before. Never had I been so dumbfounded or confused. Flowers? In exchange for abduction? It was as macabre as it was ridiculous.

In a large hall, he twisted me around so that I was forced to face his throne. Only his throne was not alone. No, beside it sat another, equal in height and prominence, the only distinguishing feature the flowers that adorned It.

"This is your throne," Hades said, his lips twitched in a smile as he misconstrued my silence for one of glee. "This is where we will rule together."

"Rule the Underworld?"

That was when my knees buckled.

CHAPTER FIFTY-SIX

P ROMETHEUS WOULD TESTIFY TO THE PAIN THAT A GOD CAN
suffer. I cannot imagine the torture he endured as that eagle
relentlessly fed upon his liver. Day after day, pulling the
flesh, stripping it from his bones and muscles, only for the wound
to heal and the agony to continue. I would not dare to compare
the throbbing that pulsed in my skull when I woke to the suffering
that Prometheus endured at the hands of Zeus, but suffice it to say,
when I opened my eyes, the pain I felt was more acute than a simple
headache, though why it was there, I did not recall at first.

The differences in my surroundings struck me slowly and
subtly; the texture of the sheets, the silk—slipping over my legs as I
moved to sit upward—was thinner and lighter than that on my bed
on Siphnos. And the intense aroma of mint so much stronger than
home. Then, there were the sounds. Every morning of my existence
I had woken to birdsong. Every morning on Siphnos, waves lapped
over pebbles as the tunes of thrushes and blackbirds roused me from
a slumber. But no birdsong met my ears. No hint of life at all.

The memories of my abduction hit me square and fast.

"No!" I scrambled onto my hands and knees, the black silk sliding beneath my fingers. My pulse raced. I was on a bed. A marriage bed. Scampering onto the pillows, I pulled my knees up to my chest, fighting the urge to gag as I pressed a hand against my belly. Had he taken me? Had Hades dumped me on this bed to violate me while I was too weak to protest? Why would he not? It would be no different from how his brother had taken my mother. The dizziness was swirling again. My vision narrowing, a blackness seeping in around the edges of what I could see. Digging my nails into my thighs, I forced myself to feel the pain that emanated from my own grasp. Whatever had occurred, I could not change it, but I would not allow myself to become vulnerable again. That was the thought I held on to. I would not become vulnerable again. I would not. With that one thought repeating over and over, I forced my breath to deepen, slowly at first, and then to a point where I could open my eyes and view the situation with some degree of objectivity.

There was no doubt the room had been prepared for a marriage night. Vases upon vases of flowers—many already wilting—surrounded the gilded bed, and yet there were no bruises upon my skin. No tenderness in my flesh. No pain within my stomach that might occur had a god as powerful as Hades placed his seed within me. After a few more moments, I was certain he had not yet taken what he had considered his, though the thought offered little comfort. He would come for me in here, and there was no way I could escape. All I could do was prepare. I pulled the silk sheet up over my knees and held it there. My heart knocked against my ribs. My breath hollow as the fear caused my hands to tremble. I would be prepared.

Steeling myself with the same grit and false confidence I had shown when I entered the palace, I swept my gaze around the room, searching. I did not know what it was I was looking for. Only that I would know it once I saw it. A large copper bath glinted at one end of the room, while on the table by the bed were amphorae filled with wine and water. Next to those stood a table with a large, mirrored glass and countless brushes and combs, no doubt for me to primp and prime myself as my husband desired. The thought was enough to draw my attention back to the amphorae and vases.

Smashing one would provide me with a shard that I could defend myself with. But from what? I would not kill the god of the Underworld with a piece of pottery. Even a mortal would not be foolish enough to consider that. But what other option did I have? I would not be like Danae in her tower, kept away from the world. Worse even, for at least Danae felt the sunlight as it streamed through the opening in her roof. She could feel the coolness of rain as it fell onto her, in all its forms, and bask in the morning birdsong. Danae remained in the Land of the Living. Whereas I was with the dead. Alive in a glorified tomb.

With my mind now more focused on my immediate situation, new questions arose. How long had I been in this room? Had Hades maintained a watch over me? Were there slaves waiting outside the door who would barge in and restrain me if I attempted to leave? I strained to hear, but other than distant groans and creaks long beyond the palace, I could hear very little. The silence inched its way under my skin. Prickling me. Tormenting me. Was I meant to wait here until summoned? The feelings of immurement rose within me again and with it a newfound strength. I had not spent decades fighting for my freedom only for it to be snatched from me again without a fight.

Steeled with a new energy, I swung my legs from the bed, plucked a small cup from the table beside me, and wrapped the pottery in the silken fabric of the bedsheets. After one final listen beyond the chamber, I raised my hand and slammed the cloth-covered cup into the wall. The thud was soft, muffled by the fabric, but the structure of the cup collapsed beneath my grip. Edging back to the table, I opened the fabric, studied the broken fragments, and selected a single shard—small enough to be concealed within my grip, but long enough to pierce through a throat or eye.

I do not know how long I stayed there, that shard of pottery digging into my skin. There was no dawn chorus to announce the day had begun. No sheaths of sunlight to splinter through the clouds and bring about Eos's painted dawn. There was nothing other than myself and the creaks and whistles of this world I had been dragged into. Still, I clasped that shard long enough to draw blood, which fell drop by drop, only for its color to be lost in the darkness of the silk sheet. He was waiting; I was certain of it. Waiting for the moment I dropped my guard. Then he would attack. Then he would bound through the door, ready to pin me and take me. But I was ready, and I would not let that happen.

It is hard to say how long I waited in that room. At times I thought a day must have passed or even a year. And yet the incident of the earth opening was as fresh as if it had been mere minutes before. With every sound, my tension tightened. I jolted and started, the skin on my knuckles stretched so tight that my bones shone white beneath them. Never did my gaze waver from that doorway. Yet no one stepped through it. Not once did the door budge, even by the smallest fraction. He was not coming for me. So I had no choice. I had to go to him.

CHAPTER FIFTY-SEVEN

I HEADED STRAIGHT, IGNORING THE TWISTS AND TURNS OF THE corridors for fear I would not find my chamber should I wish to return at haste. Around me, lamps offered a smokeless glow that, when stared at directly, was as bright as daylight. Polished mosaics glinted on the floor while the shard of pottery remained concealed in my hand. Even though my steps were tentative, I knew exactly where I was heading, and it did not take me long to find it: the throne room.

He did not see me at first. He sat upon his throne, his fingers steepled, his gaze lost in the space where his fingertips and thumbs met. He was not wearing his cloak. Nor was the scepter in his hand. There was no indication of his helm—gifted to him by the Cyclops to allow him the gift of invisibility—and wore none of the gold that he, as ruler of all the world's hidden wealth, owned. Had I seen him in passing, I would not have presumed this unsuspecting man was God of the Underworld. For he appeared little more than a shepherd or a farmer.

"I did not know you were awake. I would have sent someone to help you," he said, without raising his head. "Did you find everything you need? Did you bathe?"

The question sounded earnest, though it could easily have been rhetorical, for as I glanced down at my hands, I saw the mud and dirt from clawing at the earth was embedded beneath my nails. My robe, which had been pristine and white when I left Siphnos, was now in tatters around the hem, the mud staining in streaks on the thin fabric.

"It...it does not matter," he said quickly, raising his head to face me. "Come, join me. You must be hungry. I have had food prepared." He stood up from his throne and walked the length of the hall. Wordlessly, I followed him through to a small antechamber where a table big enough for all the gods of Olympus was laid out with food. Fruit, meat, salted cheeses. My mouth salivated at the sight. Yet I did not take a seat.

"How long was I in that room?" It was the first words I had spoken to him, but rather than respond, he picked up a platter and placed pieces of food onto it. "How long?" I said again, more pointedly. This time, he raised his head to look at me.

"How long?" he asked.

"Hours? A day? How long have I been down here?"

His lips moved before he spoke. "I...I am not sure. Does time matter?"

"Does time matter?" His question was so obtuse, yet he seemed truly puzzled by it. He was more like a child bewildered by the rising and setting of the sun than a god.

"Yes, yes, time matters," I said. "Time always matters." Thoughts of my mother floated through my mind and knotted my insides. Even after all the decades I wandered with the nymphs, she would start pacing the earth the instant the sky colored with the sunset, for fear I would not return. And this time, I had not. A deeper compression squeezed me tightly within. "It matters."

Hades nodded solemnly, though did not reply immediately.

"Will you sit?" he said after a moment. "If things are not to your satisfaction, I can arrange an alternative meal. Perhaps you would rather have wine than water? Or ambrosia?"

"I am not hungry," I said, looking down at the filled plate and ignoring the gnawing in my gut. The thought of dining with him repulsed me. However polite and genial, he was my abductor and captor. He stared at me, and turned his gaze toward the food before it came back again to me.

"Will you not have a morsel?"

This time, I did not grant him a reply. Tension wrapped itself around us, like the vines on the pillars of the portico. His tension, I noted, as much as mine.

"I will find out about the time for you. Someone here will know," he said after a pause, his voice cracking as he drove away the silence that was blooming. "Until then, there are fields here where you can pluck flowers, if you wish to do so. The Elysian Fields. You like to pluck flowers, I know. I can take you there myself. You will find everything you dream of them. More flowers than even Olympus. More than you could find in Cythera and Eleusis combined. You could make garlands for eternities with what I have for you here."

He was animated now, finding his stride with his words, yet I broke his streak, for what he said made me nauseous.

"You have seen me. Watched me," I said, cutting across him.

"I…I saw you in Olympus." He fumbled. The stuttering returned. "I saw you in Zeus's palace garden. Making garlands there."

His eyes avoided mine.

"You are lying. I did not pluck flowers from Zeus's garden and certainly would never have woven garlands from something that had been in his possession. My mother would have forbidden it, even if he had grown the most perfect blooms in all of Hellas. You have watched me. You have watched me since I left there."

As I spoke, I knew it was the truth. He would not have found himself so enamored after one meeting too fleeting for me to recollect. But if he had watched me, watched me in my wanderings, silent and hidden, cloaked by his helmet, then that would offer something more in the way of explaining his infatuation.

"Tell me," I said, garnering the strength of my mother and father combined. "Have you watched me?"

Hades's fists were clenched at his side, and for a heartbeat, I feared I had misjudged him and that he would storm out, the way he had done by the horses, or worse still, turn his anger to me. But he did not.

"Once. I watched you once with your nymphs, plucking flowers. Only the once."

"My nymphs?"

He nodded. "There were three of them. And you were dancing together, holding hands. And singing. You...you wore the garlands as you laughed."

I stepped back, both relieved by his truthfulness and horrified by this invasion of my privacy. I could not guess when that had been. There had been countless incidents when we had behaved in such a manner, but not in recent years. Not since I had begun wandering on my own.

"And since then. Have you watched me since then?"

He shook his head rapidly. "On my honor as your husband, it was not deliberate, I assure you. I stumbled on your presence by accident. Though I will confess I stayed and watched longer than I should."

I could hear the truth now as easily as the lies before. If Zeus had been in possession of such a helmet, I dread to think what situations he would have infiltrated himself into. Gone would be his less than subtle ways of changing into a snake or a swan to trick his victims. Oh, how his voyeurism would have been free to run rampage. Not that it didn't already. Yet Hades had merely watched me. Wanted me and watched me.

"I swear, on my honor," he repeated. "I know that means little to you now. But beloved, I swear I will prove myself to you. I will prove to you that I am a good man."

He reached out to take my hand, but I pulled away from him. For his part, he did not attempt to grab me again, though perhaps he would have done, had we not been interrupted.

"My lord, you are needed."

The voice caused Hades and I to turn simultaneously to the doorways where one of his servants, Ceuthonymus, slunk into the room.

With a long sniff, Hades cast off the reticence he had shown to me. His voice was sharp, the fraying edge of a temper apparent in his tone.

"Now is not a good time," he said. "I will find you when I am done."

Had Zeus, or any other god of Olympus spoken to a servant in such a manner, the lower being would have scuttled off before they took another breath, but Ceuthonymus did not move.

"This is important, my lord."

"I said—"

"I am not hungry…" I interrupted, longing for my solace as much as Ceuthonymus longed for his master's attention. "You must see to your needs. My presence here should not affect that."

With a deep inhale and purse of his lips, Hades nodded at me, before pushing himself back up from the table.

"I will be as swift as I can," he said. "Please, treat this home as your own. There are clean robes in your chamber. And oils for the bath. I will see that it is run for you now."

And before I could say another word, he strode toward the door.

CHAPTER FIFTY-EIGHT

After Hades's departure, I was swift to return to my chamber, though not before collecting a simple platter of food. I would not eat in his presence, under his watch, and dine like true husband and wife would, yet I would not deny myself the pleasure of food either. That was my thought, though, when I reached my chamber, my appetite evaded me. Perhaps I would pick at some fruit later, I considered. Though when would later be? I was still no closer to knowing how long I had been there. I knew only too well how the years of gods and mortals weaved and tangled with no consistency. Perhaps I had already been gone a decade? Perhaps the sun was only just setting up on the Land of the Living and my mother only now beginning to pace the ground as she waited. I continued to contemplate a question I had no answer to while staring at the intricate fresco on the ceiling, when a knock on the door roused me from my thoughts.

I sat upward, this act of privacy alien to me after so many centuries on Siphnos. A few seconds later, the sound came again.

"Come in," I said with all the confidence I could muster. The door creaked open, and though I did not recognize the face who stepped into my chamber, I knew without doubt that I was staring at a nymph.

"Excuse me, my queen. You have a visitor," she said.

"A visitor?" I made no attempt to hide the surprise in my voice. "I think you are mistaken."

With bent knees, she bowed her head.

"Forgive me, my queen, but I am not. They have asked for you by name and they are waiting in the throne room."

The title of queen addled me, but the nymph looked fearful enough without me rebuking her for the false title.

"I will be there shortly," I replied.

Time, of course, is an abstract concept to most gods, but I will confess, I waited longer than good manners would necessitate. Was this some kind of trick by Hades, I considered. For who would travel to the Underworld to see me? In all my centuries on earth and before then on Olympus, I had never once received a visitor.

Despite my confusion, I was aware that my current attire was not fitting to greet anyone, even in the Land of the Dead. And so, while this unknown guest waited, I stripped from my soiled robe and stepped into the bath. My knees and shins were covered with the same black dirt that caked my nails. My hair was sticking to my face, and small stones were stuck deep into the soles of my feet.

I could count the number of baths I had taken in my eternal life. The number of times I had submerged my body into a stagnant pool. After all, how could such an experience compare to the running bubbles of a fresh spring, as minnows darted around my feet? Yet that bath was luxury. Lavender eddied around me. The scents of rose petals seeped into my skin. And then, by choice, I closed my eyes.

When I opened them again, the water continued to steam,

although the rose petals and lavender had clustered at the edges of the tub. I dipped back below the surface, rinsing my skin clear before standing up and taking the towel that was placed on a stool beside me. Only when I was dry did I realize that I was without clothes.

It was then that I saw the chest of dark wood with a brass clasp placed in the corner of the room. Hades had thought about flowers and oils in the bath. It seemed unlikely he would have neglected clothes for me to wear.

My hunch proved correct, although what I found was unlike anything I had seen before. In the Land of the Living, I had worn only white pelops. A standard sign of the purity with which my mother and the world viewed me. Core. Maiden. Yet not a hint of white glimmered in these piles of silken fabric. Deep reds, dark browns, blacks even. Colors of the Underworld were all I found.

I hesitated, the darkness alien to my eyes. What would it mean if I were to wear such an item? That I was succumbing to Hades's desire to make me queen? No, I shook my head at the thought. I was surviving this place, while I figured a way to escape it. I picked a garment of midnight blue and wrapped it around me. Cut perfectly to measure. The fabric finished at my ankles so that I did not trip as I walked. When it was tied, I opened another chest. A smaller one. Jewelry, the likes of which I had never seen, spilled outward. Broaches and necklaces. Bangles and earrings. Gold and silvers inlaid with garnets and rubies and ambers and as many gemstones as I could hope to view in a lifetime. I studied them for a minute, as mesmerized as I would be by a field of flowers, before closing the lid. I would accept his clothes, yes, but not these other gifts. Clothes were a necessity. Gems were not. Whoever the visitor was, I was as ready as I could hope to be to greet them. With my heart hammering, I headed to the throne room, my feet already having learned the route.

Her back was turned to me, and all that was visible was the back of her long cloak. Yet as I cleared my throat, she turned to face me.

"You are not harmed."

A visible sense of relief washed over her face, as she buried her head swiftly in her hands before regaining her composure.

"No, I am not harmed," I said, struggling to understand who, or what, I was seeing. The woman herself was confusing, for she bore no signs of physical age. I could have been looking at a young maiden or an old crone. Her image seemed to change constantly, being at once both and neither.

Sensing my confusion, she stepped forward and cupped my cheeks with her hand.

"I am friends with your mother," the woman said. "She sent me to check on you."

"Friends with my mother? My mother has no friends." I replied. Perhaps it was impudent to say such a thing, particularly before I had even inquired of her name, but I would not be fooled by trickery. "Or at least no friends that we have seen in the last millennia in our isolation."

"It is a new friendship indeed," she replied. "Although I can assure you it is true. We met while she was searching for you. She called for me to help her, and I came. Just as I have come here to help you." It was then I knew who stood before me. Someone who could travel between the Land of the Living and the Land of the Dead. Someone who Hades would allow into his home. Someone old and powerful.

"You are Hecate," I responded. Hecate the witch. Hecate, older than even my grandfather and whose renown was so great that even Hades would not dare dispute her presence here. Hecate had come to my aid.

"I am, Goddess. And I am so very honored to meet you."

I did not know whether to laugh or cry. Like all children regardless of age, I had wished that somehow my mother would be able to sweep in and save me from this fate, but how? How could someone who did not wish to leave her home possibly rescue me from the Underworld? And yet she had found a way. Beyond all faith I had had in her, she had found a way to reach me.

"How is my mother?" I imagined her shriveled up, weeping at the sea, the nymphs' arms wrapped around her, unable to offer her comfort. I assumed Hecate had been drawn by my mother's grief and unceasing wailing. Yet my perceptions were swiftly proved wrong.

"She has been strong. Fearless, although her journey to meet me has not been without pain. We met in Eleusis. That was where she was looking for you."

I frowned.

"You are confused. You must mean Siphnos? My mother is fearful of all places beyond our island."

Hecate offered a small, wry smile.

"That may have been the case before, but I can assure you she has traveled to a great many places in search of you. She will not rest until you are returned to her. Neither of us will."

This proclamation was nearly as unfathomable as me attending to a guest in the palace of Hades. My mother had left Siphnos? Glee lifted my heart, only to be replaced by a sudden terror. Her journey was unlikely to have been without pain. What state would she be in when I returned? If I returned.

"Daughter," Hecate said, placing her hands upon mine and lowering her voice, while swiftly casting a gaze around the hall. "Tell me, have you eaten since you have been here?"

"Eaten? No." I shook my head. The platter of fruit that I had taken to my chamber remained untouched.

She glanced around us. "Good. Do not. The food in this place is the food of the dead. You will be trapped for eternity should you consume it. Now, I cannot stay. Your mother needs me, but tell me, can you stay strong? She will see that you are released from here. I promise you. She will fight Zeus himself for your return. Now tell me, is there anything you need?"

I shook my head again, feeling the prick of tears sting behind my eyes. "Must you leave me so soon? Can you not stay a little longer?"

The witch scanned behind her, her eyes lingering on the doorway. Eyes that some believed could see the past, present, and future. With a small smile, her gaze came back to me. "I must leave. But I will return. Soon. I promise I will return soon."

CHAPTER FIFTY-NINE

URING THOSE FIRST WEEKS IN THE UNDERWORLD, I learned that a day is marked by more than the rising and the setting of the sun. There are, after all, parts of the earth where the sun will shine constantly, without a hint of fading, or where it will fail to rise above the horizon for more than but a few hours. For Hades, and those of us within the palace, night and day in the Underworld were dictated, quite simply, by food.

As in the Land of the Living, breads and porridges were placed out in the dining room for the first meal of the day, while beings retreated to slumber once the largest meal of fish and legumes had been consumed. Though I had no need or desire for the foods, I, too, fell into the rhythm dictated by these meals. I rose with the clattering of the breakfast bowls, then spent my waking wandering the palace grounds, longing for the hours when I could return to my chamber and close my eyes.

Hecate's departure struck me deeply. Her absence—the absence of a woman I did not even know—caused a gaping hole to arise in my heart. And yet, in that hole was a spark of hope. My mother was coming for me. She had braved the lands beyond Siphnos. If Hecate was to be believed, Demeter would brave Zeus himself, and she would have to secure my freedom, for it was Zeus himself who had gifted me to Hades.

Hades had forbidden me to leave the palace grounds until I was more accustomed to my new home, yet there was plenty to keep me occupied inside the boundaries of the moat. For hours I gazed at the white poplars, which swayed lazily back and forth despite the lack of breeze. Of course, it was not the poplar trees that held my attention so intently but the wraiths that drank from the lake beside them. For each of them, I would imagine a story. Their past life. Their past loves. Their birth and death. Hour after hour, I spent weaving these souls a history that existed only in my head. One was a tradesman, whose ship had been blown off course and steered into the Strait of Messina, where he and all the crew had been devoured by Scylla. Another was a farmer, whose love of wine had seen him take a tumble from which he never rose. Not all the tales were so morose. For some I wove long lives, filled with the type of love I did not believe I had ever known. I gave them children. Grandchildren. Friends who wept at their death. My mind and my imagination were my greatest source of comfort. My mind, my imagination, and my powers.

The desire to play with my strength came early one morning, upon my stroll toward the lake. A large vine crawled up the outside of the palace. Deep green, with a purple hue, the leaves were gargantuan, but the plant itself was without a single bloom. I had passed the same vines before, but that morning I decided to act. To wield it to my will.

With no indication of how Hades would respond to my interfering with the flora of his world, the adjustment I made was small. Barely a dozen minute black flowers scattered the length of the vine, but each time I passed, I added more and made them larger and more vibrant. Perhaps it was some kind of test, not only of myself but of Hades. To see how far I could transform this palace with my blooms before he confronted me on the matter. But he did nothing. Even when I added thorns to the vines and bright white flowers as big as dinner plates that gleamed like the catkins on the pillars, he did not mention them. For Hades did not give up his desire to charm me.

I do not know how long I had been in the Land of the Dead when we were seated in the courtyard together, as had become common. The open space was far grander than my home on Siphnos, and even Olympus, and offered us ample room to keep a distance.

Since Hecate's visit, Hades had not offered me a morsel of food or even suggested that I join him in the dining hall. Perhaps he hoped I would choose to eat with him of my own volition, but despite the courteous manner, he was still my captor.

As we sat in separate corners of the courtyard, my attention was occupied by a dark purple bloom that I had never encountered before.

"I wonder if I would find you in the Land of the Living," I said, stroking the delicate petals and inhaling the aroma they released. "You would look beautiful in a crown in Peisinoe's hair." I imagined the nymphs, how they were aiding my mother in her search for me, keeping her company while Hecate went about her travels.

"You are lonely." Hades's voice caused me to start. "You are lonely here."

His casual tone did not irk me as greatly as the fact that Hades had approached *my side* of the courtyard without an invitation.

"Are you surprised?" I said, seeing no need to bite my tongue. "How could I not be lonely? I have no one here to talk to."

"You have me. I am always here for you. But I understand you do not view our relationship in that manner. I wish you to know I told the witch Hecate that she was welcome to stay as your companion, if you so desired. But it was your choice. Your decision. I will not thrust her presence on you if you do not wish for it. However, if you would like, we could summon her immediately."

Summon her immediately. I did not doubt he had the power to do such a thing, but it was the way he said *we* that caused me to hesitate. My powers, like my experience of life, had been bound by the limitations my mother had placed on us both. How great would I be if those binds were lifted? I could but dream.

In the silence that followed, I dismissed Hades's offer. Hecate had told me a truth; she needed to return to be with my mother. Besides, if the witch spoke the truth, there would be no need for company at all. I would be released soon enough.

"That is a generous offer," I answered. "Perhaps you will allow me to think on it."

"I do not need to allow you to do anything. This is your home. Your kingdom. You have as much sway here as I do. Or at least you will in time."

His eyes moved away from me as his hands fidgeted with his robe. I barely knew him, yet already I had learned so many of his mannerisms. There was something he wished to say to me. Something that pushed the limits of his comfort. Ruling the dead he could do without a second's thought, but an intimate conversation with a goddess was well beyond his skills. Dread lurched in my stomach as I feared this was to be the night he asked to take me to his bed. After all, he would not wait forever. Every night, I feared he would wake me to take what he thought of as his. And though that night had not yet come, I was certain his patience would not last forever. I stiffened, tension gripping my muscles as I prepared for his words.

"I…I thought perhaps you would like me to take you to see your kingdom," he said, his lips pursing so much between his words, they were near inaudible.

"Sorry?"

"Our kingdom." He straightened his back and spoke with a little more self-assurance. "You have seen nothing but the inside of the palace and the poplar trees. There is a great deal of beauty here. Perhaps as much as you will find in the Land of the Living. I hope to show it to you, so in time, you will learn your way to travel these lands yourself."

My thoughts snapped to a single answer. *I do not need to learn my way. I will be gone soon.* But given the request I had expected him to make of me, it felt churlish to refuse such a simple offer.

"I would appreciate that," I said.

That was the first time I saw the God of the Underworld smile. Truly and genuinely. It was his first smile in my presence, and from the stiffness of his cheeks, I wondered if it was the first smile he had ever formed, at least in the presence of another. The thought caused a light chuckle to leave my lips.

Immediately Hades's face fell.

"Something has amused you? You are mocking me."

"No, no," I said hurriedly. "Not at all. I was merely thinking…" I did not know how to word myself. Desperately, I wished for my mind to think of a lie. To think of a way to cover the truth from him, but there was none.

"Yes?" he pressed.

With a steeling breath, I locked my eyes squarely on his.

"I was thinking how strange it was to see you smile."

If any comment could have caught him by surprise, this was it. The god's eyes bulged from his head, and I feared he had taken my words so badly that he would rescind his offer immediately, but he did not. Instead, he remained with his gaze down a moment longer.

"We shall go to the Elysian Fields. You will find all the flowers you could wish for there. You can make posies and garlands until your heart is content. Whatever flora you wish for, fern or flower, it will be there. I will make sure of it."

"That is very kind," I answered honestly. "But there is something I would rather see first."

"Anywhere, my queen. I will take you anywhere."

I nodded and thought through my answer only briefly before I replied.

"I wish to see the river Styx," I said.

CHAPTER SIXTY

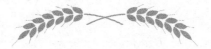

O F ALL THE RIVERS IN THE UNDERWORLD, THE RIVER STYX
is the one the mortals regale the most tales of. The boundary that separates the Land of the Living and the Land
of the Dead. I suspect that is why Hades believed I wished to see it.
To see how close I remained to the land that had been my life for so
long. The land we both knew I longed to return to. But that was not
the only reason I wished to go there. There was something else there
I needed to see.

We walked silently away from the palace and past lakes of deepest
blue. Wraiths and demons alike passed him without acknowledgment. There were no accolades or libations offered to the god. No
trains of nymphs and admirers that followed him. No parades like
his brothers reveled in.

Hades walked by my side, across the Plains of Judgment and
the Vale of Mourning. Soft hillsides with well-trodden paths that
meandered lazily through the soft grasses. By instinct, my hands
brushed against the foliage, and a spray of colors erupted at my
fingertips. A flash of fear struck, as I worried that casting my color

on this place would invoke an anger in Hades, yet he said nothing, even as the blooms spread out in front of us. Even as I let them grow higher and brighter than I ever had in the Land of the Living, for even when I roamed the earth free from chaperone, I feared my mother's rebuke. Her words, about my powers attracting the attention of the other gods, had been so deeply ingrained within me that I never allowed myself the freedom to explore the real strength of my power, the way I started to do that day. From a distance, I heard the great growls of Cerberus and the calls of the kings as they cast their judgments on the dead.

When we reached the river Styx, a boat was approaching us. The Ferryman, Charon, stood at the helm, his punt deep in the water, as he pushed against the riverbed toward us. The small rowing boat would have been full with half a dozen passengers, yet there was nearly double that number clinging to one another. All with a look of fear upon them.

The passengers included several elderly men and women, but also those far younger. One in particular held my attention: a child who sobbed intently. My heart burned for her, but it was a pain that was short lived. She was dead, yes, but fortunate still, for Charon had already pocketed her payment and she was traveling across to Hades's dominion. It was not the ones who made it to this side that I had wanted to see. It was the others.

The other side of the river Styx swarmed. A murmuration of souls, trapped between the Land of the Living and the Land of the Dead, swamped the riverbank. How deep their numbers went, I could not tell: tens? Hundreds? Thousands? It was possible. Shouting and screeching, they pushed and shoved as they clamored forward, grabbing the tattered remnants of one another's robes as they attempted to move closer to the river. Several were knee deep in the water, wading out into the lapis lazuli river, fighting against the currents that Charon had managed with such ease. I stared transfixed as the water pushed them back against their own shore, or worse still, dragged them under. These were the ones who did not have payment for the crossing. Those who had been buried without the coins that Charon required. Or not buried at all. These were destined to spend all eternity in neither place. Trapped in an agonizing existence, never to find peace.

"Do any of them make it?" I asked Hades, gesturing to a young woman. She had been swimming strongly. So much so that she was nearly halfway across, but then a current must have caught her feet from beneath, for she was yanked under the water. When she rose again, coughing and spluttering, she was barely a foot from where she started and lacked the strength to try again.

"No, they cannot make it by swimming. They cross on the boat with the ferryman, or they do not cross at all."

Next, my attention moved to two young children, ankle deep in the water. The pair held on to each other's hands so tightly that, had they still been human, their bones would have shattered. Children. Trapped for all eternity.

"Are there always so many?" I asked. The number was unfathomable. As far as I could see in either direction so far, I suspected the souls might stretch all the way back to the Land of the Living and someday even Olympus itself.

"Their numbers are always ever growing. But currently, they are arriving in droves." He stared outward at the scene, a slight bite on his lower lip. A pause, heavily laden with Hades's unease, settled between us. There was more to this scene than I understood. Certainly enough to unsettle the God of the Underworld. But before I could question what that may be, Hades turned his attention back to me and continued. "When death sweeps through a family, many arrive without payment. Often those who still live are too ill to perform the correct preparation. And those who are alone when they die have no one left to perform the rites."

"Surely there is something you can do for them? It is not right. It is not right that they are not allowed entrance. It is through no fault of their own."

"It is not of my doing. It is their mortal family's responsibility to ensure they are sent with the correct payment to cross."

"So they are forever to be punished for the wrongdoing of their family?"

"Some, yes. It is unfortunate, I agree, but that is the way it has always been, and the way it will always be."

Even in death, mortals were held by the bounds of others. Was it ever possible, then, for one to be truly free, when even in death they were beholden to another?

I had not been aware that Charon's boat had departed until I noticed it approaching the opposite bank. My toes curled as I knew what scene would unfurl. Hundreds of wraiths scrambled over one another, battling and beating their way for a seat on the tiny boat, only to be pushed aside for those who had the coins. This was how it would always be. How it always had been. And it caused a pain so sharp in my chest it was as though my heart had been pierced.

"We should leave now." Though it was my thought, it was Hades's voice that spoke. "You have seen enough."

CHAPTER SIXTY-ONE

I DID NOT RETURN TO THE RIVER STYX AGAIN AFTER THAT DAY, although the images of the wraiths remained etched in my mind. Did time move differently for them? Did it soar like the centuries we passed on Olympus, where an entire mortal's life could pass in the length of a meal? Or did it drag, each hollow rasping breath reverberating around their withered forms?

Soon after, Hecate visited me again, and this time, I greeted her with open arms. Although I found her embrace far colder than expected.

"What is this?" I said, plucking a glimmering snowflake from her hair. "Snow? From where?"

Her eyes twinkled, and even though we were alone, she leaned in closely before she spoke.

"It has grown cold in the Land of the Living," she responded, with an elusiveness I could not place, though I paid it little mind. I thought of what Hades had said at the river Styx: how the dead were arriving in droves, old and young alike. Was this cold something to do with that?

Pushing the thought away, I spoke again to Hecate.

"Can you stay for a while?" I asked her, "or must you return to my mother straightaway?"

The solemnity of her gaze as she glanced at the melting flakes said it all.

"She is suffering?"

"She does not talk of the pain of losing you, but I am fearful. Fearful that even when you do return, a part of her will forever be changed by her actions."

She was already changed, I wanted to tell her. Every incident in my mother's life, whether it had been forced upon her, or she had taken it willingly, had seen her changed. I doubted Demeter would even recognize the young Titan first freed from her father's stomach should she meet her face-to-face.

"You should go to her," I said as I squeezed the witch's hand a little tighter. "Let me walk you to the gate."

At this, it was Hecate's turn to show a modicum of surprise.

"Hades will let you travel that far on your own?"

"It is my kingdom, too. For now."

Together we walked through the palace, but we did not reach the gate, for when we reached the throne room, a crowd was gathered like I had never seen before.

For the first time since I had arrived in Hades, Charon was in attendance in the palace. No longer holding his long punt, or surrounded by a swarm of wraths offering him their coins, he was recognizable from his white bedraggled hair and the shred of fabric that clung to his emaciated frame. But he was not the only unexpected figure in the room.

On the ground by his master's feet, all three heads of Cerberus lay flat against the cold obsidian floor. I had never seen him before, but it was difficult to believe this was the same beast I had heard growling in the distance. His tongues laid out lazily from the sides of his mouths. His stomach rising and falling with a soft gentle breath. He appeared as placid as a farm dog raised from a pup by children, though I made no attempt to test that theory. Perhaps I would have had I not been so distracted by the other figures in attendance.

Three cloaked figures stood tall, their frames, shapes, and faces lost behind the dark sweeps of folded fabric hoods, but I did not need to see them to know who they were; they were the judges of the dead. Those who weighed up the actions of the once living and decided which part of the Underworld the soul should be sent to. They were responsible for condemning the most wicked and vile souls to Tartarus, the same infernal depths where Zeus kept all those he feared or had condemned to suffer an eternity of torture. Those the judges believed were most worthy were sent to the Elysian Fields, and others would remain in the Asphodel Fields. I knew little of these places. I had not yet been permitted to stray far from the palace by myself and truthfully had no inclination to visit. The desire would come, however, far sooner than I had expected.

The judges did not appear to be ascertaining any soul's worth; instead, they were deep in discussion with Hades. Their attention, I noted, rested solely on a man before them. A man dressed in a red robe with oiled hair. In his hand he held a beautifully ornate lyre. Though it was not his hair or instrument that caused me to stifle a gasp as I reached beside me and grabbed Hecate's hand, it was his opacity. Every mortal I had seen in this place was a wraith. Insubstantial in their form. Veil-like in their translucency. And yet this man was as dense and corporeal as the stones of the palace walls.

"He is living?" I whispered. "How? How is a living mortal present in the Land of the Dead?"

Her lips pressed tightly as she observed this stranger with a mixture of curiosity and concern.

"I do not know, Goddess. I do not know."

Our voices were barely whispered, and yet Hades turned to face us. Warmth glimmered in his eyes.

"My queen, I am glad you are here. Come, take your seat. This young man has trespassed from the lands of the living to join us here. He even managed to bribe his way past Charon without payment, I might add." His eyes flickered to the ferryman, and I wondered what punishment would be inflicted for such an indiscretion, for certainly it would not go without notice. "He has come here to plead with me, as King of the Dead, but let him see what my queen thinks of his words. Come, let us listen to him."

For all the time I had spent in the Land of the Dead, this was the first incident in which I had been called upon to act as queen, and I was torn. I could, of course, refuse. Protest that I was not his wife. That I would be leaving him as soon as I could, but I hesitated. I did not wish to humiliate the god, for my own benefit as much as his. I could not imagine how he would respond to me opposing him directly in front of such an audience. And while he did not so much as raise a hand to me, gods and powerful men do not need to dirty their own hands. They have shown that often enough. Should I upset him, I was certain he could punish me. And so wordlessly, I dropped Hecate's hand and trod slowly up to the dais, where I took my place on my throne.

A throne is but a seat, but one with power. Power that coursed through me the instant I took my place. On Olympus, I had never been granted a seat. At the wedding of Harmonia and Cadmus, it was only the twelve most powerful Olympians who had been offered thrones. The rest of us lesser gods were required to mingle with those below us. But here the throne was mine. And not a throne of twelve, but a throne of two. I had not believed Hades when he had said that I would be the ruler of his kingdom with him. I had envisioned myself like Hera or Amphitrite. A wife when required. A burden when not. Certainly never an equal. But as I took my seat, a realization of what all that power could bring struck me. The realization of what I could be. Of what I already was in Hades's eyes. At the thought, a thousand black blooms appeared around our thrones, twisting and tangling them together. Blooms the likes of which I had never created before.

Several pairs of eyes widened at the sight, though not Hades's. Within his eyes I saw a glimmer of a smile meant only for me, and when he crossed the hall and took his seat beside me, he rested his hand on mine and a bolt of energy surged through me. A torrent of power that swelled through my core. I stifled a gasp, closing my eyes as I allowed this strength to crescendo within me. In that moment, I did not feel like the daughter of Demeter. I did not feel like Core, the maiden, whose power was forever kept subdued for fear of the attention it could attract. I felt like a goddess and a queen in my own right. I did not move my hand away.

"Tell me, who are you, and why are you here?" Hades said to the mortal, who had remained gazing absentmindedly at his instrument. Upon being addressed, the man dropped to his knees, holding his lyre a mere fraction off the ground.

"I am Orpheus, son of Oegrus." He looked up from his bowed head as he spoke. "I am a musician. Apollo himself gifted me this lyre, and I have been bestowed by the tuition of the muses. They themselves have spoken of how my gift is as great as they possess."

He paused after this introduction, and Hades's eyebrow arched upward. The silence extended a fraction longer before he spoke.

"A bold claim, indeed. And a lyre from Apollo. Truly impressive, but it does not explain why you are here, Orpheus, son of Oegrus. It does not explain how you persuaded Charon to carry you across the river or why you have tamed my beast and persuaded my judges to lead you here. I assume that you have not come merely to bear witness of my hospitality. You want something."

Fear shone from this mortal, Orpheus, and yet he held steady, and I found myself thinking of my mother's lover, Iasion. The way he had spoken to Zeus at the wedding, before an audience of gods and men. Girded by love, he had possessed unfounded confidence. He had hoped that love, when shown with enough deference, would appease the mighty god. Unfortunately for Iasion, his assumption was proved false. I hoped for Orpheus's sake that his fate was not the same.

"I am a married man," Orpheus continued. "My wife, Eurydice, is the mother of my children. The most gentle and beautiful being that roamed the earth." At this, his eyes darted to me with a flash of fear. I suspect he feared I would dispute this claim. When I did not, he continued, although his pace was quickened. "She was wronged. A man tried to take her. He attempted to force himself upon my beloved. But she fought him. She fought him and she escaped his grasp. Yet her rejoicing was short lived, for as she fled one monster, her mind and heart still racing, she trampled on a serpent. It is the poison of that serpent that brought her here to you. That killed her."

My heart ached. Tears gleamed in this man's eyes as he clutched a curved arm of the lyre. None of us needed to hear any more of the tale. We knew why he had come to the Underworld, yet it was Hades who spoke next.

"You have come here to join her?" he said. "There are far easier ways to reach my land than the journey you have taken. For I am sure you are aware, no person who steps foot in my lands leaves again."

At this comment, I shuddered. Goddess, queen or otherwise, it made no difference. None of us left without Hades's permission. Yet the mortal did not share my response. Instead, he lifted the lyre a little higher and raised himself to his feet.

Orpheus shook his head. "I am sorry, you misunderstand me. I did not come here to join her. I came here to ask you to release her to me. She is young, my lord. She deserves a longer life."

"She deserves a longer life?" Hades punctuated his words. Gone was the stuttering man who greeted me in privacy. Here was the ruler we had heard so much about. "Orpheus…that is your name, is it not? Orpheus, if I granted every soul who *deserved* a longer life the ability to return to the Land of the Living, how many souls do you think I would have here? Tartarus would remain full, of that there is no doubt. But the Asphodel meadows would be lacking. And as for my Elysian Fields, why, the heroes that do not die young are few and far between. By all accounts, I believe those fields would be empty."

Once again, the mortal dipped his chin, but as he bowed deeply, he took a step closer to the god. Cerberus, who previously had remained silently dozing, lifted his left head, seemingly interested in the proceedings.

"I understand, great god. Your rules are just and fair. And I would never expect you to return her to me without something in return."

"And you believe that you have something to offer me?" Hades said. Had the comment been spoken by his brother Zeus, it would have dripped with arrogant amusement, but with Hades, the words came with a genuine interest. "Please, I am eager to hear."

At this, Orpheus bowed even more deeply than before.

"I wish to offer you a song. A single song, during which you may consider my request. If my music touches you, in the manner that it swayed your companions, and you understand that is just a fraction of the love and devotion that Eurydice brought me, then you will return her to me. That is what I ask of you."

The hall swelled with silence that even Cerberus's breaths could not break. All eyes remained of Orpheus and his lyre, though it was Hades's word we awaited. Finally, when my lungs quivered with anticipation, he spoke.

"Play."

CHAPTER SIXTY-TWO

A COLLECTIVE BREATH HELD FIRM IN THE AIR. A SILENCE balanced on a knife-edge. Hades's hand was still upon mine, yet at some point we had shifted so that our fingers now intertwined. A memory stirred deep within me: an image of hands held, fingers interlocked. My heart stirred beneath my ribs, though no clarity or further images formed from such a sensation. A moment later, the mirage was snatched from me, just as Orpheus plucked his first notes.

Every being in the hall was poised to listen as the melody rose from his instrument, though the music we heard was far from that of a simple lyre. From that first solo tone to every one of the thousands that followed, we were in rapture. High notes reverberated in the pillars of the hall, causing the hair upon my arms to rise, while the base tones resonated with such depth they permeated into my very bones. Orpheus commanded music as Poseidon does the seas, the harmonies ebbing and flowing beneath his touch. My heart swelled as I leaned in to hear more and, understanding my yearning, Orpheus began to sing.

His voice was as lyrical as his playing, the pitch never faltering as it trembled with a vibrato that would have caused mountains to part. The tune of the lyre alone would have been enough to keep us mesmerized, but with his voice, he had transcended the skills of a mortal. He was, as he said, gifted by the gods and the muses.

I gasped as if I had been submerged in the iciest of water. Water from which I could not escape. No longer was I in the throne room, listening to the melodies of a grieving man, but standing beside a river in a place I did not recall. Memories surged through me, one after another, a rushing tide, too fast for me to catch a breath. A cool stream, the water tumbling over the rocks. A tree, with long, delicate leaves, bowing down to the earth as they swayed in the breeze. And a taste of sweet fruits and fresh berries on my lips and of her lips upon mine.

A woman. The minute her face filled my mind, it flooded it. Though it was not just her face I saw. Her smile, the touch of her fingertips. The arch of her spine when it curved in ecstasy. Her voice. Her laughter. Her words of true love. And the ones I responded with. My stomach lurched at the reflections. Memories, but how? And who was she? The question had barely formed in my mind when her name returned to me. And with it, every thought and pain that I had requested the muse to suppress. Ione.

The name shook me to the core. *Ione.* I spoke it over and over again in my mind. Ione. The only woman I had ever loved. The woman who had seen through my weak lies and frail excuses to expose the goddess beneath. The woman who had held my heart so completely that with her loss, I had struck her memory from my mind.

Orpheus's song continued to play around us. The deeper pitches sung out as he plucked at the thicker strings, and his voice matched with perfect tone, yet I did not listen to him. It was only Ione that I could hear, her coquettishness that first day we met. Her breathlessness as we made love over and over again. And I heard my own voice, too, the cries of grief that rose from my shattered heart at losing her. Pain twisted around my ribs. How long ago had that been? I tried to fathom. How many decades or centuries had I allowed myself to be stripped of the most precious memories my sheltered life had? And how could I have thought that a life without these memories was any form of life at all?

I did not realize that Orpheus's song had come to an end or that the throne room had descended to silence until Hades spoke. His voice grating and crass against the sounds we had heard and the memories that had risen with me.

"You do indeed have talent. I will profess I have never heard such a melody played in these halls. And there is no denying you have touched my wife with your skill."

Hades turned to look at me. In the mugginess of my memories, I looked down at my hand, where his fingers were still interwoven with mine. But I did not see his hand, merely a lack of Ione's.

Pulling away from his grip, I wiped away the tears that streamed down my cheeks.

"Tell me, my love, do you think that it is true, that our guest has been blessed with the gift of the muses?"

The memory of Mnemosyne, and her words of how only a muse's gift would be able to erase her actions, swam around me.

"I do not doubt it," I said.

"So, what is your opinion? Should we grant him his wish of returning his wife to him? This is as much your decision as it is mine." He spoke quietly, as if we were the only two in the room. "You are queen here. What would your judgment be?"

The stillness in which my so-called husband observed me caused my body to tense. Not so much as his eyelashes flickered as his gaze bore into my mind, and I feared that it had done exactly that. He had seen what I had seen. Ione. Our love. As the silence spread out between us, I understood that I needed to answer, yet the memory of my lover had taken my words and replaced them with tears.

"True love deserves every moment together that can be granted." My mind barely even flickered toward Orpheus as I thought only of myself. Of the limited time I had been given with the woman I loved. I did not realize the importance of my words until Hades stood up from his throne.

"The queen has spoken. You may be reunited with your wife."

Orpheus dropped to his knees, his lyre clattering to the ground as he buried his head in his hands.

"Thank you. Thank you."

"Do not thank me yet. I cannot simply allow a person to walk from here. Not when so many souls are deserving of this gift. So there will be a condition. And if you break this, you will lose your wife forever."

"Whatever the condition, whatever the task you set me, I will achieve it," Orpheus replied.

At this, Hades turned to me. I suspect he wished to discuss what would be a suitable stipulation for the musician to agree to, but I could not offer anything. I could not even bring myself to think of Orpheus or his wife, or even Hades. Instead, I stood up from my throne, dipped my chin to all of those present, then addressed Hades.

"You will excuse me. I must retire," I said. I did not respond as I left the hall, my broken heart attempting to piece itself back together.

I was trapped in the Underworld, but there was a glimmer of hope here. I could see Ione, and I needed to do so before my mother set me free.

CHAPTER SIXTY-THREE

M Y HANDS AND LEGS TREMBLED AS I TROD AWAY FROM THE throne room, slowly at first, barely able to register the movement of my feet. Then, as I reached the columns of the portico, I picked up the long fabric of my robe and ran. My feet slammed against that cold obsidian floor.

A thousand screams filled my head as I pushed open the doors to my chamber. But rather than collapsing on my bed or couch as I had done so many times before, I pulled back the curtains to stare at the Land of the Dead. To stare at a view I had kept hidden. For what was out there that I could possibly want to see? Now, I had learned the answer. She was there. Ione was there.

How could I have allowed myself to forget her? The question rang over and over in my mind, never forming on my lips for fear of who could hear. How could I have let myself believe that a life without our memories was better than the knowledge of our love? How much of a fool could I be?

More foolish than I had ever anticipated. That much I knew for certain. For I had lived centuries since her death and seen not a glimmer of love. Not even a faint wavering of something that could have developed had I given it the chance. No. Hades and his hand in mine was the closest to intimacy and affection I had experienced since the death of my beloved. That thought struck uncomfortably within me, yet I pushed it away and observed the view in front of me. A sense of hope burning inside. Perhaps this was why destiny had brought me here, to finally make peace with Ione. To leave her, knowing that I had said the final farewell that our love deserved.

A hundred horizons spanned out beyond the line of cypress trees and the shimmering moats. Watery light glimmered, luminous, but without any of the radiance cast by the sunrays. In the distance, it grew weaker still, dim and faded as it tumbled over the slopes away from me. There were a hundred thousand places that Ione could be, but I refused to let my optimism fade. Instead, I thought again of Hades and his hand in mine. Hades knew every soul in his Underworld, and I did not doubt the love he felt for me was as real as he had ever known. And now I would test that.

"Goddess, is everything well?" Hecate stood in my chamber, concern etched into her brow. "You left abruptly."

Words stumbled on my tongue. I had been so consumed by my own thoughts that I had not considered how my departure would appear.

"I am well, thank you. The music reminded me of the living. Of my old life, that is all."

The witch observed me for a minute longer, before she bowed her head.

"You will be free again, Goddess. You will be free again."

And as she left, I wondered if she knew that I had never been truly free at all.

Hour after hour, I waited in my chamber, rehearsing what to

say to Hades. I heard the clattering plates of supper come and go, smelled the early morning baking of bread, but still I remained in my chamber, determined that when I next spoke to my husband it would be to ensure my reunion with Ione. But how would I secure such a meeting?

It did not seem appropriate to mention her as my lover to Hades, but I wanted to keep as close to the truth as I could. She was a dear mortal whom I had the greatest love and affection for. That he could believe. She was someone who had been stripped from my life before I was given the chance to bid her farewell. That in my isolation, her loss had hit me harder than anticipated and that this reconciliation would be the greatest show of love he could offer me. Yes, those words would work well.

Once I had fixed on what to say, I opened the boxes of jewelry that I had kept closed since arriving and chose the first stone I laid eyes upon. A garnet. A hefty stone that fell just above my heart. I matched it with wide silver bangles, which I wore around my biceps.

After adding thick rings of kohl around my eyes, I scrutinized the reflection that stared back from the mirror. If ever there had been a queen of the Underworld, this was her image. The regality. The beauty. Staring at myself, I recalled the sense of power I had felt sitting upon the throne beside Hades. How at ease I had felt with it. And how at ease I was with this image, too.

Once ready, I wasted no time heading to the throne room. My heart pounded more fiercely than it had done that first day I roamed these halls with the shard of broken pottery in my hand. It felt like a lifetime ago. But I walked with a surety now.

One figure was present in the throne room when I arrived, although it was not, as I hoped, Hades. This should not have come as a great surprise to me. After all, there were countless beings, wraiths, and lower Gods of the Underworld that served Hades in his role as ruler, and I interacted with many, always showing curt politeness. Despite how I saw myself, Hades had made me their queen, and that was enough for most, but there were some who visibly objected to my presence. Who grimaced at the flowers I made bloom, and sneered as I refused the palace food. Some would flinch and recoil whenever Hades referred to me as queen. More so than perhaps I did myself. And this daimon who stood before me, Ascalaphus, was the worst of them all.

Ascalaphus's place was not in the palace. He was an orchardist, charged with keeping the trees and orchards of Hades rich and ripe and abundant. You would think that with our similar passions, we would have found some mutual ground, but perhaps that was why he took such a strong dislike to me.

For a moment, I considered retreating to my chamber and waiting for Hades to return. But I had little time to waste. And so I cleared my throat and spoke to the daimon. Hades considered me queen; it was time to see just how well I could play that role.

CHAPTER SIXTY-FOUR

I AM SEEKING MY HUSBAND," I said, in the most regal manner I could muster. Though the word *wife* flew fluently from Hades's lips, this was the first time I had used the word husband, and it quivered on my tongue. A sneer of satisfaction rose on Ascalaphus at my obvious discomfort. Yet I refused to so much as shift my footing.

"Our lord will return shortly. He is meeting new arrivals. They are arriving in droves: children, innocents. Though I am sure your witch has already told you plenty."

His eye glinted.

"I know my husband finds the death of any innocent soul a burden," I said neutrally, although there was something in the way Ascalaphus's lips twitched that made me think he found my answer humorous. I pondered his comment a moment longer and thought of the snowflake upon Hecate's shoulder. A cold spell, that was all she had told me. Was there more to it than that? More that I should know?

Manners dictated Ascalaphus should respond to me or dismiss himself from my presence. Yet he remained stoic and silent. A sneer still coiling on his lips. This was a battle of wills. He wished for me to retreat. To leave. To admit defeat. Perhaps, at another time, I would have insisted on his dismissal, but my mind was preoccupied with thoughts of Ione. Besides, I had no intention of waiting for Hades in the chill of the throne room.

"Tell my husband I will wait for him in the courtyard," I said. Yet before I could even turn to leave, Ascalaphus spoke again.

"You will stay here, you know. There is no way out."

I stopped. A clenching across my chest contracted as I turned to face him.

"I am the queen," I said. "I rule over every being in the Underworld, yourself included. Why would I wish to leave?"

His face contorted. His mouth twisting into a snarl, yet he did not relent.

"I have seen. I have seen the way the witch whispers into your ear when she is here. Well, I can whisper into my Lord's ear too. I whisper, and he listens. He has always listened to me." An icy shiver ran down the length of my spine, and I wished my robe had a more modest covering of my arms and shoulders. For though I now knew Hades was a god of integrity, the same could not be said for his men.

"You forget your place." It was possibly the first claim to authority I had made in my life. There was no need to speak in such a manner in Siphnos, yet I found that with this newfound voice came a strength I had not imagined. My shoulders shifted back as I stepped toward him. "I am not only your master's wife. I am not some weak mortal queen. I am the child of Zeus. Daughter of Olympus. While I am sure your lord would be most displeased to hear how you have been pestering his wife in his absence, you should understand he is not the only god in the Underworld to be feared." With a twist of my wrist, I formed a tangle of thorns at his feet. Not enough to trap him, or even touch his skin. Just enough to warn him.

He tried to maintain the snarl on his lips, but Ascalaphus's eyes betrayed him. A flicker of fear replaced the arrogant gleam that had been there. "Tell Hades that I will wait in the courtyard for when he arrives," I said. "No, better still, go find him and tell him."

With that, I turned and left.

Despite the inner strength I had displayed, a small tremble still afflicted my knees as I retreated to the courtyard and dropped onto a couch, lying flat so that I stared up at the blackness above me.

Now that I had allowed the memories of my lover to return, they came in unending torrents. The way I had felt seeing her bathing in the stream. The anticipation of feeling her hands touch me, even after we had been meeting for over a decade. The way I had collected posies for her and made a bed of soft flowers for us to lie upon when we made love. The agony I had felt upon her death. I could feel it all. But that agony would not last, for I was going to see her again.

I had been waiting for only a short while when footsteps alerted me to a presence outside. Sitting up, I ensured my robe was suitably fitted and my necklace hung straight, and with a bracing breath, I readied myself with my rehearsed words. But it was not Hades who appeared, but Ascalaphus, and in his hands he held a silver platter.

Without waiting for an invitation, he strode into the room and placed the fruit down on the table in front of me.

"I assume that you would not consider an offer of sustenance pestering?" he said. I swallowed, wishing I was faster with my retorts. But I was not quick-witted, and my silence gave Ascalaphus great satisfaction. "May I suggest the figs? They are delicious. I have grown them myself in my orchards." When I did not move, his eyes glinted with venom. "Some would consider it poor taste to decline such an offering."

"And others would find it poor taste to insult a queen. You will leave me now. And you will not enter again unless I summon you."

His lips pursed, his eyes flicking to the food and back again before he turned on his heel and left.

"You can take the fruit too," I told him. "I will not be needing it."

As much as I hoped Hades would be swift to join me, it was not the case, and soon, I could no longer sit on a couch and wait for him. So instead, I turned my attention to the plants, adding flecks of brightness to the mass of dark petals and flowers that filled the space. With my hands I grew yellows and oranges and all the hues of the sunset and sunrises that I missed so greatly. Petal after petal, I painted an image in the blossoms that even Eos would be proud of.

"This is a transformation indeed."

I twisted quickly around, the flower in my hand turning bright white at my surprise.

"My Lord."

"I startled you. I am sorry." Hades stepped forward and took a flower in his hand. Originally the amaryllis had shared the same bloodred hue as almost every other flower in the palace, yet it was now a pale blue, iridescent so that shimmered in the lamplight.

"I do not believe I have ever seen a petal of such color. Are there plants like these in the mortal lands?"

"Not exactly," I admitted, having taken liberties and inspiration from the fish that darted below the surface of the water in Siphnos. Never before had I considered using my powers to create something new, yet now that I had, I could see the endless possibilities of such a talent. "Does it displease you? These changes?"

"On the contrary. This is what I hope for. That you would make this your home. You could paint the walls lavender and carpet my throne room with a bed of daisies if it would ensure your contentment in this land."

His words were earnest, and the gaze with which he studied me was all a wife could hope for. But I was not his true wife. I had secrets. I had Ione.

"Did Orpheus and his wife return to the Land of the Living?" I asked, as the silence induced a corkscrewing of my nerves. Hades's eyes lifted to me, the creases deepening into great ravines. Confusion masked his face. "Orpheus, the musician," I clarified. The god blinked away the confusion, and, much to my surprise, scoffed dismissively.

"Whatever actions the musician took are no longer of significance to me," he said. He had accepted Orpheus into his home, and offered both him and his wife freedom, so his reaction was odd. Beneath the nonchalance, an anger simmered. Anger at Orpheus? But why? Surely it could not be anger at me, not when he had been so affable only moments before.

This was not the way I had intended to begin our conversation. The solemnity that now held him radiated through to me. Was he less pleased with my rearrangements of the courtyard than he implied? For I could not figure why a mere mention of Orpheus would cause such a sudden change in attitude. Stepping forward, I placed my hand on the arm of his cloak.

"Is something wrong?" I asked quietly. At my question, Hades stared at me as if I had yelled in a tongue he didn't understand. His head cocked to the side. His lips twitching. His eyes went to my hand, which I hastily withdrew. "I am sorry. I did not mean to intrude." I edged backward. Immediately, the great god was shaking his head. His look of solemnity replaced with fear.

"No, no. You did not. You did not intrude. No... Thank you.

Thank you for asking. I am not used to conversation such as this. Questions and such. It is…still new to me."

I nodded, struck again by the kaleidoscope of contrast this good had shown me. Perhaps that is what drew him to me. These shared unconventionalities between us. We were both gods yet had lived our lives separate to those most like us. I did not say any more, hoping that he would continue. And he did.

"There have been deaths today. Many deaths."

"Is that not always the case?" I asked, confused that such a thing in this place would warrant his concern.

"Sometimes. Sometimes there are great wars that will bring the soldiers to us in droves, but this is not like that. These are not soldiers who are dying. Not warriors or victims of pillaged villages."

"Who are they then?"

"They are everyone. Throughout the entire earth. Old and young alive. Starving. Freezing. The world is not what it was. It is not natural."

I had stopped listening. Deaths from the cold. I saw in my mind the flashes of snow that had speckled Hecate's coat and the glimmer in her eyes. I knew exactly what it was. In that moment, I saw the icy hint that lightened mother's fingertips on the journey back from Samothrace, when we had left my brothers there to be raised by their grandparents. I recalled the frost that had spread out from beneath my mother's knees at Meliae's death. And in that moment, I knew. She was the one who was bringing about the death. Demeter was coming for me. Doing whatever it took to free me. And she was close. My time here would be coming to an end. If I were to say my peace with Ione, then it would need to be soon. It would need to be now.

CHAPTER SIXTY-FIVE

H ADES WAS MOURNING. I COULD SEE IT IN HIS POSTURE, AND
I wondered briefly how many souls he had silently
mourned for, alone, down here, without anyone to grieve
with. Perhaps I should have asked him. Offered him the opportunity
to unburden his woes as a true and good wife would have done.
But, despite how he saw me, I was not his wife. I had my own grief,
which he alone could relieve. Finally dropping the petals in my hand,
I crossed the courtyard to take a seat on a couch. All the preparation
and confidence with which I had hoped to broach the subject of Ione
was rapidly fading, yet the desperation remained.

My throat cracked and crackled as I shifted position.

"There is something you wish to ask me?" Hades said, and for
an instant I believed that he was able to read me as I had learned to
read him, but he spoke again. "Ascalaphus told me that you wished
to see me."

"Yes. Yes." My voice was breathy. "There was something I wished
to ask, but if this time is not suitable for you—"

"Now is the time we have, so tell me, how may I be of service?"

Hope flickered within me.

"There is a woman," I began. "A mortal woman, who is now here in the Land of the Dead. I wish to see her."

At this, Hades looked at me with a newfound curiosity.

"She has died recently?"

"Several centuries ago."

An elongated pause stretched between us and Hades's tongue flicked from his mouth to dampen his lips. I did not know him well, but already I saw the words forming in his mind. Words he did not wish to say. After all, what god would remember a mortal after so many years, had their relationship not been intimate?

"It is not what is done. Disturbing the souls."

"Snatching maidens from where they pluck flowers in meadows is not what is done," I countered him. "Nor was allowing Orpheus to return to his wife, but you did it for him. For their love."

"And you love this mortal?"

I had walked into my own trap. One I had been intent on avoiding. I wanted him to know nothing of Ione, yet I knew that without some confessional, he would not take me to see her, and on my own I could lose a thousand lifetimes traipsing over the Elysian Fields in search of one soul.

"She was a significant part of my life," I attempted. "I knew her from a young woman, all the way to her death, and I was never granted the luxury of a farewell." I held his gaze, speaking firmly, although whether my actions reinforced my words or accentuated the part of the truth that I had neglected to say, I cannot tell. As I remained silent, Hades's eyebrows shifted upward by just a fraction.

"You tell her only of me now? Why not when you had first arrived here? If she was of such great importance to you, I would have thought you would have made this request many moons ago."

His reasoning was valid, yet I could not respond with the truth. If I told him of Orpheus and how his music had returned Ione to my mind, he would question why I needed to invoke the power of the muses to remove one who was simply a friend.

"I did not know you well enough to know that you grieved," I answered, finding the words more truthful than I had expected. "I did not know that you would understand my grieving. But I see you now. I know how you grieve yourself, for mortals you never even knew. That is why I asked this of you now."

His gaze lowered from mine. His inhalations were loud and strong enough to push the air.

"I will grant you this meeting you desire," he said. "The meeting to say farewell. But there will be conditions."

"Conditions?" *Conditions like those he placed on Orpheus,* I thought, and found myself wondering whether the musician had met them. "Are these conditions I am likely to disapprove of?"

"I do not know you well enough to say," he said truthfully. "But I think not. I think you will find them fair."

I did not reply. My silence alone indicated my desire for him to continue. He understood.

"Firstly, you will not go alone," he said. "You may have considered yourself independent in the mortal world, but you do not know this place well enough. I will have Ascalaphus go with you."

The daimon's name juddered within me.

"Can it not be another?"

"Ascalaphus's position means he has the time to aid you. His trees do not require constant attention. And his knowledge of the Underworld is nearly as great as mine."

Still, I was not satisfied by this answer.

"Do you mean him to spy upon me?"

"No, I do not." Hades's words were pointed and sharp, and his jaw locked as he attempted to hide his irritation. "I wish for him to keep you safe. To ensure you are not lost. This is not negotiable, and if you will not agree, then there is no point in me raising my second condition."

It was my turn to bite down. Grinding my teeth, I forced my chin into a nod. "Fine, I will accept it. I will accept a chaperone, but only to guide me there. He is to sit at a distance from us while we talk so that he cannot hear our conversations."

"I believe that is fair."

"What is the other condition?"

A tight knot coiled its way around my spine, for I feared I already knew what it were to be. I had been living in this palace as queen and as Hades's wife. He called me such to every god and wraith we met. And yet he had not taken me. He had not claimed me on the couch or in my chamber. I did not doubt that would be my second condition, but how I would respond, I did not know. To give myself to another for the chance of seeing Ione, was that a trade I was willing to make? I believed it was. And readied myself for my answer, as Hades spoke his second condition.

"I wish for you to change your name," he said.

"Excuse me?"

"Core. That is not a name. That is not even a title. Maiden. Is that how you want to be known?" My mouth fell open as he continued. "I do not wish to speak ill of my sister, but it baffles me as to why she would give one so magnificent such a name. You have the blood of two Olympians running through your veins, and yet she has had the world refer to you as nothing more than a child of the meadows?"

The way his voice slanted upward showed he wished for me to

respond. To slander my mother, perhaps. But I remained sternly silent, and his request hung in the air. Maybe he thought I was so repulsed by the idea that I could not force words from my throat, but that was not the reason for my silence. My silence came from another voice rattling around in the depths of my memory. Only one other in my life had ever thought I was more deserving of a name beyond Core. And that was Ione.

"You wish for me to take another name?" My voice was little more than a whisper.

"You should have been blessed with a name fit for a goddess from your birth," he said, each of his words clamping tighter around me. "I cannot change that, but I can offer you this. A rebirth as the queen. If you agree, then I will grant you what you wish. I will allow you to find this mortal soul."

Tears pricked my eyes, but why I cannot say: the anticipation of seeing Ione again. The pain at the truth of his words. Either way, my chin dipped in a nod.

"I will."

At my acceptance, his face broke into a smile so true, I could feel it within my soul.

"Thank you," he said, and dropped from his seat onto my couch. Kneeling on the ground before me, he took my hands and kissed them, before rising to his feet and saying, "What should I call you now, my queen?"

To choose a name is a gift few of us are granted, though I wish more were allowed that freedom. A name is not merely a cluster of sounds, it is the identity we offer to others before we even show our face. Names are rich with our history and heritage. They help shape our place in the world. Until that point, my name, Core, had marked me as nothing more than a maiden. Innocent and I. A child. The old me was gone, and the new one would ensure I never became that nameless maiden again.

"From this point on," I said. "I will be known as Persephone."

CHAPTER SIXTY-SIX

Once I knew I was to be reunited with Ione, impatience took hold. It rattled me as it had all those years ago when our relationship was new and the nights between our visits felt infinite. I felt as I had during those first festivals, when I was forced to stay with my mother for days on end, and my body would pulse with desperation to see her. Those few mortal hours—when I was unable to see or speak or touch her—were too much for my inexperienced heart to handle. And now those same desperations had returned with force.

No matter how deep my longing was, I wished to keep it from Hades. He had granted me his blessing, but he could remove it just as swiftly, and so, with my new name keeping my head high, I returned to my chamber to pace the room while I waited.

I did not sleep that night. Nor even close my eyes. Instead, I ran through every memory of Ione and imagined how elated she would be to see me. I imagined how her laugh would lift my spirits so high they might well return to the Land of the Living without my body. How we would weep and kiss and speak of our endless love. Because it was endless now. I saw that. Not even death had changed it.

In my impatience, I was out of my chamber and pacing the throne room before Hades had even woken.

"Your desire to see this woman is so strong, I wonder if I should be concerned," he joked when he joined me. But I was in no mood for joking, and it was unlike him to jest at all, let alone in reference to one of his souls.

"Is it not surprising that I wish to see someone from my former life? A reminder of what I was before I was forced here against my will?"

I saw the pain flash across his face, and had I been in a better mind, I might have attempted to appease him, but I could think of nothing but myself. Besides, I had spoken the truth. Hades had promised to reunite me with Ione; now he needed to make good on his promise. "Is Ascalaphus prepared? I wish to leave immediately."

At my words, Hades strolled and took a seat upon his throne. "Ascalaphus has the orchards to attend to, and other duties he must oversee."

"Duties more important than dealing with the needs of his queen?" I responded. My acerbity was unexpected, even to myself, yet a smile twitched at the corner of Hades's mouth.

"You are, of course, correct. His queen's wishes should be his primary concern. Persephone."

The name rippled through my skin, absorbing this new truth. Power and a sensation close to happiness surged through my body for the first time since I had arrived here.

"Why do you not wait in the courtyard?" Hades suggested. "Or perhaps take a walk beyond the palace. I will inform you when Ascalaphus has returned."

My instinct was to refuse this suggestion, for his order was reminiscent of my mother's behavior, yet I did not wish to pace the throne room with increasing aggravation until the orchardist arrived.

"Thank you, I shall." I said, and I left without so much as a bow to my king.

When Ascalaphus finally came to find me, I was surprised to discover that he was not alone but that Hades accompanied him.

"Your wait is over, my love," he murmured.

A gasp of relief flooded from my lungs, cut short by his words. Not queen. Not Persephone. But *my love*. It was not the first time he had referred to me with a term of endearment, yet this time the remark grated more deeply than ever. I was not his lover. I was Ione's, and his words were like a scalding burn. I bit my tongue and ignored the tang of blood that filled my mouth.

"My Lady Core. I have been instructed to take you to a soul." Ascalaphus bowed emphatically, a show entirely for my husband's audience.

"My name is Persephone," I responded, looking down my nose in a manner that I had learned from the orchardist himself. "It is more fitting for a queen, do you not think?" I moved forward and linked my arm into my husband's. "Thank you. Thank you for this kindness. I will not forget it."

At this, Hades tipped his head slightly to kiss my cheek. He had, of course, kissed me the night before, upon the back of my hands, yet this was so unexpected I jerked away from him. The pain of my rejection flashed on his face.

"I trust you will find your way there," Hades said, slipping his arm out from mine. I reached outward with my fingertips, to thank him again, but he was gone before I could touch him, leaving Ascalaphus and me alone.

The power that I felt only moments ago had diminished,

although the orchardist did not display as much glee at my husband's abrupt departure as I expected. Had Hades still been present, I would have thanked him for his aid, but he was not, and I was no longer in the mood for niceties. "Do you know where we are to go?"

Ascalaphus's eyes narrowed on me. "Ione. Borne of Erastus in the city of Aegina. Our Lord has told me already. I suggest you stick close to me. It would be a terrible tragedy if you were somehow to lose your way."

CHAPTER SIXTY-SEVEN

T HE WALK TO FIND MY FORMER LOVER WAS SLOW, BUT I HAD
no one to blame for that but myself. As much as I wished
to see Ione, I found myself constantly drawn to the sights.
The rivers weaved and whitened as they coiled and turned and cut
through the shallow landscapes. Gossamers of cobwebs glinting with
pearls of dewdrops trapped in their threads. Trees, bright white firs,
with needles as delicate as dandelion seeds.

I walked on well-trodden pathways, and less-worn trails. Steps,
cut into rocks, wove up and down so often it was impossible to see
whether we had risen or fallen over the duration. It was after a while
that these stone steps, rising upward, finally broke into an open field.

A small gasp escaped my lips, not for the beauty, but for the
expanse. This was a meadow like none I had seen before. As far as
the eye could see, a spread of flat land stretched outward, covered
with flowers. Or rather, with a single type of flower. No variation of
blooms graced this meadow, no burst of color to add vibrancy to the
muted light. Every plant that grew between the grasses was the same,

with identical star-shape blooms open at the top of the tall stems. The yellow stamen, the only pinpricks of color in this sea of white. You did not need my affinity with nature to recognize what these flowers were. Asphodel.

The tightening within my chest was immediate. The shortening of my breath as my ribs squeezed tight around my heart and lungs. The Asphodel Field. Surely there had been a mistake. This was the place where the unremarkable were sent. The ordinary. Those who had done no great deeds, nor terrible ones. It was void, not only of plant life and color but of laughter, of joy, of any emotion at all. This was existence, nothing more, and my Ione was part of it.

Gasping for breath, I watched as a soul to my right bowed low and plucked a flower, which it promptly placed in its mouth and began to chew. Even while the stem hung from its mouth, it was already reaching for the next bloom.

"I believe the woman you are looking for is over there?"

I did not need to see Ascalaphus's face to know a sneer of glee was smeared across his face. Nor did I need to see where he was pointing, for my eyes had already found Ione. Or what remained of her.

Every part of her was there, from the curves in her fingers, to the gentle slope of her shoulders and yet, so much of her was gone. Her image was diaphanous, her form insubstantial, and the way she plucked and shoveled the asphodel flowers into her mouth caused a nausea to sweep through me so great that my knees buckled. Pain seared through me. How could this be my Ione? How could this wraith, with gray sallow skin and hollow black eyes, be the person I had loved so deeply?

With staggered breaths, I forced myself forward. My heart knocking against my ribs as I approached her.

"Ione?" I said, softly. Then a little louder. "Ione?"

Still she made no movement, other than to continue her collection of the petals on which she gorged herself. "Ione, it is me, my love. It is your Core."

It was my name, and not hers, that elicited her first reaction. Her hand, still hovering above the asphodels, did not move to pluck it, but her head cocked toward me.

"Core?" she said my name with faint recognition, though no sooner had the sound left her lips than she had returned to the flower. Before she could pull the petals from the stem, I grasped her wrists, bending at the knee so that I gazed up at her.

"Ione. It is me, my love. I am here." She tilted her head to the side again, her nose scrunching as if detecting a vaguely familiar smell. "Ione, my darling, it is your Core."

Her eyes offered only the slightest comprehension, as if she were staring at a faintly familiar face. A hawker in the agora. A family from a nearby village. Not the woman she loved.

"I knew a Core once," she said, quietly. My throat tightened as my breaths drew thinner and thinner. "She was to make me immortal. Am I immortal? She said I could be immortal."

Tears pooled in my eyes and ran down my cheeks faster than I could wipe them away.

"I am here, my love. I am your Core. I am here for you." I tried to clasp her face toward me, but her eyes were clouded, once again, gazing at the white flowers.

"What is wrong with her?" I span around to face Ascalaphus. "Why is she like this?"

"Like what? A wraith? This is what they are all like here. The spirits who feed on the asphodel flowers."

As I looked around me, I knew he spoke the truth. These spirits were not whole, not in appearance, nor in themselves. There were no sparks of laughter in these fields. No carefree dancing. Not even the bickering of men and women. Nothing but apathy. Apathy and asphodel. And in that moment, I knew what I must do. Once again, I turned to Ascalaphus.

"We are to take her to the fields of Elysium," I said.

At this, he shifted, his eyes widening in surprise.

"That is not where she belongs. She was judged. Fairly as all the souls were. She belongs here."

"She was judged on the assumption that she was only a mortal. Every hero patronized by a god is there. Tell me, how many heroes are in these lands? How many men and women that gods loved in matrimony or friendship are in this place? I will tell you. There are zero. Of course there are. Because why would a god love anyone who is not exceptional? They would not."

How his face contorted. I was a bitterness that he had to swallow day in and day out, but this was new to him. This ordering.

"This is not how things are done."

I did not raise my voice. I did not shout and yell and stamp my feet as my father would have done had someone immediately refused his request. Instead, I lowered my voice, so it was near a whisper, barely loud enough to hear over the whistling of the wind through the grass. And yet he heard. He heard every word.

"I am the queen here. And as your queen, I am telling you that this woman does not belong in the asphodel fields and she will not remain here a minute longer. Now will you take me there, or will I have to explain to Hades why you disobeyed me? And while I speak to him, I will list every snide word that you have spoken to me since my arrival." He was not being spoken to by Core but by Persephone, yet still he did not respond immediately. "I will not tell you a second time."

Finally, with a glower that burned as hot as coals, the orchardist bowed his head.

"As you wish, my queen."

CHAPTER SIXTY-EIGHT

I FOLLOWED ASCALAPHUS BLINDLY, ONLY OCCASIONALLY SHIFTING my gaze from Ione to ensure I remained sure footed. We did not return down the same path we had taken to reach there but tread down a trail covered with black stones.

"I am hungry," Ione said every few footsteps. "I wish to eat."

"Soon, my love. Soon."

I quickened my pace until I was level with Ascalaphus. "How much further must we travel? She is weak."

"How much strength do you expect the dead to have?" he responded. A hundred retorts whirred around in my head, yet I swallowed them down, for none would help me arrive at the Elysian Fields any swifter.

I would not have put it past Ascalaphus to have taken us the longest, most winding route just out of spite, but finally a stream formed in front of us.

The stream was unlike any I had encountered in the Underworld, where the waters ran deep and the beds were lost in the shadows of their own darkness. This water ran clear, sparkling as it tumbled with a gentle current. A cool sense of calm rose from it.

"We must walk through the stream," Ascalaphus said.

I let him go ahead, still not trusting his actions entirely. Although this time, my distrust was misplaced.

It was a transformation unlike any I had seen. Even through the gates of Olympus. As the water covered our feet, we passed from the expanse of the Underworld and into somewhere entirely new. The Elysian Fields. Paradise. A perfect bliss for all honored enough to roam in it for eternity.

My attention fell first—as it always did—to the plants. The flowers, not just asphodel, but crocus, and irises, orchids, and cyclamen. Too many to name, all blooming at the fullest flower, filling the air with pollen. And the trees. So many great trees, laden with fruit so ripe that their sweetness pervaded into the air.

"These are your orchards," I said to Ascalaphus.

"Some of them."

"Good. Then please fetch her some food. Anything. Apples. Peaches. Pomegranates. She enjoys pomegranates."

I assumed he would meet my request with disdain, but instead Ascalaphus nodded mutely and milled away from Ione and me toward the trees. As she left, Ione reached for yet another white bloom from a nearby asphodel flower.

"Be patient, my darling. Ascalaphus will bring you something better to eat, my love. Please wait."

I moved to force the flower from her hand, only for her eyes to flash with anger and looked at me like a wild dog from whom I was attempting to steal a bone. Hastily, I retreated and searched around me. Ascalaphus ambling slowly back toward us, as if there was no urgency.

With my attention still half on Ione, I raced to Ascalaphus, grabbed the fruit from his hand, and brought it back to her.

"Here, my love. Here. Take this. Eat this. Eat this."

It felt as though I were feeding a child, forcing the fruit between her parted lips, but little by little the juice fell over her tongue, and a spark of clarity returned to her eyes. Grabbing the fruit from me, she pushed an entire plum into her mouth, only spitting out the stone, before grabbing another fruit from my hands. This time, a peach. I watched on as, for the first time since her death, her hunger was finally satiated. Only then did her attention shift from the food.

"Core?" Her voice was sweeter than any tune Orpheus could have played. "Core, how can it be?"

Oh, how I held her. How I pulled her into me and breathed the sweet scent of her hair as I brushed the soft skin of her cheek.

"I am here, my love. I am here."

As she pulled herself away from me, her eyes moved to her surroundings.

"The Elysian Fields? How can this be? How can this be? How are you here? How?"

"There is much to explain, my love. Much. But we have time now. Please, let us sit."

Too stunned to object, she lowered herself to the ground, and I noted Ascalaphus watching from a distance.

"I will be one moment," I said to her, before striding across to my chaperone.

"Thank you. Thank you for bringing me here. You can attend to your orchard now. I will call for you when I am ready to leave."

His eyes narrowed on Ione, who continued to chew on the food. With a single side step, I blocked his line of sight.

"I will let you know when I need your aid," I said again.

"I am to ensure you are safe. How can I do that if I cannot see you?"

He was playing games. Trying to laud power over me. But I was the one with power, and I was no longer afraid to use it.

"I assure you, I will not move from this place. I believe it would be of your benefit to tend your trees."

I gestured behind him, where several leaves in his orchard had begun to blacken, as though afflicted with a fast-acting blight. As he watched on, blackness spread down the leaves and branches and down to the trunk. It took him less than a second to realize the cause.

"Stop it!" he yelled, his skin a garish green.

"Of course," I smiled. "As I said, I will call you when we need you."

With that, he scurried back to the trees, which were once again turning green.

When I returned to Ione, I dropped to the ground on my knees beside her.

"I thought I would never see your face again," I said, clasping her face in my hands and kissing each of her cheeks and then her lips. "You knew. You knew you were to die, and you did not tell me?"

"How could I? How could I allow one second of your sadness? I am sorry, But I could not leave the earth knowing that I had brought you sadness, my love. And now you have done this for me. You have brought me here. How? Why? You can cross to the Land of the Dead?" I could feel the desperation with which she drank my image in. For it was the same desperation I felt for her. The same overwhelming need to believe this was truly real.

"A great deal has happened, my love. A great deal indeed."

With her head upon my lap, I told her how, when I was walking in the meadow alone, Hades's chariot had risen from beneath the earth and stolen me. I told her how I was now his wife, though only in name, but how he saw me as his queen.

"You have grown stronger," she said, observing me. "You are more assured of yourself. There is a new strength in you. One that you lacked on Earth."

"Do you think so?"

"I do. Whatever has caused these changes, I am pleased for you, Core, my darling."

Very little time had passed since I had taken a new name, but as it was a condition of us being together, I felt it important to tell her of this.

"Actually, my name is no longer Core. Hades did not think it was fitting. He requested I choose myself a new name."

She paused, eyeing me inquisitively. "That is great news indeed. Tell me, what name did you choose?"

As eager as I had been to tell her of this new title, I hesitated. Would she love me less if my name were different? No, that was ridiculous. She was the one who had first suggested I was worthy of more. She was the one who had wanted this. Besides, it was a name only. It did not change me.

"Persephone." I said. "My name is Persephone."

Her smiled broadened and her eyes glinted with life, transforming her wraith's body to the woman I had first fallen so deeply in love with.

"Persephone. It suits you," she said. "It suits you very much."

Oh, how I wished to kiss her. I wished to kiss her so much that my lips throbbed. There was no sign of Ascalaphus in his orchard, but even if he had been present, what did it matter? Gods took lovers constantly. Goddesses too. Besides, my marriage was not permanent, nor physical. And so I leaned forward and placed my lips on her.

"I cannot stay here for too long," I said, when we finally broke apart. "Hades will be waiting for me."

"But you will return?"

"If I can. But once Demeter secures my freedom, then my life here will be over."

She nodded knowingly. "Even this day, this single day, is more than I could have dreamed of."

"As it is for me, my love."

How I wished I could stay there. Lie down and live my eternity in that meadow beside her. But it was not for me. I knew that.

"Close your eyes," I told her. "It will be easier if you do not have to see me walk away. And it will be easier for me if I know you are not watching. Please, my love, close your eyes."

As she did as I asked of her, I planted a final kiss upon her lips and left.

For the first time I could remember, in both the Land of the Living and of the Dead, I moved with lightness in my heart. I did not hold anger for the past but only a sense of gratitude for this moment and all that had gone before. That sense of lightness and peace remained in me for the entire walk back to the palace. Until I saw Hades.

CHAPTER SIXTY-NINE

NEVER IN ALL MY TIME IN THE UNDERWORLD HAD I SEEN his face so dark with anger. His eyes shone only with a blackness that caused Cerberus to cower at his feet, although the anger was not aimed at his beast. It was aimed at me.

"You moved a soul! You moved a soul to the fields of Elysium? Without even consulting me?" His voice raged. A thunderous growl of primal power, that before his abduction would have sent me running. But I had primal blood in my veins, too. Power he had encouraged me to foster.

I had not planned on keeping Ione's relocation hidden but had hoped that I would be the one to break the news to him. Behind me, a sneer of satisfaction rose on Ascalaphus's lips.

"I could not leave her there." I heard the desperation in my voice, yet Hades seemed not to notice.

"That was where the judges placed her! That was where she was supposed to be. You have no right to interfere."

"No *right*?"

My meekness lessened, and emboldened by the power of my new name, I locked my gaze on the great god Hades. "You are the one who told me I am Queen of the Underworld. That I should act as though this is my kingdom, too."

"And you are the one who has made it perfectly apparent that you will not stay here. That when the witch and your mother come for you, you will race across the rivers without a backward glance."

His words tumbled back at me. Perhaps, had they been aimed at Core, they would have knocked her into silence, but this was not the case.

"Can you blame me?" I spat the words in rage. "This is how I am treated in a place that you insist is my home. My first action, the only decision I have made beyond what clothes I can wear, and this is how you respond? You wanted a queen, and yet you are speaking to me as a wife."

Not since that first day when he captured me had I raised my voice in such a manner. Never in all the centuries of my existence had I responded with such unadulterated anger. But Hades brought forward in me a fury like no other.

"If you wish me to even consider this my home, then you will leave her where she is. You move her, and I will not say another word to you. I swear, I could remain here for all eternity, and I will not offer you a single word."

His jaw locked and a snarl close to that of his dogs reverberated through the halls. I braced myself for his next tirade when he turned to Ascalaphus and the other servants that had gathered for the entertainment of his wrath.

"Leave us!" he shouted. No one needed to be asked a second time. Even Cerberus pined only once at his master's heels before he scampered out the door.

If I had felt fear at Hades's wrath, it was little compared to the fury of his silence.

"You have humiliated me," he hissed.

"You wish to talk as to who has suffered the greatest humiliation?" I asked. "You stole me."

His eyes rolled, as if the time that had passed now excused his actions.

"Have I not tried to make this your home since? I welcomed you the best I know how. I have not forced myself upon you as your husband."

"How gracious." I snapped back.

He sucked on his teeth as he paced around the hall, barely managing two steps before he turned back to face me.

"If she is to stay where she is, there are to be conditions."

I scoffed at his remark. "Always conditions with you."

"Yes, Persephone, conditions. For I am the ruler of many. If there are not conditions, then chaos reigns. Chaos in which pain is inflicted on those who do not deserve it. So I set boundaries. I enforce rules. For the good of the many and of the few. But if you do not wish to hear my suggestion, then leave. I will see your lover is returned to the Asphodel Fields immediately."

It was the thought of Ione, in her diaphanous state, that forced me to my hold my tongue. That and the other word he used. My lover. He knew. He knew what she was to me, and that gave him all the power.

"What are your conditions?"

"Every hour that you spend with her, you must spend with me in equal measures. And not in silence. You must talk to me. Tell me of your childhood, of the places in the Land of the Living that you have loved the most."

"That is it?" I scoffed. "I am to talk to you? So you can learn everything of me, and I will know nothing of you?"

"What is it you wish to know? You only have to ask."

There was indeed a question I had about the God of the Underworld. But I did not say so much to him.

"Perhaps" was the answer I offered.

"I will tell you anything you wish to know. I wish to keep nothing hidden from you, Persephone."

I chewed his words over in my head, though there was little I could say to object. I would not see Ione returned to the Asphodel Fields, and he knew that.

"That is all you ask of me?"

"That is all I ask."

And so our agreement was made. Time with Hades for time with Ione. Time with my husband for the woman who had been as a wife. A simple exchange. Or so I thought.

PART THREE

PERSEPHONE

CHAPTER SEVENTY

Hecate leaned against the gnarled trunk of a birch tree, watching silently as I raged. All around us, the world was swallowed with white. The mountains that for millennia had remained lush and green and sprayed with flowers were nothing more than a pure unblemished sheet. A white so pristine that the sun's reflected rays could have blinded any who looked upon it as fiercely as the true sight of a god. Not that the humans looked to the gods anymore. Not the way they had. The harvests had been lost, submerged by the endless flurries I set on to their lands. The trees bore no fruit, the branches laden only with the heavy weight of snow. Animals' last breaths frothed in the frozen air, which had stolen their lives. Which had stolen so many lives.

Do not think me callous for the death of the humans. It should not have happened at all. No, the guilt lies with my brother entirely. The instant I knew he was to blame for Core's disappearance, I stormed the halls of Olympus. Not since Iasion's death had I stepped upon that mountain, and I did not so much cast an eye toward my old home. My beloved palace, which I suspected was now home to another of Zeus's offspring. No, I headed straight to his brazened hall, where he lounged upon his throne. Lounging like he had not heard my thunderous footsteps. So arrogant a creature he was, that as I approached, he yawned. Yawned. Yet despite his nonchalance, my wrath was not unnoticed. Musicians who were playing in the corner of the room stumbled over their notes when I approached and looked to my brother, who waved his hand carelessly. My presence was meaningless, and the music should continue.

Beside him, Hera sat stony faced. That young, powerful, compassionate goddess was gone. There would be no use in pleading with her. Besides, what sway did she have over Zeus anyway? None that mattered.

"Sister, this is a surprise. I did not believe you graced us with your presence on Olympus anymore," he said.

"You allowed him to take her. You allowed him to take my daughter."

"I am not sure I know of what you speak."

"Do not lie to me!" I bellowed. It was not some screeching wail of an upset mother. Now, as my lungs rattled the bronze pillars of the palace and birds fled their roosts, I had the voice of a god, and for the first time since I had been freed from the belly of my father, my presence caused a flicker of fear to cross my brother's face. I lowered my voice to a hiss. "Do not lie to me. You allowed Hades to take my daughter. And I wish her to be returned to me now."

At these actions, the musicians halted again. Their hands now trembled with such force they could not perform. As a collective, they stared at Zeus, awaiting instructions. Oh, how I wished Zeus had commanded them to play, just so he could hear how they quaked at my presence. But he was far too wise to let me hear the effects of my own power, and with a flick of his wrist offered them the response they had hoped for.

"Leave us," he said, then, turning to his wife, added, "You too." As the musician picked up the instruments and scuttled hurriedly away, Hera hesitated. There is no age to the gods. Certainly that no mortal could see, and yet I noticed how the fleck of light within her irises had grown dull and her lips turned down at the corners. However she looked on the outside, she was old now. Old and tired. When Zeus offered her no further response, she rose to her feet.

"It has been too long, Sister," she said, each step from the dais slow and deliberate. When she reached me, she took another step, and leaned in, as if to kiss my cheek. For the briefest instant, I believed she were to offer me some sisterly comfort, but instead her voice hissed like a serpent in my ear.

"You will not get your way," she whispered, before straightening up and offering me a smile so icy it could have frozen all the water in Hellas.

I watched the queen leave the throne room and waited until Zeus and I were entirely alone before I spoke again.

"I do not know why he has taken her," I said, holding my ground. "And I do not wish to know. All I wish is that she is returned to me."

"It is not that simple," Zeus said, his legs still slung over the side of his throne like a carefree youth. "You have kept our child hidden long enough."

"Our child?" A bitter laugh rattled from my lungs. "She is not your child. She is nothing to you."

"She is the daughter of two Olympians. It was wrong of me to show less of an interest in her than my other offspring. This matching is perfect. Hades requires a wife. He will require someone powerful. Someone who has powers that match his own."

"She is a child."

"No. No, Demeter, she is not. You have created her in such an image, because that is what you wish to see her as. She is a goddess. An old goddess. And a goddess should marry a god."

My throat was thick with tears I would not let him see, for the knowledge that he would misconstrue them as weakness. My tears did not come from sadness or weakness. It was anger alone that spurred them.

"Fine. If she must marry, then she can marry. I will allow that. But not Hades. Not him. You chose him to spite me. You chose him so she would be hidden from me. So she would be in a place where I cannot go."

"I did not choose her." Zeus raised his voice as he swept his feet onto the ground. "I did not choose this for her, Sister. Do you think I care so greatly about you and your misery? You place too much importance on yourself, Demeter. I must confess I do not think you have crossed my mind for the last millennia, since that scene you made at the wedding. No, this was not my choosing. Hades wished for Core. For her only. And as I have already told you, I understood the power in such matrimony. She should consider herself blessed to be betrothed to one so respected."

"Respected? Believe me, Brother, I have the same respect for the great lord of the Underworld as I do for you." Were my words wise? No, but they were the truth, and sometimes the truth is far stronger than wisdom.

The sigh that rattled from Zeus displayed the same impatience a mortal adult would show for a young child who refused to eat, or to sleep at night. He spoke of respect for the gods, and he showed quite clearly how that same respect did not extend to me.

"You fail to the see the consequence of what you wish for, Demeter. Hades is the ruler of the Underworld, but he also controls all the world's wealth. If we anger him, it would be in his power to strip the mortals of it all. All the gold and brass that they use for their offerings. Gone. All our temples, barren. It is the consequences of your actions we must think of here. That is why she will stay where she is."

"Consequences?" I repeated quietly.

"Exactly."

Oh, that word burned within me. It lit a fire the likes of which I did not know I possessed. Though I refused to show him. Instead, I bowed low. I bowed to him as if I were a mortal. As if I were overcome by deference and awe. As if I were the Demeter he had rescued all those millennia ago.

"I understand, Brother. I do. But tell me, dear Zeus, what use is all the bronze and all the gold, if all the humans who desire it are dead?" I did not wait for a response, but I turned upon my heel with my head held high and marched from the room without so much as a backward glance.

CHAPTER SEVENTY-ONE

DESPITE MY CONFIDENCE IN THE HALLS OF OLYMPUS, I returned to Hecate as unsure as I had been before I confronted my brother. There was a way to make him listen, I knew that. But it came at a cost. One the mortals would need to pay if I was ever to be reunited Core. I did not know if I had the strength to see it through.

"You are the daughter of Titans, Demeter," Hecate said as she took my hand. "Why are you waiting for your brother's permission? It is time you took back what is yours. It is time you released your power. Show them exactly how much they should fear you."

And so I did.

I had not started with snow. I had certainly not intended to bring around such dissolution of life. But I started with frost. A delicate white crispness that coated the earth with glittering crystals. Yes, some life had been lost, but much remained. The hardy perennials and plenty of vegetation continued to grow and offered enough sustenance for the mortals to survive. Had Zeus acted then, we would never have reached a point where the mortals truly suffered. But he took my actions as frivolous. As a fatuous reaction. A tantrum. And so, then I brought about the true winter.

At first, the mortals found joy in the pristine snow that drifted down from the heavens. Adults and children alike span in circles, laughing and dancing as they caught the flakes on their fingertips and tongues, mesmerized by the fleeting existence of something so beautiful. The same way I had been mesmerized by their fleeting existence for so many centuries. But as the snow continued to fall, their laughter faded away. And in its place came their cries.

Still, Zeus did nothing.

"I think it has been long enough. You should speak to him again," Hecate said several months after Core had been taken from me. The mortal deaths were now in the thousands, and the landscape of the Earth had changed beyond recognition. "It is time you address him again."

"He did not listen before. He cannot listen. He needs to see what I can do."

"The mortals have all but ceased their worship. There was barely a hecatomb to be found at the Panathenaia. Families were all too busy with funerals and burials to pay tribute to a god that cannot protect them from this misery."

"That cannot protect them from me, you mean?"

Hecate stepped forward and took my hands between her own. She had remained my loyal companion. Leaving me only to visit Core in the Underworld. The greatest friend I had possessed, beyond the nymphs who had betrayed me.

"Zeus will not wish for another year of suffering such as this one," Hecate replied, breaking my stream of thoughts. "He will want to end this suffering. Believe me. Besides..." Her words faded into nothing.

"Besides?" I pressed.

"Besides, I worry for you. I worry what you are doing to your power with these actions. The cold, the snow, the ice. I am concerned that it is affecting more than just the mortals."

I understood what she was saying. Of course I understood. The bitter iciness that had swallowed the mortals' lands had come from inside me. And every second that I allowed it to reign over the Earth, it also reigned in me. And the longer something entwines itself around you, the harder it is to break loose.

Not that I said that to Hecate. No, at her words, I merely flicked my hands from her grip and wafted my fingers above the earth. Such a small action, yet its power was magnificent. All around us, the snow melted. The white bed sank down, glistening as it drained into the earth below it. For an instant, dead grass, dull and flat, remained where the snow had been, but as I raised my hands, those sodden brown blades turned lush and green, widening as they grew upward from the ground. Soon the entire space was blanketed in a grass so verdant, its scent weaved like smoke into the air. But I did not stop there. No, I let the wheat grow, and the flowers and trees. An oak tree towered above us. Its branches reaching upward and out. Only when its leaves shaded us from what little warmth the sun had to offer did I turn to Hecate.

"Are you still concerned about me now?"

"More than ever. Please, go to Zeus. Speak to him again. He will not refuse you."

I gazed out at the green land, and allowed myself a breath of that warmth air, rich with pollen and petals and the scents of all things I had brought into this world to worship, but as my head fell into a nod, all that I had grown withered, and succumbed once again to the snow.

"Fine, I will go again to Olympus," I told her.

CHAPTER SEVENTY-TWO

To the untrained eye and ear, the palace of Olympus was the same site of magnificent splendor it had always been. The same bronze pillars glinted endlessly; the same marble floors shone so brightly they could have aided Theseus in his quest. And the same aroma of ambrosia and wine wafted through the hallways on which the same elaborate tapestries hung. But mine was not an untrained eye. Nor was my ear unaware of the subtle differences that had occurred since my last visit.

I heard the strain in the nymphs' tunes, as they struggled to maintain an upbeat melody, and the whispers that passed between them at the end of each song. I saw the glances exchanged by those lesser gods as they hurried away from the throne room, fearful that Zeus's temper would be unleashed upon them. I felt the tension, invisible but wrought, that wrapped itself around those beautiful halls and gripped the air. One more sharp tug could bring the entire palace down. A sharp tug that I fully intended on engendering should I so need to.

A mixture of pride and guilt bloomed within me. Of course, I had not wished to bring about this melancholy on anyone other than my brothers, but I was glad I had, for they would never underestimate me again. As I strode through corridors, my head remained as high as I had ever held it within these walls.

No more did I view the palace with trepidation. No longer did I fear Zeus's presence, as the sight of him flooded my mind with images of my rape. Nor did I see him in the same sense of awe as when he had first freed me. No, I did not fear or admire this god. I simply despised him, more than I would ever have dreamed possible.

"Zeus." I had dressed in white for the occasion. Not for purity, but for ice. Cold and unrelenting. My robe shimmered like the snow I had created as I walked into that throne room.

This time, the musicians and other gods did not wait for Zeus's instructions before packing up their instruments and scurrying away from my sight. With the slightest hint of a smile, I stood and waited patiently until only Zeus and I remained. Then I crossed the hall toward him.

No longer was Zeus lounging on his throne, impervious to my rage. Instead, my actions seemed to consume his thoughts. He was seated at the edge of the hall, on a small wooden stool. From there he could observe the Land of the Living. Every inch of that world stretched out beneath him. And every inch of it was white.

"This is what you wanted," he said, not turning to face me as I approached. What a change this was, I considered, from how he barely acknowledged my presence the last time I arrived.

I waited until I was beside his stool, standing so that my head was high above his, before I spoke.

"This is not what I wanted. This is what you have brought about on the mortals you claim so greatly to love. I wanted nothing but my daughter."

His gaze remained lost on the word below us, his thumbs pushing repeatedly into his palms. The action was a reflection of his apprehension. Fear even. And I loved it.

"She is his wife. There is nothing I can do," he spoke placatingly. "I am sorry, but she must stay there, in the Land of the Dead."

I did not grow angry as I would have once done. I did not even feel a stab of pain in my heart. Instead, I crouched by just a fraction so that he could hear my words as I whispered in his ear.

"I would save your pity for yourself, great Zeus. Because if my daughter is not returned to me, then this will never end. I promise you that."

And then, as if he were not the great god that I had feared for decades, but merely my younger brother who had tormented me for years, like so many siblings did, I crouched down and kissed him gently on the top of his head. A glistening sheen of ice crackled on the surface of his skin.

"Think wisely, Zeus," I said.

CHAPTER SEVENTY-THREE

I T WAS WITH A MIXTURE OF TREPIDATION AND GLEE THAT THOSE next days passed. Zeus would return Core to me. I did not doubt it, but I wished to make him suffer as much as I could while he made me wait. With the Anemoi, the gods of the winds, we whipped up a storm so fierce it ripped trees from the earth with their roots still clinging desperately on. The snow did not stop, not in morning or night. The rivers and lakes froze with layers of ice so thick that an axe was needed to break it, and even then, the time it took to gather water turned men's fingers and toes purple with cold. Zeus would come to me soon. I knew it. And I knew exactly where I wanted him to meet me.

The rocky fields of Tenos were a far cry from the place Zeus had stolen my confidence and freedom all those millennia ago. But I was no longer a victim, and reclaiming this land was one of the last things I could do to cement that.

I sat with my eyes staring out at the sea. The whitecap waves were circled by sea birds, not yet brave enough to dive into the rough waters in search of food.

"Soon," I whispered to them. "Soon, I will return the calm to you."

It was then that I heard the footsteps crunching on the snow behind me.

"I was unsure where to find you, Sister. It is difficult to see when you have turned the entire world white."

I held my tongue. After all, why would Zeus recall the importance of this land to me? When you have made so many suffer, I suspect they all become as one.

He remained standing as he spoke. Keeping a distance behind me, almost as if he were afraid of what I might do to him. *Good.*

"Make this end now and I will send Hermes to fetch your daughter," he said.

"Fetch my daughter and I will make this end now," I replied.

I twisted my chin over my shoulder just to see the anger glowing in his eyes.

"You do not achieve anything by this. The mortals are not worshipping you, either." He spat his words at me, as if his desperation would somehow soften my resolve.

At this, I stood up from the ground and took slow steps toward him. Each one I savored. Each passing second a triumph. Then, for the first time since that incident all those millennia ago, I placed my hand on him. My palm pressed flat against his face, as if he were an elderly man whose faculties were failing him. Who needed the comfort of a woman in his last frail hours.

"My dear, foolish brother. When will you see? I do not need the mortals to worship me. I worship myself. I see my own worth. I always have. That was why I would not do as you and the others suggested, limiting crops one year so that I may gain greater libations in the years that followed. That is why I am as content in a field with nothing but wheat and soft grass as in a palace with a thousand servants. That is why none of your threats will ever work on me again." I smiled softly, brushing my hand down the side of his cheek. "When my daughter is by my side, with a promise from both you and Hades that she will never set foot in the Underworld again, then the winter will pass."

The anger boiled within him. A burning rage that pulsed through the veins on his head as he pressed his lips tightly together.

"I will send Hermes to fetch her as soon as he returns to Olympus."

Smiling, I dropped my hand. "I would hurry, Brother. I hear a cold spell will hit tonight. And you know how frail your precious humans are."

CHAPTER SEVENTY-FOUR

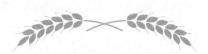

A s Zeus scurried back to Olympus, I also departed Tenos, but in a different direction.

Knowing that Core's release would be imminent, I sought out Hecate, instructing her to inform my daughter while I went to Taenarum, the entrance to the Underworld.

I waited for Hermes in the place where a free-flowing, bubbling spring had once existed. Now, an icicle as large as a stalactite held firm in its place, glistening and glittering in the light. I pressed my hand against the ice, allowing the cold to seep into my skin. I do not know when I learned about my affinity with the cold. It must have been within me from birth, of course, but for so many millennia I had repressed it. Seen it only as a flaw. A defection in my godliness that must be kept hidden. But now I saw the beauty in it. Beauty in its bleakness. In its ability to bring stillness to the world. There I remained, while the sun rose and set, until I heard the gentle fluttering of wings.

"Goddess, I apologize for making you wait," Hermes said as he approached. "Such weather is not conducive to swift flying, but that is a problem that will be rectified soon, is it not?"

The messenger god is my nephew by birth, yet his rise in Olympus had been after my departure and to me, his purpose was little greater than that of a carrier pigeon. Albeit an important one. His light blond hair was brassy against the whiteness of the snow. The fluttering wings on his flat cap a gaudy yellow, rather than soft gold. He was a caricature of youth. But he was Zeus's messenger. I could not hope to have Hades release Core unless Hermes was by my side confirming the god's orders.

"You are here now. We should leave. The sooner my daughter is returned to me, the sooner you may return to flitting around in the sun."

As I moved toward the entrance of the Underworld, he darted around and blocked my path. "I must apologize, Goddess, but you are not permitted in the Underworld."

"Not permitted." I bristled. "My daughter is there, and I must ensure she is returned to me."

Hermes did not move. For all his youth, he held his position with more conviction than his father had managed during our last interaction.

"Goddess, Demeter," Hermes dipped his head as he spoke. "I apologize for this, truly. But you have not been given permission to enter this land, not from Zeus or Hades."

"Surely what you see around you is indication enough of how I value my youngest brother's permission?" I said, gesturing to the bleakness around us. "Believe me. I should have marched across those rivers moons ago. I will not stand to be separated from her any longer." Hermes remained unmoving.

"Indeed, and understandably so, but it is you I fear for. If you were to trespass into his world without his permission, Hades would be well within his right to hold you captive. Please. Consider your actions.

Consider the desperate irony if, on the day your daughter is finally granted her freedom, you were trapped for all eternity from her."

I will confess my opinion of Hermes changed that day. I still find his incessant fluttering and the way his feet refused to rest upon the earth, even when it is mere inches below his feet, an extreme irritation. But he spoke the truth to me. And for that, he earned a modicum of my respect.

"Fine, I will wait, but if you do not return by nightfall, then I will hunt you down myself."

And with that, he left.

CHAPTER SEVENTY-FIVE

Y OU ARE STILL HERE," IONE SAID, AS SHE SAW ME APPROACH across the fields. It was remarkable how similar the land looked to our own sanctuary in Tegea: not merely the willow trees, but the meandering river and the languorous slopes of the hillside. Not to mention the way the wind rippled through the long stalks of grass in a great tide, as if the entire Earth longed to be water.

"Hecate is certain it will be any day now," I responded. "Would you rather I had already gone?"

"Never." Ione wrapped her hands around the back of my neck and kissed me softly upon the lips. "You know I would never wish to be without you. But I understand. I do."

We kissed again, softly, tenderly, and then with more passion. This was our third meeting, although each one we treated as though it were our last. Each kiss we savored as though we would never again feel the softness of each other's touch. And when we parted, we promised love eternal.

My chaperone remained, although we had come to an impassive truce. At that moment, he was off in the far distance, tending to red apples that were gleaming on bowing branches. Since I had blighted his orchard, he had been notably more respectful, although I did not doubt his disdain for me had grown.

"Will you have the chance to tell me of your departure?" Ione asked. "Will I know when you are to leave?"

"I suspect not, but I will send for someone. Ascalaphus or Hades, perhaps. They will come and tell you. But you are not to grieve."

"Grieve? When I have had a goddess in both life and death? I have been granted a love greater than I could have dreamt. I shall miss you, but I shall not grieve." She kissed me again, though as I pressed toward her, I noticed the sweetness of her lips. A familiarity that went beyond the mere flavor of her kiss.

"What do you taste of?" I said, kissing her again and pressing just a fraction harder.

Grinning, Ione pulled herself away from me and leaped from the ground.

"I cannot believe I had forgotten. Look, I wished to show you something," she said, pulling me up by the hand. "Look at what I found. An entire field of them. Do they not look just like those which you brought for me?"

She pulled me to where a small mound of pomegranates lay on the ground. The red leathery skins shone with freshness, and even at a distance I could smell the tart aroma that emanated from beneath the thick cocoons. With a single hand, Ione grabbed one and tossed it over to me. "Smell them," she said, pressing another against her nose and inhaling deeply. "Tell me, have you ever smelled something so fresh in all your life?"

She passed the fruit to me. Following her guide, I placed the skin beneath my nose and breathed in the scent. The sharpness struck senses I had almost forgotten existed.

"That is truly magnificent." The scent alone was enough for me to salivate, but when Ione plunged her fingers into the skin and pulled apart the flesh, a small groan escaped my lips.

"Here," Ione said, scooping out a handful of sweet gems and offering them to me. "They are delicious. I already eaten an entire one before you arrived."

My body cried out for the food. I could not recall how long it had been since I had eaten, or what my last meal had been. In the palace I continued to refuse Hades's food of the dead, though I had seen every feast he served: pig heads served up on a platter. Fishes, scales and bones so perfectly intact they should have still been swimming. But this. This pomegranate was not like that.

"I do not believe I should," I said, taking a step back. "Hecate warned me."

"She warned you about Hades's food, did she not? The food he offered you in the palace. How could this possibly be the food of the dead? I plucked it from a tree myself. A living, growing tree. Can you not see for yourself how the leaves grow and fall? Could anything which is not living create leaves which grow and fall?" I hesitated slightly. "I can take it to you if you would prefer." she continued. "You can pluck one yourself, then decide if you wish to eat it."

My eyes were locked on the seeds so sweet they glistened with sugar. And how my stomach growled for it. Not once, in all my time in the Land of the Dead, had my stomach growled for any of the food on offer. Surely that meant something. Surely that meant that this, Ione's offering to me, was acceptable.

"I will just have a single seed."

My lover laughed. "One seed? You cannot have one pomegranate seed? Who would do that? At least take a handful."

She dug her fingers into the flesh, causing several seeds to spill out as she scooped a handful and passed them to me.

"No, that is too many," I said, tipping the contents back into her hand until what remained on my palm was a mere half dozen. Six single pomegranate seeds.

"I am certain it will be fine," she said. "Besides, who is here to see?"

I glanced across the fields to where Ascalaphus tended his trees. All I could make out of him was a small shady figure moving about within the depths of the orchard. Far too far away for him to ascertain my actions, and there was no one else about. No one who could see us.

I took a single seed and popped it into my mouth. The intensity of flavor was so deep I gasped. The zesty tang, everything I had craved while trapped down here. Bright, and vivid. Like a cloud exploding on my tongue.

Next to me, Ione's smile widened. "See, I told you they were amazing. You should have the rest. Go on."

I looked at the seeds in my hands, then back to my lover. Before shaking my head.

"One is enough," I replied.

Disappointment clouded her face, though it was swiftly replaced. "Surely you can have these few? For me?"

And so for her and me, I ate the remaining seeds in my hand.

"Every time I eat pomegranates in the Land of the Living, I will think of you," I told her.

"And every time I am awake, I will think of you," she replied.

Later that evening, we kissed and bid each other farewell as if it were the last time we would meet. I told her I loved her and would always love her. Then she closed her eyes, and I walked away. For I had a bargain to maintain.

CHAPTER SEVENTY-SIX

MY LIFE HAD FALLEN INTO A RHYTHM MUCH LIKE THE ONE it had in Siphnos. I would sleep in my bed, bid Hades good morning, then leave to while away the hours with Ione. Then, spurred into motion by Ascalaphus, I would leave and return to the palace to spend the evening with Hades, anticipating that perhaps that might be my last night, before I would return to the Land of the Living.

Hades and I did not spend our nights as husband and wife, at least not in a carnal sense. There was an element of trust between us. Even, perhaps, a friendship. Days passed, and soon I had visited Ione over a dozen times, and after each visit, as I had promised, I spent equal hours with Hades.

"Some of the gods in Olympus say that Zeus tricked you. That he and Poseidon ensured you would receive the Underworld to rule," I said to him one night. It was the question that had burned through me the longest, though it took many days to find the courage to ask it. "Is this true? Did they?"

"I suspect they believe they did," he responded with more of a riddle than an answer.

"What does that mean?"

He topped up his goblet before he leaned back on the couch and replied. "I knew what they had planned, and I also knew that fairness was not within Zeus's capacity. Do you think, if I had chosen the Land of the Living that he so desperately wanted, he would have allowed me to keep it? Do you think he would have allowed his brother, who he had freed from the belly of his father, to be ruler of the kingdom that he desired? The same kingdom that he had slain his father for? No, the wars would have continued. And I have no desire for war. Let them battle up on the Land of the Living and on the seas. The souls have been through enough. Here we rest. That is all I ever wanted."

Never did I doubt the earnestness with which he spoke to me. Never did I feel fearful in his presence. And as the evenings progressed, we found ourselves sitting closer together while we exchanged our tales. It was on one such night, where we lounged beside one another, that Hades questioned me about Ione.

"This mortal that you meet, she must mean a great deal to you," Hades said. He no longer ate in my presence, aware that I would not indulge in his food. A hazy yellow light shone through the open roof in broken shards, breaking the tiles of the courtyard with its beams.

I was lying on a couch, now as at ease in the garments that he had provided for me as I was in my previous white robes. I had even taken to wearing gems around the palace, favoring still the garnet. In this place, I was Persephone. That was how I thought of myself. Strangely, I believed I had always thought of myself as her.

"She did mean a great deal to me," I said, in answer to Hades's question. "She does."

"Because she was your lover?"

My muscles tensed. I had wondered from that first fight if Hades knew the nature of my relationship with Ione, but he had not mentioned. I stumbled for a response.

"I am sorry, I have made you uncomfortable," Hades said. "That was not what I meant to do. I am still finding it difficult to navigate what is acceptable between a husband and a wife."

It was hard in such situations not to feel some compassion toward the god. I did not doubt that he could make a most suitable husband for someone. Perhaps, I recall thinking, he could have made an adequate husband for me had our meeting not been so tainted.

"You do not need to apologize," I said. "This is your home, and you should speak as openly as you wish to anyone in it. Myself included. Ione and I are grateful for this time to say goodbye," I said, evading his question in a manner than I hoped would not seem rude. "It is a luxury I did not think we would be granted."

Hades nodded before his expression tightened and he gnawed at his bottom lip. Again, I had learned the sign and knew there was more to come, and so I waited.

"There is no need for it to end. If she is what makes you happy in this world, then I will never take that from you. Not as long as you are here."

I waited for a condition, as I was certain he would place upon the offer, but none came. As a pause stretched between us, I found myself thinking of Demeter. How different yet similar she and her brother were. Truly, their only wish was to make me happy, but neither of them understood what was needed to make that happen.

"May I ask you something? Something I hope you will answer truthfully," Hades said, drawing my thoughts away from my mother.

"It is your home. You may ask me anything you wish."

"It is *our* home," he stressed. "I hope that soon you will start to see it as that. But I'm glad to hear this. Why? What is the appeal of this mortal? You are a god. You could have anyone of your choosing. So why did you choose her?"

"Ione?"

"Yes, why was she the one to whom you gave your heart?"

In all the time we had shared, all the grief I experienced and even my trip to the muse, this was a question I had never asked myself. I had never asked myself why her. That, to me, was like asking, why air to the mortals? Why grass to the cattle or water to the fish? How could there have been anything other than her? She was the beginning of my existence. And yet, how did I say that to Hades? How did I tell him that when true love strikes you, you do not ask why, you just wish to hold on to it for all your life is worth and hope it does not slip away?

"Sometimes I feel like I did not have a choice. That she caught me in a web like a spider that first time I saw her."

"That is all?"

"No, I do not think that is all." I pondered the truth a little more deeply. I did not have to answer him, I knew that, but I wanted to. As strange as it was, I had found with Hades a friend with whom I now had no secrets. Never had I experienced such a thing beyond Ione. Even with the nymphs I had kept secrets. Hades and I had struck our bargain, and I had no reason for falsehood. To find someone I could talk with openly was a breath of fresh air in this darkened underworld.

With Ione, I was entrapped by those dark eyes and the way her simple words enticed me to follow her into the water, but it was my decision to return to her and keep returning, decade after decade. Something about Ione caused me to risk my mother's wrath, and to see beyond the illusions of youth and beauty. That is not the same as being caught in a web. For a fly does not stay in a web out of choice. It would flee the first chance that it got.

"In truth, I think it is in the way that she viewed me and listened to me."

"How so?"

Hades was sitting up, leaning forward, absorbing me like a student listening to the words of a scholar.

"Ione did not feel the need to protect me. She did not see me as weak or incapable."

"Why would she, when you are neither of these things?"

I smiled to myself. "That is kind of you to say."

"I'm not loading you with false flattery. It is the truth. I hate to speak ill of another god, but if my sister has made you feel that, then that is a failing on her part."

I could not offer a reply, for though I had thought the same myself so many times, I would not speak ill of my mother. Not to Hades, not to any of the gods who did not understand the loss of a loved one. Yet through my silence, he found more to say.

"Persephone." Hades leaned forward. "Tell me in honesty, do you not see the change within you? The power that you have found in this place? Every day I watch it grow. I see you claim your place as queen. The Land of the Living does not deserve you. You deserve to be worshipped in your own right, not as some shadow to your mother. And I will do all in my power to ensure that happens."

A tightness swelled in my throat. A prickling heat. He was keeping me here to ensure I was worshipped as a queen, was that what he was saying? It would have sounded absurd, if I had not grown to know this man and his inability to lie.

"Hades…" I began, yet I had no words to continue. He, however, had more still.

"And while we are speaking so freely, I will tell you another truth," he said. "If her belief in you was the reason that you fell in love with your Ione, I am truly saddened." His eyes were downcast, his tone quiet as he spoke.

"Why?"

"Because I believe your love for her formed because she was the first person who made you see your true strength, and if I had gotten there sooner, perhaps it would have been me you fell in love with instead."

It was I who turned my eyes down now, not because I did not want to reply, but because I needed time to sort my response. There were words I wanted to say, needed to say, but in my heart, I feared they would come at a cost. The cost of this friendship that I was, against all odds, beginning to rely on.

"You stole me." The words cracked in my throat, and this time the phrase was uttered almost as a question.

Hades nodded slowly, his eyes finally lifting.

"There is nothing I can say that will change those actions. But I will tell you this, in all earnestness. Thanks to your friendship, I am not the same man I was when I claimed you, and I will spend all eternity regretting my decision and the blind arrogance that led me to believe you could ever love a captor." He paused, still looking at me. As our gazes met, I noticed the watery sheen that filled his eyes, though before I could even be sure what it was, he blinked it away. "Perhaps I am wrong. Perhaps you would never have loved me at all."

That night, as Hades walked me to my chamber, I let my hand fall a little distance from my hips, and when his fingertips found mine, I did not snatch my hand away but let our fingers interlace.

When we reached my chamber, he dropped my hand and kissed my cheek, and I felt the slightest pang of something in my chest. Something undefinable and unexpected.

"Your meetings with your friend have done you good," he said, as he stepped backward. His words were all it took to flood my mind with Ione. Ione, who for the briefest second had slipped away from me, in replace of this god. I cleared my throat, fighting the flush of heat I knew was coloring my cheeks, and readied to bid him good night, but Hades was not done. "If you wish to bring her to the palace, you have my blessing. We could set up a chamber at your discretion."

At your discretion. My heart should have leaped. It should have seen fit as to burst out of my chest, but rather, a heavy weight pushed down on me. In that moment, I saw myself as Hades saw me. As a woman he had fallen in love with, foolishly and rashly. And now he offered the greatest gift he could see: to bring my lover into his home. Yet it was not a thought that brought me joy. To have them here together felt wrong. A trespass on both their emotions.

"That is a kind offer, but quite unnecessary," I said.

A small smile flickered on the corner of his lips, and though it didn't quite form, I felt it in my chest.

The next day, I chose not to visit Ione.

CHAPTER SEVENTY-SEVEN

Each morning, I rose, expecting that day to be my last in the Underworld. Occasionally I would spend it solely with Hades, learning more about the land he considered me queen of and the beings that resided within it. Mostly, though, I visited Ione, if only for a short while. Each time, we would act as though it were my last visit, believing our time together had come to an end. Yet as the days passed, it became harder and harder to believe my departure would ever happen.

"I feel today is to be the day," I said one morning when I met her. "My mother will come for me today."

"Did you not say that yesterday too, my love? And the day before."

I laughed. "Perhaps I did, but today I feel certain. There is something in the air."

"I believe you," she said, resting her head on my shoulder and falling into silence. Pauses between our chatter were not uncommon, but this one stretched on, filling our previous bliss with something unpredictable.

"What is it?" I asked, unable to bear any tension between us. "Is something wrong?"

"Nothing is ever wrong when I am with you." She smiled, but a glimmer of sadness shone in her eyes.

"Ione?"

Lifting herself off my shoulder, she picked up a stone from the ground and turned it over in her hands. Her eyes still evading mine.

"I wished to ask you something," she said eventually. "Or rather, I hoped you could ask Hades for me."

I sat upright. Even in her old age, Ione's sense of playfulness had never faltered, yet she was looking at me with a solemnity that I had rarely encountered.

"What is it you require? He will not return you to the living. I have told you, your life was not cut short. He will not break a rule such as that."

"I understand. Of course. I do. That is not what I wish to ask for."

"Then what is it?"

Her eyes moved upward to the sky, then lowered back down to me.

"I wish to drink from the river Lethe," she said, after a deep breath. "I do not need to return to the Land of the Living. I know I will not be given the honor of returning to a new life as a mortal. I understand that. But I do not wish to be with these memories. You understand, my love, don't you? It had taken centuries for them to fade. If I am to be here, without you, then I must be fully without you. Please, ask him. Ask him if I can forget you were ever here."

A pain throbbed deep in my chest. She wished to forget me. To be rid of all the love we had shared in the Land of the Living and beyond. I could have been angry, but I was not. For I knew better than any the truth of her desire. No aoidoi would ever recite great poems of our love, but I did not need them to. It was our love. Ours alone.

With my thumb, I caught the tears that trickled down her cheeks. "I will see to it."

"But not until you leave."

"When I leave."

I readied my lips to kiss her again, when Ascalaphus called me.

"Queen Persephone, we should return to the palace." He was the only person in the entire Underworld that could cause my skin to prickle at the sound of my name. Which was perhaps why he said it so often. Still, I did not grant him so much as a second glance as I kissed Ione on the lips.

I did not need to tell her to close her eyes anymore. This was the routine that we had fallen into. Before my lips had even left hers, she had shut them. I would commit this image to heart, I swore to myself as I left. I would commit each wayward strand of hair and inflection of her skin to memory and would never let it go. With tears stinging my eyes, in the same manner they had each time, I left her.

We had just reached the edge of the fields when Ascalaphus stopped.

"What is it?" I said. "Is something wrong?"

His lips pursed, pinching his face.

"I have an obligation in Tartarus. Something I should have seen to this morning. It is far longer for me to return to the palace with you than to cut back through the Asphodel Fields, but I am supposed to accompany you always."

"You do not need to accompany me anymore, Ascalaphus. I have walked this way dozens of times. I can already view the lake. Go."

"It is the king's wish that you are not alone."

"If the king has issues with this, then he can raise them with me. It will not be your wrongdoing."

At this, Ascalaphus bowed his head deeply. "Thank you, my queen."

As I walked back to the palace, trees and flowers of the deepest reds and greens sprung up around me, more mammoth than anything the Land of the Living could sustain. The freedom to expand my powers had seen me push myself beyond the abilities of even Demeter and with it came the desire to push them further still. That day, I considered how I would like to turn the entire Underworld red with blooms. I would seek Hades's opinion, but he would agree.

I smiled and a sensation swirled through me, one I had not experienced in so long, it took me a moment to recall what it was. I was content. Despite these unforeseen circumstances, I had found a genuine happiness. Was it enough to replace the feel of cool air as it swept off the sea, or the taste of spring water on my lips? I did not know. But perhaps. Just perhaps it could be.

At the palace, Hades himself noted the change. I was transforming our thrones when he found me that evening. The seats themselves were similar in shape and size. Gold and black and not of my taste. The white flowers that had adorned mine upon my arrival had long since withered and died, and since taking a seat next to Hades to hear Orpheus's tunes, I had taken it upon myself to embellish them in whatever manner my mood dictated. Sometimes, I would curate two entirely different styles, one for Hades and one for myself.

During such times, I would cover his throne in flowerless vines. Creeping figs that blanketed the seat in dense small leaves. Ferns and ivy. Deep greens that layered upon one another to create a mesh of darkness. I would contrast mine with the brightest of colors. Dandelions, paperflowers, and spring parsley would burst with yellow as if my throne was made of sunlight. The antithesis of his. Other days I would adorn mine with the color of the sky.

Cornflowers, sea holly, chicory, and bluebells would create a wall of bright blue, so vivid I could squint and believe I was staring upward in the Land of the Living. However, that day I created something more cohesive to bind us.

Purple was the color I had chosen. Wisteria and passionflowers. Clematis and nightshade. They grew from the edge of Hades's throne, their dark stems disappearing under thickening green leaves as they reached the top of his chair, only to burst into a sea of purple that cascaded down onto my throne.

I had grown so used to Hades's glances and stares that by this point I found a strange comfort in his eyes. Yet, that night, it was too much for even me. As I lifted my head to look at him, he quickly lowered his eyes in a manner that made me chuckle.

"There is something you wish to say?" I said.

Without looking, I knew how his mouth was opening and closing as he struggled to find the words, and am certain that to some, this would be an infuriating trait. The inability to spit the words from his tongue resulted in every conversation taking three times longer than necessary, but I did not mind. Perhaps it was after years of having Demeter state her opinions so firmly, without room for negotiation or consideration. This uncertainty from a god endeared him to me. There were many things, in fact, that endeared Hades to me.

Finally, he spoke.

"You look like a queen," he said quietly, then again, a little louder. "Today, you look like you are the queen here. That you are comfortable in this role."

I considered his statement. Yes, I was far more at ease in the palace. More willing to accept aid to fix my hair, and I now thought of the chamber I slept in as *my* chamber. But how could he truly consider me the queen when I refused to offer my husband the one thing that custom dictates a wife should? Still, he had not shared my bed, or even kissed me beyond my cheek or hand. Each night he walked me to my chamber, and each night I thought, or rather tormented myself with the thought, that this would be the night his lips found mine. Would I want that? I did not shirk his touch, but would now instigate it, resting my head against his shoulder as we sat together, or clasping his hand as we walked. But such actions were granted to close companions, were they not? My friendships had been limited to nymphs, and I had known no men other than my brother. Beyond that, the only romantic attachment I had formed was with a female mortal. One whom I still loved. Perhaps that was why I became so confused about my emotions in Hades's presence.

"I believe you are right," I said, responding at last to his words. I was Queen of the Underworld. Yet the next morning, it all changed.

CHAPTER SEVENTY-EIGHT

WHEN I ARRIVED AT THE PALACE GATES THE NEXT morning, Hecate was waiting, scratching Cerberus's chins. Not a word passed between us, yet as she looked up from the beast and met my eyes, I knew.

"She has done it? She has persuaded Zeus to free me?"

"She has."

Breathlessness rendered me mute. I was to feel the true warmth of sunlight on my cheeks again. I was to lie upon the grasses and feel the cold sweetness of spring water on my feet. Somehow my mother, Demeter, had changed the hand of Zeus, and brought me my freedom from Hades. Freedom. The word tripped in my mind, replacing the elation that swept through me with a tangible fear.

Freedom was my right, but in some ways I had experienced more of it in the Underworld than at any point in the Land of the Living. I had been free to be myself, unashamedly. Free to test the limits of my power. Free to grow. Something I had never experienced with my mother.

Once the thoughts began to tumble, there was no relief. I thought of Ione. Of that last kiss I had placed on her lips as she closed her eyes and waited for me to leave. Had either of us truly believed that it was to be our last kiss when I had said it to her so many times before? And what of Hades? Only a few nights before, we had been laughing together in the courtyard. Not a frivolous polite titter, but a true, full-bellied raucous laughter as I told him of the mischief I had seen among mortal children in the Land of the Living. As we struggled to regain our composure, it was impossible to picture the man who I had once so vehemently despised, I recoiled at his touch. Hades was—beyond my mother and Ione—the closest I had ever grown to another being. I spoke the truth to him, and he had turned me into a goddess I was proud of. A queen.

"How long?" I asked Hecate, aware that I had not yet responded. "How long will it be until I leave?"

"A day. Perhaps a little longer. Zeus will send your brother Hermes to deliver the news to Hades."

"Of course he will," I muttered. Of course Zeus would not face his brother and admit his mistakes in front of an audience. And to call Hermes my brother was almost laughable, though I would not say such a thing to Hecate. In all this, she was the least deserving of anybody's wrath. She had come to my mother's aid and mine. She had placated Hades, and she had offered me a light in the Underworld before I had found my own.

"Are there any affairs you wish to get into order?" Hecate said. "People you wish to say goodbye to?"

People. I admired her diplomacy. I thought again of that last kiss with Ione and the promises I had made to her; I would send someone to tell her of my departure and request Hades take her to the river Lethe so she could drink away her memories. We had said goodbye in every meeting that we had. Every word we had spoken to each other in this next life was a farewell. An extra blessing granted to us. Yes, there was a farewell I needed to offer, but it was not to Ione.

He was sitting on his throne, his hands crossed on his palms.

"You have heard." It was not a question, and he did not even raise his head to me as he spoke. "You are happy. You must be happy?"

It was the same thought I had had to myself. I should be happy. Yet a deep weight was pushing down on my shoulders. Why did I not feel lighter? I moved to take my place on my throne next to him, only to hesitate.

"It is yours. It will always be yours, Persephone," he said, kindly.

Nodding silently, I took a seat next to him. A silence formed between us, so thick and tangible I could have believed it was all that existed.

"I have missed the sunlight," I said, speaking as much for my sake as his. "I have missed the breeze and the sea and the taste of honey. I have hidden none of this from you. I have never hidden the fact that should the chance arise, I would return to the Land of the Living."

"No, you offered me the kindness of never faking happiness in my home."

The words cut sharply, first for their tone, but also for the untruth within them.

"I have been happy here. Not at first, perhaps, and not always, but there have been many moments of happiness. True and real."

"With your lover."

"With you as well. In these palace walls." I turned and took his hands. "Hades, there is much that I regret of our meeting. Much that has brought me great distress, but I will not leave the Underworld the same soul which arrived. I was a goddess, but you made me a queen. I had power, but you were the one who showed me how to be powerful. Yes, I will leave here, but my time as your wife, in whatever sense we take that word to mean, is carved in the very fibers of my soul. It has shaken my past and woken me to a future otherwise unimaginable. And I have you to thank for that."

When I finished, my hands were clutching his. Grasping so hard, my knuckles shone white, as if I were fearful of what might happen if I were to let go.

"Your words were pretty indeed, but you did not speak the entire truth."

I loosened my grip.

"I promise you I—" Before I could continue, he silenced me with a finger to the lips.

"I knew exactly how powerful you were the first time I saw you. Every person here understood it, too. It was only you who needed to see it."

For the longest while, silence swept over us. The low groans of the wraiths that drifted outside the palace sounded not like the drones of the angry dead, as I had first thought, but more of a soft, deep hum. An assurance that I would never be alone in this place.

"How long do I have left here?" I asked, our fingers once again entwined.

"It will not be long now. Hermes is on his way. He will be swift."

With the realization that our time was to draw to a close, I recalled my promise to Ione and recited her request to drink from the river Lethe. A sad smile drifted onto Hades's lips.

"It would be a hard request for me to deny, given how deeply I understand her grief at being without you. I only wish the water offered me the same luxury."

At this, I removed my hands from his. "Do you mean such a thing? That you wish to forget me."

His head shook. A sad laugh rattled through his chest.

"Never, Persephone. Never."

As his laughter faded, his hand rose to my cheek. Our eyes locked on one another. There was a tremble between us, and for an instant, I thought it was me. That I was the one afflicted by the sensation, but as I stared into the endless depth of his eyes, I knew that my composure was completely steady. This was not just friendship, I realized with a clench of my heart. Not a sensation that had grown simply because of proximity. Not my hand, nor my breath quivered, even as I tipped my face toward him. It was not out of pity that I kissed my husband on his lips that day, as if he were my lover. It was not out of some sense of duty or obligation or some misguided sense of guilt that I was leaving him. No, it was because at that moment, I wanted to kiss him. I wanted to feel his warmth against mine. I wanted us to be close. It was a kiss that began with tenderness although grew quickly with a passion I had not anticipated. Fervor I had not expected rolled through me, as, for the first time in all these months, at this precise hour, I saw in him everything he had hoped I would.

"I wish for you to take me, as your wife," I said, my words gasping in his ears. "I wish to be with you."

He broke away and held my gaze with as soft a tenderness as I could ever have hoped for. His eyes glazed with tears.

"No," he said simply. "Not now. Not when I am about to lose you. Not when I can never truly be yours."

My heart was as torn as it had ever been. The desire to stay in the Underworld, with Ione and my husband, my two great loves, at odds with the desperation to return to the sunlight. I was pulled from each side, with a force equal in magnitude. Had Hades known such a thing, I believe he could have taken me as his wife upon the couch, for perhaps that would have been the single grain of sand to tip the scales. To keep me there with him.

My lips were once again on his when a throat cleared behind us. Still, we did not jerk apart in the manner that one might expect of two who had been caught in the depths of their first kiss. Our hands remained clasped as we turned to where Hecate was standing in the doorway.

"There is someone who wishes to speak to you both," she said.

"Goddess," Hermes flitted above the ground, only resting his feet upon it as he dipped his head in a bow. "Our good father Zeus sends his apologies for the miscommunication," he said.

"You mean that he thought he could offer me as a wife against my will with no repercussions?" I replied, icily.

As Hermes frowned, I found a great deal of satisfaction in his confusion. We had not known each other when I was in the Land of the Living, but we had, naturally, known of each other. He had expected to greet Core. The maiden. The peaceful goddess who fled conflict and hung behind her mother. But Core was gone, and Hermes found himself faced with Persephone.

"Zeus's apologies mean nothing to any of us," I said. "And we are both aware the only reason he is here to is to appease my mother's wrath."

"Which I am learning her daughter has inherited," he grinned.

Ignoring his attempt at humor, I turned to Hades. "Thank you. Thank you for your hospitality. For all you have done. I will never forget you." I stood up, prepared to fill my lungs with my last breath of the Underworld, yet before I could part my lips the doors to the throne room swung open. And there, illuminated by the lamp light, stood the orchardist, Ascalaphus. He strode forward until he was level with Hades.

"My lord," he said, bowing deeply. "She cannot leave this place. She has eaten the food of the dead. She must stay here for all eternity."

CHAPTER SEVENTY-NINE

T HE BREATH FLEW FROM MY PARTED LIPS AS IF IT WERE NOT merely my lungs that were emptied, but my very soul. Ascalaphus had righted himself now and stood tall in front of Hades and Hermes, an audience to his spectacle. Beside me, Hecate took my hand, her eyes asking me a single question. I shook my head hurriedly.

"She would not do such a thing," Hecate said, stepping forward. "She knew that this day would come, and I had warned her. I had warned her not to touch any of the food offered to her in the palace."

A slow smirk spread across Ascalaphus's face. A sinister grimace that twisted his features in the most grotesque manner.

"It was not in the palace that she ate the food," he said.

I had forgotten. Truthfully. The moment stored away in the back of my mind, along with a hundred thousand others I'd spent with Ione.

Hades had not yet looked at me but continued to view Ascalaphus with a mixture of confusion and disdain.

"Persephone is your queen. Think carefully before you accuse her of something you may later regret."

"I have no need to regret my words, for they are the truth, my lord. I have the evidence here with me now." As Ascalaphus turned to the doorway. I knew, with a sinking heart, exactly what evidence he would provide.

It was as if every ounce of warmth had drained from the earth. Every hint of color and joy ebbed away.

"No," I whispered, my voice trembling as I fought back the tears that clogged my throat. "No, she cannot."

She did not look like a wraith as she stepped into the palace. If anything, she looked golden. Even more so than when I had seen her bathing in the river. She moved with elegance, gliding across the floor. Her gossamer robes reflecting the lamplight.

"Ione," I whispered, as Ascalaphus grabbed her by the wrist and yanked her before Hades.

I should have moved to loosen his grip. I should have moved to free my love from the grasp of this venomous daimon, but there was no strength within me. I was paralyzed by fear. The hissing and spitting of the oil lamps were the only sound that echoed around in the expansive throne room.

"Tell him," Ascalaphus spat at Ione. "You cannot lie to the God of the Underworld. He will know, and you will receive the punishment of Tartarus." When he yanked his hand for a second time, it was not I who came to the aid of Ione. It was my husband.

"Enough!" Hades's voice bellowed like I had never heard before. Hecate, for all her strength, did not flinch, unlike Hermes, who flew backward like a small child frightened by an animal. It could have been humorous to see an Olympian god act in such a manner, but there was no humor in that hall.

At Hades's command, Ascalaphus dropped Ione's hand, but Hades was not done. In slow steps, he approached Ione. His pace was tentative, so as not to frighten her, for we could all see how she quaked.

"There is no need to fear me," Hades said. "Or anyone in this room. You have none to fear if you speak the truth. Do you understand that?"

Ione's eyes remained trained down on her feet as her chin dipped in a nod.

"Good. I am sorry for the manner in which you have been brought to me, but I must ask you to tell me the truth. To lie to me will only do more harm to all concerned. Is that clear?"

Once again, she nodded.

The tears lodged in my throat had stuck tight, swelling to form a lump that could not be swallowed.

"Ione," I whispered, willing her to look at me. "Ione, please." Beside me, Hecate squeezed my hand.

Though my lover ignored my pleas, my husband looked upon me, with expression I could not fathom. Was it pity, possibly? Or hurt. Perhaps both, or neither. His gaze lingered upon me, absorbing all the regret that I could feel seeping from my skin.

"Tell me the truth, my child, so we can all move on with this day. Did Ascalaphus speak the truth? Did you see your queen eat the food of the dead?"

That second stretched out for a thousand years. Tens of mortal lives must have passed in the time it took for Ione to take a single inhale. My heart fought to beat its way through my ribs. A pain searing through my very soul.

"She has eaten with me. She has eaten the seeds of a pomegranate."

CHAPTER EIGHTY

DEMETER

I DID NOT KNOW HOW LONG I WAS EXPECTED TO WAIT IN TAENARUM for Hermes to return with my daughter. I estimated, of course. I estimated how long it would take him to reach the river Styx, though there would be no need for him to wait for Charon to ferry him across to the other side, after all. What was the purpose of winged sandals if not to evade hindrances such as rivers and ravines?

Pacing up and down the hillside, I counted the minutes in my mind before realizing the futility of my actions. It could take him hours to reach the palace, even with his ridiculous sandals, and I could not keep pacing in such a manner. So instead, I took a seat by the spring.

This would not be the world that Core saw upon her return, I thought, and rested my hand against the frozen tendrils of ice that had once sprung from the spring. At my touch, water ran through my fingertips. No, she would want to see the world as she remembered it. Full of color and life. Full of flowers. The thought of Core's face appearing through the gateway was enough to melt the frost. And then, from the cold earth, the flowers began to grow. So many flowers. Every one I could think of. Every color and size, with aromas so luscious that the buds had barely opened when butterflies and bees flocked to them.

When flowers filled my view as far as I could see, I began to pluck them, wrapping them tightly, one then another to make her a crown. And then, when it was done, I made a second one with identical blooms. Mother and daughter together, that was how it was supposed to be.

There I remained with my two wreaths as I waited for my child. I waited and waited. I waited until the sun had sunk so low on the horizon it seemed to have set it alight with golden embers that burned a deep red on the distant trees. The flowers in my hands began to brown and wilt. If Core was not there soon, I would have to create new crowns, I mused. Then I heard the footsteps approaching me from within the cave.

It took every modicum of restraint within me not to run to her. Instead, I slowly stood and walked toward the entrance. There my feet remained fixed on the ground, until there in front of me, a silhouette came into view. A single silhouette, petite, slight, and wearing a winged helmet.

Only when Hermes stepped forward into the light did I know he was alone.

"Goddess," he said, bowing. "I am sorry. It is not possible for your daughter to join you. There was a complication."

"A complication?" Ice re-formed on the ground by my feet. "Where is my daughter?"

"She...she cannot leave. I am sorry. This is the ruling. She cannot."

"I have an agreement with Zeus." My tongue smacked against my teeth as I spoke, punctuating my every word. "Where is my daughter?"

"I am sorry."

"I am done with this," I gritted my hands by my side and, with all the force I could muster, bellowed, "Zeus!"

I did not bring snow or ice. No, I brought a blizzard the likes of which the world had never known. Hailstones the size of boulders hammered the earth. Smashing rocks and buildings alike. I did not stop as it rained down around me. I would freeze every inch of land and water, if that was what it took. "Zeus!" I did not relent from that storm. Hermes took to the sky, battling the winds that howled around him, knocking him back and forth as he fought for his retreat. "Where is my daughter? Return her to me!"

Sometimes I think back to how many human lives were lost because of my actions that night. Sailors caught out at sea, their boats broken by the shards of ice that crashed against their hulls. Priestesses in their temples, whose candles were blown out with the gusts of wind before the cold took them. And the farmers who could not fix a fire to save their family from the ice. And I feel for them. I feel the slightest tendril of guilt. But only the slightest.

When Hermes returned, Zeus was by his side. His tanned skin as pale as the whites of his eyes.

"You will kill every mortal on Earth with this scene of yours. Is that what you want?" he said, having to lift his voice above the howling of the wind.

"You promised my daughter would be returned to me," I said to him. "You promised you would return her."

"I am as confused by this matter as you are."

"Forgive me if I do not believe you."

He stepped forward and placed his hand against mine. A sensation that sickened me to the core. The touch of his skin was identical to all those years ago, when he had taken my hand in a promise of love and brotherliness and had defiled me. I should have thrown him to the ground. I should have emasculated him as he did to our father, but I did not need Zeus emasculated. I did not care what happened to him. I cared only for one thing. For my daughter.

"I will fix this, Sister," he said, his hand still on mine. "I will go to Hades now and fix this, I promise."

I snorted. "I learned long ago that your promises mean nothing to me. I will come with you this time."

His expression hardened.

"That is not what is done."

"No? Then, you should listen to the prayers that your precious mortals are calling to you, for it will be the last ones they can give you."

CHAPTER EIGHTY-ONE

PERSEPHONE

A HEAVY SILENCE FELL OVER THE THRONE ROOM. IT WAS impossible to believe this was the same hall I had sat in only hours before, kissing Hades upon the lips and questioning how much it would hurt to leave him and this life in which I was queen. Less, I discovered, than knowing I would never see the sunlight again. That I would never feel the grass of the living world under my feet or wake to the chorus of birds that rang out every morning as dawn broke.

"My Goddess," Hermes said, breaking the silence that had engulfed us all. "I should leave now. You know how the messenger life is. Constantly on the move."

He did not wait for a farewell or offer one more than a dip of his chin before he fluttered away on his wings. Somehow, with Hermes's departure, the tension became even more pronounced. Ione was kneeling on the floor, Hecate motionless beside me, and even Ascalaphus had the sense not to show his satisfaction.

As the silence bloomed around us, I did the only thing I could believe to do. I begged.

"Hades, please. I did not even realize it was the food of the dead. It was six seeds. Six pomegranate seeds. Surely you cannot keep me trapped here for that?"

He, like Ione, could no longer look me in the eye.

"It is not I that am trapping you, my love. This is the way of the Underworld. You are bound to it now. You are bound to it in a manner that I cannot undo."

"But Eurydice. Orpheus's wife? You freed her. You allowed her to leave."

Once again, his eyes evaded mine as he shook his head.

"She did not leave."

"What?" I bristled. "What do you mean, she did not leave? Hades? What do you mean by this?"

His jaw clenched, his lips pressed tightly together in a thin line.

"She did not leave. The condition I set upon Orpheus, I knew he would not meet it. He could not. His wife was bound here."

"You tricked him!" I said, disgusted. I had believed that he was above all that trickery. Above the games of his brothers. And yet here he was, toying with mortals, as if they did not hurt and live and love like we did.

"I did not trick him, Persephone." He reached for my hands as he spoke, but I snatched them away. His tone hardened by a fraction. "I did not trick him. He made his way through the Underworld. He completed a feat that few mortals have ever managed. Few gods. You wanted me to tell him it was pointless? That all his efforts were for nothing? A wasted journey. I am sorry, I could not do that. I could not beat down a man who had already been so consumed by grief that he would risk the Land of the Dead."

"He will think it is his fault. That he did not do enough to save her."

"And for that, I am sorry, but that is the way that you choose to see it."

Perhaps his words made sense, but I was unable to hide the disgust in my voice. "And how would you see it?" I said. "How else is there to see it?"

"I believe I gave a man hope. That for a few seconds his heart was without the burden of grief. For a few moments, the woman he loved walked close behind him. His grief was already there, Persephone. I could not change that. I merely gave him a few moments free of it. Surely you, of all people, know the lengths someone would go to rid themself of grief?" I had not realized until then that he knew, but the tenderness with which he gazed at me showed it all. "It was not until Orpheus's song that you wished to see her. That was when the memories returned. You forget how I watched you always. I watched then, and I saw the change within you."

I stumbled backward, unsure why this revelation would strike me so deeply. Perhaps because I could not deny it.

"What now?" I said to Hades. "What do I do?"

"We live as we have done," he said. "You as my queen. My wife. And…" He did not finish his sentence. His lips twisted as he shifted his gaze to Ione. From there, his eyes moved slowly back to me. "My offer still stands. Now you know you are here permanently, perhaps you would like to reconsider it. For me to find her a place in the palace."

At this, Ione let out a small whimper from the ground. I barely glanced at her. Instead, I spoke again to Hades.

"Will you please give us a moment's privacy?" I said.

"Of course." Without so much as a gesture, Ascalaphus and Hecate left the hall with the God of the Underworld trailing behind them.

Ione and I were together and alone in the throne room of the Underworld. I had imagined a thousand scenarios in our hours whiled away by the river in Tegea. I had talked of taking her to Siphnos, of course, and though she had rejected talk of immortality, my hope persisted that perhaps she would change her mind. That we would have an eternity to reside together wherever we desired. But I had never imagined this. Never imagined eternity together in the Land of the Dead.

She cradled her head in her knees, stifling her sobs.

"Ione?" At the sound of my voice, she sat up straight. Tears glistening in her eyes.

She scrambled toward me, wrapping her arms around the bottom of my legs. Crouching down to her level, I brushed the tears from her cheeks. Tears of a wraith, glistening and white and sharp enough to pierce my very soul. Tipping her chin upward so that her eyes met mine, I spoke with hushed tones.

"Did you know, Ione? Did you know what those seeds would do?"

Her breath shuddered as she inhaled. "He told me if you ate the fruit, it would give you power. Power to be as strong as your mother. As strong as Hades."

"And you believed him?"

I lowered my gaze. Ione had never been naive in the Land of the Living, but she was a mortal. She had always been a pawn of the gods whether I had seen it before now.

"There is joy to be found in this, my love," she said, running her fingers through my hair. "We can be together. Together forever. I thought I had lost the chance, but we have it now. We have eternity together."

I stepped back, tugging her hand from my head, unable to fathom the words that she were saying, or the gentle smile that graced her lips. Despite all the tears, she found happiness in this outcome. She was happy that I was still here.

"Did you wish for this?" I said, standing. "Did you wished for me to be trapped?"

"No my love. I wanted you to be free. To be a queen. To be powerful, Persephone. This is what you are meant to be. Not your mother's underling, as she controls your every action. He told me the seeds would do that."

"And you took the word of Ascalaphus rather than consult me?" My voice raised to a shout, and icicles formed on the vines above us. Drawing in a deep breath, I forced the chill to recede from my fingers. "I have power, Ione. Power that grows every day. If you had truly seen me for who I have become, you would have known that."

I watched as Ione pulled herself to standing as she grappled at any frail fragment of hope she could find.

"We are not trapped. Did you not hear Hades? He said I can live here with you. Just like we always dreamed of."

"To live with me and my husband."

"But you do not think of him that way."

"I do not know how I think of him. But I deserve the rights to choose my own destiny. And you have taken that away from me."

I believe I said the words as much to spite her as anything, but that kiss was still there in my mind. The way my heart had burned at the thought of leaving him. Not like this, of course. No, it had never burned like this. But it was enough. Enough for me to be a true wife? I believed so. I took another step back so that I could view her in her entirety.

"You are right. I have choices now. And I must choose what is best. What is best for me. And me alone."

"Pers—"

"Please, don't!" I turned in a circle, unable to stem the whirlwind in my mind. "Please, I need to think."

She stepped toward me, encroaching on the space I so desperately needed.

"My love, what is there to think of? We are together now. As it should be. You cannot live without me. You cannot. Nor I without you, please, my darling."

"Please stop telling me what I can and cannot do!" I raised my hand. I cannot say why. I certainly did not intend to strike her, for I had never struck anyone in my life, but the anger that had bled into me was enough for me to cause a flicker of fear in both myself and Ione.

I drew in a breath. The words I needed to say teetering on my tongue. Though before I could speak, the door swung open again.

"Core, my darling. Core. I am here. I am here for you now."

CHAPTER EIGHTY-TWO

I HAD DREAMT OF MY MOTHER AND IONE MEETING. I HAD THOUGHT perhaps I would persuade Demeter to visit Tegea, where Ione would prepare a picnic for us. Or else I would simply arrive back in Siphnos as the sun set, Ione's and my fingers interlocked. I had imagined countless ways the two would meet one another, but never had I imagined this. Me with my hand raised above my lover as she cowered on the floor of the throne room in Hades. My half brother, Hermes, standing in the doorway with my father himself. Zeus. Zeus had come for me.

"Mother?" Edging away from Ione, I studied the figure in front of me. She was, without doubt, my mother, and yet she was unrecognizable. It was her stance. The way she was standing tall, like she had never done before.

In the silence, I realized she was scrutinizing me with the same keen eye. Her gaze lingering on my new attire, the kohl round my eyes, the twisted curls of my hair so different to the goddess she had birthed and raised.

"You are here," I said, finally.

"My darling. My darling, Core. I am here for you now."

Beside her, Hades recoiled at this name—this nonname—with which my mother addressed me. A recoil I felt in myself.

"I am Persephone now," I said to her, as softly as I could. "It is a name that is more fitting for a goddess, do you not think?" I felt the child in my voice as I spoke. The girl, hungry for the approval of her parent. What would I say if she disapproved, I wondered fleetingly. Could I return to Core? That nameless maiden? No, I knew that much.

My mother's eyes glinted with tears. "I think it is most suitable for a goddess," she said. "Persephone. Now, come. I am to take you home."

As she reached out for my hand, I found my gaze casting around the hall. It had filled again quickly. Zeus, Hades, Hecate, Hermes, Ascalaphus. Not since the wedding of Cadmus and Harmonia had I been surrounded by so many immortals. Yet the sober faces told me that this was no celebration.

"She cannot leave," Ascalaphus piped up.

"Silence!"

Hades, Zeus, and my mother's voices were enough to send the orchardist cowering back against a pillar. The smug satisfaction of earlier was well and truly gone. But immediately afterward, the silence settled again.

It was my mother who spoke next. "Hermes, take Co—Persephone to the Land of the Living. Zeus and I will follow when we have this matter sorted."

Never had I heard her command another god, but not all present were ready to bow to her command. One in particular bristled.

"Persephone stays. Whatever discussions we are to have, my wife has more right to be here than anyone else." Hades's eyes met mine with a nod. Whatever I decided, he would stand by me. That was the truth of his love. He loved me enough to let me leave.

"Fine," my mother said, with a haughtiness more suited to Hera than Demeter. "I will make this brief. This marriage is a farce. A trickery. She is a goddess of flowers, of nature. You cannot possibly believe she has a place here."

"I believe Persephone has a place wherever she chooses, as is her right as a goddess," Hades replied.

"And that is what you believed when you stole her from me? When you trapped her and held her captive? She is *still* captive."

My mother's pain was so raw, it tore at my heart. Yet so did the realization of Hades's words that followed.

"That is not true. She has not asked to leave for months. She has made this place a true home. One where her powers are not bound by her mother's fear."

My mother's eyes turned to me, shining with tears. *Was it true?* her look asked. *Was it true that I no longer asked to leave?* My lips parted, as I tried to offer her some assurance, yet I could not. For I could not, in all good consciousness, recall the last time I had asked Hades to set me free. Certainly not since Orpheus had freed my memories and I felt the power of that throne.

"Mother—" I began, but before I could continue, Hades was speaking again.

"Demeter, I can assure you, I will be burdened with my wrong-doings against your daughter for all eternity. But do not speak as if she is powerless or not aware of her own abilities. And do not act as if you are knowledgeable of her wants or desires, for you made no attempt to learn of them when she was in the Land of the Living. As far as I am concerned, Sister, your presence here is only toler-ated because of Persephone's love for you. If she so wishes, I will gladly cast you out of this domain myself." Hades's voice had risen substantially, as his hand trembled at his side. No one, me included, dared speak, for who could contradict a truth so succinctly given? In the silence that followed, Hades drew a long breath into his lungs, stemming the tremble to his hands. "All of this is beside the point," he said, his tone far softer. "She ate the food of the dead. She is bound to the Underworld by powers older than any of us."

Demeter's eyes glistened as she gazed at me. "What did you eat?" she asked. I opened my mouth to speak, but a lump had lodged in my windpipe.

"Six pomegranate seeds," Ascalaphus spoke from the edge of the room. "From my orchard. Six seeds are what she ate."

At his voice, my mother turned and looked down her nose at the daimon as if he were excrement on her shoe.

"Who is this?" she said.

"This is Ascalaphus. A servant to me."

"He is the one who told me to feed Persephone the pomegranate seeds." All eyes turned to Ione, crumpled on the ground. "He was the one who told me I should make her eat."

"Is that true?" Demeter said, stepping forward to Ascalaphus. "It was you who did this?"

"I did nothing." His voice was a sneer, and I wondered if stupidity, as much as malice, played a part in his actions. "I did not persuade her to eat the food of the dead. I did not *offer* her the food."

My mother's disgust radiated from her as she turned to Hades.

"Brother, this daimon is yours?"

"He is yours now," Hades replied. "Do as you wish."

I did not know what was to come until it happened. With a flick of her hand, Demeter let out a mighty bellow. The force of wind that she created blew through the halls, though it was aimed only at

Ascalaphus. The daimon flew backward, his scrawny body slammed into the pillar, and dropped to the ground. A moment later, when he rose again, he was no longer in a human form. But a screech owl.

From the mosaic floors, Ione emitted a terrified whimper, though fear was not my first thought. A deep pang of guilt struck me square in the chest. How much must Demeter have been through to change in such a manner?

"Six pomegranate seeds," Demeter said as the screech owl flapped its wings around the top of the hall. "That is what we are debating here? That is not a meal. That is not even a cup of wine. Surely you cannot think to hold her hostage for such a thing?"

"She has been queen," Hades said, bristling at the word *hostage*, despite the truth it held. "But this is beyond my control. She is bound to the Underworld."

"Bound," my mother repeated. "Again you use this word, *bound*. What does that mean?"

At this, Hades pressed his lips together, and his eyes looked slowly at me. The pain. I saw it. I saw the insecurity. "It… It… It means."

"Spit it out!"

"Mother!"

I could not comprehend the manner in which she was speaking, no more than I could comprehend how Hades had once again been reduced to the stuttering, insecure god that I had first encountered upon my arrival there.

"She will not survive in the Land of the Living. She will wither," he said. "Her powers, her strength, are linked to here. To this place. To the Underworld. Its food is now her life course."

The air seized tight in my lungs, and I was not alone.

"How can that possibly be?" My mother's voice was now a faded warble. "She is a goddess of life."

"Yes, but now of life and death," Hades said. "I... I am sorry. I cannot do anything to change this. Believe me, if I could alter this, I would."

She was lost. I could feel her hopelessness, for I too felt it. After all, what is the purpose of power, if not to save the ones you love?

"Persephone, may I make a suggestion?" To all our surprise, it was Zeus who had spoken. Zeus, who until then, had remained silent, stepped forward. Never had my father addressed me in person. Not as Core. But now, standing here as queen of the Underworld, I was finally worthy of his attention. That was how it felt, although whether I was pleased or repulsed by this, I cannot say.

"You are bound to the Underworld, and this power, which seems to suit you well, is linked to it."

"So I have been told."

"Then this is my suggestion. You return to the Land of the Living with your mother."

Given what we had heard, it seemed like folly. "I cannot return."

"You can. You return to the Land of the Living with your mother. Then, when your power wanes, you return here. Regain your strength. Feed from the food of the dead. Then return. You will lead two lives: one in the Land of the Living, one in the Land of the Dead. Hades, would that appease these binds which have been placed on her?"

Hades blinked, then nodded. "I believe it would." He caught my gaze, the smallest hint of a smile glimmering in his eyes, but before I could return it, Demeter stepped forward.

"No, it is not enough. You promised she would return to me. You promised she would be mine again. She is meant to be with me! This is not enough. I will see that the entire Earth freezes. And this time I will not stop with the Land of the Living."

"Mother, stop." Slowly, I stepped toward her, and in that moment, I knew truly that Core was gone. That only Persephone remained. A queen. One with power and strength and compassion. All eyes were on us as I took her head and tilted it toward me, to place a kiss on her forehead. I had missed her more than words could say. At the touch of my lips, she crumpled into tears and collapsed into my arms.

"I was meant to save you. I was meant to rescue you."

"You have," I whispered to her. "You have done so much for me. You gathered the gods for me. You transformed the world for me."

"But it is not enough."

"It will have to be."

CHAPTER EIGHTY-THREE

I DID NOT BID ZEUS FAREWELL. I DID NOT THANK HIM FOR HIS presence down in the Underworld, since he was the reason I was there. Yet before he left, he held my gaze and nodded to me, offering an acknowledgment that I had never before received from him. I was a goddess now. Not only in blood but in his eyes and in the eyes of all the Olympians. Though it was not the Olympians whose company I required.

Hecate had taken my mother from my arms and ushered her up into the Land of the Living on the promise that I would follow swiftly, once my farewells were spoken.

Soon, only three of us remained in the throne room. Myself, my husband, and my lover, who was still crumpled on the floor, sobbing.

"I am sorry you have not gained the outcome you wished for," Hades said. There was a distance between us. A gap that I wished to close, although I found myself unable to step toward him.

"I believe this may be the outcome I desired. Though I did not realize it," I said.

"Is that so?"

"It is." My feet found the motion to take a step toward him, and in a mirror image he moved toward me. We were still not close enough to touch, yet I could hear the drumming of his heart and the rattle of his breath as he fought to slow it.

"When I return. I will do so as your queen. In every sense," I said. "But I must ask for one thing from you."

"Anything."

"Loyalty." Such a simple word, and yet it meant so much. "Do not lie to me. Do not hide things from me. And if I am to rule, I am to rule as your equal."

"That is the only way I ever wanted it," he replied, his eyes wide and tear-filled.

"Then I will be your queen."

I bowed my head. All these months in each other's company, and it was an act I had never before performed. To bow to my king. To my god, to my husband. As I should have expected, Hades returned the gesture, although when he lowered himself, he took my hand and kissed it. When he rose, we stood side by side. King and Queen of the Underworld.

"And what of your lover?" Hades said, with a glance to Ione. "Her fate is of your choosing. Any offer I have made stands, now and always."

Despite her attempts to stay hidden and remain oblivious to our conversation, Ione's head rose from her knees. With her bloodshot eyes she looked directly at me, and I found myself thinking of what Hades had said to me one day in the courtyards. She had found me first. Was that all it was? Was the fact that she was the first person to show me affection the reason I fell so deeply for her? No. No, I did not believe so. She and I were meant to have a lifetime together. A lifetime of love and passion that would open my eyes to a world I had never allowed myself to dream of. But that lifetime had passed. It had passed, and we had been granted more time still. Perhaps that was where my mistake had lain all along. It was time to let go. Our eyes met, and she nodded almost imperceptibly.

"She will return to the Elysian Fields," I said. "She will be there, with the heroes and the others who have felt the true love of a god. But, as she wished before, she will not remember. She will not know that the queen who resides over this place holds her heart. Instead she will drink from the river Lethe and with her soul cleansed, will return to the Land of the Living. She will return with her eyes open to all the beauty and splendor there is. And when she is there, she will find love. Not with a god or a goddess. Nor with one who she must keep hidden in the shadows or leave before their time. But to a mortal. An equal in every way. Ione will love again. She deserves to love again. We both do." I stepped forward and planted a single kiss on the top of her head. "Goodbye, my love." And with that I turned and left.

EPILOGUE

I AM THE DAUGHTER OF OLYMPIANS. I AM THE GODDESS OF THE Underworld. I am Persephone.

This was my story.

A hurricane of flowers awaited me in the Land of the Living. Meadows fit to burst with a cascade of buds that burst into life as I walked by them. When I reached my mother, who stood beside a spring, she placed a crown of flowers upon my head and bowed gently.

"Persephone."

"Demeter."

We did not return to Siphnos that day. Nor the days that followed. Never did my mother even mention the name of the island to me, as we moved from one land to the next, our hands held, the silence between us enough for now. Over the years, we spoke. She told me of all she had endured in my absence. Of Poseidon and Hecate and the kindness strangers had shown her. And in turn, I told her of Ione, and of Orpheus, and of course, Hades.

Six months. That is how long I remain in the Land of the Living. Six months before the draw of the Underworld grows too strong for me to ignore. For six months, I live with my mother, feeling the heat of Helios's sun upon my face, and breathing in the scent of fresh herbs and spring blooms. After which, I return to the Underworld. To my husband, who is as loyal and tender as I could ever hope for. My mother has not yet mastered her grief. The winter still comes whenever I depart, though it fades again when I return to her side. As it will be for all of time.

READING GROUP GUIDE

1. Consider the long-lasting effect Zeus's assault has on Demeter. How can you trace it through her character arc?

2. Compare mother and daughter. In what ways are they similar? How are they different?

3. *Daughters of Olympus* features a number of women who suffer great loss but remain dignified and kind. Why do you think that is?

4. Demeter is convinced Core is naïve though her daughter is centuries old. Do you agree with her?

5. Core believes Demeter is weak for mourning Iaison because their relationship was brief. Do you think her relationship with Ione is more meaningful?

6. Ione consistently refuses immortality though Core begs her to accept it. Why do you think she does this? What would you do under the same circumstances?

7. How does Core change in the Underworld? Describe the differences between Core and Persephone.

8. Hades believes he can simply take Core as his wife and keep her against her will. What makes him realize he's in the wrong? Do you think he atones for what he's done?

9. Core chooses to forget her lover entirely rather than remember losing her. Do you think it's possible to ever truly forget heartbreak?

10. What did you make of this reimagining of a classic myth? What surprised you?

A CONVERSATION
WITH THE AUTHOR

The story of Hades and Persephone has been retold many times, across many genres. What made you decide to put your own spin on it?

It is such a well-loved story, it's impossible not to be drawn to it. For me, it was the tale of the two women that attracted me the most. Mother and daughter, trying to do their best by each other, unaware of the hurt their actions could cause.

In balancing the threads between Demeter and Persephone, how did you make sure each woman had her own voice? How did you handle crafting the same scenes from two different perspectives?

I wrote this book in the order that you read it, meaning I went through all of Demeter's initial scenes before then tackling those same events as Persephone. (Or, at that time, Core.) It was important to me that I showed how perceptions of the same situation can change according to a character's perspective—even as far as experiencing the same conversation but hearing different things. A character's interiority shapes how they view the people and the world around them, and I wanted to explore that.

In many myths, mothers are often cast aside or left as a footnote. Why did you decide to give Demeter such a prominent role?

As a mother, I resonated so strongly with Demeter's desire to hide Core from the world and keep her safe. I cannot imagine the heartbreak she felt in failing to do so and understand completely why she would go to such extremes to find her daughter. But I also saw how those same actions, her overbearing nature and the way she stripped her daughter of her freedom, could easily have been the thing that drove Core away. Demeter's story is at the heart of it all, which is why I no longer wanted it left as a footnote.

***Daughters of Olympus* breathes life into Core/Persephone by giving her a life *before* being taken into the Underworld. Can you talk a little bit about that?**

The earlier we start in a character's life, the more we can view their transformation, and transformation is at the heart of this book. To be known simply as Core—Maiden—would be devastating enough for anyone, but for a goddess, it seemed even more cruel. I wanted to show that Persephone was a person in her own right even before she became Hades's wife. Writing her earlier life allowed me to do that while at the same time highlighting the magnitude of her evolution from a sweet, demure daughter of gods to Queen of the Underworld. It also allowed me to demonstrate her loyalty, not only to her mother and Hades but also to Ione, who she remained with throughout Ione's entire mortal life. It was the loss of Ione that finally allowed Core to understand the grief her mother suffered.

You've written a few mythic retellings. Was there anything different about writing this one? Were there any unique challenges?

This retelling is the first one I have done that focuses solely on the gods rather than the mortals of that time, and it threw up a few challenges. For example, writing the scene where Demeter gives birth as a horse to a horse and making it seem entirely realistic was definitely new to me! There were also some pretty heart-wrenching scenes too that I knew needed a careful balance to ensure they did not come across as gratuitously violent or unnecessarily shocking.

Memory is a powerful theme in this story. When you first started writing *Daughters of Olympus* did you plan on that?

No, it wasn't my initial plan, but as I wrote these women and their backstories, it became clear how much of them was shaped from the past, and that is the case for all of us. Without Demeter's loss, she may well have been an entirely different mother to Core. Core knew this, which was why—in my retelling—she didn't want to be burdened with those same memories of heartbreak.

Demeter's rage is deadly. Do you think it's warranted?

Absolutely! She had to show Zeus that she was willing to take everything from him. If he had accepted this from the start, she would never have gone to the extremes she did. (Can you tell I'm on Demeter's side here? It was definitely Zeus's fault she killed all those people, not hers!)

What do you hope readers will take away from this story?

There is a lot to unpack here. The relationships between parents and children are at its core. Sometimes our vision of what is right for our child may end up harming them in the long run. As a parent, I know that is one of my own fears. But also, this story showcases the power of personal growth, regardless of when in your life it may happen. Demeter did not find her true strength until Core was taken from her. Persephone only stepped into her power when she was free from the burdens of her mother and allowed to find out who she was for herself. I think that is something we should all remember: we can constantly grow and evolve, if we accept the opportunities to do so.

ACKNOWLEDGMENTS

Writing *Daughters of Olympus* has been such a gift, and there are so many people I would like to thank for bringing this story to life. To the wonderful team at Sourcebooks and in particular my editor, Jenna. Thank you so much for all your patience and faith in me. Working with you has been an absolute joy, and I am so grateful for your help in making this the best book it could possibly be.

The cover, which continues to take my breath away, is the work of Holly Ovenden. Thank you so much for creating such a spectacular piece of art.

I owe a sincere thank-you to Anna Venkus and the marketing team, who have helped this book reach people. Also, for being so patient with me when I repeatedly messed up the different time zones for meetings. Sorry! I promise I now know that GMT is not the same as British Summer Time!

To all of my readers and reader reviewers, including those on Instagram and TikTok. What you do makes a massive difference to an author's life. Thank you from the bottom of my heart.

Erica from MoanInc. has been supporting me since the very beginning of my journey, and her opinions on my stories mean so much to me, so I really hope she enjoys this one. I also owe a debt of thanks to Olivia from Maldon Books for all she has done to help me.

To my agent, Nicola, who reached out to me all those years ago, thank you for believing in me and for never letting that belief fade. To Carol, I would not be here without you, (Or Nigel, for doing all the cooking and dog walking while Carol was helping me.) and to Mags, whose gift of a laptop meant that I could leave my house and still work! Thank you. It really was a gift that changed my life.

Given that this is a story about a mother and daughter, it would be wrong not to mention Elsie. Sorry if I can sometimes be a bit of a Demeter when it comes to parenting, but hopefully after reading this, you'll know it only comes from a place of love. You are magnificent.

Lastly to Jake. I don't have enough words to thank you for everything you do. I would not be writing without you. I would not be the person I am without you. Every book has you at the very heart of it. Thank you for being my best friend.

ABOUT THE AUTHOR

Hannah Lynn is a multi-award-winning novelist. Publishing her first book, *Amendments*—a dark, dystopian speculative fiction novel, in 2015. Her second book, *The Afterlife of Walter Augustus*—a contemporary fiction novel with a supernatural twist—went on to win the 2018 Kindle Storyteller Award and the Independent Publishers Gold Medal for Best Adult Ebook.

Born in 1984, Hannah grew up in the Cotswolds, UK. After graduating from university, she spent fifteen years as a teacher of physics, first in the UK and then Thailand, Malaysia, Austria, and Jordan. It was during this time, inspired by the imaginations of the young people she taught, she began writing short stories for children and, later, adult fiction.

Now settled back in the UK with her husband, daughter, and horde of cats, she spends her days writing romantic comedies and historical fiction. Her first historical fiction novel, *Athena's Child*, was a 2020 Gold Medalist at the Independent Publishers Awards.

ATHENA'S CHILD

The story of history's most infamous monster—
and the men who made her into one....

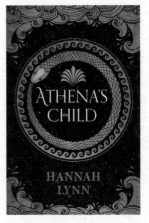

To be young, beautiful, and innocent is a curse. Knowing this, Medusa, the loveliest of her sisters, seeks sanctuary in the goddess Athena's temple. But she soon realizes that a woman among gods can never be safe—especially once she's caught the lecherous eye of the mighty Poseidon. A victim of his desires, Medusa is blamed for them and, to avoid the unjust wrath of Athena, flees.

Perseus, naïve and desperate to prove himself, embarks on an impossible quest to kill this woman-turned-monster. But he and Medusa are pawns, their fates irrevocably interwoven by the hands of spiteful gods... And Medusa will do all she can to avoid becoming the monster they say she is.

Medusa's truth has long been lost. History tells of conquering heroes, of men with hearts of gold. Now it is time to hear the story of how history treats women who stand their ground. It is time to remember Medusa.

"Full of adventure, anger, bitterness, and manipulation by the gods...
Fans of Madeleine Miller will enjoy Lynn's take on classic mythology."
— *Booklist*

For more Hannah Lynn, visit:
hannahlynnauthor.com

A SPARTAN'S SORROW

She is a mother, a queen, a villain. However we remember her, her wrath will never be forgotten.

Clytemnestra is no stranger to pain. As a wife and queen, she bears it with stoicism. But when her husband does the unthinkable, sacrificing one of their daughters to appease the ruthless gods and bring himself glory in battle, Clytemnestra is forever changed.

No longer will she stand by, a mere witness to the brutal games of gods and men. She will play by their vicious rules. She will rise to power, cut down those who oppose her, and protect her remaining children, whatever the cost. But revenge is as venomous and unforgiving as a snake, and Clytemnestra's actions will change her family in ways she could never imagine.

A Spartan's Sorrow is a nuanced story of power, loss, and bitter betrayal—a story of the rise and fall of history's most infamous queen.

For more Hannah Lynn, visit:
hannahlynnauthor.com

QUEENS OF THEMISCYRA

Sisterhood is worth fighting for...

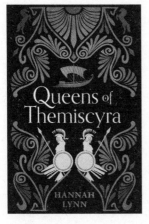

In ancient Themiscyra, Hippolyte rules as queen of the Amazons with her sister Penthesilea at her side. Feared throughout Greece, their skills on the battlefield are unrivalled. But when a ship lands on their shores, it brings something more dangerous than the threat of war: Theseus, the legendary king of Athens.

Swept away by a love unlike any she's ever known, Hippolyte leaves her people. In her stead, Penthesilea leads the Amazons with a ferocity that spreads terror across the Aegean.

But not all men of myth are heroes, and back in Athens, Hippolyte finds herself trapped in her new life. She's a queen without her people, a warrior without her army, and a mother separated from her family. But she remains an Amazon, and she's ready to fight. And across the sea, Penthesilea is ready to do the same…

For more Hannah Lynn, visit:
hannahlynnauthor.com